Romantic Times praises bestselling author Bobbi Smith

"*Arizona Caress* is a sensitive, fast-paced, satisfying love story. Chalk up another winner for Bobbi Smith!"

"*Sweet Silken Bondage* is a double-barrel romance that captures your imagination and your heart!"

Bayou Bride
"Ms. Smith's wonderful characterization and sparkling dialogue are what make her such a fine storyteller!"

Other *Leisure Books* by Bobbi Smith:
LADY DECEPTION

THE OFFER

Rafe's smile faded as he turned serious. "I have a proposition to make you."

Brandy went cold. She sensed she knew what was coming, and wondered how she would ever hide the shame of it all from her mother. "Yes?"

"I have been fighting off women ever since I came of marriageable age. You were witness to that the other night."

"What does that have to do with me?" She was staring at him, confused, wondering where he was going with this.

"I have come up with a plan that would suit me well. You owe me an outstanding amount of money, and you have no funds with which to pay me. I have an arrangement of sorts in mind...."

"What kind of arrangement?"

"I want you to marry me."

BOBBI SMITH

THE LADY'S HAND

LEISURE BOOKS NEW YORK CITY

A LEISURE BOOK®

May 1999

Published by
Dorchester Publishing Co., Inc.
276 Fifth Avenue
New York, NY 10001

ISBN 0-8439-4598-2

This book is dedicated to my friend Louie Reuther, who died January 9, 1996. Louie's talent, intelligence, kindness, generosity, and unfailing good humor marked him as a rare man, indeed. If I've learned nothing else from his early passing, I will always remember to do that act of kindness now, so there will be no regrets tomorrow. Thanks, Louie. I loved you a lot.

I'd also like to thank the Florissant Romance Readers' Book Club from Annie's Book Stop in Florissant, Missouri and, in particular, their president, Sharon Kosick, for all their support over the years. They are wonderful women who support the romance genre 110%! I treasure their friendship and their honesty. Thanks Elaine Kramer, Barb Forir, Barb Gaston, Sharon Burt, Jan Gaines, Nina Horack, Sharon Keeney, Renee Koch, Princess Moll, Merry Morrison, Donna Reeves, Ann Royer and Liz Thomas. You're terrific!

Prologue

Rafe
1845

It was late when the carriage carrying Charles Marchand and his fourteen-year-old son, Rafe, turned into the drive at Bellerive Plantation. They were excited, for they were almost home. Tied to the back of the carriage was a handsome Arabian stallion.

"Mother's really going to love him, isn't she?" Rafe asked his father.

"He's the perfect gift for her."

"Do you think she'll be surprised?"

"Absolutely. I told her we'd be gone at least through the weekend. She has no idea that we're bringing her an early birthday present." Charles smiled at the thought of his beautiful wife. Alanna meant everything to him. He loved her more than life itself. Lately, though, he had sensed that she wasn't happy, and he hoped this extravagant gift would please her.

When the carriage drew to a stop before the house, Rafe immediately climbed out.

"Come on! Let's hurry!" Rafe urged. "She won't be in bed yet. We can give him to her tonight."

Charles's smile broadened at his son's eagerness. He had to admit that he, too, was anxious to see Alanna's reaction to their present. He envisioned a wonderful night with her after Rafe went to bed. "All right, let's go. I'll send one of the servants to get our bags," he said as he descended from the vehicle.

They untied the fine Arab and led him to the hitching post in front.

"Let's get her!" Rafe ran ahead of his father, up the few steps to the veranda, and was reaching for the doorknob when the door swung open.

"You're back early . . ." George, the butler, looked from Rafe to Charles. If he was surprised by their unexpected return, he did not show it.

"We've got a surprise for my mother, George."

"I'm sure she will be surprised, sir," he replied as he glanced quickly at Charles.

"Look at the present we brought her!" Rafe told him in a conspiratorial tone, afraid she might be close by and overhear.

The servant stepped outside and saw the magnificent Arabian. "He's beautiful."

"Where is Alanna, George?" Charles asked as he entered his home.

"In your room, sir."

Rafe took the steps two at a time in his hurry to find her. Charles followed at a more dignified pace, but his excitement was equal to his son's.

From the foyer below, George watched them go, shaking his head sadly.

Charles saw that the master bedroom door was closed, but he thought nothing of it. Without knocking, he and Rafe opened it and walked in.

"Mother!"

"Alanna, we're . . ." Charles stopped, frozen in place. "What the hell?" He stared in disbelief at the sight of Alanna lying naked in the arms of another man.

"Charles!" Alanna's expression was haughty, her voice icy as she casually drew a sheet over herself.

Rafe said nothing. He stood a little behind his father staring at his mother and her lover. As he watched, the man bolted from the bed and grabbed his pants. Rafe was young, but not so young that he didn't know what was going on. He glanced up at his father and saw the fury etched in his face.

"Get out of my house, Lawson!" Charles thundered, recognizing the man.

Without a word, Lawson snatched up the rest of his clothes and fled.

"Rafe, go to your room," Charles ordered without looking at his son. His condemning gaze was focused only on his unfaithful wife. "I have to speak to your mother privately."

"But . . ."

"Go!" he roared.

Rafe all but ran from the bedroom, closing the door behind him as he went out. He made his way to his room and locked himself in, but the sounds of his parents' furious voices reached him even through that closed portal. He listened in horror as everything he'd ever loved and believed in was destroyed.

"Aren't you going to say anything, Charles?" his

13

mother taunted. "Or are you just going to stand there staring at me?"

"What is there to say, Alanna?"

"Perhaps actions would speak louder than words. Why don't you come here and finish what John started?" She gave a tempting, husky laugh.

"I wouldn't touch you if you were the last woman on the face of the earth."

"Oh, come now, Charles. You know I can make you forget all about this."

"How long, Alanna?" His father's voice sounded strangled.

"How long, what?"

"How long have you been unfaithful? How many men have there been?"

"Oh, Charles, you're such a fool." She laughed mockingly this time.

"I'm a fool because I loved you, Alanna."

"Loved me? You're hardly man enough for me. Why do you think I've taken so many lovers all these years? I married you for your money, Charles. That was all I ever cared about or wanted from you. I never loved you."

"I want you out of this house. Be gone by morning. Do you understand me?"

"I've always understood you. Far too well, in fact." She laughed again. "Don't worry, I'll be gone long before morning, and I won't look back—ever."

"What about our son?"

"What about Rafe?"

"Be careful what you say to him." There was a very real threat in his father's voice.

"I won't even talk to him. Why should I? You do it. You know I never wanted any children."

Rafe stood unmoving in the middle of his room,

his hands clenched into fists. He had adored his mother, yet now he understood why she had always kept him at a distance and rarely showed him any real affection. *She had never wanted him. . . . She had never loved him or his father. . . .*

The sound of the master bedroom door opening and closing jarred him, as did the sound of his father's heavy tread passing his room on his way downstairs. Rafe wanted to go to him, to see if he could help in some way, but he knew this was not the time. He could only imagine his father's pain. Rafe stood in the middle of his room, his heart breaking. He refused to acknowledge the tears that burned in his eyes.

Rafe did not speak to his father the rest of the night. He heard his mother leave the house and drive off in the carriage in the early morning hours. He didn't sleep at all that night.

The following day his father sent a servant to a neighboring plantation with the Arabian as a gift. Then Charles had all of Alanna's things taken from the house and burned. He spoke only briefly to Rafe, telling him tersely that she had gone and wouldn't be back. Charles retreated into the study and locked the door. Rafe didn't begin to worry seriously about him until a week passed. Desperate to find a way to reach his father, Rafe sought out George for help.

"What can I do, George? He can't stay in there forever," Rafe said worriedly.

"He'd like to." George put a kindly, supporting hand on his shoulder. "You're gonna have to be strong for him, Master Rafe."

He looked up at him, frowning. "I don't understand."

Bobbi Smith

"Your father loved your mother very much. She was his life."

"And she hurt him . . . deliberately!" The look in Rafe's eyes hardened at the memory. "I hate her for what she did! I'm glad she's gone!"

"But your father is never gonna hate her and he's never gonna be glad she's gone."

"But how can he still care after what she did?" Rafe didn't understand.

"That's what's tearing him apart inside. That's why he's locked himself in the study and is drinking himself to death."

Rafe's expression was troubled as he struggled to understand. "Will you come with me and see if we can get him to come out?"

George wanted to help, and they walked toward the locked study together. George knocked.

"Mr. Charles? Master Rafe would like to speak with you." They waited for a response, but none came. He knocked again. "Mr. Charles?"

"Go away! I don't want to see anyone," he finally answered in an irritated rasp.

"I need to see you . . ." Rafe panicked at how strange his father sounded. Something was terribly wrong.

"I don't want to see you or anyone!"

"Father . . . Please . . ." Rafe couldn't believe that even his father didn't want to see him. He felt alone and lost.

"Mr. Charles, we're not going to leave until you come to speak with us," George insisted, seeing the boy's desperation.

Finally, they heard footsteps coming toward the door and the sound of the lock being turned. When the door was opened, Charles stood before them, a shadow of his former self. He was unshaven and un-washed. His eyes were red from the sleepless nights he'd endured. He reeked of liquor, and Rafe recoiled from the harsh scent.

"Are you all right?" the boy asked.

Charles turned his back on them without speaking and returned to his desk. He slumped in the chair, staring at them with a bleary-eyed gaze. "What do you want?"

Rafe couldn't believe his condition or the haunted, almost dead, look in his eyes. "I need you."

Charles's gaze sharpened for a moment as he looked at his son. "Don't." The word was harsh and cruel. "Don't need me. Don't need anyone. You can't be hurt if you don't need anyone."

"You can't go on like this." The change in his father was so dramatic that Rafe knew he needed help.

"Your words are more true than you know," Charles said flatly. "Your mother's never coming back."

"So?" Rafe raged, furious at what she'd done to his father and to him. "We don't need her! You should be glad she's gone. We'll be all right, the two of us. I know we will."

Charles stared at his son, seeing the anger in him and knowing there was nothing he could do to help. Alanna had always been his one weakness. He had worshipped her, and now that all-consuming love was destroying him.

God knew, if she walked through that door right now and asked him to take her back, he would. A week without her had seemed an eternity. He still wanted her . . . desired her. Yet, his tortured mind would not stop conjuring up the devastating image of her with Lawson. He had seen the look on her face as the other man had possessed her, and he knew he would never forget it. He would take that torment to the grave with him.

"It's good that you don't need her, Rafe, but . . ." His voice trailed off as he would have said, "but I do." He dropped his head into his hands in an exhausted motion. "George, get Rafe out of here. I need to be alone."

"But Papa . . ."

"Go, son." It was an order.

Rejected by his father, Rafe looked up at George with pain-filled eyes. The servant just shook his head solemnly as he led him from the study. They hadn't gone far when they heard the key turned in the door again.

It was much later that night, as Rafe lay awake in his bed worrying about his father, that the sound of the gunshot split the silence. Rafe raced downstairs to find George beating on the door, trying to get in. In desperation, the two of them broke it open.

The sound of Rafe's cry when he saw his father lying on the floor would forever haunt George. The servant knew it was the death of the boy's innocence he'd heard in that cry. He tried to keep Rafe from going any nearer, but the boy pushed past him and dropped to his knees beside his father's body. Rafe picked up the note that lay on the floor near his father's hand:

I can't go on without Alanna.

At the funeral, Rafe watched coldly as his mother played the role of the widow to the hilt. She sat with him, weeping when it was deemed appropriate, but he could not help thinking that her thoughts were on

John Lawson and how quickly she could get back to his bed. She paid scant attention to him, and that was fine with Rafe. He knew that her own pleasures were all that concerned her.

At the reading of the will, when the lawyer asked her what her plans were for her son, she'd immediately directed the man to send him away to school. Rafe hadn't said a word in opposition, for he'd had no desire to be anywhere near her. She had not spoken to him except in passing since his father's death, and Rafe was certain that she had no intention of allowing him to interfere with her plans. She never returned to Bellerive after that day.

A week after the funeral, Rafe left Bellerive for a private boarding school up north. His mother never came to see him during all his years there and she never wrote to him.

Years later, when he was informed of his mother's death in a carriage accident, Rafe felt nothing.

Brandy
Natchez, 1848

It was dark as the two shabbily dressed, barefoot young girls crept through the lush, flowering garden of the stately mansion.

"We shouldn't be here," Mary Magee whispered nervously as she clutched at her adventurous companion's arm. She wanted to stop Brandy from going any farther. They were getting too close to the house, and they might get caught.

"Hush," Brandy O'Neill returned in a low voice. "There's something goin' on tonight that I want to see."

"How do you know there's something going on?

Have you been here before?" The girl glanced at her friend in surprise, wondering what a poor girl from Natchez-Under-The-Hill was doing coming up here by the rich folks.

Brandy nodded. "I sneak up here all the time just to look around. Someday, I'm gonna be this rich, too," she answered with a conviction unusual in someone so young. "Someday, me and my mama are gonna live in a big house just like this one. We're gonna have fancy dresses, lotsa food, and servants to wait on us, hand and foot."

Mary shook her head at her fantasy. "You're dreamin'. You ain't never gonna be a lady."

"Oh, yes, I am! Maybe you're happy livin' the way you're livin' right now, but I'm not. My mama deserves a better life, and I'm gonna see that she gets it. Ever since Pa died, she's been workin' herself sick trying to support us with her sewin'. One day, I'm gonna be taking care of her so good that she'll never have to sew for anybody again."

"How're you gonna do that?"

"I don't know, but I will. Now, come on."

"But what if they catch us?"

"They're not going to catch us if you just stay quiet."

Brandy led off again, heading down the path that wound through the carefully manicured grounds. As the pair moved ever closer to the house, the faint and distant sound of music came to them.

"They havin' a party. . . ." Mary said under her breath.

Brandy nodded. "Look."

She pushed aside the branches of a low-growing shrub to reveal a view of the balcony off the ballroom. The double French doors to the ballroom were open wide, and inside, beneath the light of the glowing chandelier, they could see the handsome, elegantly dressed men squiring the magnificently gowned ladies about the dance floor.

Mary gasped at the beauty of the scene.

Brandy only stared, watching dreamily as the couples spun around to the music. For just that little time, as she hid there watching from the darkness, she could forget that her future was bleak, that she and her mother lived from day to day, struggling just to pay the rent on the single, rat-infested room they let in the town below the bluff. She could forget that she hadn't eaten a full meal in a week. She could believe, if only for a little while, that the future was going to be just as wonderful as she dreamed.

Chapter One

The mood among those gathered that evening in the gentlemen's saloon aboard *The Pride of New Orleans* was one of anticipation. The men had heard about the beautiful lady gambler named Brandy who was a regular on the steamboat, and they were eager to get a look at her. Rumor had it that she was one talented poker player, and they were more than ready to test their gaming skills against hers.

"I've listened to all your talk about this Brandy for over an hour now, and you're all making her sound like some paragon of womanhood—young, beautiful and smart. Is she really that special?" asked Kevin Berra, a darkly handsome young man who was making the trip north to expand his carriage trade business to points upriver, as he stood drinking straight bourbon at the bar. He didn't think there was a woman alive who could live up to what they were saying.

Dan Lesseg, a prominent young attorney from St. Louis who considered himself a connoisseur of woman, answered easily, "Brandy is more than special. She's magnificent."

"Why, thank you, Dan." Brandy's sultry voice came from the back of the room as she made her entrance through a private door.

"I only speak the truth," Dan told her, turning toward her to give her a courtly bow. He smiled broadly as he watched her cross the room toward him.

Kevin looked up and, along with the others, decided Lesseg's assessment had not been in the least exaggerated. Brandy was a fine-looking woman. Her ebony curls were perfectly coiffed up and away from her artfully made-up face in a style that set off her green eyes, sparkling now with good humor. She wore a form-fitting, off-the-shoulder satin gown, deep scarlet in color, that emphasized the flawlessness of her creamy complexion. Her figure was breathtaking, and to a man, they thought her stunning.

"Evening, gentlemen," Brandy purred as she stopped at her favorite table. Lifting her gaze to find everyone still watching her, she smiled and asked in a tone that held much promise, "Anyone for a friendly game of poker—stud?"

Several of the men almost tripped over themselves in their rush to take a chair. Impressed as they were by Brandy's beauty, an hour later they were even more impressed by her gaming skills. Several men had been overconfident, believing no woman could outplay them, and their pockets were much lighter for it.

"You are one helluva—er, excuse me, ma'am, one heckuva poker player, Miss Brandy," Sam Foster said in admiration as he threw down his cards and leaned back in his chair. An elderly man who'd sat in on his share of poker games in his lifetime, Sam realized that this lady was as good as her reputation claimed. She had soundly trounced him on several hands, and she'd done it all honestly.

"Are you quitting on me already, Sam?" Brandy asked with a friendly smile. She liked the way he'd accepted his losses with grace.

"I'm afraid so, my dear. Mrs. Foster only allows me to lose so much on my travels, and I fear I've reached my limit."

"A wise woman, your wife."

"Very," he agreed, grinning as he stood to leave. "Thank you for an enchanting evening."

"My pleasure." And she meant it. She'd won several hundred dollars from Sam in the course of that one hour.

His vacated chair was soon filled by another man wanting to test her ability, and play continued. It was well after midnight when the game finally ended. Brandy looked up to find the *Pride*'s captain, Ben Rodgers, at the bar.

"Good evening, Ben," she greeted the tall, gray-haired steamboat owner.

Ben's gaze was warm upon her. "You look beautiful, as always."

"Why, thank you, sir. You do know how to turn a girl's head." Her smile was real, for Ben was a true friend.

"Are you ready to call it a night?"

"I think so. Will you walk me to my cabin?"

"I'd be delighted."

She rose from the table and left her winnings with the barkeep. Ben then escorted her from the saloon.

Brandy and Ben Rodgers had met when Brandy was just fourteen years old. Ben had been foolish enough to walk the streets of Natchez-Under-The-Hill alone in the wee hours of the morning, and two men had attacked him in an alley. The pair had been in the process of beating and robbing him when Brandy had heard the commotion from the small boardinghouse room she shared with her mother. Most folks wouldn't have cared or gotten involved, but Brandy had roused her landlord, and together they'd frightened the attackers away.

Ben had been groggy and bleeding when they'd helped him inside. Brandy and her mother had taken him into their room and had doctored him and kept watch over him through the night. They'd sent him on his way the following morning with only a headache and a few bruises to show for his ordeal. Ben had seen how poor they were and had offered to pay them for their help, but they'd refused any money from him. He'd realized how proud they were then, and he'd told Brandy that if she ever needed anything, anything at all, she had only to ask.

Brandy had held his offer in her heart, but had never called upon him. Only when her mother's health had begun to fail and they'd had trouble supporting themselves had she approached Ben with the idea of letting her gamble on his boat. She'd learned how to play from a retired riverboat gambler who'd lived in their boardinghouse and befriended her and her mother. He'd taught her everything he knew before he died, and she'd proven an apt pupil. Brandy had been confident that she could earn a living for her mother and herself by gambling, and she hoped Ben would give her the chance to prove it on his riverboat. If he refused her, her only alternative means of livelihood was too horrible to consider.

At first, Ben had been hard to persuade, for he'd been concerned about her safety. She'd pressed her argument, assuring him that she would be an attraction for his boat and, with all the people around, her virtue would be assured. He'd finally relented on a trial basis. When everything she'd told him had proven true and the *Pride* had become known as the steamboat with Miss Brandy aboard, he'd realized they had something special going.

"Did you have a profitable evening?" Ben asked when they were alone on deck.

"It went very well. The men were an easygoing bunch tonight. It's always more fun to play when no one minds losing."

"When was the last time *you* lost? Two trips ago?" Ben knew how talented she was. She had a gift for keeping track of which cards had been played and knowing who was holding what.

"Yes, and it wasn't pretty," she answered with a grimace, remembering that night all too clearly.

They paused by the rail, and Ben glanced down at her to find her gazing out across the moon-kissed Mississippi. Her expression turned dreamy as she stared out at the twinkling lights of a majestic plantation house in the distance. She sighed softly.

"Is something wrong?" Ben asked.

"Oh, no. I was just remembering my fantasy from when I was little."

"What fantasy?" He was curious.

"It seems so long ago now . . . a lifetime really . . .

but I always fantasized about living in a big house like that one and having lots of servants, beautiful clothes, and plenty of food to eat."

"My mother always used to say, if you're going to dream, you may as well dream big," he agreed.

"You know, when I was ten, I found a secret path into the gardens of one of the big houses in Natchez. I used to sneak up there at night just to get a look at what was going on. Sometimes, they had big parties, and all the ladies would be wearing pretty gowns and the men would look so handsome all dressed up."

"You're lucky you didn't get caught." He chuckled at the thought.

"I know." She laughed, too, as she remembered how scared she used to be that someone would find her hiding there, watching everyone. "Reality does have a way of intruding on childish dreams, doesn't it?"

"It does, but never give up your dreams, Brandy. We all need something to inspire us to keep going."

"All I need for inspiration now is a good poker hand. Winning is far more fun than losing."

"And more profitable, too."

"You're right about that." Brandy laughed again. Ben did know how to make her smile.

"How's your mother?"

She turned away from the view and the bittersweet memory of her pointless, youthful fantasy. "Much better. With the money I'm bringing in now, I've managed to rent a small house and even hire a servant to stay with her while I'm gone."

"Good. Tell her I said 'hello' when you get back." Ben was glad that things were working out for them.

"I will."

They moved on down the deck. He bade her good

night when they reached her cabin and waited until she was safely inside and had locked the door before leaving. Life had been rough enough on Brandy so far. The least he could do was make sure she was safe when she was with him.

Inside her room, Brandy slowly undressed, then donned her nightgown and climbed into bed. For just a moment before she drifted off to sleep, she allowed herself to remember all the dreams she'd treasured for so long in the innocence of her youth.

"Oooh, I hate Cynthia Gaultier!" Lottie Demers hissed to her younger sister, Rachel, as she watched the other woman dancing with the man she loved.

"I can understand why," Rachel agreed, her gaze focused on the same couple. "Cynthia's petite, gorgeous, rich and dancing with the man you want to marry. What is there to like about her?"

"Shut up!" Lottie snapped in irritation. "I'm richer than Cynthia, and I'd make Rafe Marchand a better wife."

"You may think so, but what about him? You know all the talk has it that the man has no interest in marriage."

"I don't care what everybody else says, I know I could make him happy if he'd just give me a chance!" Lottie sighed audibly as she watched the object of her unrequited affections waltz by. She imagined herself in his strong arms, gazing up at his ruggedly handsome face, her hand on his powerful shoulder, the heat of his hand at her waist, his body moving in rhythm with hers. . . . Color tinged her cheeks as her pulse quickened and her throat went dry. The man was gorgeous, and she had to have him. "I have got to find a way to get that man to marry me."

"Don't you think that's going to be a little difficult when he hardly knows you exist?"

"He danced with me earlier," she declared defensively.

"You practically threw yourself at him," Rachel pointed out.

"So what? When I see something I want, I go after it, and I want Rafe Marchand." Lottie's green eyes flashed fire as she looked at her sister.

"If you figure out how to do it, let me know."

"I've got to think of something. We're leaving for Memphis tomorrow, and I won't get to see him for weeks and weeks."

"Well, while you're plotting to get him to the altar, I'm going to get some more punch. You want some?"

Lottie glanced at Rafe once more, then stood up to follow her sister. "All right. Let's go. Maybe he'll come over to the refreshment table when he's done dancing with Cynthia, and I'll be able to talk to him again."

Rachel said nothing, for she knew it was pointless to try to distract Lottie. Once her headstrong, spoiled sister made up her mind, there was no stopping her. She wished Rafe Marchand luck, for Lottie had a bulldog's tenacity when she was after something.

Rafe Marchand seemed to be enjoying himself as he squired the lovely young Cynthia Gaultier around the ballroom floor. To all outward appearances, they looked the perfect couple. She was blond and beautiful. He was tall, dark and handsome. But in truth, Rafe was merely going through the motions. Pretty though his dancing partner might be, she was husband-hunting, and he had no desire to fill that role in her life or anyone else's. After the disaster of his parents' marriage, the farther he stayed away from the institution, the better.

When the melody finally ended and Rafe was able to take his leave of Cynthia, he was glad. He thanked her for the dance and headed out the French doors to the veranda. Behind him, a very disappointed Cynthia watched him go, a lovesick expression on her face.

Relieved to be alone and away from the crowd, Rafe stared up at the star-spangled sky and breathed deeply of the honeysuckle-scented night air. The sound of a steamboat's whistle on the Mississippi drew his attention, and he moved to the railing to watch the brightly lighted steamer churn past the plantation's landing. In the morning, he, too, would be on a steamer heading north. He almost wished he was already on board. The Natchez social scene with its fortune-hunting debutantes bored him.

"Rafe . . . I'm so glad you came out here. I've been wanting to get you alone all night," Mirabelle Chandler said in a seductive voice as she appeared out of the shadows nearby.

Without waiting for him to speak, she went straight into his arms and kissed him passionately. She was smiling when the kiss ended. His embrace was every bit as wonderful as she'd remembered.

"I've missed you," she said softly, moving out of his arms to look up at him. Her gaze was hot with promise.

Rafe was not the least bit surprised by her boldness. The thirty-two-year-old, voluptuous blond widow was a wanton lover, and he'd enjoyed sharing her bed on several occasions. His taste in females ran to women like her—the more sophisticated ones who knew what a man's needs were and catered to them with no strings attached. "I've been busy."

"Too busy for me?" she pressed.

"You know how I feel about commitments, Mirabelle," he reminded her harshly.

His words stung, but she tried not to let it show. He'd been honest with her about his aversion to marriage from the start of their relationship. He would share her bed occasionally when it suited him, and that was all. She answered with an ease she wasn't feeling, "I had one husband, darling, and one was enough."

Rafe chuckled at her reply, his irritation gone. "Would you like to go back inside and dance?"

"Waltzing in the ballroom with you wasn't quite what I had in mind. I was hoping we'd share a much more intimate dance. . . ." She trailed her hand down his chest suggestively, remembering how exciting it had been between them. "We could leave right now. My carriage is around front. . . ." She kissed him once more, pressing herself fully against him in invitation.

He felt her willingness, and, had circumstances been different, he might have taken her up on her offer, but tonight he couldn't. "Your offer is tempting, but I fear I must decline. Marc and I are leaving first thing in the morning for St. Louis."

"Pity. We do dance so well together." Her disappointment was real.

"Rafe?" The sound of Marc LeFevre's call interrupted the privacy of the moment.

Mirabelle saw the other man standing at the open French doors looking out at them. "I hope your trip goes well. I'll see you when you get back."

Rafe nodded as she moved away.

"Hello, Marc," Mirabelle said to the tall, fair-haired man who passed her on her way inside.

"Evening, Mirabelle," he responded.

Marc had been looking for Rafe for the past few minutes.

"Did I interrupt anything?" he asked with a knowing smile as he glanced back to watch Mirabelle enter the house.

"No, Mirabelle had just decided to go in."

"It must be difficult to be the most eligible bachelor around and have all the beautiful women throwing themselves at you. There are at least three young ladies inside who would love to get you to the altar."

"So why don't you marry one and take some of the pressure off me?" Rafe countered good-naturedly.

Marc's cheerful mood tempered a bit. His beloved wife, Jennette, had been dead for over a year now, yet the pain of losing her was still with him. Marc doubted he would ever marry again. "I loved Jennette too much. No other woman could take her place."

"What you had was very special," Rafe agreed.

"And that's exactly what you need—a good wife to make you happy," Marc joked, knowing how his friend felt about the issue.

"The happiness you and Jennette had in your marriage was the exception, not the rule."

"Well, there are more than a few gorgeous females inside who would love to prove you wrong. They'd be delighted to show you that they could make you as happy as Jennette made me. There are a lot of happily married couples, you know." Marc believed in the beauty and sanctity of marriage.

"We could argue that point all night and never agree."

"You're impossible."

Rafe shrugged. "The only reason I can think of for a man to get married is to have children, and I'm not ready to tie myself to a female for that reason just yet."

"But you want children some day, don't you? As good as you are with Merrie and Jason . . ."

"Yes, I want children. It's the wife part I have trouble with."

Marc wished his friend wasn't so jaded. He understood his background, though, and knew there was little he could do to change him. Instead of pressing his point, he simply changed the topic to the reason he'd been looking for him in the first place. "We're starting up a poker game. Do you want to lose some of your fortune to me tonight?"

"I'm in," Rafe replied with a grin, "but I don't plan to lose—not to you and not to anybody. When I play poker, I play to win."

"That's what they all say," Marc said, but he knew Rafe could be as ruthless and hard at the poker table as he was at everything else he did. "Let's go. They're waiting for us."

Chapter Two

The LeFevre carriage drew to a stop on the landing in Natchez-Under-The-Hill. As the driver climbed down to unload the bags, Rafe and Marc descended and turned to help Marc's two children, four-year-old Merrie and six-year-old Jason, and their nanny, Louise, down from the carriage.

"Uncle Rafe, I'm so glad we get to go with you on this trip," Merrie said happily, looking at him with glowing eyes. He wasn't really her uncle, but she called him that out of love. Certainly, if she could have picked an uncle out of all the men in the world, she would have picked Rafe.

Rafe smiled tenderly at the petite blond beauty as he lifted her in his arms and set her on the ground. Merrie was his goddaughter, and in her he saw all that was good about the world. She was innocence and beauty personified. She was totally unspoiled and completely lacking in cunning and selfishness.

"I'm glad, too, sweetheart. We'll have fun."

"I know. I don't like it when you go away without me," she went on, holding tightly to his hand. "I think you should keep me with you all the time."

"I would, Merrie, but your father might have some objections to that. Wouldn't you miss him?"

Merrie looked at her father, who was watching her with Rafe. "I would miss Papa a whole lot. . . ." she said thoughtfully, trying to decide how she could please both herself and the men in her life.

"We'll have to talk this over," Marc said as he and Jason, along with Louise, led the way toward the steamer they were taking to St. Louis, *The Pride of New Orleans*.

"It would be easy, Papa. Uncle Rafe could just come live with us and then we could be together all the time," Merrie announced, perfectly happy with her solution to the dilemma. It seemed so simple.

Rafe listened to Merrie's logic and had to fight down a smile. He wondered what Marc was going to do with her in a few more years. He was amused by the thought of his friend trying to deal with Merrie as a high-spirited young woman.

They were just nearing the ramp to board the *Pride* when a barrel broke loose on the back of a passing freight wagon. The heavy container crashed to the ground and careened wildly toward Rafe and Merrie.

"Look out!" the driver shouted as he realized the danger.

Rafe heard the warning and had only enough time to snatch Merrie up and get out of the way of the rolling barrel. Merrie clung to him as he saved them both from harm.

"Uncle Rafe!" she cried in a breathless voice as

they watched the barrel smash into some freight stacked nearby.

"You're all right now, sweetheart," he said, holding her to his heart. The thought of anything happening to her unnerved him.

Merrie was trembling as she reached up to kiss his cheek and then nestle against him.

A feeling of protective tenderness swept through Rafe, and he understood completely the depth of Marc's love for his children.

"Rafe! Merrie!" Marc charged back down the ramp to make sure they were uninjured.

"It's all right," Rafe assured him as the driver ran toward them, too.

"You all right, sir?" the driver asked worriedly.

"We're fine," Rafe answered.

Marc was furious. The possibility that Merrie might have been injured left him outraged. He turned on the driver. "It could have been serious! Check your tie-downs better next time, before somebody really gets hurt!"

"Yes, sir." The driver saw the anger in the man's expression and quickly moved away.

"You're sure you're all right?" Marc asked again.

"Don't worry, Papa. Uncle Rafe saved me," Merrie said adoringly.

"So he's the hero of the day, is he?"

Merrie nodded, smiling brightly at both men as they headed up the walkway to the steamer. Rafe did not put her down again until they were safely on board.

Brandy had already boarded the *Pride* and had been walking toward her cabin when she'd heard the driver's warning shout. She left her bags on deck and hurried toward the gangplank just in time to see the little girl snatched from the path of deadly destruction to safety by the dark-haired, handsome man. She watched a moment longer, wanting to be sure all was safe, and found herself enchanted by the scene that unfolded below.

Brandy couldn't hear what was being said, but it touched her heart to watch the way the man cradled the child protectively to him and the way the girl hugged him and kissed his cheek. Brandy guessed he was her father, and she envied them their loving relationship. Her own father had died when she was very young, but she could still remember how safe she'd felt whenever he'd held her.

Rafe, Marc, Louise, Jason and Merrie ate in the dining room that evening, enjoying the sumptuous fare. When the meal was over, Louise took the two children back to their room to put them to bed for the night.

Kevin Berra and Dan Lesseg had been sharing their table, too, and when the nanny and children had gone, they engaged Rafe and Marc in conversation.

"Have you been to the bar yet?" Kevin Berra asked Marc and Rafe after introducing himself.

"No, not yet," Rafe answered.

"You're in for a treat then," he told them.

"What kind of treat?"

"You'll get to meet Brandy tonight."

"Who's Brandy?" Marc asked.

"You haven't heard about Miss Brandy, the best poker player on the Mississippi?" Dan Lesseg put in with a grin. "I lost about two hundred dollars to her last night."

"And you're smiling?" Rafe was surprised by his casual attitude toward losing. He seemed the kind of man who liked to win, not lose.

"You'll have to meet her before you'll understand."

"She sounds interesting."

"Brandy's more than interesting. Why don't you come down to the bar with us now? She should be there soon, if she isn't already, and you can see for yourself."

Rafe and Marc agreed, thinking they would enjoy another good poker game tonight. Rafe had won handily the night before, much to Marc's chagrin, and he was looking forward to a rematch.

All rose and headed for the men's salon. As they went, Kevin and Dan related what little they knew about the elusive lady gambler.

"There's a lot of mystery about Brandy," Kevin said. "Very little is really known about her past."

"And many men have tried to convince her to do more than gamble with them, but for all their efforts, Brandy remains aloof. She refuses all advances," Dan added.

Rafe was intrigued. He was beginning to believe that the voyage to St. Louis might turn out rather interesting after all.

They entered the men's salon to find that it was already crowded. A group of men were standing around a table toward the back of the room, concentrating on the action there.

"She's here," Kevin said, pointing toward the crowd.

Rafe and Marc were curious, but first they went to the bar with Kevin and Dan to get a drink. Rafe bought the first round, and bourbons in hand, they made their way to join the men who were watching the game in progress.

Rafe and Marc managed to find a place to stand directly across the table from the woman they'd heard so much about, and they understood immediately what Kevin and Dan had been saying. It was no wonder men didn't mind losing to her. Brandy was beautiful enough to distract even the most accomplished poker player.

Rafe's gaze went over Brandy appreciatively. Her skin was flawless, and, from what he could tell, her figure was, too. He decided that even without the rouge and lip color she wore, she would be lovely. He watched her play for a while longer and realized that she was as good as the other two men had said she was. Still, he prided himself on his own card-playing prowess and was not about to let a mere female best him at the tables.

"Are you going to play some poker tonight?" Marc asked Rafe, already knowing the answer.

"I wouldn't miss it for the world." He smiled wolfishly, knowing he was going to enjoy the evening to come.

"Me, too."

Brandy had been concentrating fiercely on her cards, but she sensed someone new staring at her. When she finally won the hand and raked in her winnings, she looked up. It was then that her gaze collided with the stranger's intense blue-eyed regard.

Brandy recognized him immediately as the man she'd seen earlier on the levee with the child. She had thought him good-looking then and very much a father figure, but right now there was nothing fatherly about him. In fact, he was far more attractive than she'd originally thought. Darkly handsome, he had an aura of power and almost danger about him. He stood well over six feet tall. His shoulders were wide and powerful and filled his tailored jacket to perfection. Brandy decided that his wife was one very lucky woman.

"Evenin'," she said in a welcoming tone meant just for him.

"Good evening, Brandy," Kevin and Dan said eagerly in unison. They were standing nearby and thought she was talking to them.

Rafe knew she'd been speaking to him, but he only tipped his head slightly in acknowledgment of her greeting.

Marc was standing beside him, and he smiled at the exchange. He thought Brandy one outstanding example of womanhood and knew this was going to be a very interesting evening.

"How are you tonight?" she asked Kevin and Dan, tearing her gaze from the stranger to glance over at them.

"Just fine, and you look like you're doing fine, too," Kevin said, seeing her winnings piled before her.

"So far, it has been a profitable night for me, but it's early yet," she told him. "You know how Lady Luck is. One minute she's on your side and the next . . ."

"I'll say," whined Tom Jackson, a heavy-set man with beady eyes and thinning gray hair. He'd been drinking too much and had lost quite a bit on the last hand. "I wish Lady Luck would find me tonight."

"Me, too," a player near Rafe said as he stood up, quitting the game. "G'night, Brandy."

"Good night, James." She smiled at him as he moved off to the bar.

Rafe moved into the vacant chair, ready to test his

card-playing abilities against her.

"Do you like to play poker, Mr. . . . ?" Brandy asked as she shuffled the deck. Her movements were sure and deft.

"Marchand, Rafe Marchand, and yes, I've been known to enjoy a hand now and then," he answered easily.

"Ante up, gentlemen," she said as she slid her own money forward to the center of the table and then began to deal.

Rafe and the other four men at the table tossed their money in the pot with hers and were ready to play. Marc looked on, waiting for an opportunity to join in.

Three hands later, Rafe realized that Brandy had rightly earned her reputation. She was shrewd, played smart, and knew when to cut and run. As much as it irked him, for he had only won one hand so far, he had to admit that he admired her skill. She was good.

When another man dropped out, Marc took his chair.

"Welcome to the game," she greeted him, thinking him attractive in a wholesome, honest-looking way.

"My pleasure, believe me."

"We're playing five-card draw," she said as she deftly dealt the hand.

"Have you been doing this long, Brandy?" Marc asked as he picked up his cards.

"I learned how to play when I was young, but I've only been on the *Pride* for about six months."

"Well, we're glad you are," one of the other men put in.

"Thank you. I enjoy being here. Where else could I spend every evening with such handsome, entertaining men?" she answered lightly.

Tom Jackson grumbled something, but they ignored him.

An easy banter developed at the table, for everyone was enjoying themselves—everyone, that was, except Jackson, who continued to drink and lose and complain.

"So, Miss Brandy, will you join me for a stroll on deck later this evening?" John Boyer, asked, his gaze hungry upon her. He had been wanting to get her alone since he'd first set eyes on her, and after six whiskeys he was emboldened to make his move.

"Why, Mr. Boyer, I do appreciate your kind invitation, but I make it a point never to mix business with pleasure. I do not socialize with the passengers."

Boyer was confident that he could change her mind. "I'll show you a good time."

Brandy managed to control the urge to tell him what he could do with his good time. She had seen the look that was in his eyes many times before from a lot of other men and knew exactly what he wanted from her . . . and it wasn't just a good time. "You are a charmer, sir, and I'm sure we'd have a delightful time together, but I never make exceptions to my rule. I wouldn't want any of the other gentlemen to get the wrong impression. I'm here to gamble, nothing more."

Several of the men who'd known Brandy for a while chuckled over Boyer's lack of success.

"Told you so," one said under his breath.

"You can't blame a man for asking." Boyer good-naturedly shrugged off her rejection. "I'm usually pretty successful with women."

"I'm sure you are," Brandy agreed, and then, to

lighten the mood even more, she turned to Rafe. "And so is Mr. Marchand, judging from what I saw earlier today on the levee. Tell me, sir, do you make it a practice to go around rescuing young ladies in distress? And when you do, do they always reward you that way?"

Rafe grinned lazily. "You were watching?"

Brandy was amazed at how the smile transformed him. For one brief moment, the guarded aloofness about him was gone. "That young lady certainly adores you. You must be quite wonderful to inspire such devotion."

"I have my moments," Rafe returned.

"What happened?" Boyer asked eagerly, thinking something exciting had gone on.

"Well, a certain young lady kissed Mr. Marchand right there in front of everyone, and from the look of it, I do believe he enjoyed every minute."

"Indeed I did," he answered. "What man wouldn't want a beautiful female kissing him?"

"She seems to love you very much."

Boyer was listening more and more avidly to their conversation.

"The feeling is mutual. I'd do anything for her." His expression darkened, and a note of bitterness sounded in his tone as he went on, "Innocent beauties like Merrie are rare treasures."

Brandy saw the change in his expression and heard the edge in his voice and wondered at it. "Spoken like a true father."

"Father?" Boyer croaked in confusion.

"Godfather," Rafe corrected. "I'd claim Merrie as my own any day, but I think Marc might have something to say about it." He nodded toward Marc.

"That I would," Marc put in. "I'm rather fond of her myself."

"She's very lucky to have both of you."

"Father? Godfather? How old is this 'Merrie'?" Boyer blurted out in frustration.

"My daughter is four," Marc supplied.

Those gathered around the poker table laughed at the revelation, while Boyer looked disappointed. Only Jackson didn't respond to their banter. He was too caught up in worrying about his losses.

"Are you going to talk all night, or are we going to play cards?" Jackson demanded impatiently. Brandy had finally dealt him a decent hand, and he was ready to play. He was sure this one would be a winner, and he'd be able to recoup all his losses.

"Of course, Mr. Jackson." She smiled at him as she studied her own cards.

Jackson totally ignored her attempt at friendliness. He just slugged down another straight shot, then pushed his glass aside in a rough manner. He led off the betting.

The play was spirited. The betting turned heavy.

Brandy concentrated solely on the game. She was aware of each man's mood. She watched for slight changes in their expressions and the way they hesitated over drawing a card. She noticed how they held their cards, too, for that was important. She understood all the nuances of playing poker and used that knowledge to her advantage. It rarely failed her.

Jackson's complaining had made Brandy aware of his dire financial situation, and she paid particular attention to him, watching from beneath lowered lashes. She wished that he'd quit playing long ago, before things had gotten so far out of hand, but compulsive gamblers rarely stopped on their own.

When Boyer and another man folded, Brandy knew she'd been right about their hands. She grew more confident. Finally, the last bet was placed and Brandy called, spreading her winning hand out on the table for all to see.

Rafe stared at her cards in irritation, realizing she'd beaten him again.

"Thanks for a great game, gentlemen," she said as she reached out to rake in her winnings. "I appreciate your generosity."

"Hold it, woman!" Jackson snarled as he stood up suddenly, jarring the table and knocking his chair over.

The room fell silent at his violent move. Everyone stared at the out-of-control, drunken gambler.

"You were cheating!" Jackson accused her. "I know you were! That pot is mine!" He went for his gun.

"I wouldn't do that if I were you," Brandy ordered in a cold voice. In her hand, a small but deadly derringer was already pointed at Jackson's heart.

Brandy had reacted so quickly to his threatening move that no one had even seen her draw. A shocked murmur ran through the crowd.

"What the hell?" Jackson froze just as his gun cleared the leather of his holster. He turned ashen at the sight of her gun on him.

"Hell is exactly where you're going to end up, if you don't stop and think about what you're doing, Mr. Jackson." Her green-eyed gaze was cold upon him. "I don't cheat. I don't need to. Now, don't do anything stupid. I'll use this gun if I have to."

"But that money's mine! I had two pair!"

"That money is not yours. I had three of a kind, and that beats what you had and what everyone else

45

had at this table. If you can't afford to lose, you shouldn't play."

"You can't talk to me like that after you been stealing from me and everybody else all night long!" He looked around for moral support, but found none.

"The game was a fair one, Jackson," Rafe asserted, his hand sliding toward his own sidearm. As crazy drunk as Jackson was, he wanted to be ready just in case the man started shooting. "I've played with cheats before, and this lady is not one of them. Her game's an honest one."

Jackson was sputtering mad. "She ain't nothing but a whore! Doing what she does! Cheating honest men this way!"

"Shut up, Jackson," Rafe snarled.

Marc recognized Rafe's tone. It wasn't good to push Rafe, and Jackson would have realized it if he hadn't been so drunk.

"We all lost, Jackson. Not only you," Marc said sternly, wanting to diffuse things. "Why don't you just turn around and walk on out of here?"

"But she . . . !"

Brandy lifted her weapon for emphasis. She had kept it poised and ready. If there was one other essential thing that old gambler had taught her years ago, it had been never to bluff with a gun—if you draw it, plan to use it. He'd shown her how to handle one and where to aim for maximum effectiveness. She'd never had to fire it in a situation like this before, but the way things were going, it looked like that might change. Her gaze remained riveted on Jackson as she awaited his next move.

The room was tense and silent.

"Well, Jackson? What's it going to be?" Brandy demanded.

Chapter Three

Jackson stared down her gun and began to tremble. "But my money . . ."

"It's not *your* money anymore," Brandy repeated. "Quit while you're ahead."

"Ahead? How can you say I'm ahead?" Jackson was growing even more furious. Besides his losses, he'd been outgunned by a female. "I've lost everything!"

"You're still alive, aren't you?"

"What's the trouble here?" Ben Rodgers demanded as he charged into the salon backed by two burly deckhands. He'd heard there was trouble in the men's salon and had wasted no time coming to Brandy's aid.

"Trouble?" Brandy looked up at Ben almost innocently, yet the gun did not shift from its target. "I don't think there's any trouble here, Captain. Is there, Mr. Jackson?"

Jackson knew he was defeated. He'd lost his money, and now he'd lost his pride.

"No. There's no trouble here." He backed down, shoving his gun back in his holster.

"Good." Ben was relieved, but he still kept an eye on the drunken passenger. "Then let's get you out of here and see what we can do about putting you ashore. I don't take kindly to poor losers with hot tempers and guns on my steamboat."

Ben and his two men led the cursing Jackson from the saloon.

It wasn't until they'd gone that Brandy realized just how tense she'd been. When she lowered the gun, her hand started to shake. Even so, she managed a slight smile.

"Nothing like a little excitement to liven up the night," she said as she put the gun back in the hidden pocket in her skirt.

All the men were impressed by her nerves of steel in facing down the drunk. They complimented her on her quick thinking, admiring her even more than they had before.

"It's a hazard of the trade, gentlemen," she remarked with seeming ease. In her heart, though, she realized just how close she'd come to shooting a man, and she knew she would be on edge for the rest of the night. "Shall we continue play? Now that Mr. Jackson has left us, there's room for one more."

One of the onlookers quickly took Jackson's seat, and the gambling continued as if nothing unusual had happened.

Brandy retired for the night about an hour later. She made a quick, quiet exit and retreated to her cabin, locking the door behind her. She was still tense and nervous as she tried to sleep.

* * *

When Brandy had gone, Rafe and Marc stood at the bar with Kevin and Dan.

"So, what did you think of our Brandy?" Kevin asked.

"She's everything you said she was and more," Rafe agreed. "I can't believe how well she handled Jackson. It's not easy to back down a mean drunk, but she did it."

"And without even flinching," Dan praised her. "How did she manage to draw so fast?"

"I don't know, but I'm glad I never made her mad." Kevin was impressed.

"She knew exactly what to do and how to do it," Rafe said.

"It could have gotten ugly in here if she hadn't been ready for him," Marc said.

"Very ugly. Let's hope the captain puts Jackson off the boat first chance he gets. Brandy doesn't need to be putting up with his kind," Dan remarked.

"Don't worry," the bartender said, overhearing their conversation. "Captain Rodgers won't let Jackson out of his sight until he's put him ashore. He's not about to take any chances with Miss Brandy's safety."

Later, after Kevin and Dan had gone, Marc and Rafe moved to sit at a table. They were more than mellow as they enjoyed one last bourbon before calling it a night. Marc looked thoughtful.

"You know, Rafe," he mused out loud, a gleam in his eyes, "I think I've figured out the solution to your problem."

"What problem?" Rafe looked at him, puzzled. He couldn't imagine what Marc was talking about. Life was generally good—he had Bellerive; he had money; he had a few friends. What problem did he have? What could be wrong?

"You know . . . your problem . . . the way the women are always throwing themselves at you. Well, I've figured out how you can put a stop to it." He paused and took another drink, feeling rather pleased with the brilliance of his idea.

"Really? And just what is your solution to my 'problem'?"

"I think," he announced with as much seriousness as he could muster, "you should marry Brandy."

"Have you been drinking something besides your usual bourbon tonight?" He stared at Marc as if he'd lost his mind.

"No, I haven't, and this would be perfect—you and Brandy, happily ever after." He grinned, obviously feeling no pain.

"Why don't you and I go see the captain right now? We can arrange for him to perform the ceremony first thing in the morning," Rafe countered sarcastically. "Of course, there is the problem of asking the bride if she wants to be a part of this. . . ."

"Hear me out." Marc held up a hand to shut him up. "Admit it, there isn't a female within a hundred miles of Natchez who could hold a candle to her. Brandy is beautiful."

"So? What does her being good-looking have to do with anything?"

"Not only is Brandy gorgeous, but she's smart, honest and just about the bravest woman I've ever seen. Not to mention the fact that she's damned good at poker. She beat you tonight—and not just once." Marc was grinning widely. He knew how much his friend hated to lose.

"Tonight was only one night of many," Rafe assured him. "It's a long trip to St. Louis, and believe me, by the time we get there, I'm going to be on the winning end." He fully intended never to lose to her again.

"I'm telling you, she'd make you the perfect wife."

"Right. Once we're married, we could open a gambling den in the front parlor at Bellerive. That would really impress everyone who came to visit."

"Since when do you care what people think?"

"I don't, and I don't give a damn about getting married, either."

"Don't be so quick to reject the idea. Besides, I'm not through yet." Marc continued with his argument. "Brandy also, and this is probably the most important part for you to remember . . ." He paused for emphasis, " . . . Is very good with a gun."

"What does that have to do with anything?" Rafe demanded incredulously as he stared at his friend. He could not imagine why Marc thought having a wife who could use a gun would be a good thing.

Marc was trying to keep a straight face as he answered, "Because, my friend, she could use it to run off all the other women who are constantly chasing you!"

"Oh, sure, I can just see me introducing Brandy to Natchez society while she's packing her gun just in case Mirabelle or some of the debutantes show up."

Marc laughed out loud. "Granted, Brandy may have a few rough edges, but she could learn. Hell, if she can bluff her way through a poker game, she could bluff her way through a society ball. All she'd need is a new wardrobe and a few lessons in etiquette, and she could fool everybody."

"I don't want to get married."

"Well, if you *were* looking for a wife, she'd be perfect," Marc concluded, finishing the last of his bourbon. "Think about what I've said."

"Oh, I'll do that," Rafe replied, ready to say anything just to silence his friend.

"Good." Marc was quite proud of himself for having come up with such a great idea.

Brandy had been lying in bed trying to fall asleep for the better part of an hour when she finally gave up. Tossing off her covers, she rose and started to dress. The memory of her showdown with Jackson was still haunting her, and she hoped a few minutes out on deck under the starry night sky, listening to the sound of the paddlewheel and the distant call of the night birds, would help her relax.

Donning a demure day gown suitable for a lady of quality traveling by steamer, Brandy left her cabin and went to stand at the rail. Dressed as she was, she bore little resemblance to the Brandy who'd just passed the night gambling with the men. Her face was washed, all traces of her makeup gone. She looked innocent. Her hair was unconfined, brushed out in a glorious, shining mass of curls about her shoulders. It was the look Brandy had hoped to achieve, for she didn't want to attract any notice. She just needed some peace.

The warmth of the night was a velvet caress. Brandy was enjoying her time there, when suddenly the steamboat slowed and began to glide in toward the bank where she could see the lights of a small settlement burning. This was not one of their regular stops, but she knew what Ben was doing: putting Jackson ashore.

On the deck below, Brandy could hear the sounds

of men's voices arguing as the steamer closed in on the riverbank.

"I don't care what you say, the woman's a cheat and a whore!" Jackson was shouting in a slurred voice.

"You're wrong, Jackson, and I suggest you shut up. You keep pushing me, and I just might decide to throw you over the side and let you swim to shore."

"To hell with you!" Jackson came back at Ben. "The slut's probably sleeping with you. She's probably up in your bed right now just waiting for you to get back there—"

There was the sound of a fist connecting with solid flesh and a grunt of pain.

"I warned you to hold your tongue," Ben snarled at the man. "I won't hear any such remarks about Brandy. She is a lady and my friend. She will be treated right by you and everyone else on my ship."

The steamer reached the bank, and the deckhands who were helping Ben quickly put out the gangplank for Jackson.

"Get off the *Pride*, Jackson. I don't want your kind on my boat!"

Brandy could hear the man's vile curses as he made his way down the ramp to the muddy bank. She stepped back into the shadows, not wanting anyone to see her there and know that she'd overheard his ugly comments.

"One day you'll all get yours! That slut will, too! Just wait and see!" Jackson's voice echoed hollowly through the night.

"Pull up the ramp, boys. Let's get out of here." Ben's orders were curt.

On the deck above, Brandy stood alone in the darkness, feeling the bite of Jackson's ugly accusations. Ben had been staunch in her defense, but she feared that every man on board, no matter how nicely they treated her to her face, really believed the same thing. Her heart ached at the thought.

Rafe parted with Marc at his cabin door. He was heading on to his own room when he realized they were slowing and moving in toward the shore. He heard the argument between Jackson and the captain on the deck below and started to go see if he could help. He quickly realized, however, that the captain had things well under control and didn't need him.

Moving on toward his own room, Rafe almost didn't notice the woman standing back in the shadows. When he did see her, he didn't recognize her, merely thinking it strange that a lady would be out on deck at this time of night alone.

"Are you all right, ma'am?" he asked as he drew near.

Brandy had been so intent on listening to what was going on below that she hadn't noticed his approach. Her breath caught in her throat as she found herself staring up at him in the darkness. "Why, Mr. Marchand . . . you surprised me."

"Brandy?" Rafe frowned as she stepped forward into the light, then gazed down at her, amazed by her transformation. The woman he'd just spent the evening playing poker with was a temptress. The woman standing before him looked for all the world like a genteel Southern lady. Rafe was spellbound. Gone was the face paint and seductive gown. He knew it was crazy, but as attractive as he'd found her before, he found her even more so now.

"Isn't it dangerous for you to be out here by yourself?" he asked, concerned.

"Is it, Mr. Marchand?" she challenged, wondering at the strange, breathless tension that gripped her because he was near. A moment ago, she'd been almost in tears, but now her heart was pounding a frantic rhythm. She told herself it was only because he'd surprised her. That was all.

"Call me Rafe, please."

"All right, Rafe. And no, I'm not worried about being out here alone." Brandy looked up at him, a hint of a smile curving her lips.

He stared down at her mouth, suddenly wondering what it would be like to taste of her sweetness, then remembered her rule that she never got involved with passengers. He smiled easily, wondering if he could be the man to get her to break that rule. "I've seen how you handle a gun. You'll get no trouble from me."

"You know, I've never had to fire that gun yet. Usually just showing it convinces the drunks to back down, but Jackson was not a good loser."

"That's the understatement of the year," Rafe agreed. "I liked the captain's idea of letting him swim to shore."

"I did, too," she said with a laugh.

"He's gone now. You won't have to worry about him anymore."

"Jackson may be gone, but there will always be men like him. . . ."

"You handled the situation very well."

"I was lucky this time. Who knows what I would have done if he'd actually drawn his gun. Somebody could have been killed—and all over money." Her words were heartfelt.

Rafe had thought her hard and a bit brazen to do

what she did for a living. He had thought her completely motivated by money, but now . . . An emotion foreign to Rafe stabbed at him as he realized there was more to her than he'd thought. He felt a twinge of conscience over his earlier remarks to Marc.

"Well, I'd better be going in now," Brandy said as the boat churned its way back to midstream.

"May I walk you to your cabin?" he offered in his most gallant manner.

"No, thank you. Good night."

Brandy turned and walked away without a backward glance.

Rafe stared after her. He was accustomed to women fawning over him, vying for his attention. He'd expected her to welcome his escort and even encourage him once they reached her cabin door. He'd been wrong. She had turned him down flat. His mood turned black.

Rafe stayed where he was, watching her until she'd disappeared inside her cabin, but she never once looked his way.

Scowling, Rafe went to his own cabin. As he lay in his bed much later courting sleep, the memory of Brandy's transformation and Marc's "solution" would not let him rest.

Brandy lay awake in her own bed staring up at the ceiling. It had not been one of her better nights. Dealing with Jackson had been upsetting enough, but then there was Rafe Marchand. She knew how to handle men like Jackson, but Rafe . . .

Brandy closed her eyes, yet a vision of Rafe haunted her. She found herself mesmerized by his dark, compelling good looks. There was something about him that drew her to him like a moth to a flame. She'd had to force herself to walk away from him when they'd been on deck. Her rule about not getting involved with the passengers was a steadfast one, and she would not break it—tempted though she might be.

She tossed and turned, knowing it was going to be a long night.

Chapter Four

Ben sought Brandy out first thing in the morning. He wanted to make sure she was all right after the excitement of the night before.

"Join me for breakfast?" he invited her when she answered his knock.

"That's the best offer I've had all morning," she said. They often breakfasted together, and she enjoyed his company.

They made their way to the dining room and were seated at a quiet table so they could talk.

"I put Jackson ashore last night," he told her once they had settled in.

"I know. I heard."

"You did?"

She nodded. "I couldn't sleep, so I went out on deck late for a breath of fresh air."

"I'm sorry you had to listen to that. He was an ugly one to deal with."

"Thank you for defending me." Her eyes met his across the table.

"He needed to be set straight about you," Ben said gruffly. "I didn't want to leave any doubt in his mind that you're a lady."

"From what I heard, you were pretty forceful about it." She was smiling.

"Some men don't understand plain English. You have to add a little emphasis for them to get the full meaning."

"Let's just hope we never run into Mr. Jackson again."

"That would be fine with me, too. But you take care," he cautioned. "There are a lot more dangerous men out there than just Jackson's type. He was just a stupid, mean drunk. No doubt he's all sobered up this morning and regretting everything he said and did. It's the other ones you have to keep a look out for. Remember that."

"I will. The last thing I want is trouble—from anybody."

Ben knew it wasn't easy for her, especially when situations arose like the one last night, and he admired the way she was handling herself.

When they'd finished their meal, Brandy accompanied Ben as he made his way to the pilothouse.

Marc regretted his late-night drinking far more than Rafe did, for Jason and Merrie, along with Louise, were at his cabin door bright and early the next morning wanting him to eat breakfast with them. Dutiful father that he was, Marc dragged himself from the comfort of his bed to join them.

After eating, they went out on deck to take a walk. It was then that Jason caught sight of the captain.

The boy's eyes rounded as he realized that this was the man who commanded the whole boat. Without waiting for his father's approval, he ran straight up to the uniformed man where he was standing talking to a lady.

"Are you the captain?" he asked, awed by his uniform and bearing.

Ben had seen the youngster running toward him and had stopped talking to Brandy long enough to speak to the boy. "Why, yes, I am. I'm Captain Ben Rodgers, at your service. And you are?"

"I'm Jason," he replied, elated to have met a real live captain. "I never got to meet a captain before. Do you really pilot the ship and everything?"

"I have river pilots to help me. But, yes, I do a little of everything on the *Pride*. My favorite part is talking to my passengers and making sure they're having a good time on board. Are you?"

"Yes, sir! Your ship is great."

"I'm glad you like her." Ben found the boy's candor entertaining.

"Captain Rodgers, I'm sorry if Jason is bothering you," Marc said as he caught up with his son. "Ma'am." Marc greeted the lady in passing, then took a second look. "Why, good morning, Miss Brandy."

"Good morning, Mr. LeFevre. How are you today?" She smiled at the sight of him with his children and nanny. She recognized the little girl as the one Rafe had rescued back in Natchez.

"We're just fine," he replied. "Come on now, Jason, I'm sure the captain has a lot of work to do."

"No, no. It's perfectly all right. In fact, I was thinking perhaps Jason would like to have a tour of the pilothouse. What do you say, young man?"

"Could I?" Jason looked eagerly at his father for approval.

"You wouldn't mind?" Marc did not want to pester the captain, for he knew how busy he must be.

"Not at all. It would be my pleasure. Why don't you come along, too? Brandy? Would you like to join us?"

Brandy declined, saying, "I think I'll just sit on deck and read for a while. You all enjoy your visit."

"It was nice to see you again," Marc said and meant it. He had a distant memory of his drunken conversation with Rafe the night before and recalled that he'd told him Brandy was potential wife material. Looking at her now, dressed as a Southern lady, he knew he'd been instinctively right. Her beauty was natural. She could easily pass for a lady. When he'd been drunk, he'd thought it an outrageous suggestion. This morning, as he looked at her, he suddenly knew there was more to Brandy than just being a gambler.

"Jason and I will be back in a few minutes, Louise."

"Of course, sir. Merrie and I will be fine."

"So, you're the lovely Merrie?" Brandy remarked, kneeling down before the little girl who held such an esteemed place in Rafe Marchand's heart.

"Merrie, this nice lady is Miss Brandy. Can you say hello?" Marc introduced them before he followed Jason and Ben toward the pilothouse.

Merrie gazed up at Brandy, her regard assessing, as if she were looking into her very heart and soul. "You're very pretty and nice, too," she pronounced.

"Why, thank you. So are you. It's no wonder your godfather thinks so highly of you."

"You know Uncle Rafe?"

"I met him just last night."

"He's wonderful."

"He feels the same way about you."

Merrie beamed at her words. "I want to marry him when I grow up, 'cause next to my daddy, he's the man I like best. But Uncle Rafe just laughs and tells me he's too old for me."

"So your uncle isn't married?"

"No. Papa says Uncle Rafe doesn't ever want to get married, but if he did decide to get married, he'd probably marry me."

"Why doesn't he want to get married?" This news surprised her. From the look of him, she'd have thought that Rafe Marchand could have had any woman he wanted.

"I don't know." The child answered simply. "I think being married would be fun."

"I do, too. Merrie, I was just going to my room to get a book to read. Would you like to sit out on deck and read with me?" Brandy looked at Louise for her approval, and she was pleased when the nanny smiled and nodded.

"Do you have any good books with pictures?" Merrie asked.

"I most certainly do. Do you like books?"

She nodded. "My Papa reads to me a lot when we're home. It's fun looking at the pictures and figuring out what the words mean."

"Wait right here with your nanny, and I'll see what I've got in my cabin that you might enjoy. I'll be right back."

Merrie and Louise sat down in two chairs on deck to await her return.

"Did you find any?" Merrie asked when Brandy returned a short time later.

"I have one I think you're going to enjoy."

Brandy drew a chair over and sat down next to Merrie. They began to page through the book. It was Brandy's favorite—an illustrated children's Bible, a gift from her mother when she'd been about Merrie's age. She carried it with her wherever she went. They paged through it slowly, looking at the pictures of Noah and the Ark, and the pictures of angels and the devil.

"My papa says that Mama is an angel now."

"Your mother's in heaven?"

Merrie nodded as she met Brandy's regard. The look in her eyes made her seem very old. "She died last year. It seems like a long time. Sometimes, now, I don't even remember what she looked like."

"I understand."

"You do?"

"Yes, my father died when I was young. It's just been my mother and me ever since, but sometimes I miss him real bad."

"I would miss Papa and Uncle Rafe, too, if anything ever happened to them. I bet you're lonely."

"I am some days, but I still have my mother."

"Mothers are nice."

"I think so, too. Mine is one of the nicest people I know."

"Are you going to be a mother?"

"Not any time soon," Brandy answered, stifling a laugh at the innocence of Merrie's question. "Someday I'd like to be, but you have to fall in love and get a husband before you can become a mother."

"Sometimes things are complicated, aren't they?"

She sounded so mature and so perplexed by it all that Brandy did laugh out loud this time. "I'm sure it's not as terrible as it seems. After all, you're very young and have a lot of time yet to make all your dreams come true."

"Do you dream a lot?"

"I used to. In fact, I was just talking to Captain Ben the other night about how I used to dream of living in a big plantation house when I was little."

"You don't dream about it any more?"

"No, not any more. Besides, most of the time, now that I work with Captain Ben, I get to live on the *Pride*. That's probably even more fun than living in a big house."

Merrie's eyes lit up. "You get to live on this steamboat? That would be fun. You get to go places and meet lots of people."

"That I do," Brandy agreed.

A short time later, the men returned.

"Merrie! Captain Ben invited us to sit at his table and eat dinner with him!"

Merrie was impressed. "Can Miss Brandy come, too? She's nice. I like her."

"Of course she can," Marc answered.

Brandy was touched by the child's open acceptance of her, and Marc's quick agreement to her joining them.

"I'd love to if Captain Ben will have me," she teased.

"It is an honor to have you grace my table any time," Ben said as he started off to take care of business. "I'll see everyone this evening."

"Uncle Rafe! Guess what? The captain invited us to have dinner with him at his table tonight. You want to go?" Jason asked eagerly as he spied Rafe coming down the deck toward him a short time later.

"You met the captain, did you?" Rafe asked.

Jason excitedly told him all about his tour of the pilothouse and his visit with Ben. Rafe found his enthusiasm contagious and agreed to join them.

"It must be nice to get to sleep late," Marc remarked to Rafe when the nanny had taken the children off to play.

"I was up later than you were last night," he countered. "When I was on my way back to my room, there was some trouble on deck. The captain was putting Jackson ashore and things got a little rough." He related what had transpired with the drunk. "I ran into Brandy right after it happened, and she'd heard all of it."

"It must be hard on her, knowing people are always thinking such things."

Rafe shrugged. "She chose the job. Nobody forced her to take it."

"That's true enough, but I'll tell you what. I was right about one thing."

"What?"

"There's more to Brandy than meets the eye. She was with the captain this morning looking like a regular lady. With the right clothes, she could fool anybody. Oh, and she'll be dining with us tonight, by the way."

Rafe said nothing. He remembered all too well how she'd disdained his offer to escort her to her cabin the night before. It would be an interesting evening.

It was dark when dinner was served. Jason was given the seat to Ben's right, and the boy gloried in being so close to him. Ben found the youth an entertaining companion and answered his multitude of questions with patience and good humor.

Brandy took extra care in dressing for dinner that night. She selected a suitably demure gown that would reflect well on the captain and his guests. As she made her entrance and crossed the room to Ben's table, the men all turned to watch her, while the "good" women all whispered cattily behind their fans.

"Good evening, Merrie . . . Gentlemen . . ." she greeted them as she reached the table.

Rafe, Marc and Ben stood, and Ben pulled out the chair on the other side of him for her.

"Evening, Brandy," he said.

"Hi, Miss Brandy," Merrie chirped, glad to see her new friend again. "Uncle Rafe's eating with us tonight, too."

Brandy had been aware of Rafe's presence since the minute she'd entered the dining room.

"Mr. Marchand," she said coolly, her gaze sweeping over him quickly to focus on Marc as she slipped into her chair. "Mr. LeFevre."

"Marc, please," he insisted. "I'm glad you could join us."

"Good evening, Brandy," Rafe said with an appreciative gleam in his eyes as he gazed at her across the table. There was no denying her beauty, and tonight she was, by far, the fairest in the room.

The men sat back down and the meal was served. Conversation remained general. Merrie dominated Brandy, as Jason questioned the captain nonstop about the workings of a steamboat.

Rafe watched Brandy with Merrie and was impressed by her interest in the child. Most of the females he associated with had little time for children. They were more concerned with the latest fashions and gossip and thought little ones a bothersome, noisy lot. Rafe had to admit that he'd held much the same thoughts about children, too, until Jason and Merrie had come along. Now, he found their youthful honesty and exuberance far preferable to the jaded musings of the social set.

Jason finally ran out of questions for Ben as dessert was served. Louise appeared to claim the children as they finished off the rich concoction. When it was finally only adults at the table, it was Marc's turn to ask a question that he'd been wondering about.

"Captain Rodgers, how did you and Brandy become acquainted?"

"I'm proud to say that Brandy and her mother saved my life many years ago, and I've been indebted to them ever since." He went on to tell them the circumstances of how they'd met.

"But how did Brandy end up gambling here on the *Pride*? Was it your idea or hers?"

"It was mine," Brandy told him. "I approached Ben about nine months ago with the idea of letting me sail with him. He didn't think much of it at first."

Marc was surprised by the revelation and looked over at Ben. "You didn't want her? But it's such a good idea, and she certainly draws customers."

"Those were the exact arguments she used on me, but I was worried about situations like we had last night with Jackson," he explained thoughtfully. "Brandy finally managed to convince me that things would be all right, and so far, I have to agree with her. It was a great idea."

"But why would you want to gamble on a riverboat?" Marc turned to Brandy.

"My mother's health is failing, and I had to find a way to make enough money to support us. I learned how to play cards when I was young, and because Ben was my friend, I knew I would be safe on the *Pride*. So that's when I asked him for the chance to prove myself."

"If your mother's so sick, what aren't you with her?" Rafe cut in, wondering at her tale.

A wave of personal guilt swept over Brandy, and with it came the inevitable anger—anger at herself for the situation she found herself in and anger at him for questioning her motives. How dared he so arrogantly question her decisions?

"We have no other family. This is something I have to do." With great dignity, she rose. "If you'll excuse me?"

She was gone from the table before anyone could say any more. The men were barely able to get to their feet as she swept from the room, her head held high.

Ben looked over at Rafe. "I don't take kindly to anyone offending Brandy. You have no idea what her life has been like, so I recommend that you refrain from judging her. Good night, gentlemen." Ben rose and left the table.

When he had gone, Marc shot Rafe a condemning look. "I can't believe you said that to her."

"All I did was ask why she wasn't with her sick mother."

"She'd already said that she had to earn a living for them. The women we know have either fathers or husbands to take care of them. Brandy doesn't, so if she doesn't work to support them, who will?"

"Why doesn't she just get married? She could have any man she wanted," Rafe challenged.

"Maybe like somebody else I know, she doesn't want to get married," Marc shot back.

Rafe scowled.

Chapter Five

At a table toward the back of the dining room, Lottie and Rachel Demers sat with their parents.

"Look, Rachel! I can't believe it! Rafe Marchand is on this boat!" Lottie grabbed her sister's hand under the table in her excitement.

"I can't believe it either. And here you thought you weren't going to get to see him for weeks. What do you suppose he's doing on the *Pride*?" Rachel responded.

"I don't know, but this must be fate bringing us together. Isn't it wonderful, Papa?" Lottie looked over at her father.

"Absolutely," James Demers said, spying the rich planter as he left the room.

"He is so wonderful, Daddy." Lottie sighed. "He danced with me at the ball the other night." The memory of being in Rafe's arms as he swirled her about the dance floor had fed her fantasies ever since.

"Lottie wants to marry him," Rachel told her parents conspiratorially.

"He would make a good son-in-law," Helene Demers said, her eyes narrowing greedily. "Bellerive is a magnificent showplace." She smiled as she imagined her daughter hostessing balls at the plantation.

"I've heard his finances are in even better shape than the plantation," James added.

"But how do I get him to propose to me, Papa? I love him. I'd do anything to be his wife."

"These things take time," he cautioned.

"Rafe can have any woman he wants. Somehow, I've got to convince him that he wants me."

"I'm sure he'll be at another ball soon, and you'll get a chance to speak to him again," her mother told her.

"I hope so." Lottie sighed, watching Rafe until he disappeared from the dining room. "But I wish there was something more I could do to encourage him."

James's mind was racing as he tried to think of ways to throw the two of them together. "Well, for a start, you and your sister could go for a walk on deck right now."

Lottie brightened at the thought of getting the chance to speak with Rafe. "We will. Come on, Rachel."

"We'll see you a little later," they said, smiling at how quickly their daughter caught on. Lottie might not be the prettiest girl in the world, but she was smart.

"What do you think, dear? Can we convince Rafe Marchand to marry our precious daughter?" Helene asked.

"I'm sure there's some plan we can come up with that will work. Though from what I've heard, he's in no hurry to marry."

"Perhaps there's some way we can change that. . . ." Helene was thoughtful, her scheming mind already searching for ways to catch herself a rich son-in-law.

"Well, what do you think, Rachel?" Lottie asked as they followed Rafe and Marc at a distance down the deck. "Should I just corner him and ask him to marry me? Or should I be more subtle?"

Both girls giggled.

"Do you know what kind of competition you have for his affections? Why, Mirabelle is after him, and so is Cynthia . . ."

"I know, but I'm still a virgin, which Mirabelle can't claim, and I'm far richer than Cynthia. Still, I have to think of some way to make him propose. It's a long trip from one dance at a ball to the altar. . . ."

"But if he doesn't love you . . ."

"Love?" she scoffed. "He doesn't have to love me now. I can make him fall in love with me later. I love him. That's all that matters. He's just got to give me the chance to prove it."

They fell silent, their minds traveling devious avenues until Rachel, the more conniving of the two, looked up. Her eyes were alight with an inner glow of excitement.

"I think I've got it!"

"What is it?"

"If Papa and Mama agree, this is what we'll do . . ." She quickly outlined her strategy to claim her sister the husband of her dreams. "What do you think?"

"Do you think it will work?"

"How could it fail?"

"But won't he hate me for it?"

"Maybe for a minute, but then you'll have him for your husband, so what does it matter? After a little while, he'll forget all about it, and you'll live happily ever after." Rachel sighed, thinking herself quite brilliant.

"I love it," Lottie agreed. "Do you really think I can pull it off? It's awfully daring—and dangerous, too."

"Do you want to marry Rafe?"

Lottie didn't have to think about the answer. "I can do it." Her words were firm with conviction.

The two began to plot in earnest. They needed to confide in their parents and knew it would take at least another day to set their plan in motion.

Brandy channeled her anger into her game that night and won. She bested Rafe Marchand for several good-sized pots and felt a sense of immense satisfaction when she saw a flash of annoyance in his regard. She enjoyed putting the arrogant man in his place.

The rest of the men were attentive and kind that night, paying her compliments and flirting with her constantly. She enjoyed their company, and laughed and flirted back. As she was leaving for the night, though, her gaze met Rafe's assessing one from across the room, and the guilt that had haunted her earlier returned.

Once she reached her room, Brandy sat in silence, staring down at her small portrait of her mother. Sighing, she held the picture to her heart. There was nothing she'd rather do than stay home and be with her mother, but circumstances being what they were, she couldn't . . . not and survive. She had to work for a living and gambling on the *Pride* was the only way she could earn enough to make ends meet. Her mother understood that and supported her in her efforts, but that didn't ease the guilt Brandy felt because she truly enjoyed what she did. She reveled in the challenge of a good card game, of bluffing her way out of a tight hand and of winning large pots from rich men. As Miss Brandy on the *Pride*, the men vied for the chance to match wits with her over their poker hands as they tried outrageously to charm her. But how many of them would even have deigned to speak to her, let alone flirt with her, had she been working as a mere maid or seamstress? Not a one, she was sure.

There was no denying the truth, for Brandy was a completely honest person—especially with herself. She loved gambling on the *Pride*. She loved dressing up in pretty dresses and being the center of attention. She loved winning, too, for it let her know that at least she was as good as they were at gambling—if nothing else. But always in the back of her mind was the image of her mother, ailing and lonely, awaiting her return.

A single tear traced down Brandy's cheek as she put the picture back on the small nightstand and went on to bed. There was no resolution to her situation.

The following day passed quietly. Brandy kept to her room except for an early morning walk about the deck. She found herself looking forward to the coming evening, and especially to facing and beating Rafe Marchand again.

For some reason, Brandy felt the need to look even more stunning than usual that night. She styled her hair up away from her face and dabbed a touch of scent at all her pulse points. The gown she wore was less revealing than others, yet even more suggestive. Of dark blue satin, it clung to her figure like a second skin, more than hinting at the lush curves beneath. She donned paste diamonds at her ears and throat to complete the ensemble. She felt daring and confident as she made her way toward the side entrance to the men's saloon.

"Good evening, gentlemen," she purred in a throaty voice as she came through the door.

The legion of men who were waiting for her responded enthusiastically to her arrival. Soon she was surrounded at her table, dealing smartly, returning their clever remarks with witticisms of her own. She felt a niggling of disappointment when there was no sign of Rafe. Forcing herself, she concentrated on the cards and her job.

The game was going smoothly except for the farm boy who kept gawking rudely at her while he played.

"You know, Miz Brandy, if you're holdin' a pair like you already got, that'd be one hell of a great hand . . ." He laughed loudly at his own innuendo.

The other men shot him silencing glances, but he ignored them.

Brandy winced, but said nothing as she continued to play with grace and elegance. When, to her dismay, the boy won the hand, she covered her irritation with a smile.

"My, oh, my." He leered at her. "Since I won the hand, does the rest of the 'lady' come with the pot, too?"

"Shut up, Jones. Don't talk to Brandy that way," one of the other men told him.

"I kin talk to her any way I want. If she's in the men's saloon, then she knows what she's askin' for and what she's gonna git," he declared, reaching across the table to snare her wrist. "What d'ya say, sugar? What did I win from you?"

Brandy was tempted to slap him, but she controlled her temper. "You won the pot, sir, and that's all."

"Oh, I think I won more than that." His grip tightened as she tried to pull away.

"This wasn't a game of stud. If it had been, I doubt the others would have let you join in."

Jones's expression darkened at her insult. "Look, lady . . . I'll show you a stud . . ."

"*Lady* is right, son." The cold, hard sound of Rafe's voice cut through the room. "Now, take your hand off her. The only thing she deals is cards."

The threat in his tone stopped Jones, and he glanced around at Rafe to find himself staring into a pair of the deadliest eyes he'd ever seen.

Rafe had walked in to find the lout taunting Brandy and was immediately furious.

"*Now*, boy," he ordered, deliberately humiliating him.

Jones's hand dropped away, and he glared up at the stranger who had dared to interrupt him. "I won the hand."

"And that's all you won. Now, get the hell out of here if you can't act like a man." Rafe turned to look at Brandy. "Evening, Brandy," Rafe greeted her. He glanced back at Jones. "You staying in the game or clearing out?"

Jones was furious. He snatched up his pot and stomped from the room.

"Thank you, Rafe." Brandy hated to have to thank him, but she did breathe a little more easily with the other man gone.

Rafe took his seat and gave her a slight nod.

"You're in?" she asked.

"I'm in," he replied.

"Since the company has vastly improved, shall we play stud this time?" she asked daringly, looking around the table.

"Whatever you want, Miss Brandy," the men replied. "None of us will give you a hard time."

"I think I feel like a game of stud tonight," Rafe replied with a crooked smile.

Though Jones's words and actions had annoyed Brandy, at Marchand's response, her heart did a strange flip-flop.

"Stud it is," she replied, giving him a smile in return.

Several hours later, as the night wound down and play ended, Brandy graciously took her leave. It had been a very prosperous evening for her. As she always did, she left her winnings in the safekeeping of the bartender and retired to her cabin, pleased with the way things had gone.

Lottie and Rachel spent hours creating the perfect plan, and they were ready to tell their parents about it at breakfast the next morning. Before they could broach the subject, though, their parents brought up the topic of Rafe.

"Lottie, I ran into Rafe Marchand in the bar last night," James told them.

"You did? Did he say anything about me? How was he?" Lottie asked, eager to know everything that had transpired.

"He was just fine, and, no, he didn't say anything about you."

"Oh." Lottie sighed heartbrokenly, wishing that he had.

"I mentioned that we were all traveling upriver. He said that he might attend the social after dinner tonight." James doted on his daughters and spoiled them. Whatever they wanted, he saw to it that they got.

"I hope so. I want to do something to get his attention, and I want to do it now. This trip is the perfect time. You know, Papa . . . Mama . . . Rachel and I have come up with an idea. But we're going to need your help to make it work."

"You've got an idea of how to get him to propose?" her mother asked, wanting to hear their plan.

"Yes." She quickly told them the plot they'd devised.

When James looked up at his oldest daughter, he was smiling. "It's brazen and will take a lot of nerve, but if it works, you'd have him at the altar the following day."

"I want Rafe Marchand, Papa. I'll do anything to get him."

"All right. We'll do it," Helene agreed.

"Now, listen carefully, girls," James began. "This is what we have to do. . . ."

All were smiling widely when he finished explaining his part in their strategy.

"Papa, you're brilliant."

"Thank you." He was gloating, more than pleased with what they'd come up with. Soon, Lottie would have a husband and he'd have a rich son-in-law.

"Tonight's the night, then?" Helene asked, excitement glowing in her eyes.

"Yes. I'll be in the men's saloon keeping an eye on things. Once he leaves, I'll wait about twenty minutes and then follow. That should give you plenty of time to maneuver him where you want him. Think you can do it, Lottie?"

"When I want something, Papa, I get it."

"That's my girl. This will work. I'm sure of it."

The prospect of having Rafe Marchand in the family more than satisfied Helene and James. Suddenly, they didn't mind having had only daughters for their offspring anymore. This was going to be wonderful—once all the shouting was over.

After dinner that night on the *Pride*, there was dancing in the grand salon. Rafe had wanted to go with Marc to the bar, but had run into James Demers and had been cornered into a business conversation. James was asking Rafe about how he'd been upgrading the stables at Bellerive when the ladies joined them.

"You remember my daughters, Lottie and Rachel, and my wife, Helene, don't you, Rafe?" James asked.

"Of course. It's lovely to see you ladies again."

"It's good to see you, too," Lottie managed, barely able to contain her excitement. Her gaze was hungry upon him. He was all she'd ever wanted in a man, and all she could think of was that soon he was going to be her husband. Brazenly, she asked, "Shall we dance? I do love this melody."

"Of course." Rafe saw no way out. Ever the gentleman, he offered her his arm and squired her out onto the dance floor.

Lottie was in heaven as they moved about the room. Surely her feelings were not all one-sided. She glanced up, hoping to find his gaze upon her. Instead, she found him staring off into the distance.

Determined to monopolize his thoughts, she started to talk.

"Why are you bound for St. Louis, Rafe?"

"Business, I'm afraid. This is not a pleasure trip." Rafe found her attempts at conversation irksome. He caught sight of Brandy with the captain across the room. She had just looked his way when Lottie began to talk and he was forced to pay attention to her.

"Pity. I do love St. Louis. We could enjoy it together, you know. There are a lot of things we could do. . . ." She fluttered her lashes at him.

"Perhaps, if there were time, but from the looks of things, I'm going to be very busy."

"Well, if you find a moment, I would love to spend more time with you."

"I'll keep that in mind."

Rafe was glad when the dance ended and he could take Lottie back to her father.

"Thank you for the dance, Lottie. Now, if you'll excuse me?"

"Of course." Lottie sighed rapturously. When he was out of earshot, she turned on her father. The look in her eyes was determined. "I'm going to marry him, Papa. He's the only man I want."

"Then we'll do it."

"Tonight?"

"Tonight."

Lottie was smiling brightly at the thought of what was to come. Rafe Marchand didn't stand a chance. And once he was caught, she was going to make him a wonderful wife.

Rafe finally escaped to the men's saloon and enjoyed a bourbon at the bar. When Brandy arrived and took her place at the table, he remained at the bar, watching her play from a distance. He told himself that he hadn't really been eager to see her tonight, that he only wanted to win back what he'd already lost. But after dancing with the clinging Lottie, being around Brandy was like a breath of fresh air.

"Good evening, Brandy," he said as he joined her game some time later.

"Hello, Rafe," she welcomed him, trying not to think about the way she'd felt when she saw him in the other woman's arms on the dance floor. "Your friend Marc, here, is having a lucky night. This is the third hand he's won in a row."

"It's about time," Marc laughed. "After last night, I was beginning to wonder if I should ever play poker again."

"Obviously, you should," Rafe said, seeing the winnings stacked before him. "I had a bad night last night, too. Let's see if my luck's turned and I can lighten your pockets a little."

Play began again.

An hour later, Marc leaned back in his chair. "Well, I think I've taken enough of your money for one night," he announced with a chuckle. He had continued his winning ways and was feeling more than pleased with himself.

"I think you should stay longer, so we can all have a chance to win our money back," Rafe said, knowing full well that Marc was quitting because Merrie and Jason would be at his door at the crack of dawn.

"I'll give you another chance tomorrow. Miss Brandy, thank you for a delightful evening."

"Good night, Marc."

The other gamblers were glad to see him go. They, along with Rafe, hoped their luck would change for the better now that he was gone.

Only Rafe proved the beneficiary of his departure, though. He won the next game and smiled to himself. He'd taken the time over the last few nights to study Brandy's style of play, and he had come to recognize a subtle difference in the way she sat at the table when she held a good hand. There was a slight shift in her shoulders, a straightening of her back, that gave her away, and winning this hand had just proven his theory. He was going to enjoy winning back everything he'd lost to Brandy and then some. It might take him a night or two, but he was going to do it.

"It looks as if Marc passed his good luck along to you. I could use a friend like him," Brandy said.

"So could I," one of the other men said, sighing over his losses.

"Me, too," another added as he studied his cards hopelessly.

Rafe just laughed as he raked in his winnings. "I'll tell him you all said so."

Rafe finally quit the game and left the bar at midnight. He'd had his share of bourbon, but was not drunk. He was merely comfortable as he headed for his cabin.

Brandy continued to play. As long as there were men there willing to lose their money to her, she was more than happy to oblige. She noticed how odd the man named James Demers had been acting. He had been drinking heavily all night and seemed preoccupied with watching Rafe. He had paid particular attention when Rafe left the room, and since then had been nervously checking his pocketwatch every other minute or so. At one point, the man said something to the bartender and then laughed at his own remark, raising his glass in toast to himself. Brandy hadn't been able to hear what he'd said, and when the hand ended, she excused herself to go speak with the barkeep. She called him down to the end of the bar so she could talk to him privately.

"Is something wrong, Brandy?" he asked, wondering at her unusual move in seeking him out.

"No. I was just wondering what Demers was laughing about."

"It's strange. After I poured that last bourbon, he checked his watch and said that by this time tomorrow he'd have a rich son-in-law. Then he toasted himself. I don't know what the hell he was talking about."

"He didn't mention any names?"

"No, he was just mouthing off about some man his daughter was in love with and how they were going to be married very soon."

Brandy remembered Rafe dancing with the woman earlier that night. She frowned. Her instincts were screaming that something strange was going on. "He sure got nervous when Marchand left, didn't he?"

The barkeep nodded.

"I think I'd better pay Mr. Rafe Marchand a call. I owe him since he helped me with Jones. He could be in for a big surprise. Tell the boys I had to retire for the night, and I'll see them tomorrow."

"They won't be happy. They're all waiting for you to come back."

"Give them a round on me."

"Whatever you say," he agreed, seeing the determination in her gaze.

Chapter Six

The deck was deserted and all was quiet as Rafe reached his cabin. He went in, thinking only of the comfort of the bed that awaited him. He threw the covers back and started to undress, unbuttoning his shirt. He had just shrugged out of it when a knock came at his door. Rafe frowned, thinking it had to be Marc. He didn't stop to put his shirt back on, but hurried to open the door.

Rafe had been prepared to see Marc. The last person he'd expected to find at his door was Lottie Demers, but there she was, staring up at him with a hungry look in her eyes. He could almost feel the heat of her gaze upon him, and he was very sorry that he hadn't taken the time to put his shirt back on. "Lottie?"

"Evening, Rafe," she said softly.

"Just one moment . . ."

He turned, meaning to grab his shirt and put it on,

but she was too quick for him. In the time it took him to reach for the garment, she had slipped inside the room and was closing the door.

"Lottie? What are you doing? You shouldn't be in here. It's late, and I was just about to go to bed. . . ."

"But I needed to talk to you, Rafe. It's important." Her voice was breathless.

"This is hardly the time or place for a nice young lady like you to be paying a single man a visit. If your father were to catch you here, there'd be hell to pay."

"But, Rafe," she said with a note of desperation. "I have to talk to you in private. Please . . . It'll only take a minute. . . ."

"No. Not tonight. I'll be more than willing to meet with you in the morning, but not here in my room tonight."

Lottie realized she was getting nowhere and knew her father wouldn't be along for another few minutes to entrap them. She had to stall. She had to get Rafe into the bed and she had to do it now. In a brazen move, she began to unbutton her bodice. "Rafe . . . The way I feel about you . . ."

"Lottie, I want you out of here," Rafe warned, in no mood to deal with her.

"I know it's crazy. . . . But . . ." She blurted out, "I love you!"

"You have to leave now!" he said in a stern voice that would have left anyone else quaking.

Not Lottie, though. She knew her wedding was as close as tomorrow morning. Just as soon as her father showed up, everything would turn out perfectly. "Rafe . . . I want you . . ."

Rafe backed away from her and was reaching for the door, getting ready to leave himself, when suddenly the door opened and Brandy rushed in. She took one quick look around and went straight into his arms, ignoring his stunned and wary expression.

"Thank heaven you waited for me!" she said, linking her arms about his neck and pulling him down to her. In a rushed whisper, she said, "Play along with me!"

"Brandy, I . . ." Rafe wanted to know what she was doing there, but there was no time.

Brandy kissed him full on the mouth to silence him. It was a passionate kiss, and Lottie couldn't believe what she was witnessing.

"How can you want *her?*" Lottie gasped at the sight of the man she wanted embracing Brandy. "Rafe, this is ridiculous! She's beneath both of us! She's nothing but a hussy!"

At that particular moment, her father came bursting into the room, followed by another man from the bar. James had thought he would find his daughter in Rafe's embrace and have won himself a son-in-law. Instead, he found Rafe and Brandy wrapped in each other's arms, and Lottie looking on in tears.

"What's going on in here?" James bellowed as he and the other witness looked on in shock.

They had all heard that Brandy didn't give out her favors. They realized now that everything they'd heard about her had been wrong.

Brandy broke off the kiss and glanced archly at him. "Why, Mr. Demers . . . What are you doing here?"

"I was about to ask you the same! My daughter—"

"Your daughter was just leaving," Rafe spoke up. "And if I were you, I'd keep a more careful watch over her. The young lady is quite headstrong and is going to get herself into trouble if you're not careful."

"But she's in your room and you're half-undressed!"

"The woman I want is right here in my arms," Rafe said smoothly. "I told Lottie that this wasn't a good time for a visit, but she came in uninvited anyway."

"Rafe knew I was due here at any minute, and he didn't want to embarrass the poor innocent little girl." Brandy said each word with emphasis, letting them know that they fully understood that Rafe had been set up. "Think how devastating it would be to her reputation if it was learned that she had been in Rafe's room—unchaperoned."

James paled. "But my daughter has been compromised—"

"Your daughter was foolish enough to push her way in here when Rafe was expecting me. Her reputation will be in tatters if word of this gets out," Brandy pointed out.

"As would yours."

Brandy shrugged as if her own situation was of no import. "I've dealt with worse than gossip in my life, but I'm not so sure about Lottie."

James gnashed his teeth in frustration. Their wonderful plan had failed. Lottie had done everything right. She'd gotten into Rafe's cabin in time, and he himself had appeared on schedule, but somehow, things had turned out badly. There was no way to force Rafe to marry Lottie now. James would never have guessed that Brandy and Rafe were involved, but he had seen her in his arms.

"Come on, Lottie. This is no place for you."

The young woman looked crushed as she quit the room with her father and the other man following her. They closed the door behind them, leaving Rafe and Brandy alone.

Brandy immediately moved out of Rafe's arms. His kiss had been powerful, more exciting than she'd ever dreamed, and that frightened her. It had felt right to be in his arms, but she knew she had to fight the feeling.

"There. Now we're even. You helped me with Jones, and I just saved you from a trap. I'll just wait a second longer to make sure they're gone, and then I'll be out of your way." She started for the door to listen to what was happening outside.

"Wait a minute. How did you know about this?"

"I didn't. I was guessing, but my instincts warned me that something was wrong from the way Demers was acting in the bar after you left. It looks as if they had it all planned. Evidently Lottie wanted to marry you so badly that they cooked up this scheme to force you to the altar."

"But Demers caught *us* together. How do I know that you're not a part of their plot? What do you want out of all this?"

"Me?" She stared at him in outraged disbelief. "What makes you think I want anything?"

"Every woman wants something," he replied snidely.

"Believe me when I tell you this, I don't want a thing from you. Nothing happened between us, and even if there is any talk, it will pass. Don't worry, Mr. Marchand. Unlike Lottie, I didn't come in here to force you to marry me. You don't owe me a thing."

Then she was gone, without another word.

Rafe's frustration grew as he stared at the closed door. He couldn't believe what had just happened. One minute he'd been ready for bed, and the next he'd been saved from a conniving plot to force him into an unwanted marriage.

Rafe smiled ruefully. Brandy was one amazing woman! She had put her own reputation at risk for him, coming into his room like an avenging angel. And how had he repaid her? He'd insulted her.

Rafe thought about the way she'd looked as she'd quit the room. He had seen the fire of pride and defiance in her eyes as she'd told him she wanted nothing from him, and he thought he'd never seen a more desirable woman.

Unable to relax, he strode about the cabin. He stopped his pacing suddenly and shuddered at the realization of how close he'd come to being forced to the altar. Raking a hand through his hair in a weary motion, he sighed. If he was already married, he wouldn't be having these problems, but he had no desire to wed. Only the thought of having a son or daughter tempted him even to consider marriage.

Rafe imagined a son or daughter with Brandy's quick wit and bravery, and he knew that offspring would be a child to behold. When he recognized the direction of his thoughts, he frowned and pushed the idea quickly away. Brandy wanted nothing to do with him. She'd made that abundantly clear.

Rafe stretched out on the bed. He wondered what Demers was going to do about what had happened there tonight. If the other man was smart, he'd keep his mouth shut. Certainly, Lottie's reputation would suffer dramatically if the events that had transpired were revealed, but there was no telling what the other man might do. If he was angry because his plot had been foiled, he might try to hurt Brandy. Despite undercurrents of suspicion about her, Brandy's reputation had been unsullied—until now. Now, however, there definitely was some truth to the gossip, and if Demers wanted to, he could make things difficult for her.

The more Rafe thought about it, the more it troubled him. Brandy had saved him from a horrible fate—a marriage to Lottie Demers—yet she had wanted nothing in return; in fact, she had disdained the thought. Still, she would be the one to pay the price for coming to his rescue, and he had to find a way to ensure that she didn't suffer for that.

Chapter Seven

Brandy was in the middle of dealing when she saw Rafe enter the room. She tensed, then forced herself to relax. She had been seething ever since she'd left him last night. How dare he accuse her of plotting with James Demers! The thought still had the power to infuriate her, and as Rafe claimed the chair directly across from her, she vowed to make him pay at the poker table tonight for his insults the night before. She was going to trounce him soundly.

Despite her attempt to reveal nothing of what she was feeling, Rafe had seen the way her eyes narrowed when she spotted him across the room, and he'd known the night was going to be an interesting one. He was ready for the game to come. He had been thinking about it all day, and he knew what he had to do. It seemed a stroke of fate that the man sitting opposite Brandy had chosen that particular moment to quit the game. Rafe took the seat in a casual motion.

"Good evening, Brandy,"

She glanced at him and managed a phony smile of welcome.

"Mr. Marchand, how nice to see you again."

"The pleasure is all mine, believe me," he returned, and he meant it. He had told Marc about how Brandy had rescued him from Lottie's trap, but he had not said a word to him about his own plan. He would tell him later. For now, he just was going to do what had to be done. "What game are we playing this evening?"

"Draw," she answered quickly. She no longer thought teasing banter with him amusing. She knew him for who he really was now, an arrogant, conceited bastard, and she didn't like him. In a way, she was even sorry she'd saved him last night. She rather thought he and the Demers girl deserved each other.

Brandy dealt efficiently as she joked with the others at the table. No one noticed that she was irritated, and she was glad. This was her job; it would not do to let her emotions get the better of her.

As play began, she sensed right away that there was an edge to Rafe's game that hadn't been there before. It was a simple matter to read the others at the table. The man on her left, Morrison, was definitely no card sharp. If he held more than a pair of deuces, his left eye twitched. Williams sat on her right, and she knew when he was bluffing for he had the nervous habit of clearing his throat then. The third man at the table, Hagan, was a little more difficult to read. The only clue she ever had that he held a good hand was when his knuckles whitened as he held his cards. And then there was Rafe. She had marked him over the last few nights as a solid, cautious player, but she had never been able to read his cards by his expression or any nervous reaction. Tonight, he seemed even more guarded than usual as he bet heavily and steadily.

Brandy was not concerned when she lost a few hands. It was to be expected. She knew the risks and took them. She dealt again and was pleased with her hand. She had three queens, a seven and a four. Rafe took one card on the draw and raised. Williams dropped out; Morrison followed. Brandy threw away the seven and four and drew an ace and a three. It wasn't her best hand of the night, but she wasn't disappointed. Three of a kind was solid.

The crowd standing around the table drew in closer, sensing that something exciting was about to happen.

Rafe raised again. Hagan stayed. Rafe's expression was mild as he looked directly at Brandy. "Your bet."

She felt a twinge of nervousness at his steady, unwavering regard, but she did not give in to it. She continued to match him dollar for dollar in the betting. The stakes were high and getting higher.

Hagan finally dropped out, sensing that their hands were far better than his own.

"I bet five thousand," Rafe announced calmly, a slight smile curving his lips. He watched Brandy closely as he pushed the amount into the middle of the table.

A shocked gasp sounded in the room from the onlookers.

A frisson shivered down Brandy's spine as she stared at her three queens. Her own funds were dangerously low, but the pot to be won was a big one—enough to take care of her mother for many months.

Besides, she refused to lose to this man. She would not let him back her down. She was going to match him dollar for dollar, bet for bet. Brandy looked up at Rafe, but could read nothing in his expression. Drawing a deep breath, she knew she had to go for it.

"I match your bet and call," she declared fiercely, certain that she was going to win.

"You have the money?" Rafe asked.

"*If* I lose." She emphasized the *if*. "I'm good for it."

Rafe smiled. He had her right where he wanted her.

James Demers was among those who'd gathered around the table. He had been drinking heavily all night and was watching the game with interest.

"You of all people, Marchand, should know that she's good for it," he slurred. He stumbled back to the bar muttering under his breath, "Marchand can always take it out in trade."

Rafe stared straight into Brandy's eyes, challenging her, daring her. "I trust you to pay your debts, just as I always pay mine," he said in a low, soft voice. "Let's see your cards."

Brandy nodded and spread her hand on the table.

Rafe was quiet for a moment, letting the tension build. Then he smiled easily. "A straight beats three of a kind."

He laid down his cards—a heart straight, king high.

She went pale, but said nothing.

A roar of approval erupted in the room. Side bets that had been placed on Brandy and Rafe were paid off.

"Looks like you're a winner, Mr. Marchand," she said tightly, trying to cover her shock and horror.

93

"Did you ever doubt it?" he countered as he quickly counted out the money to see exactly what she owed him.

Brandy was feeling sick to her stomach. It was the first time she'd ever lost so badly, and inwardly she railed at herself for letting her emotions interfere with her gambling. She had wanted desperately to beat him, and now she would pay, and pay dearly, for giving in to that weakness.

"You owe me five thousand dollars. When can I expect to see the money?" Rafe asked, deliberately pressing her.

"Tomorrow." The word was choked from her. "I'll pay up tomorrow."

He nodded, his gaze catching and holding hers.

"If you gentlemen will excuse me?" Brandy rose from her chair.

All those gathered around complimented her on the fine game she'd played. She bantered with them easily, appearing unaffected by her loss. But in reality, she knew she was in dire straits. She had another six hundred dollars in her room, but that was all the money she had left in the world. She wondered what she was going to do.

That night was one of the longest, most terrible ones she'd ever spent. She did not sleep, but paced her room endlessly, searching for some way to find the money to pay Rafe. She knew he was ruthless. She knew he was heartless. She knew he expected payment.

In desperation, in the middle of the night, she left her room and went to knock on Ben's door. He was surprised to see her, but let her in after taking the time to quickly dress.

"What's wrong?" Something had to be terribly

amiss for her to seek him out in the middle of the night.

"I made a terrible mistake tonight," she confessed, trembling. "I was playing cards with Rafe Marchand and the betting went high—too high. I should have gotten out, but I was sure I had a winning hand." She refused to confess to Ben that she'd wanted badly to beat the other man.

Ben looked sympathetic. "How much do you need?"

In all her time on the boat, she had never gotten herself into any tight situations before and Ben was more than ready to help her out. He had seen how Brandy and Rafe had reacted to each other at dinner the other night and knew sparks had flown between them. Rafe Marchand had impressed him as a man to be reckoned with, and he knew she had to make good.

"Nearly five thousand."

Ben stared at her in shock. "I could scrape up a thousand, maybe fifteen hundred, but that's all I have."

"I understand." She sounded defeated. "I have six hundred in my room, and that's all I have left." She lifted her troubled gaze to Ben's.

"Maybe he'll . . ."

She interrupted him, knowing what he was about to say. "Don't even suggest it. I don't think Rafe Marchand's the forgiving type."

They shared a look of misery as they searched for a solution.

"I shouldn't have kept playing. I knew there was something different about him tonight. He was so cold and determined. It was almost as if he wanted nothing more than to beat me badly. And he did."

"You have to talk to him. Go to him and see if he'll take partial payment. I can spot you a few dollars to start you up again, and then maybe he'll give you time to earn it back and pay him off."

"You're too good to me, Ben."

"I just want to make sure you're all right. I was afraid something like this might happen, but I hadn't expected it from Rafe Marchand."

"He's one of the men you warned me about, isn't he?"

Ben nodded, his expression serious. "He's ruthless and thinks only of what he wants. Be very careful when you talk to him."

"I will."

"Do you want me to go with you?"

She shook her head quickly. It was bad enough that she was going to be humiliated before Rafe. She didn't want a witness. "I'll go in the morning and see what kind of arrangements we can make. Perhaps he'll be agreeable to terms."

She turned, ready to go back to her empty room and lie awake the rest of the night hours. Ben reached out and took her arm.

"It'll be all right. He may be a hard man, but he's not a monster."

"I hope you're right."

"Here, take what money I do have. It might help." He handed her the money he kept in his cabin, which amounted to about nine hundred dollars. Even with her six hundred, she was far short. "If he agrees to terms, I'll give you more when we get back to New Orleans."

"Thank you."

With that she was gone. Ben sat down heavily on his bed and rested his head in his hands. This was his worst nightmare. This was what he'd feared. This was what had worried him. This was why he'd tried to keep her from coming on board. He had thought after all these months that things were working out well. He'd been wrong, and now it was too late to save her from what could be a very ugly situation. He hoped Marchand proved to be a decent sort, but he couldn't know for sure.

When the knock came at Rafe's door the next morning, he'd been expecting it. He had been up since dawn, planning the way he was going to handle Brandy. If her story about her mother was true, he was certain she wouldn't be able to get the five thousand, and that would leave her right where he wanted her. She might not have heard Demers's remark last night, but he had, and he was certain others had, too. As independent as she was, he knew their upcoming conversation wasn't going to be pretty, but he didn't care. He already knew what he wanted from her in the way of payment, and he intended to get it.

He opened the door to find Brandy standing before him, looking every inch a lady.

"May I come in?" she asked.

Rafe held the door wide for her to enter; then he closed it behind her. At the sound, Brandy felt trapped. She maintained her stoic demeanor, though, and revealed nothing of her inner turmoil.

"I had hoped you would be here."

"I've been expecting you. Do you have the money?" Rafe was not going to waste time on niceties. When Rafe knew what he wanted, he went after it—with a passion.

She opened the small purse she was carrying and

started to take out what money she'd brought with her.

For a moment, Rafe went still. He had been sure that he'd driven the stakes up high enough to bankrupt her. He'd felt certain that she didn't have enough to pay the debt, and now . . .

"Here." She held out a wad of bills. "There's nearly fifteen hundred there. I can pay you the rest over the next few months."

The uncertainty that had gripped him for a minute was gone in that moment, and Rafe knew he'd won. The feeling was heady. He was going to force her to his bidding whether she liked it or not. The thought made him smile. His was not a kind smile, though, but the smile of a victor in his triumph.

"I'm afraid that won't do. When you made the bet, I believe you said you were good for the full amount." He didn't even reach for the money.

"And I am. Just give me a few months to make up the difference." It seared her soul to say the words to him. She had hoped he would agree right off and there would be no bargaining. She owed him, she knew it, and he would get his money.

"I'm not a bank, making loans. I think the words you used with Jackson were 'If you can't afford to lose, don't play.'" His expression was hard.

"I see."

"Is there a problem getting the rest of the money now?" he asked, wanting her to admit openly that she could not pay up.

"I don't have it. I only have this."

Rafe fell silent as he stared at her from across the room. Even humiliated and despairing as she was, she was standing proudly before him, and he thought she had never looked more beautiful.

"Is there any kind of payment agreement we can arrange?"

"As a matter of fact, I had considered one option. . . ."

Brandy swallowed nervously. Fear gripped her. Ben had warned her of men like him—ruthless, driven, they took what they wanted, when they wanted it, and damn the consequences.

All along Ben had argued that her virtue was at risk, and now she understood why. No doubt, Rafe was going to ask her to become his mistress. She was horrified. For all of her exposure to men and gambling, she was an innocent to the more intimate ways of men. Protected as she'd been by her devotion to her mother, she had never been involved with any man, let alone learned the ways of a courtesan.

"And your option is?" she asked, her chin up, her gaze fixed on him. She was not willing to appear weak or frightened before him as she awaited his announcement.

Rafe's smile faded as he turned serious. "I have a proposition to make you."

Brandy turned cold. She sensed she knew what was coming and wondered how she would ever hide the shame of it from her mother. "Yes?"

"I have been fighting off women ever since I came of marriageable age. You were witness to that the other night."

"What does that have to do with me?" She was staring at him, confused.

"I have come up with a plan that would suit me well. You owe me an outstanding amount of money, and you have no funds with which to pay me. I have an arrangement of sorts in mind. . . ."

"What kind of arrangement?"

"I want you to marry me."

Chapter Eight

"You what?" "Stunned" barely described what she was feeling as she stared at him.

Before she could say any more, he held up his hand to stop her. "I want you to marry me."

"That's it? Just marry you and the debt's canceled?"

"No, there's more. We both know how the other feels about marriage." There was a sneer to his voice as he spoke.

Brandy swallowed, expecting the worst, though she couldn't imagine much worse than being forced into a marriage she didn't want with a man who didn't love her. "Like what?"

"I want a child."

"You *what?*" Now she really was shocked. "I don't understand."

"It's simple really," he went on coolly. "Neither one of us is disposed to marriage. I think it's the one thing we have in common, but no matter how I feel about that venerable institution, I have always wanted children. So my offer to you is this—we'll marry, I'll claim access to our marriage bed until you are with child, after which I won't bother you again. You will bear the child for me, and once the baby is born, you will be free to go, your debt to me paid in full."

"You're crazy. . . ." She was staring at him in total disbelief. He sounded so cold, so unbelievably callous, that she didn't know what to say.

"Hardly, my dear Brandy; I'm merely practical. I feel it's quite a bargain. I shall never have to worry about being trapped into marriage again and I will have a child. You will have your debts paid in full, and when the time comes for you to leave, I'll make certain that you are provided for. It wouldn't do for the mother of my child to be gambling on a steamboat anymore. What do you say? Do we have a deal?"

"Why are you so set against marriage that you would plan something like this?" She was staring at him, trying to come to grips with his proposition. "You want a child, yet you don't want a mother for that child. I don't understand."

"It doesn't matter to me whether you understand or not. If you agree to my terms, once the child is born, it will be mine and you will be free to go."

Silence reigned. Brandy's mind was racing, her thoughts in turmoil. She couldn't believe that this man would so heartlessly make such a cold-blooded arrangement.

"Well?" Rafe pressed.

"You're serious about this? You wouldn't rather take the money I've got now and let me pay you the rest over time?"

"You heard my offer. Take it or . . ."

"Or what?" She came back at him, frantically searching for a way to escape what he had planned for her. It was impossible. She knew how special the mother-child relationship was, and she knew in her heart that if by chance she did conceive and bear him a child, she could never leave it. Yet, what alternative did she have but to agree? She was trapped.

"Do I really have to spell it out for you? Suffice it to say, people who don't pay their debts suffer the consequences."

"You wouldn't dare." Her voice was a horrified whisper.

"There's much I would dare, Brandy. Now, you've heard the terms of my offer. What's your answer?"

"I need time . . ." she agonized.

"I want your answer now." Rafe chafed at her reaction. Of all the women in the world he could have proposed to, he'd picked her, and now he had to blackmail her into marrying him! "If you walk out that door, I rescind the offer. Do you agree to the marriage or not? If so, arrangements can be made while we're in St. Louis. If you do not, then . . ."

Brandy knew there was no escaping the consequences of her actions. She lifted her gaze to him, the look in her eyes cold and disdainful. She wanted to defy him, to tell him that she had no intention of accepting his horrible proposal. Marry him, have his baby and then leave . . . The idea was abhorrent to her. As she stared at Rafe, she couldn't imagine what kind of life he'd led that would lead him to think that any woman could desert her own flesh and blood. She wondered if he had a heart.

"You're serious about this."

"I've never been more serious." There was granite

in his tone. "Do you agree to the deal or not?"

Brandy was stricken. "I agree . . ." she began.

Rafe did not allow himself to smile as he quickly said, "Wise choice, my dear fiancée."

She raised her chin slightly in defiance. "I'm not through yet." Her voice was clipped, indicating her barely contained fury. "I agree—as long as you consent to *my* terms."

He lifted one eyebrow mockingly. "I hardly think you're in any position to dictate terms to me."

Brandy refused to grovel. He might have trapped her, but he would not defeat her. She looked him straight in the eye with a daring she wasn't feeling. "I agree to your terms but only on one condition . . ."

"And that is?"

"That you allow my mother to accompany me and to live with us during the duration of our 'agreement.' "

"Ah, your mother again. How could I have forgotten?" His expression was totally devoid of emotion as he answered her. "I don't care what you do with your mother as long as I never have to deal with her."

"There will be room for her in your home?"

"I think it's safe to say that we can find a room for her."

"Then I agree to your terms."

Only now did he allow himself a triumphant smile. "Good. As my intended, I expect you to conduct yourself as a lady at all times from now on."

Brandy stiffened at his insulting words. "I have always acted the lady."

"From here on out, there will be no more acting. Now, you're going to become one."

"You bastard!" Her temper flared out of control. All her life she'd been treated as someone less than quality. No matter that she had fought hard to live a clean life. It would have been far easier to sell herself in a brothel or work in a tavern than to do what she did, yet she was constantly condemned for her choice. She raised her hand to slap him.

Rafe saw the explosion of fury in her and anticipated her move. He snared her wrist and dragged her against him. "This is hardly the way to treat your intended, my dear."

"You . . . !" Brandy was pinned against the hard-muscled width of his chest as she glared up at him. Never before had she been so defeated and helpless before a man, and she didn't like it. She didn't like it at all.

"Ah, ah, ah," he scolded sarcastically. "Lesson number one will be in learning to control your temper. It would behoove you to be nice to me."

"Why?"

"Because I can make your life a living hell if I want to."

"It already is."

Rafe stared down at her, his eyes boring into hers, seeing the resentment and hatred there. He felt a twinge of regret, but dismissed it. He had not wanted her devotion or her affection. Any emotional involvement would make things too complicated. All he wanted from her was a child. After that she would be free to go.

Still, as Rafe held her pinned against him, he remembered the kiss she had given him the other night and felt a stirring of desire within him. He knew it would be no hardship availing himself of their marriage bed. He lowered his head, intending to kiss her, wanting to taste her sweetness again.

Brandy read his mind and quickly broke free. "Sir,

if I am to be a lady, then I must become one, not merely act like one in public. I hardly think a good Southern girl would be caught in her fiancé's room unchaperoned. Do you?"

Thwarted by her quick thinking, he found himself chuckling in spite of himself. After all, it had been her spirit and courage that had impressed him from the start. "You're absolutely right, Brandy, my love," he said in his most courtly way, giving her a slight mocking bow. "Oh . . . there is one other thing I want you to keep in mind."

"What?" Her gaze was hard and suspicious upon him.

"I want everyone to think ours is a love match. Remember that."

She shot him a withering look. "I am feeling a bit weary after all this excitement. I think it's best if I go back to my room and rest for a while. It's not every day that a lady is swept off her feet by such a romantic proposal."

He ignored the bite of her words as he grinned at her. "Allow me to escort you to your cabin, my sweet."

"It's not necessary." She was piqued by the fact that he was laughing at her. She found absolutely nothing funny about their situation.

"But I insist, *darling.*"

Brandy knew this was one argument she couldn't win. "Then I would be delighted to have your company, sir." She used her most affected manner and accent.

Rafe opened the door and then offered her his arm as they started from the room.

"You'll join me for dinner this evening?" It was a statement, not an invitation.

"Of course." Brandy was tempted to ask if there was any way she could avoid it, but already knew the answer. She had lost her soul to the devil, and the devil was Rafe Marchand.

She shivered as she took his arm and felt the power there. He was a man to be reckoned with. Though her expression didn't falter, her spirits sank as she wondered how she would ever go through with the bargain she'd just made. Somehow, she had to find a way to earn enough money to pay him back in full before the time came.

They did not speak as they made their way to her cabin.

"Until tonight," Rafe said as he left Brandy at her door.

"Tonight."

Brandy was emotionally numb as she closed and locked the door behind her. She realized as she did it just how foolish it was to lock the door against Rafe. There would be no keeping him out of her life. He had just taken it over. There could be no hiding from him. He owned her, body and soul.

Exhaustion claimed Brandy. She lay down on her bed fully dressed and fell into a fitful sleep. She did not dream, and when she awoke in the afternoon, she did not feel rested.

Rafe met Marc on deck. The children were off playing with Louise, and that gave them time to talk.

"Did Brandy meet with you today?"

"Yes. I spoke with her this morning and everything is settled."

"I'm surprised she had that much money, judging from the things she said the other day."

"She didn't."

"You let her off?" Marc was surprised.

"Not exactly. We've come to an agreement of sorts."

"What kind of agreement?" Marc asked shrewdly. He could always tell when Rafe was trying to keep something from him.

"Brandy and I have decided to get married."

"You what?" Marc could not have been more surprised. He stared at his friend as if he were seeing him for the first time in his life. "You're getting married? Why?"

Rafe was surprised that he didn't want to tell his best friend the details of his upcoming nuptials. "Suffice it to say that she's a beautiful woman. I proposed. She accepted. We're going to be married in St. Louis."

Marc shook his head in disbelief. "You're getting married . . . ?" he repeated, staring at Rafe suspiciously. Then suddenly Marc started laughing. "You took my advice! For once in your life, you listened to me! Congratulations, Rafe. You couldn't have picked a better woman. I think the two of you will live happily ever after." He clapped Rafe on the back. "Let's go have a drink to celebrate."

"Don't say anything to anyone else yet. Brandy and I still have details to discuss."

"It's enough that I know. Come on. I'm buying!"

The men's saloon was relatively deserted, and they settled in at a table in the back that would afford them privacy as they talked.

"Have you thought this through yet?"

"I've given it all the thought it needs. After that little scene with the Demers family the other night, I realized I had to do something. It's one thing to get married of your own choice. It's another to be blackmailed into it. It was pretty unnerving to find myself cornered that way."

"You were very lucky. If it hadn't been for Brandy—"

"Precisely, and that's what made me realize I had to take some action to make sure it never happened again."

"So you proposed."

"That's right."

"And she said yes without hesitation?"

"She did have a few concerns. . . ."

"Such as?" Marc knew it was getting interesting now.

"Her mother."

"What about her mother?"

"Brandy wants her to live with us."

"And?" Marc wondered how Rafe had handled that one, feeling as he did about mothers.

"And I agreed."

"You surprise me. I would never have dreamed you'd go for marriage, let alone acquiring a live-in mother-in-law, too."

Rafe's expression hardened as he explained harshly, "I told her it was fine with me as long as I didn't have to deal with her. There's plenty of room at Bellerive. I shouldn't have to be bothered by the old woman."

"Does Brandy know about Bellerive?"

"No, we really haven't gotten that far."

"So, she basically knows nothing about you except that she's marrying you?"

Rafe grinned. "I guess I'm so overwhelmingly wonderful that she didn't care about the rest."

"Right," Marc drawled. "How are you going to handle all this? How are you planning to pull this off? Is she going to keep gambling until we get to St. Louis?"

"No. I think after last night, she's officially out of business."

"There won't be many happy customers in the bar tonight."

"That's not my problem. I can't have my fiancée gambling in a saloon every night."

"But that's who she is," Marc pointed out maddeningly.

"That's not who she's going to be. You said yourself that first night that she could bluff her way through society. Well, now she's going to get the chance, but I don't want her to be bluffing. I want to transform her into a lady who will fit right in at Bellerive. I think it's safe to assume that not everyone has heard of Miss Brandy on the *Pride*. Once she's established as my wife, I'm sure she'll be accepted."

"Even so, you're going to have to do something about her wardrobe. And what about manners and decorum? If you want her to fit right in without question, you're going to have to make sure she can handle any social occasion with ease."

"Any suggestions?" Rafe hadn't thought this far ahead. He was just glad that he'd gotten Brandy to agree to his plan. A year from now, if everything went well, he'd have a son or daughter and be free to do exactly as he wanted again—not too bad a deal, considering.

"She needs someone who can tutor her about all that."

"What's wrong with us?" Rafe suggested.

Marc gave him a pained look. "What do we know about all that female stuff like entertaining company and running a home? She needs a woman's influence, the kind of training young girls get at a finishing school."

"Well, she's got about two weeks to learn everything before we have to go back."

Marc frowned. "Bluffing her way through a party is one thing. Living a whole new way of life is another. You know, Jennette went to an exclusive school in St. Louis. We might be able to find someone there who can help us."

"Let's look into it as soon as we dock." Rafe was beginning to realize how complicated this was going to be.

"There is one other thing. . . ."

"What else?" Rafe sounded irritated.

"Brandy's going to need a chaperone, or at least some kind of companion, until you're married. It wouldn't do for her to be compromised before the wedding."

"You're beginning to sound like we're talking about Merrie."

Marc laughed. "Believe me, if this was Merrie's wedding we were planning, I wouldn't let you within ten miles of her without a chaperone until the wedding day."

"You don't trust me with your daughter's virtue?"

"I don't know a sane man who would, so I'm appointing myself Brandy's protector. If you want her to be a lady, you must treat her like a lady."

"My experience with ladies hasn't been all that wonderful, but if you insist I play the gentleman, I will."

"I'm proud of you. I know it won't be easy for you." Marc laughed.

"I'll make the effort."

Chapter Nine

"Are you all right? What happened?" Ben asked worriedly as Brandy answered his knock at her cabin door. He had been thinking about her constantly since she'd left him to go speak to Marchand, and he wanted to make sure she was all right. As he stared down at her now, he couldn't tell by her guarded expression how she was.

"I'm fine," she answered, agonizing momentarily over what to say to Ben. She knew she had to tell him what had happened—or at least part of it.

"Why don't I believe that?"

"Come on in. I'll tell you all about it."

She held the door wide, and he went to sit at her small table and chair.

"Did he agree to terms to let you pay him off?"

"Not really."

"I don't understand."

"We did come to an agreement of sorts." At Ben's

expectant look, she went on, not waiting for him to ask more questions. "I was going to tell you this a little later. Rafe and I . . ." She paused to swallow. "Rafe and I are going to be married when we reach St. Louis."

"You're *what?*" he bellowed. "I know you practically owed the man your soul, but this is ridiculous. We could have paid him off a little at a time."

"Now don't be furious. . . . I agreed to this." She tried to calm her friend. "It was my decision."

"But why, Brandy? I've never heard you say much about the man, and now you're going to marry him! Do you love him?"

She gazed at her friend, seeing the very real concern in his expression. "I don't know. All I know is that if I agreed to marry him, my debt would be canceled. So I agreed."

"He forced you into it."

"What other choice did I have? I owed him. It was a debt of honor."

"But did you owe him your life?"

"I'm not sacrificing myself."

"You might very well be. We don't even know the man. Who knows what he's really like?" Ben was very worried.

"I've seen him with Marc LeFevre's children. Any man who is kind to children can't be all bad. It'll be all right."

"How can you be sure?" He didn't want to think that she'd been forced to sell herself.

"Because he's even agreed to let my mother come live with us."

"He has?" Ben was taken aback by this news. It did improve his thoughts about Marchand, but the whole thing was happening much too fast to suit him.

"Yes, he has. And you know, it could have been far worse. He could have asked me to be his mistress or something."

"He'd have been arriving at the gates of hell if he had," Ben declared, anger surging through him at the thought.

Brandy went to Ben and hugged him. "You are such a good friend to me."

When she moved away from him, there were tears in her eyes. Ben was her only friend, the only one she could count on. Otherwise, with her mother so far away, she was alone in the world. Still, she couldn't tell him everything. She couldn't tell him how Marchand wanted her to bear him a child and then leave. It was too terrible even to consider, let alone talk about.

"I care about what happens to you, Brandy," Ben told her in earnest. "If this is what you want, then I support your decision. But I have to tell you, I still have my doubts. And I'm telling you right now, that if Marchand doesn't treat you right, all you have to do is send word."

"Thank you. You'll never know how much your friendship means to me."

"You're sure about this?"

She was quiet for a long minute before looking up at him. When she did, she managed a smile. "Yes."

Ben touched her cheek gently, then turned to go. She might think that he was satisfied with her situation and wasn't giving it another thought, but that wasn't the case. He intended to pay a visit to Mr. Rafe Marchand. Passenger or not, the man was going to hear from Captain Rodgers.

Rafe had just left Marc after finishing up their drinking in the saloon and was heading back to his cabin when he came face to face with the captain.

"Mr. Marchand, I'd like to have a word with you," Ben said, his expression revealing nothing of what he was feeling. Though Brandy seemed satisfied enough with the arrangement, he just wanted to make sure that Marchand knew he'd have him to deal with if he didn't treat her right.

"Captain." Rafe was not surprised by his interest. "Would you like to go to my cabin or would what you have to say be better aired on deck?"

"Your cabin would be best. This is a private matter between you and me."

Rafe led the way. They did not speak again until they were inside Rafe's room, facing each other in the male animal's age-old way of confrontation.

"Brandy has told me that she's agreed to become your wife." Ben made the statement, then waited, wanting to judge Marchand's reactions.

Rafe was a master at revealing nothing of his emotions. He had been wondering how much Brandy had told the captain, and he was glad that she had merely informed him of their coming marriage. He met the other man's gaze squarely. "She did accept my proposal. We'll be married while we're in St. Louis."

"I can't say I'm happy about this . . . your rushing her this way." There was a subtle but unmistakable threat in his tone.

"It was her decision."

"So she says, and if it's what she wants, then I'm all for it. But I can't help wondering, why did you ask her to marry you?" He knew Rafe was a man of means, and Brandy was a lady gambler. For all that they had worked so hard to keep her reputation spotless, he still didn't trust this man's motives.

"Have you looked at her?" Rafe asked him with a slight smile. "She's a very beautiful woman. Not to mention that she's smart and one helluva poker player."

"Except for last night," Ben said bitterly.

"Yes . . . except for last night."

"Listen to me, Marchand. Brandy is a wonderful woman who deserves far better than life has dealt her in the past. I care about her and am concerned about her welfare. It would not sit well with me to see her abused in any way."

Rafe tensed at the challenge in the captain's words. "You need have no fear on that account. As my wife, she will be held in the highest esteem."

Ben regarded him silently for a moment, then nodded. "I do not know how the two of you came to this agreement, and it is truly none of my business. I will, however, make it my business if I feel something is amiss in all this."

"Brandy will suffer no harm while she is under my protection," Rafe replied, wanting to assure the captain that all was well so he'd go on his way. It seemed his beloved fiancée encouraged more protectors than she knew. First, Marc had lectured him, and now Captain Rodgers. He almost resented the fact that the two men cared so much for her that they thought he needed to be warned about the proper way to treat her. "Once we are married, you need not fear for her circumstances. I own Bellerive plantation and have invested in numerous other industries. Her financial status will be secure. Until the wedding, I have plans to provide her with a companion, so as not to compromise her reputation in any way."

"I appreciate your diligence in these matters. She's worked hard to maintain her dignity on this steamer and I'd hate to have any untoward rumors start now."

"There is one thing we need to discuss. I'm sure she's already told you that she won't be gambling any more."

"I'll have the barkeep make her excuses. It's only two more nights to St. Louis, so I think everyone will be able to deal with it."

"Good. Then we understand each other."

"Yes, and I wish you every happiness. Brandy is a wonderful woman, and she deserves a bright future. I hope everything works out well for the two of you."

Ben left Rafe, not quite sure what to think of all that was going on, but as long as Brandy had no complaint, he would be happy for her and hope for the best. Marchand seemed a straight enough fellow. He prayed that he did right by her.

Brandy took great pains dressing for dinner with Rafe that evening. She was determined to show him that she was a lady, and her selection of gown and hairstyle were made with that in mind. As she sat before her mirror at the small dressing table in her cabin, she found her thoughts drifting to the future and to what her life was going to be like.

There was no denying that she was attracted to Rafe Marchand. She had been from the moment she'd first seen him, and it was difficult to imagine the quirk of fate that had brought them together this way. Yet, here she was, promised to him in marriage.

Brandy tried to be logical for a moment and analyze what she really knew about the man, but it wasn't much—he was kind to children, could play a mean hand of poker and could back men down when necessary. As far as personal things went, though, she knew practically nothing about his life or his home. She wondered dazedly what she'd gotten herself into. He dressed well and expected her to be a lady. Obviously he was not a poor man, but she had no idea what the future held, and it was frightening.

Brandy gazed at her own reflection in the small mirror and set her expression in a composed look that revealed none of her inner torment. She clung to the anger that came with the memory of his demand that she bear a child and leave, for in that anger was her strength.

The knock at her door jarred Brandy from her thoughts. She knew it was Rafe. Rising, she smoothed her skirts in a nervous gesture and then went to open the door. She paused one moment to gird herself for the evening to come, then swung the portal wide and faced the man who'd claimed her for his own.

"Evening, Rafe," she greeted him. He looked devastatingly handsome tonight in the dark suit that he wore.

"Good evening, Brandy. Are you ready to go to dinner?" His gaze was admiring upon her. She looked ravishing.

"Yes," she said a bit more breathlessly than she'd intended.

She took his arm and closed the door behind her as they started from the room. His body at her side was a heated branding iron.

Rafe was completely aware of Brandy's touch on his arm. She wore a heady fragrance that spoke of sensuality and seduction, and he found himself longing to taste of her again. Even as he had the thought, though, he knew he must deny himself. As she had so clearly reminded him earlier that day—if he wanted her to be a lady, he was going to have to treat her like one. He could well imagine how she would react to any advance he might make right now.

"I spoke with Ben this afternoon," he began. "He seemed concerned for you, but I put his misgivings at ease."

She was surprised, but not overly so, knowing Ben. "I didn't know that he was actually going to seek you out. I tried to assure him that this was something I wanted."

" 'This'?"

"Our betrothal," she said aloud and blushed a little at the intimacy of it. "Obviously, I wasn't convincing enough if he thought he had to speak to you personally about it."

"He just wanted me to know that he wanted what was best for you, and I think I managed to convince him that you would be safe with me."

"Good." She didn't want Ben to harbor any doubts. She had enough of her own to go around.

They reached the entrance to the dining room and asked for a quiet table so they could talk. They were shown to a secluded one at the back of the room. Once they were seated and their order taken, she turned to him.

"Rafe . . . ?"

He glanced at her, waiting for her to go on.

"Tell me about yourself. I barely know you, and yet in a few days we'll be married. Do you have any family?"

"My parents are dead, and I had no brothers or sisters. Marc is the closest to family I have."

"You must have been lonely growing up," she remarked, trying to understand this man who would soon be her husband.

He shrugged his indifference. "I didn't notice. I was too busy when I was away at school, and now I'm too busy running Bellerive."

"Bellerive?" she repeated slowly, her heart skipping a beat at the mention of the well-known plantation.

"I own Bellerive plantation. It's outside of Natchez. You might have heard of it."

"I have." Brandy couldn't believe what he was saying. If it hadn't been so sad, it would have been laughable. Her childhood fantasy was coming true, yet it was proving to be more of a nightmare than a dream.

"My father built it, and since his death, I've been working at improving it."

"Tell me about it."

"The house is large, over twenty rooms. My father built it to last for generations." He paused as memories of a happier time came to him, but he quickly pushed them away. "My means are substantial, so you will want for nothing as my wife."

Brandy hadn't been thinking about money. She'd been dreaming about the fact that she was actually going to be living her childhood fantasy—she was going to be one of the ladies at the ball, at least for a little while. But reality intruded with the realization that this was no love match between them. Rafe wanted her only as a brood mare. She would want for nothing only for as long as she fulfilled the terms of their agreement.

Her heart ached as the truth forced its way into her thoughts. There was no hiding from it. As much as she would have liked to pretend that her future was going to be happy, she knew better.

"I'm eager to see your home."

"Our home," he corrected with emphasis as their food was served to them.

"Yes . . . our home." She didn't truly believe what she was saying. She would be a mere passer-through at Bellerive, staying only until he'd gotten what he wanted from her.

"I've also taken on outside business interests. That's one of my reasons for this trip; I have a meeting scheduled with one of the owners of a shipping firm I've invested in. I decided long ago not to trust my fate to the whims of nature and planting. Too many fortunes are lost that way. I've diversified my investments, and shipping is just one of them."

She heard the toughness in his tone and knew he was a force to be reckoned with.

"So, tell me about yourself, Brandy," he said, studying her across the table as they began to eat. "Tell me about your family."

"There isn't much to tell. My father died when I was young, and my mother supported me up until a year ago with her sewing. When her health began to fail, it was up to me to find a way to earn a living for us."

"That's when you turned to Ben?"

"Not at first. Oh, I knew how to gamble and all, but I also knew what everyone would think of me if I did that. I tried to sew like my mother did, but I just wasn't any good at it. Then I thought about working as a maid or something, but there wasn't enough money that way to feed us, let alone rent a room. Things were getting desperate, and that was when I remembered everything Silas had taught me about playing cards and I decided to sharpen my skills. I knew from him how much there was to be made playing, and once I felt I was good enough, I approached Ben. Luckily, he allowed me on board the *Pride*. If he hadn't, there's no telling where my mother and I would be right now."

Rafe had been watching her closely as she talked, and he realized everything she'd told him before had been the truth. "Why didn't you marry?"

"I hadn't even thought of it. I'd been too busy taking care of my mother, and then once I started sailing with Ben, we both decided the best way for me to handle men was not to handle them. It was better for my reputation and for the boat's that way."

Rafe was staring at her intently. The kiss she'd given him in his cabin the other night in front of James Demers and his daughter had been wildly passionate, and from the way she flirted in the saloon, he'd thought that she knew her way around men.

"Is something wrong?" she asked.

"No . . . nothing's wrong. How do you think your mother will react to the news of our marriage?"

"She's going to be surprised, but as long as she believes I'm happy, she'll be happy for me."

"Are you going to be able to convince her that we're madly in love?" His gaze pinned her as he awaited her answer.

"Don't worry," she said flatly. "You've already made it quite plain that the world has to believe ours is a love match."

"Then smile, my dear. If you're in love, you must act like it."

He reached across the table and took her hand in his. She resisted his touch at first, then forced herself to relax.

"It may take me a while to get used to this."

"I trust you won't find it too taxing for you." He smiled at her as he spoke.

"I'll manage." Brandy found herself staring at him, mesmerized by the change in him when he smiled. Had she not known the truth behind their charade, she might have thought herself in heaven to have a fiancé like Rafe Marchand dancing attendance on her. Instead, she focused on the ugliness behind their union, needing to keep everything in perspective, needing to remember that this was all fleeting, a mere financial arrangement that had nothing to do with love and honor and commitment.

"Ben and Marc were both concerned about your reputation, so . . ."

"You told Marc about us?" She looked horrified, humiliated that the gentleman who'd been so kind to her would know her ultimate shame.

"I told Marc that you'd agreed to marry me. That's all I told him," Rafe replied, irritated that she would think him enough of a cad to tell Marc the whole truth.

Brandy lifted her troubled gaze to Rafe. "Thank you."

"As I was saying, both men were concerned about your reputation, so once we reach St. Louis, I'll be looking for a suitable companion for you. With any luck, maybe we'll be able to find someone who is well versed in the social graces, too."

"Ah, yes, I certainly wouldn't want to embarrass you with anything less than sterling behavior."

"It's a precaution that I'm taking for your own well-being."

"You're doing this for yourself and you know it," she challenged. "Heaven forbid that I might use the wrong fork and bring humiliation upon your family name."

"This is hardly about using the wrong fork at dinner, and my family name has nothing to do with it." Rafe's expression hardened at her scathing words. "I've found in business and in life, Brandy, that it is always better to anticipate the worst and prepare for it, than to be caught unawares."

"Well, since in my experience I've always had to deal with the worst, we shouldn't have any problems, should we?" she shot back at him. She hated to think that he regarded her as so unpolished and uncouth that she needed instructions in how to comport herself in public.

"The people you will be associating with when we return to Natchez are not your usual gaming-room material. It's important that you're aware of all the proper ways to do things, so you won't find yourself in a situation where you'll be feeling out of place. You will be a lady. No one will be able to find fault with you."

She gave a short, harsh laugh. "They always do, you know. I've always been aware of what the fine ladies of quality were saying about me behind their fans when I entered a room. But you needn't worry. I'll prove an apt pupil. I'll be so polished by the time we return to your home that you won't have any reason to be ashamed of me."

"It had never occurred to me that I would be ashamed of you. I merely want to make your transition as easy as possible. After all, I'm sure associating with the men in the bar for all these months is a far cry from making small talk with the ladies over tea."

"What about the men in the bar? They're expecting

me to gamble tonight. What am I supposed to tell them?"

"Ben is handling it."

"Who told him to do that?"

"When we talked, we agreed that was the best way to do it."

"That's nice of you two to take care of my business for me without asking."

"I thought it would save you from being embarrassed."

"You're saving me from embarrassment all over the place, aren't you? First, you tell me that you're hiring a companion for me to save me from being embarrassed in society," she said sarcastically, "and now you've taken it upon yourself to save me from being embarrassed in my own gaming room. I don't need you to save me. If you really were interested in helping me, you would save me the embarrassment of becoming your wife just to settle a debt that could and would have been repaid over time." She kept her voice low so only he could hear her.

Rafe tensed. "You're not backing out, are you?"

Anger flared in her eyes at his words. "I'm not backing out of anything. I just don't appreciate your making decisions for me that affect my life."

"Once you're my wife, I'll be making all the decisions that concern us."

"I hate to point out the obvious, Rafe, but we are not husband and wife yet," she said as she laid her napkin upon the table. Without another word, she rose and swept from the room, leaving Rafe staring after her in disbelief.

Chapter Ten

Brandy's anger did not fade as she left the dining room and emerged on deck. It was all she could do not to storm off in a rage. How dare he think he could take such complete control of her life?

It was bad enough that she was going to have to suffer through his wonderful etiquette lessons, but to think that she would never have the chance to gamble again upset her. She was being forced to abandon every vestige of the life she'd built for herself. Nothing would be left of the woman she was—nothing. Once she became Mrs. Rafe Marchand, her own identity would disappear, covered by a layer of etiquette, good manners and social polish.

Brandy paused at the rail and drew a shuddering breath. She'd had no idea how frightened she was by the prospect until now. She'd thought she could handle the situation, but giving up everything she'd known and loved to start a whole new life was scary.

It was all because she'd been foolish enough to let her emotions rule her gambling sense. She'd learned her lesson now, but it was too late. She was going to marry Rafe Marchand and there was nothing she could do to stop it.

"Brandy?"

She almost jumped at the sound of Marc's voice nearby. Quickly disguising the turmoil of her emotions, she turned to smile at him. "Good evening, Marc."

"What are you doing out here all alone?" He glanced around, expecting to see Rafe hovering somewhere, but there was no sign of him.

"I just needed a breath of fresh air."

"I've heard the good news of your betrothal. I think you're perfect for Rafe."

"You do?" She stared at him in surprise, wondering what Rafe had said to the man, for he sounded sincere.

"I do. In fact, I'm sure he didn't mention it to you, but the first night I saw you, I told Rafe you would make him the perfect wife. I'm glad he listened to my advice. He usually doesn't."

"It's nice to know you approve." She found herself relaxing in his company. She liked Marc. He was a straightforward, honest man, who harbored no deceit in him—unlike his friend. "I wonder how Merrie's going to take the news, though. When we last talked, I think she wanted Rafe for herself. She was saying that she hoped he would wait for her to grow up before he took a wife."

Marc laughed. "If she had to lose Rafe to anyone, I'm glad it's you. I think you're going be very happy together."

If you only knew, she thought painfully. But she

answered, "I hope so. It's rather exciting, happening as quickly as it did. Up until the moment he . . . proposed, I had no idea of his feelings."

"Once you get to know him, you'll discover that he's not quite as hard as he seems."

"I'm sure," she lied, thinking Rafe was truly one of the most calculating, cold-blooded men she'd ever met.

"Has he told you much about his family or Bellerive?"

"We talked about it a little over dinner tonight. His home sounds magnificent."

"It is, and he has one of the best stables in three counties. His father started it years ago, and Rafe's been working on building it up ever since."

"Did his parents die when he was young?"

"He was fourteen when his father died. His mother passed away a few years after that."

"Were they close?"

"He and his father were. His mother . . ." Marc paused, wondering just how much to reveal.

"What about her?"

"Let me put it this way to be kind. She wasn't a shining example of chaste and virtuous womanhood. It was a bad situation, and the world suffered no great loss when she was no longer in it."

"So his parents' marriage wasn't a happy one?" She sensed there was much more to the story than Marc was telling her, but she wasn't quite sure how to get at it without prying.

"No, and especially not at the end."

"At the end?" She was confused.

"His mother deserted the family. That's why I was so surprised when Rafe told me you two were going to marry. He doesn't hold a high opinion of women or marriage, and I had begun to wonder if he would ever take a wife."

"How terrible for him."

"Up until you, he hasn't trusted women at all. But you . . . you're different." Marc smiled kindly at her.

"Different, good?"

"Definitely different, good. Has he talked to you about hiring a chaperone yet? I mentioned it to him earlier today because I was concerned about your reputation. It wouldn't do to put you in a compromising situation."

"It was very kind of you to think of me." She smiled at him with heartfelt warmth. Besides Ben, Marc seemed to be the only man who treated her as if she were a real lady, and his respect touched her deeply. "And yes, we did speak of it."

"I have an idea where we can find someone suitable. My wife Jennette was born and raised in St. Louis. She attended a prominent academy for girls there, and I think they might be able to recommend someone for the job. As soon as we reach town, we'll look into it."

"It's awfully kind of you to help this way."

"Marc is always glad to help," Rafe said as he appeared on deck nearby to find the two of them talking and smiling at each other. For some reason, it irked him to see her being so pleasant to Marc when she'd just cut him dead in the dining room.

"It's always my pleasure to come to the aid of a beautiful woman." Marc grinned at his friend.

"Well, if you two will excuse me," Brandy said, wanting to escape from Rafe's stifling nearness. "I think I'll go on to my cabin now."

"Allow me, my dear." Rafe stepped forward and offered her his arm.

"Of course," she said sweetly, remembering his warning to convince everyone that theirs was a love match—no matter how bitter the pill was to swallow. "Good night, Marc, and thanks."

"Good night, Brandy. I'll see you in the bar later, Rafe?"

"I'll meet you there."

Marc moved off as Rafe escorted Brandy toward the steps to the upper deck where her cabin was located.

"A lady should never be on deck at this time of night unescorted," Rafe said.

"As you've made abundantly clear so many times, I'm not a lady, so it really doesn't matter, does it?"

"It matters. You're under my protection now," Rafe ground out, annoyed, yet not able to admit that he was concerned about her. When he'd first come out on deck and had seen her talking with another man, he'd been furious. In the dark, it had taken him a minute to recognize Marc, but even then, his irritation hadn't lessened. He'd seen how the men in the bar reacted to her. Didn't she realize that one of them might try to take advantage of her if they found her alone?

"I'll keep that in mind." Except for Ben, she'd never had to rely on any man. She wasn't quite sure she was going to like this arrangement if it meant Rafe would be watching her every move and dictating what she could and couldn't do.

There had been a time several years ago when she'd thought that having a handsome man sweep her off her feet and save her from all her troubles would be heavenly, but the reality of Rafe's agreement destroyed any fantasy she might have had.

"Until tomorrow, then," Rafe said as they paused before her cabin door.

"Good night." She slipped quickly inside, wanting to escape his disturbing presence.

Rafe's mood was pensive as he left Brandy and headed for the bar to meet Marc. He'd expected their relationship to go smoothly. He was getting what he wanted from the marriage, and Brandy would be coming out of the arrangement free of debt and well-off financially. It seemed a good arrangement for both of them, and it certainly was a sound business agreement. He'd even gone along with her demand that her mother be allowed to come live with them, so he didn't understand why she seemed less than satisfied with the way things were going.

Rafe frowned in the darkness. He'd told Brandy that he wanted everyone convinced that theirs was a love match. Instead, she acted skittish and resentful around him. He realized that if this was going to work, he had to play his part, too. They had one more day before they reached St. Louis, so tomorrow he would begin to make the effort. He would play the lover. He would begin to court her as if he really meant it, and maybe that would erase the hardened suspicion from her gaze when she looked at him. As he entered the bar, Rafe wondered where he could get flowers in the morning. He would have to make some inquiries.

Brandy was awakened early the following morning by a knock at her door. She drew on her wrapper and went to answer it.

"Who is it?"

"It's Molly, Brandy."

"Is something wrong?" she asked as she quickly

unlocked the door to speak to the maid who usually tidied her cabin. She could say no more as she found herself staring at one of the largest bouquets of flowers she'd ever seen. It was beautiful, breathtaking almost. "Molly?"

"Oh, I'm here, Brandy," the maid chuckled from behind the bouquet. "These are for you." She handed the flowers over to her.

"From who? Why?"

"They're from Mr. Marchand," Molly explained, nodding down the deck.

Brandy frowned, wondering why he hadn't brought them to her himself. She glanced over the top of the flowers to spot Rafe standing at the rail some distance down the deck, his gaze upon her. When she looked his way, he smiled slightly at her. Heat flushed through Brandy at the intimacy of his look, and she found herself feeling suddenly very exposed before him. Lord knew she looked a mess. Her hair was down and unbrushed. She had no makeup on. She was sure she looked terrible.

"Tell Mr. Marchand I said thank you."

"He wanted to know if you would join him for breakfast."

Brandy felt a bit giddy, and she knew it was totally ridiculous to feel that way. "Tell him I'd be delighted to join him, but it will take me a while to get ready."

"I'll tell him, and congratulations, Brandy. He told me about your engagement. I think it's wonderful!" Molly sighed romantically. She leaned closer as she whispered, "And he's so handsome!"

Brandy smiled benignly at the gushing maid as she retreated into her room with the flowers and closed the door. She stood there a moment, staring at the blossoms, smelling their sweet scent and glorying in their beauty. She didn't know how Rafe had managed to find such a lovely bouquet in the middle of the Mississippi, but she was glad he had. As she gazed down at them, she realized that no man had ever given her flowers before. She smiled.

Suddenly realizing that he was waiting for her, Brandy laid the bouquet on her bed and began to get ready. She quickly washed, then put the flowers in the pitcher on the small nightstand, not wanting their beauty to fade. Brandy had never realized how long it actually took her to get ready in the morning, and she found her heart pounding as she hurried to brush out her hair and then twist it up in a suitable style for the day. Almost half an hour had passed before she finally emerged from her room. She had thought that Rafe would have gone off to take care of some other business, and she was surprised when she found him relaxing on deck in a chair, quietly enjoying the passing scenery.

"Thank you for the flowers," she said as she joined him.

He looked up and a wide smile spread across his face as he saw her. "You're more than welcome."

"Where did you find them?"

His eyes were twinkling with good humor, but he was not about to reveal his secret source. "Just let it be said that a Marchand will go to any lengths to please his woman," he said with bravado as he rose to escort her to the dining room.

"They're lovely."

"Ah, but they're not as lovely as you."

She found herself laughing at his honeyed words. "Is there a reason you're behaving this way?"

"What way?" he asked innocently. "As if I'm smitten?"

"Well, yes . . ."

"We're about to be married. You're my fiancée. How else am I supposed to act?"

"I have no idea. I've never been engaged before."

"Neither have I, but it seems to me that if we're madly in love, we should act like it."

"Have you ever been madly in love?" she challenged.

"No. I'm new at this, but, who knows, with a little practice . . ."

"It seems to me you're doing just fine." She laughed lightheartedly in spite of herself. She had never seen this side of Rafe. He had always been so aloof and almost intimidating. Now, he was being solicitous and funny and sweet, and she found herself almost believing him.

"Why, thank you, my dear," he said in his most courtly manner. "After you."

He held the door for her, and they entered the dining room to find Marc there with the children. He saw them come in and motioned for them to join their table.

"Good morning," Brandy said as they sat down.

"Good morning, Brandy," Merrie piped up happily. "Papa told me that you're gonna marry Uncle Rafe. I'm glad."

Brandy and Rafe both looked surprised at her open declaration.

"But I thought you wanted him for yourself," Brandy said.

"I love him whole bunches, but Papa explained to me yesterday that Uncle Rafe can't wait for me to grow up." She looked at Rafe pointedly.

He leaned over and kissed her cheek. "I'd love to, honey, but I can't—not now that I've met Brandy."

"She is kinda special, isn't she, Uncle Rafe?" she said to him conspiratorially.

"She's very special," he answered, turning a warm regard to Brandy.

Brandy almost found herself believing his lies. It would have been easy to give in to the fantasy and pretend that this handsome man really did care about her, but she couldn't forget the underlying truth to their relationship. It was a bargain between them—nothing more. She would play his devoted wife until she delivered the child he wanted and then she would have to go—whether she wanted to or not. Rafe didn't really want her or care about her. It was all an act, a means to an end.

"I'm glad you think so," she replied, smiling at the both of them. It was a tight, forced smile, but neither noticed. "Your Uncle Rafe is one special man, Merrie. I'm glad you don't mind me marrying him."

"If he had to go and get married, I'm glad it's to you. When is the wedding, Uncle Rafe?"

"As soon as we can get things arranged in St. Louis."

"Can I come?"

"I wouldn't dream of having it without you."

Merrie beamed with pleasure. "Good. It'll be fun."

"What's wrong, Jason?" Rafe asked, seeing the funny look on the boy's face.

"Girls are strange. Why do they think getting married is so wonderful?"

"Because it is," Merrie argued. "Uncle Rafe and Brandy are in love, Jason. They're not gonna love anybody else the way they love each other, just like Papa loved Mama."

Jason grunted disparagingly, a sound of pure male irritation over silly female ideas of love.

Brandy felt uncomfortable over Merrie's starry-eyed description of their relationship. She glanced over at Rafe and found he was studying her with a hooded expression.

"She's right, darling," Rafe said, reaching out to take Brandy's hand. "I've never known another woman like you."

I'll bet, she thought, meeting his gaze. She expected to see deceit in his regard as he used double entendres to hide the truth from everyone, but to her surprise, he was looking at her without guile. His gaze was almost beseeching her to play along with him and make their whirlwind courtship believable to Marc and the children.

"What about you, Brandy?" Merrie was asking. "How come you fell in love with Uncle Rafe so quick?"

"It wasn't difficult," she told her. "We were playing cards, and he won not only the poker game, but my heart as well."

"I know. Uncle Rafe is easy to love. Lotsa girls love him. He's awful handsome, and he's rich, too," Merrie pointed out without bragging. "He's not like Jason!" Merrie giggled as her brother sat beside her making faces.

"Shut up, Merrie," Jason growled. "I'm glad no girls love me! I don't like girls."

Brandy couldn't help smiling as she thought of Lottie Demers and her desperate attempt to force Rafe to the altar. A lot of women really did want Rafe. She didn't, and yet she was the one he was going to marry.

Brandy thought about what Marc had told her of Rafe's parents' marriage and knew that their unhappiness had influenced his decision. She could think of no other reason why he had decided that she, of all the females who would have been delighted to be his wife, was the one he would marry.

"And they don't like you either!" his sister taunted. " 'Cause you're not nice like Uncle Rafe. Uncle Rafe is special. Right, Brandy?"

Brandy looked over at the man who would soon be her husband. Outwardly, he was the true Southern gentleman—handsome, charming, sophisticated. He gave the appearance of being completely devoted to her. Only Brandy knew the truth. "Yes, Rafe's very special. It's no wonder so many women want to marry him."

"But you're the one who got him, and you're gonna be very happy, I know it."

"You think so, do you?" Rafe finally spoke up.

Merrie nodded with a childlike confidence that Brandy wished she were feeling. The waiter came with their food then, and the conversation turned to the day's activities.

"What are you two lovebirds going to do?" Marc asked when they'd just about finished the meal.

"There isn't a lot we can do until we reach St. Louis," Rafe answered.

"Well, let me know what your plans are in the city, and I'll help with whatever I can. Jennette's folks will be thrilled to see Merrie and Jason, so I'm sure I won't have any trouble getting away if you need me for anything."

"Don't worry, I'll be taking you up on your offer."

"You're staying at the Planter's House?" Marc asked.

Rafe nodded. "My business meetings are set. It's going to be a full week."

"What about Brandy? Where is she staying?"

"I have my room here on the *Pride*," she offered.

"Yes, but how long will the boat be in town?" Rafe said. "We'll need to get you a room at the Planter's House, but we also need to take care of the chaperone situation."

"When we reach St. Louis tomorrow morning, I'll check with Jennette's family and see if they have any suggestions about finding one. They should be able to give me a lead on someone suitable for the job."

They parted after breakfast. Brandy and Rafe went to stroll on the deck together. They were quiet, neither speaking for a long time.

"Do you really think this farce is going to work?" Brandy finally asked when they found a spot where they were alone and could speak freely. She still hoped there might be some way she could convince him that this whole thing was crazy and they should give it up. They both knew the truth—he didn't love her and he never would.

Rafe glanced at her, his expression bland. "Of course it will work. We've made an agreement, and we're both going to live up to it."

"Somehow, I have trouble thinking of marriage in the same terms as a business deal. I know money is involved. But there's so much more to marriage than just a financial arrangement."

"Are you sure?" Rafe sounded harsh. "With the exception of Marc and Jennette's marriage, most of the marriages I've seen have definitely been influenced by money. Granted, it's usually arranged by the parents, who either want to keep the family fortune in the right hands or want to trap a rich husband for a desperate daughter, but it's always about money."

"How did you get so jaded about marriage?"

"I'm not jaded, I'm just honest. We have no secrets

between us. You and I both know what we're getting out of this arrangement. There won't be any surprises for us when the time comes for us to go our separate ways."

"That's true enough. I'm certainly not going into this marriage harboring any foolish notion that you love me or that we're going to live happily ever after."

Rafe glanced at her. "Good. Childish daydreams like Merrie's are just that—dreams for children. Those kinds of fantasies only make real life more difficult to deal with. You and I both know what to expect from each other, so we should get along just fine."

"Oh, yes. I know exactly what you want from me, and you needn't worry that I'll press you for more than you're willing—or able—to give."

Rafe thought she sounded as pleased with the arrangement as he was. Things were working out very well—very well, indeed.

Chapter Eleven

Dancing followed dinner that night, and Rafe and Brandy stood together at the side of the dance floor watching the other couples gracefully sweep past.

Rafe was remembering the last time he'd waltzed. Lottie Demers had been the woman in his arms, but his gaze had been on Brandy the whole time. He'd been wondering what it would be like to be dancing with Brandy instead of the other girl, and now the time had come to find out. He was certain that she would be as light as a feather in his arms and that she would move with more grace and elegance than any other female he'd known. He'd been thinking about this moment all night and he was expecting her to be eager to dance with him. After all, every woman he'd ever asked to dance before had been thrilled by his invitation.

"Would you care to dance?" he asked, turning to Brandy, his expression pleasant.

• "No . . . no, thank you," she quickly declined, not looking up at him.

At her refusal, a black scowl marred his handsome features for a moment, then was quickly masked. "Are you sure I can't coax you out onto the dance floor?" He tried again.

"I'm just not in the mood tonight. In fact, if you don't mind, I think I'll retire for the evening," she said, turning away from the dance floor.

Rafe was left to follow, and he quickly trailed her from the room. When they were on deck, he strode angrily after her. He caught up with her and took her arm to stop her progress, for she seemed hell-bent on retreating to her room.

"Are you feeling all right?" he asked, wondering at her rush to leave.

"I'm feeling fine."

"Then there must be another reason why you didn't want to dance tonight."

Brandy was cornered, and she hated it. Somehow, this man always managed to do this to her. He instinctively seemed to be able to find her weaknesses and zero in on them. She spun around to face him, her eyes flashing fire as she glared down at his restraining hand on her arm.

"Yes, there is," she told him in a tight, low voice. "If you must know . . ." It irked her greatly to say the next words, but she had no choice. "I don't know how to dance."

The confession cost her much. She glowered up at him, daring him to laugh.

"You don't know how to dance?" he repeated, staring at her incredulously. It had never occurred to him that there was a woman in the world who didn't know how to waltz. He'd thought females were born

dancing, ready to use their abilities to catch themselves a husband at the earliest opportunity.

"No," she repeated tightly, then added in sarcasm,
"Would you like me to shout it out loud so the whole
world knows too?"

"Why don't you know how?"

She couldn't believe he was so slow. Wasn't he the
one who'd said she was lacking in social graces?
Well, damn it, in this instance he'd been right, and
it irked her to admit it, even though it was true. "My
mother and I had no money for dancing lessons."

Rafe stood still, staring down at her in the moonlight. He saw all the pride she clung to and not for
the first time thought she was one magnificent
woman. Ben had told him just how rough her life
had been, and he wondered how he'd been able to
forget that. Unable to help himself, he lifted one
hand to gently touch her cheek.

"I'm sorry if I embarrassed you. It was not my intent," he said softly, his gaze catching and holding
hers. "In all honesty, I asked you to dance because I
really wanted to dance with you."

"Oh . . ." That was all she could manage. The soft
caress of his hand at her cheek thrilled her, and the
intense look in his eyes held her mesmerized.

"Would you like to learn?" he asked in a low, husky
voice. "I know we'd talked about hiring someone to
help you with etiquette and things, but this is one
lesson I would like to teach you myself."

Brandy felt herself blushing, and she was glad for
the cover of darkness to hide that telltale emotion.
Her heartbeat quickened as she imagined being held
in his arms while they moved together to the melody's sensuous rhythm. It was a heady thought.

She remembered the night she'd seen him dancing

141

with Lottie Demers and remembered, too, the envy she'd felt toward the other woman. Now it was her turn to dance with Rafe, and she would not refuse.

"I . . . I'd like that."

"My dear Miss Brandy, may I have the honor of this dance?"

He bowed in a most courtly way, eliciting a soft laugh of delight from her.

"Why, Mr. Marchand, I would love to waltz with you . . . if you think you're strong enough to bear up under my ineptitude." She spoke in her most exaggerated Southern belle drawl as she curtsied deeply before him.

"It would be my pleasure to suffer any pain just to hold you in my arms, my dear," he said gallantly.

Then, knowing she was nervous and unsure of herself, Rafe held out his hand to her and waited for her to take it. When she did, he drew her to him, holding her lightly, one hand resting at the small of her back. She felt delicate and very feminine beneath his touch.

"Waltzing is simple actually," he began. "Just put your hand on my shoulder and move with me. I'll go slow so I don't confuse either one of us."

He began to move about the deserted deck, rhythmically, swaying ever so gently to the sensuous music.

The melody was slightly muted, but that only added to the intimacy of being in Rafe's arms. Brandy was swept away by the romantic magic of the moment.

The one fantasy she held in her heart all these years was the memory of watching the handsome men and beautiful women waltzing in the ballroom at the manor house when she was a little girl hiding in the garden. It had seemed the most wonderful thing in the whole wide world, and now there she was on the deck of a steamboat in the moonlight, waltzing with the most handsome man she'd ever seen.

The magic of the moment let her forget for just that tiny space of time that Rafe was not the love of her life, a hero sweeping her away to a fairy-tale life in his kingdom. She became a creature of her senses, aware only of the warm strength of his hand at her waist guiding her, and the heat of his body searing her whenever they accidentally touched.

"You're getting it," he told her in a soft, low voice as she swayed back and forth. "I'm going to turn now . . . stay with me."

Rafe moved gracefully for a man, and she was able to follow his lead easily. She lost her step only once, and he covered for her quickly, keeping a steadying grip on her.

Brandy gazed up at him, studying the hard line of his jaw, and realized there was strength there instead of danger. She stared at the firm line of his lips, and instead of seeing a sneering conqueror, she saw the sensuous lips of the one man she longed to kiss. She lifted her gaze to his and found him staring down at her with a flaming intensity that seared her very soul.

And then they weren't dancing anymore. Suddenly, she was standing perfectly still, wrapped tightly in his arms, her body pressed intimately to his.

Rafe gazed down at the beauty in his arms and could only stare at her in amazement. She was a wonder—strong, beautiful and intelligent. She could match him word for word, argument for argument, and not give an inch. She was different from any other woman he'd ever met, and he wondered how fate had brought them together this way.

Rafe felt almost hypnotized as he bent toward her. He was intent only on kissing her. She fit perfectly in his arms. They moved together in perfect rhythm. He had to kiss her or go crazy. His hand tightened instinctively at her waist as he lowered his lips to hers.

He heard her gasp at the first touch of his mouth on hers, and she stiffened slightly as if to resist him.

"Brandy . . ." He drew back just enough to whisper her name in a low groan before meeting her lips in a tentative kiss.

The moment was ecstasy. The churning of the steamboat, the throbbing of the engines, the sound of the music all faded away to oblivion. There was just the two of them, wrapped in each other's arms, standing alone in the moonlight.

It was a kiss that dreams were made of. It was perfection and more. Romantic, breathless, passionate, they broke apart to stare at each other in amazement and confusion.

Brandy gave herself a mental shake. This was Rafe Marchand—the man who'd blackmailed her into marriage with the intent of getting rid of her as quickly as he could. There was no tender emotion behind his sensual assault. There was only lust. There was no point in her trying to fool herself.

"I have to go in now . . ." she managed hoarsely, realizing what power he wielded over her. She had never known a man's kiss to move her so dramatically before, and it frightened her to know that he could affect her so.

With that she turned and rushed away from him,

pausing to look back only once before disappearing inside her cabin.

Rafe watched her run away from him, and, in truth, was glad that she was gone. No matter that he'd wanted to lay her down upon the deck and take her right there and then. He had insisted she act the lady, and he had to treat her like one. He was more than tempted to follow her, but he held himself in tight control, watching from a distance until she was safely in her room. Only then did he head for the bar.

Marc had been coming out of the men's saloon when he spotted Rafe and Brandy dancing on deck. He'd paused to watch them and had noticed immediately how perfect they looked together, moving in rhythm about the deserted deck, completely unaware of anything save the thrill of being in each other's arms.

Marc remembered all too clearly how it had been when he'd danced with Jennette. During those precious moments, holding her had been the only thing that mattered; the rest of the world had somehow disappeared.

It was obvious to him that Rafe was finding that same joy with Brandy, and he was glad for his friend. Every man deserved that special happiness once in his life. When the couple broke apart, Marc went in the opposite direction, not wanting to embarrass them by letting them know he'd seen them. Instead, he made his way back to his own cabin the long way.

A sadness filled Marc as he bedded down in his solitary bed. He had lost the love of his life and would never again know the joy of holding Jennette in his arms, of loving her, of dancing with her . . .

He fought against the pain that threatened to overwhelm him. It was getting a little easier to battle the agony as the days, weeks and months passed, but it seemed it would never go away completely. Jennette had meant too much to him. She had been his world. He had loved her more than he'd thought it was humanly possible to love anyone, and she had been taken from him, tragically, devastatingly.

Marc had to go on. He knew it. And he did, day after day. He got out of bed and faced the world alone—save for their children, his and Jennette's. He sighed as he closed his eyes against burning tears.

St. Louis loomed ahead of the *Pride* as the steamboat churned the final mile upriver. The landing was crowded, yet the steamer had no trouble finding a place to dock.

Brandy was filled with a terrible sense of trepidation as she stood on deck with Rafe at her side. When she next boarded a steamboat to head back downriver, she would be this man's wife and her whole life would be changed.

She slanted Rafe a sidelong glance. After last night, she wasn't quite sure what to think of him. Kind had never been a word she would have used to describe him, but he had seemed kind last night. Thinking about it now, the whole evening seemed like a dream. Had this tall, silent man at her side really taken her in his arms and waltzed her about the deck in the moonlight? Had he truly not belittled her for her lack of skill? His actions had surprised and pleased her, yet she cautioned herself not to read too much into them. She had to learn to dance. Who better to teach her than Rafe? That way no one else would realize just how backward she really was.

"Marc and I have several things to take care of right away. Will you be all right here on the boat?"

Rafe's question drew her back from her thoughts.

"Of course," she replied lightly. "Do you know what our plans are going to be?"

"I'll be registering us at the Planter's House Hotel, but it wouldn't be appropriate for you move in there until the chaperone issue has been resolved. As soon as that's taken care of, we can start making the arrangements for the wedding."

"That quickly," she said a bit breathlessly.

"There isn't a lot of time. I'm hoping the priest who married Marc will be amenable to performing the ceremony for us. We'll have to see. Some insist on three weeks for the banns to run, but there's no time for that."

"We could go to a justice of the peace," she offered, thinking there was something sacrilegious about their taking their vows in a church before a priest.

"No. I won't give the gossips any reason to question our union. We'll be married in church." It was a statement that brooked no argument.

He sounded so fierce that she let it drop. If she hadn't known better, she would have thought it really mattered to him, but as he'd said, it was just to keep the gossips from talking.

When the *Pride* had finished tying up at the riverfront, Rafe turned to Brandy.

"I'll be back for you as soon as possible."

"I'll be waiting," she answered, keeping her tone that of a woman who was going to be separated from her beloved for a few hours.

Rafe found himself smiling at her as Marc appeared on deck with the nanny and children in tow.

"Are you ready, Rafe?" Marc asked as he joined them.

"Yes. I'll see you later, Brandy," he said to her in a more intimate tone.

She just smiled as she watched them go. Merrie darted back to her to give her an impulsive hug.

"Be good, sweetheart," Brandy told her.

"I will," she promised and then ran to catch up with her harried father.

Rafe and Marc shared a carriage, dropping Rafe at the Planter's House.

"I'll go on to the Davidsons' house, get the children settled in and then see what I can find out. I'll be in touch."

"Let me know. The sooner we get this over with, the better."

"I'll talk to Jennette's mother. I hope she can recommend someone to help us or at least set us looking in the right direction."

"I'll be waiting to hear from you."

Rafe went on into the hotel, booking two additional connecting rooms, in the hope that he would need them for Brandy and her soon-to-be-hired tutor and chaperone.

Chapter Twelve

Claire Patterson stood at the window of her small office on the second floor at the Wellington Girls' Academy, staring out at the busy city street below. There were so many people, rushing about town with so many places to go and so many things to do. Yet here she was at the end of another school year . . . and what had she accomplished? True, she had helped another class of young women graduate with sophistication and grace. She had inspired them to read, sing and play a musical instrument. She had counseled them when they'd had problems, dried their tears when they'd been heartbroken and cheered them when they'd succeeded. And now, the school year was just about over, and as had been the case for the last eight years, she would be alone again.

With a sigh, Claire turned away from the window and went to sit at her desk. Methodically, she began to empty the drawers into her small valise just as she had last year and the year before. Her classes for this year were over. She loved working with the girls, Lord knew she did, for without her students she would have no life at all. But there were days like today when she couldn't help remembering when she had been one of the young, happy girls graduating from Wellington.

Claire was not unhappy with her life. Money wasn't a problem, for her parents had left her very well off when they'd passed away. She spent most of her time helping others, and she'd always wanted to do that. It was just on days like today that she wished something exciting and adventurous would happen to her. It was beautiful outside, sunny and bright. The temperature was moderate. It was a perfect day for an impromptu picnic or a ride in the country, but there was no fun in riding or picnicking alone. And she was alone.

A knock came at her door, interrupting her thoughts.

"Yes? Who is it?"

"Miss Cavendish," her headmistress announced as she came into the room. "I just wanted to thank you for another splendid year and wish you a wonderful summer off."

"Why, thank you," Claire answered. She genuinely liked the headmistress. "I'll see you in the fall?"

"Absolutely. I'll send you your new schedule in August. Have a lovely summer, Claire."

"I will, and you, too."

Miss Cavendish disappeared out the door in a whirlwind of activity, and Claire was once again alone. She smiled ruefully at her own morose mood as she gathered up her things and started home. She glanced back once at her small office—the walls bare, the desktop clean—then closed the door quietly behind her.

"I have an interesting problem that I hope you can help me with," Marc told Suzanne and Roger Davidson that afternoon as he sat having tea with them in the parlor of their spacious home on Lucas Place in St. Louis. He had arrived there with the children several hours before, and now that the initial excitement of their arrival had passed, he had the time to talk to them about Brandy's need for a chaperone.

"What is it?" Suzanne asked, ready and willing to do anything for Marc. She'd adored him from the first day Jennette had brought him home, and she cherished the close relationship they'd developed and kept over the years.

"Do you remember my friend Rafe Marchand?"

"Oh, yes. He's a very nice young man," she said approvingly.

Marc explained Rafe's situation with Brandy, saying only that it had been a whirlwind courtship and was a love match. "They're planning to marry while they're here in town, but he wants to make sure that her reputation is untarnished. He needs to hire a suitable chaperone for her, someone perhaps who could even act as a tutor and help her with some of the finer points of etiquette. Can you think of anyone who might be qualified for such a job? Or at least, recommend someplace for me to look?"

"That is so romantic," Suzanne said with a smile as she looked over at her husband. Her expression turned thoughtful as she considered the possibilities; then her eyes lit up as she realized the answer to

Marc's problem. "Of course! Roger . . . what about Claire?"

At Suzanne's mention of Jennette's childhood friend, Roger smiled his approval. "Claire would be perfect," he agreed. "Marc, you should remember Claire Patterson. She was one of Jennette's friends from the academy. I think you met her on several occasions. I know she was at your wedding."

Marc frowned. "The name sounds familiar, but I don't remember what she looks like."

"Claire was never a great beauty. She's rather tall and thin. Her hair is brown and she wears glasses."

Marc looked up at Suzanne, recognition showing in his eyes. "I remember her now. She was always quiet and stayed in the background a lot. Jennette liked her, and I think they wrote to each other often when we were first married."

"Claire is a delightful young woman. She's never married, though. She teaches at the academy now, but since it's the end of the school year, that shouldn't be a problem. Shall I send a note for you this afternoon?"

"That would be wonderful," Marc said, pleased that they might have been able to solve the problem so quickly and easily. He relaxed then and enjoyed the Davidsons' company. Since Jennette's death, they'd only had the opportunity to visit twice, and it was good to be together again.

Claire had settled into her parlor with a good book and was reading when the knock came at the door. She hadn't been expecting anyone and was curious when her maid, Della, came in to hand her the letter.

"It's from the Davidsons," Della announced. "The

servant who brought it over has been instructed to wait for your answer."

"The Davidsons?" Claire repeated, a bit surprised, as she took the envelope and quickly opened it. She scanned the contents once, then reread it. "Tell him that I'd be delighted to join them for dinner tonight. I'll be there promptly at six o'clock."

Della went off to deliver her answer as Claire glanced quickly at the clock. It was already going on four. She knew she'd better start getting ready if she was going to be on time for dinner.

"Claire! Come in! It's so good to see you, again," Suzanne welcomed her as their maid was ushering Claire into the foyer.

"Mrs. Davidson, it's good to see you, too. I was so excited when I got your invitation this afternoon. What a wonderful surprise to hear from you."

"It's our pleasure, believe me. Come on in and join us. We've so much to talk about."

Claire had not expected it. Her heart skipped a beat, and her breath caught in her throat. She could only pray that her expression did not reveal what she was truly feeling as she came face-to-face with Marc LeFevre in the Davidsons' parlor.

Marc was standing at the fireplace conversing with Roger when Claire entered the room with Suzanne. He looked up and recognized her immediately, for she hadn't changed in the nine years since he'd last seen her. She was a tall, spare woman with medium brown hair tied back in a bun at the nape of her neck. She wore wire-rimmed glasses and a very nondescript, dark blue gown. She was the picture of a prim and proper old-maid schoolteacher, and Marc knew immediately that Suzanne and Roger had been right.

She would be perfect for the job, if he could only convince her to take it.

"Good evening, Claire," he said, turning to greet her with a smile. "It's been a long time."

"Marc . . . ?" She hoped she sounded normal. She hoped she sounded like anything other than the way she was feeling. Marc was there, standing before her looking every bit as handsome as he had the last time she'd seen him—on the day of his wedding to Jennette. The memories came back in a rush, and she struggled to hold them at bay. It had been nine years ago . . . nine long years. She had never told anyone how she'd felt about this man. He had been too far out of her reach. Jennette had loved him and he had loved her. There had been no point to her feelings, but she had never been able to control them where Marc was concerned.

Claire had fallen in love with him the first time she'd seen him, when he'd attended a society ball. He had been everything she'd ever dreamed of in a man—handsome, intelligent and kind. They had danced one dance that night, and she had lost her heart to him. He'd never known it, though, for shortly thereafter, Jennette had made her grand entrance.

Jennette had been beautiful and witty and charming, the belle of St. Louis that season. She'd had every man in town proposing to her, but it had been Marc Jennette fell in love with, Marc whose proposal she accepted. Claire had been happy for them and had tried never to think of her feelings for Marc again. It startled her now to be staring at him and to have those long-buried emotions surge to the fore in her heart.

"It's good to see you again. Thank you for coming,"

Roger was saying as he came forward to take her hand and press a kiss on her cheek.

She tore her gaze from Marc to speak with Jennette's father. "Thank you for inviting me. It was a wonderful surprise, especially after all this time."

They spoke at length of general things, settling in on the sofa.

"How are your children, Marc? It must have been a difficult time for them," she said sympathetically.

"It's been a hard time for all of us, but things are slowly getting better. Jason's getting to be quite a young man now, and Merrie . . ." He paused, looking to his mother-in-law.

"Well, Merrie is very much like her mother," Suzanne added with a smile.

Claire gave a soft laugh. She remembered how Jennette had always been curious about life, always asking the question no one else dared to ask, always seeing the delight in life. "Merrie must be wonderful."

"She is," Marc said huskily. "They've already gone to bed for the night, but we're going to be in town for over a week so I'm sure you'll get to see them before we have to leave."

"I'd like that."

The servant announced that dinner was ready then, and they went into the dining room.

Claire couldn't help wondering why she'd been invited to dinner after all this time. During the meal, as they spoke of all that had happened over the years, her rather active imagination teased her with the fairy-tale notion that Marc had really missed her and had longed to see her again. The logical, rational Claire knew better and refused to entertain the fantasy. She'd been invited there for a reason; they just hadn't gotten around to bringing it up yet.

As dessert was served, they finally did. Claire had been relating tales of her students to them, and it was then that Suzanne broached the subject.

"Claire, we need your help," Suzanne began, "or rather, Marc needs your help."

She met his gaze across the table, wondering what he could possibly need from her. "You need my help?" she asked, a little disbelieving. She couldn't imagine what she had that he could possibly need.

"Suzanne and Roger recommended that I speak with you about this," he began in earnest.

At those words, her heart sank even more. He hadn't thought of her on his own; the Davidsons had been the ones to mention her to him.

"I need to hire a chaperone, and tutor, of sorts, and they thought you would be perfect for the job. I understand why now," he said, meaning to be complimentary, not realizing that he'd failed miserably.

"You need a tutor for your children and you want to hire me?"

"Oh, no . . ." Suzanne put in. "It's much more romantic than that. Tell her the whole story, Marc."

Romantic? What were they talking about? Claire looked around the table. "I'm afraid I'm a bit confused."

Marc related Rafe's tale. "Brandy is wonderful. I think the world of her, but she is in need of a female companion and some social guidance. That's where you come in."

"I do?" Claire clasped her hands together in her lap, schooling her expression to one of polite interest.

"Rafe would be willing to pay handsomely for your services. It could last as long as a few months and would require you to accompany them back to Natchez. Suzanne and Roger suggested you, and I think you'd be wonderful. Would you be interested?"

Claire didn't know whether to laugh or cry. She was glad she'd fought down her foolish fantasy. Marc certainly didn't want her for herself. He wanted to hire Claire, the teacher.

"Tell me more about Brandy."

"She's about twenty, I think. She's very bright, and I'm sure she'll be a quick study. She'll need your help learning how to run a plantation house and some of the other finer arts of society."

Claire nodded and was quiet for a moment. She had thought Marc was gone from her life forever. She had thought that she would never see him again. And now . . . She gave a rueful shake of her head. Earlier that day, she'd been wishing something exciting would happen, and now it had. If she took this job, she would get to travel, to meet new people, and be close to Marc. She knew he would never consider her romantically. She was nothing like Jennette. But this way, at least, she could be with him for a little while.

"I'll take the job," she answered with conviction, not needing to think about it anymore. "When would you like me to start?"

"We can meet with Rafe and Brandy at the Planter's House in the morning—if that's all right with you?"

"That will be fine."

The rest of the evening passed in a blur for Claire. She had never in all her life done anything as impulsive as taking this job, and she was amazed at how calm she felt about it. As she lay in bed that night courting sleep, she wondered what had ever possessed her to say yes.

But she knew the answer.

It was Marc. If only for this short span of time, she would get to be near him, to hear his laugh, talk with him and love him . . . from afar.

Rafe was studying Claire with open interest. She had arrived at the rooms he'd taken for Brandy that morning promptly at nine A.M. as Marc had said she would. She was dressed conservatively and wore her hair pinned back in a bun. He couldn't tell if she was young or old, but he certainly knew that she looked every bit the formidable schoolmarm he'd been hoping to hire. He'd already decided that if she wanted the job, it was hers.

"Marc has told us all about you, Miss Patterson, and after meeting you this morning, I agree with everything he said. The job is yours if you'd like it."

Claire was pleased, but she looked at Brandy, the young woman she was to work with. "And you, Miss O'Neill? I wouldn't dream of taking on the responsibility of being your chaperone without your consent. If you feel there would be any difficulty between us that would impair our ability to work together, now is the time to say so."

Brandy had been quiet during the meeting with Claire. She listened carefully as Rafe had asked the other woman several questions relating to her background and teaching experience. She found the woman interesting and certainly no mealy-mouthed miss from the way she was handling Rafe. She met Claire's gaze and saw the kindness in the depths of her eyes. "I would love to have you as my chaperone."

Rafe and Marc both sighed in relief.

"It's settled then," Rafe said, smiling. "Now, as to your salary . . ."

"I'm sure you'll be more than generous," Claire responded, honestly caring little about the money. Her excitement was too great to be troubled with such a mundane thing. She didn't know what the future held for her, but she hoped it proved more adventurous than the life she'd been leading. "When would you like me to start?"

"Today, if you can." Rafe wanted Brandy safely ensconced at the hotel. "I've taken these rooms at the hotel for you and Brandy. Mine is right across the hall."

"I'm afraid that arrangement is unsatisfactory," Claire dictated, drawing surprised looks from Rafe, Brandy and Marc. Her tone brooked no argument. "Brandy will move in with me at my home until the wedding takes place."

"Are you sure you want to do it this way?" Marc asked.

"I have plenty of room, and it's the only way I can be sure of safeguarding her reputation. It will also be easier for the two of us to work on the finer points of her education." She looked at Brandy. "If you have your things with you, we can leave now."

"I have a few more things to get from the steamer, and I need to say good-bye to Ben. I could be at your home this afternoon."

"I'll be expecting you by one." Claire gave her the address.

"I'll be there."

"Also, you will be needing a new wardrobe. Are there funds available, and if so, how much?"

"Money is no object. Order whatever she needs."

"Are you sure?" Brandy glanced at Rafe in surprise.

"You're going to be my wife. I want you to have whatever you desire."

"Thank you." For a moment, Brandy had been touched by his generosity, but then she understood the motivation behind his largess. He didn't want her to embarrass him. She had to be beautiful when they were in public, so he would pay whatever it took to ensure that her wardrobe was immaculate. Outwardly, she was going to be turned into a shining example of delicate Southern womanhood.

"First thing this afternoon, then, we'll pay a visit to the dressmaker. Until then." Claire left, knowing she had a myriad of things to do before Brandy came to stay.

"Well, what do you think?" Rafe asked Brandy once Claire had gone.

"I think Claire and I are going to get along just fine." She smiled. "But I certainly wouldn't want to make her angry. She seems quite formidable. I bet she's a wonderful teacher."

"I'm going on back to the Davidsons'," Marc said. "If you need me for anything, just send word. I know you've got a business meeting in an hour. Shall I drop Brandy at the *Pride* on my way?" he asked.

"Thanks, Marc."

Marc went on out into the hall to give Rafe and Brandy a moment of privacy.

"I'm glad you approve of Claire. I wanted to find someone you'd be comfortable with."

"I think we'll do fine."

"Shall we plan on dinner tonight, at eight?"

"I'll be ready."

*   *   *

Ben sat beside Brandy in the carriage as they rode toward Claire Patterson's home.

"Are you sure this arrangement is satisfactory to you? It's not too late to back out, you know," he said, his expression serious.

"You are so sweet, Ben." She gave him a heartfelt look. "But it looks like Rafe and Marc have arranged everything, so I'm going to be in very good hands. Claire Patterson is a teacher at a prestigious girls' academy here in St. Louis. She's agreed to take the job of being my chaperone for the duration."

"And you liked and trusted her?"

"I did. You'll see when you meet her. You'll feel the same way."

"I wish I didn't have to leave tomorrow."

"I wish you could stay, too. It would be good to have you here for the wedding, but that won't be for at least a week."

"I've got to pull out and head upriver tomorrow; then it'll be almost three full weeks before I'm back in St. Louis again. You take care of yourself, you hear? I'll be worrying about you until I can check up on you when I get back to Natchez."

"Thank you, Ben. I don't know what I would have done without you." She gave him a bittersweet smile, knowing nothing would ever be the same again once they parted.

"You would have done just fine without me. You're a survivor, Brandy," he told her confidently.

The carriage slowed before Claire's house then, and Ben got a look at the home where she would be living. It was in a good neighborhood and the two-story brick house looked well kept. He escorted her to the door and waited with her for someone to answer. He would not leave Brandy alone until he'd spoken with Claire Patterson.

"Brandy. You're right on time," Claire greeted her as she opened the door.

"Hello, Claire. I'd like you to meet my friend, Captain Ben Rodgers. Ben, this is Claire Patterson, my official chaperone."

They exchanged pleasantries.

"I just wanted to make sure that Brandy got here all safe and sound. And I wanted to meet you."

"I'm glad you came. Any friend of Brandy's is a friend of mine."

Brandy was relieved that they seemed to like each other. When Claire went back inside, leaving them to say their good-byes, she turned to her friend with a bright smile.

"I told you you'd approve."

"I am impressed. Your Miss Patterson seems like a very capable lady. You're sure you're going to be fine?"

"I'm sure."

"Well, I'd better be heading back. You just send word if you need me—any time, any place."

"I will. Thanks for coming with me, Ben. It's good to know that you care," Brandy told him.

He gave her a quick hug and kissed her cheek. "I'll be in touch."

Her smile was teary as she bade her friend good-bye. She watched him go, then turned back into the house, prepared to face her future.

Chapter Thirteen

"Well, the first thing we need to do is go through your present wardrobe and see exactly what you have, so we know what to order at the dress shop," Claire announced, once Brandy's things had been taken up to one of the extra bedrooms.

For the first time in her life, Brandy was a little embarrassed in front of another woman. Knowing that Claire was unaware of her background, Brandy flinched inwardly as she opened her bags to draw out her clothing. She spread the four fancy dresses she'd worn for gambling on the bed, smoothing the wrinkles from the skirts. She was not ashamed of them, but they were too low-cut and far too flashy for a "decent" woman to wear in public.

"I see," was all that Claire murmured as she studied the gowns thoughtfully.

"I do have three more sedate day gowns," Brandy told her quickly, laying them out, too.

Claire picked one up and smiled. "The workmanship in this is beautiful."

"My mother made it."

"She did a fine job."

"I'll tell her you said so, or better yet, you can tell her yourself when we get to Natchez. Rafe has agreed that she can come live with us at his home, so I'm sure you'll get to meet her."

"That's wonderful. Not all men would be so accommodating of their mothers-in-law." Claire wasn't quite sure how to ask her next question, but she was dying to know where Brandy had worn her more revealing gowns. "So tell me, Brandy, where exactly did you, um . . . Well, I was wondering . . ."

"You're curious about my wardrobe," Brandy finished for her. She had known Claire would ask after seeing her clothes, and she sat down on the edge of the bed, still holding one of the daygowns her mother had made.

"Your dresses are . . . interesting . . ." Claire's expression and tone were both noncommittal.

Brandy had expected condemnation or haughtiness from her. She hadn't expected Claire to be simply curious. "When Rafe and I met and fell in love on board the *Pride*, I was working."

"You worked on the steamboat?" Claire was frowning, trying to imagine what kind of job Brandy had had where she would wear such clothes.

"Yes, I did." Brandy had been dreading this moment. She had almost left her dresses behind with Ben, but since her mother had sewn them, they meant too much to her. She girded herself for Claire's coming condemnation of her character. "I know you're wondering what you've gotten yourself into, but now you'll understand why Rafe felt the need to hire a tutor for me. I worked on the steamboat as a gambler."

"You're a gambler?" Claire's eyes rounded in amazement. Brandy looked so sweet, hardly the hardened type she would have imagined, who dealt cards and matched men drink for drink in a men's saloon.

"Yes, and a damned good one, at that," Brandy answered defensively, though she hadn't sensed any real censure in Claire's question. "That's how Rafe and I met—by playing poker—and now we're going to be married."

"I would never have dreamed you two met that way. It's so romantic."

"Isn't it, though?" Brandy tried to keep from sounding jaded. It wouldn't do for anyone to suspect that all was not as it should be between them.

"And now you're going to give it all up to become his wife." A small, secret smile curved Claire's lips and she asked, "How did you ever get into gambling?"

Brandy figured there was no point in lying to Claire. She quickly told her how she'd come to be a gambler with Ben on the *Pride*, and how careful she'd been about her reputation.

"So now I understand why it was so important for Rafe to hire me," she said thoughtfully. "It's good that he cares so much about you and wants to help you adjust to his way of life."

"I know, but it's going to be hard not being 'me' anymore."

"Oh, you'll still be you. You'll just be a better 'you,' " Claire told her confidently.

Brandy smiled at her reassurance. "Thanks."

"For what?"

"For not judging me for what I had to do."

"I think your life sounds exciting. You're going to have to tell me more about your adventures."

"It wasn't that exciting. I was just trying to take care of my mother and myself."

"And you did it. I'll bet your mother is very proud of you."

"I hope so . . . I truly do." Brandy wondered what her mother would say when she found out what had happened between her and Rafe. "But what about you? It must be wonderful to be a teacher and influence so many young lives. Tell me about the academy."

"I do love my students, and I'm always thrilled when they graduate and go on to succeed. But the one life I've wanted to change the most, I can't. . . ."

"Whose life was that?"

"My own," she sighed.

"But you're here with me now. That's a change for you."

"You're right, and that was precisely what I was thinking when I agreed to take the job."

"I think we're going to be great friends, Claire."

"I'd like that."

The two women shared a warm look.

"Well, we know one thing for certain, Miss Brandy O'Neill."

"What's that?"

"If you're going to make your debut in Natchez society as Mrs. Rafe Marchand, you are going to need an entirely new wardrobe. I don't think your gambling dresses would play too well in any of the ballrooms of the finer families of Natchez," she said with an impish grin.

"I don't know why not." Brandy laughed. "I might

be able to tell everyone that I'm a trendsetter and that it's the latest style from Paris."

"You might, but somehow . . ."

"I know. You don't think they'd believe me. I guess we'd better find a dressmaker and fast."

"How soon is the wedding?"

"Some time next week. Rafe and Marc have to meet with the priest first to set the date, and I think they're planning on doing that tomorrow."

"Then let's go shopping. What do you say? I know just the place. . . ."

An hour later, as she descended from the carriage that Claire had hired to take them to the dress shop, Brandy found she was holding her breath in excitement. She had often dreamed of shopping in one of these exclusive establishments, but she had never had enough money. She tried to look blasé as she entered the store, but she really wanted to gawk. Bolts and bolts of colorful fabric were artfully arranged on tables and along the walls, and dress forms fitted with already completed dresses were displayed about the room.

"Do you shop here often?" Brandy asked Claire in a low voice.

"I've been in occasionally, but most of what they carry is far more elaborate than what I need."

The owner approached them, smiling brightly in welcome.

"Good afternoon, ladies, and welcome." She had already eyed them critically and thought they might be serious customers. "My name is Lorna. What can I help you with today?"

"Miss O'Neill is in need of a whole new wardrobe," Claire said in her most authoritative voice. "She's getting married and must have the perfect trousseau."

"How wonderful! How romantic and exciting! Congratulations!"

"Thank you," Brandy replied, a little taken aback by the woman's eagerness to wait on them. She was finding that she was glad to have Claire with her. Claire was taking charge without being pushy or demanding.

"Will you be needing a wedding gown?"

"Of sorts," Brandy began.

"The wedding is going to be a small, intimate one, so we'll need something suitable for that."

"Of course. I have the perfect pattern . . ." Lorna started rushing about the store, pulling materials and patterns for their approval.

"She's going to need everything from underthings and negligees to daygowns and ballgowns. Shoes and stockings, too. Can you provide all these things?"

"Of course," Lorna answered eagerly, seeing dollar signs in her eyes.

"There is a time limit, too. Do you have any gowns that she could take with her today?"

"I have several that might be just the thing, and a few more that would work with some alterations."

"And the rest? How soon could you have them completed?"

"Ten days . . . two weeks at the most."

"That's unacceptable," Claire stated firmly in her authoritative teacher's voice. "We'll need everything by Friday of this week or we'll have to go somewhere else."

"Friday?" The dressmaker's eyes widened. The order was a magnificent one she dared not lose. It was obvious that these women had money, so she knew she could hire extra help to complete the job on time.

"Is that a problem?" Claire acted as though she was ready to walk away.

"No, no!" Lorna insisted. "I can do it. Your things will be ready by Friday."

"Good. Shall we start?"

"This way, please. We'll need to take your measurements and then begin selecting patterns that you like."

Lorna led them to the back to the dressing room. She called to her assistant, Kate, to come help, and they began the arduous task of planning Brandy's new wardrobe.

Brandy felt as if she were being swept along in a dream. All the clothes she'd ever owned in her life were inexpensive compared to the garments in this shop. She kept quiet, letting Claire debate with the women, and she had to admit that she was impressed by her new friend's fashion sense. It amazed her that a woman who dressed so plainly would know so much about fabric and current styles.

"Why don't you buy something for yourself while we're here?" Brandy asked Claire.

Lorna and her assistant had gone in search of another fabric, and they were left alone for a moment.

Claire glanced at her in surprise. "Me? Buy something here? No, I could never wear something like that."

"Why not? I'm sure that once we get to Natchez we're going to be doing a lot of socializing. You'll need to have an evening gown or two in your own wardrobe," Brandy urged, wanting to see the prim and proper Claire in a fancy dress. She wondered how very different she might look in a color that set off her fair skin and brought out the highlights in her hair. The way she was dressed now, she played down all of her good features. She had a nice figure and beautiful skin and an easy, bright smile that could charm anyone. It surprised Brandy that Claire didn't try to do more with herself.

"I don't know. . . ."

"If it's money that's worrying you, we can put it on my bill and just tell Rafe that it was one of my gowns."

"Oh, no. I could never do that. I have enough money to pay for it. My parents left me comfortably well-off when they passed away. It's just that . . ."

"That what? You'd look absolutely beautiful in that teal evening gown she showed me earlier," Brandy urged, remembering the way Claire had looked at it when Lorna brought it in for them to see.

Claire fell silent, thinking of the full-skirted satin gown. It had been simple, yet elegant, and she'd thought it a shame when it had proven too big for Brandy.

"You're several inches taller than I am. It would probably fit you without any alterations. Why don't you try it on? I shouldn't be the only one who's being poked and prodded and pinned today."

Lorna reappeared at that moment carrying several bolts of material and two new patterns for ball-gowns.

"Lorna, bring back the teal gown. Claire wants to try it on."

The seamstress looked amazed, then smiled. "You're right. The color would be perfect on her. I'll be right back."

She put the materials down and hurried off to find the creation she'd made for another woman who'd changed her mind. It was a stunning dress, fit for a queen, and it had annoyed her when the other woman had refused it. Of course, she'd always known someone would come along who could wear it, and it seemed that this woman might just be the one. In fact, she'd been looking at her with a rather critical eye while she'd been measuring Brandy, and she could tell that the woman named Claire had a near-perfect figure beneath the shapeless, dull day dress she was wearing. She was smiling brightly as she gathered up the gown and hurried back to her two customers.

"That was an inspired idea, Miss O'Neill," Lorna said as she helped Claire out of her gown. "I hadn't thought about having you try this on earlier, but I think you're going to find that the color is ideal for you."

Claire was nervous. It had been years since she'd bought anything so frivolous. As a teacher, she didn't have any need for fancy dresses, but maybe Brandy was right. She was going to Natchez where no one knew her. Here she was Miss Patterson, the teacher from the academy, and she was expected to behave in a certain, sedate, well-mannered, unobtrusive way. When she went to Natchez, she could be anybody she wanted to be . . . at least for a little while. An image of Marc flashed into her mind.

Claire lifted her arms and let Lorna slip the dress over her head. She'd forgotten how heavenly satin felt against her skin. The gown slid down over her body in a sensuous caress, and she didn't immediately look in the mirror as Lorna straightened the skirts about her and adjusted the neckline.

"There," Lorna said with satisfaction, stepping back to admire the way she looked. "What do you think, Miss O'Neill?"

"Oh, Claire! Look at yourself in the mirror," Brandy told her a bit breathlessly.

She wouldn't have imagined that just a change in color could do so much for the other woman, but the teal blue seemed to light up her entire face. It drew attention to her eyes. Brandy had never noticed their color before behind the glasses she wore, but now she realized that they were a fascinating blue-green that seemed to change color with whatever she wore. The gown fit her through the bodice, revealing the tops of her firm, full breasts, and then it nipped in at her slender waist. Brandy stared at her in delight, impressed by the change that one dress could make. Claire truly could be pretty if she'd give herself a chance.

Claire couldn't imagine why Brandy and Lorna looked so shocked, but when she turned to the full-length mirror behind her to take a look at herself, she understood. She stopped dead still as she stared at her own reflection.

"Oh . . ." she breathed. "It's beautiful. . . ."

"*It's* not beautiful," Brandy corrected. "You are! You look gorgeous. You have to take that gown. I know you'll have the occasion to wear it once we get to Natchez."

"Yes . . ." was all Claire could say. "Yes, I'll take this one for myself."

"A wise choice," Lorna agreed. "I never dreamed it would look so magnificent on you, but it does. That dress seems like it was made for you. I hope that the night you wear it, all your dreams come true."

Brandy smiled at the woman's kind words. "They certainly should. She looks like a fairy princess in it."

"Hardly," Claire said. She knew that no matter

how lovely the dress, underneath it she was still Claire Patterson, an old-maid schoolteacher who was playing at being a chaperone and tutor. Forcing her gaze from her own image, she turned her attention back to Brandy. "Now, what about you? If I'm going to wear this, we have to find something even more wonderful for you. Not to mention the gown you're going to wear for your wedding."

"I've found just the pattern for that," Lorna said and they turned their attention back to their original intent.

Across town, Rafe sent word to Marc that he would be done with business by mid-afternoon and that he could go to see the priest with Marc at four. The two men met near the church where Marc and Jennette were married and went together to the rectory to speak with Marc's long-time friend, Father Finn.

"Marc? Marc LeFevre? It's great to see you! Come on into my office," the priest greeted them at the door.

"It's good to see you, too, Father."

"I was so sorry to hear about Jennette. Suzanne and Roger took it so very hard. It was tragic." Real sympathy shone in his eyes.

"We all took it hard," he said solemnly.

"I understand."

"Sad news is not why I came to see you today, though, Father. I'm here as a favor to my friend, Rafe Marchand. Rafe, this is Father Finn."

They exchanged pleasantries as the priest led them into his office where they could sit down and talk.

"What can I do for you?" the priest asked earnestly, looking from Marc to Rafe.

"Well, Father, I want to get married," Rafe announced, and suddenly paused, realizing what he'd just said. He'd never voiced that sentiment before in his entire life.

"Rafe was hoping that you could do the honors, Father. He's in town with his fiancée for only a short time, and they wondered if you could marry them?"

"Right away?" Father Finn frowned slightly.

"I have to return to my home in Natchez next week, and I was hoping to take Brandy back with me as my bride," Rafe told him.

Father Finn drew a deep breath as he studied Rafe seriously. "Church law calls for banns to be published for three weeks before a wedding."

"But can't exceptions be made, Father?" Marc spoke up for his friend. "Your marriages work. I certainly loved Jennette with all my heart, and I want that same happiness for Rafe and Brandy. You've got the touch, Father."

Father Finn was laughing at Marc's good-natured teasing. "I'd like to believe that what you say is true, Marc. It would be good to know that all the marriages I perform are happy ones."

"They are. Of all the marriages I know, we were the happiest. I'm sure it's because of you. Will you do it for Rafe and Brandy, Father?"

Inwardly, Rafe was cringing as he listened to their banter. His acting had been too good. He'd convinced everyone, including his best friend Marc, that he and Brandy were really in love and that theirs was going to be a real marriage that would last forever.

Father Finn turned to Rafe, and he rubbed his chin thoughtfully as he studied him. "Well, I suppose I could arrange something if it's that important to you to be married next week."

"Thank you, Father," Rafe said, smiling widely, relieved that everything was working out.

"You're welcome, young man. Why don't you bring your fiancée by tomorrow morning? That way we can get to know each other and set all the plans for the ceremony."

"We'll be here."

They rose to go.

"Marc?"

"Yes, Father?"

"I'd love to see those children of yours. Can you bring them by for a visit? I haven't seen Merrie since her baptism."

"I'll make sure of it."

"Good."

Chapter Fourteen

Rafe returned to the hotel and was just starting inside when he noticed the sign on the shop down the street—CLARKSON AND SONS, JEWELERS. He stood unmoving for a moment, considering, then altered his course and headed for the store. A bell jingled, signaling his arrival as he entered.

"Good afternoon, sir. How may I help you today?" an elderly gentleman asked as he came out from behind the curtains that shielded the back room.

"I need a . . ." Rafe let his gaze sweep the glass display cases searching for the perfect . . . "ring." And then he saw it, glistening and shimmering in the bright light.

"A ring, sir?"

"That one . . ." he said immediately, staring at the solitaire set in yellow gold. The setting was simple, almost stark, but it served to enhance the glory of the gem itself.

The Lady's Hand

"You have an excellent eye, sir," Clarkson gushed, hurrying to unlock the case and take the ring out. He handed it over to Rafe and waited for his reaction.

Rafe didn't need to think about it. He knew a quality stone when he saw it. The ring would be Brandy's.

"I'll need a wedding band to go with it, too."

"Ah, so you've already proposed, have you?"

"Yes, we're being married in a week."

"I have just the thing." The jeweler hurried in back and returned with a thick gold band. "There, what do you think? I can have your initials engraved in it along with your wedding date, if you'd like."

"Yes, I'd like that very much. I'll take them both." Rafe made arrangements for the payment.

The jeweler enjoyed waiting on people who knew quality and appreciated it. "Your lady will be very pleased with the engagement ring, sir. You have excellent taste. The band will be ready the first of the week."

His lady . . . Rafe paused as he stepped outside, the beribboned box containing the engagement ring in hand. The jeweler's words were true. Brandy would be "his lady" in just a few more days.

He was surprised that the thought didn't bother him. Before, any time he'd considered marriage or commitment, it had made him angry. Now, he found himself actually looking forward to their meeting with the priest the next day, and it puzzled him.

It was just eight o'clock when Rafe arrived at Claire Patterson's home. The house was located in a well-established part of town that spoke of old money and comfortable living. The maid answered his knock and quickly led him into the parlor.

"Good evening, Mr. Marchand." Claire was there,

smiling in welcome as Della showed him in.

"Please, call me Rafe," he invited her. "How did things go this afternoon?"

"You'll be getting the bills soon, so you'll know," she answered, her eyes sparkling with good humor. "Actually, we did very well. Brandy's wardrobe has been ordered, and we should take delivery on everything no later than the weekend."

"Wonderful."

"Tomorrow, we begin our lessons. I think she's going to do very well."

"I appreciate your diligence in these matters."

"I truly believe it's going to be my pleasure. Brandy is a delightful young woman."

"I think so, too," Rafe answered.

"Oh, here she is now. . . ." Claire heard Brandy coming down the stairs and led the way out to the foyer to meet her. She knew Brandy was excited about the evening to come, for she was wearing one of the new gowns they'd purchased that day.

Rafe followed her into the foyer and glanced up the steps. He found himself transfixed at the sight of the sophisticated woman descending the staircase. He knew it was Brandy, and yet . . .

Her hair, lush and dark, tumbled down her back in a cascade of curls. The gown she wore was a masterpiece. The style artfully mixed the innocence of a virgin with the sensuality of a temptress, and it made his blood run hot. Low-cut without being vulgar, the dress temptingly displayed her breasts for his manly enjoyment. The waist of the gown was fitted. The skirts flared fully and swayed about her hips in subtle invitation. At her throat and ears, she wore expensive jewels whose color matched the pale blue of the gown.

Rafe's mouth went dry, and he could only stare at Brandy.

"Good evening, Rafe," Brandy said as she reached the bottom step.

"Brandy," he muttered hoarsely. His gaze moved appreciatively over her. "You look lovely."

"Why, thank you," she said with a soft, delighted laugh. "I was hoping you'd approve."

"I approve," he said hoarsely, managing a smile. "Are you ready to go?"

"If you are."

"Brandy must be home by midnight," Claire told him, hiding a smile of triumph over his reaction to her charge. It was obvious how much he loved her.

"I'll have her back on time."

Brandy donned a light wrap that matched the gown and added to the sophistication of her total look. From her perfectly coiffed hair to her satin-slippered feet, she appeared every bit the lady. She took his proffered arm, taking only a moment to cast a quick smile in Claire's direction as he led her from the house.

Rafe handed Brandy up into the waiting carriage, and as she passed him the faint, heady scent of her perfume came to him. It stirred a hunger in his already heated blood, and his grip on the carriage door tightened. He paused, standing outside the carriage for a moment under the pretense of giving her time to get settled in. In reality, he wanted time to think and to bring his raging desire under control.

Brandy was a pretty woman, and that was all. He'd made the deal to marry her because he wanted to have a child, not because he felt anything for her. He conceded that it was good that he was physically attracted to her; otherwise getting her with child might prove a disagreeable chore. Other than that, she was just another woman, like all the others. Nothing more, nothing less.

Rafe climbed into the vehicle and sat down beside her. As he did, the box containing the engagement ring jabbed him in the side. As the carriage rumbled off toward their dinner destination, he turned to Brandy.

"I have something for you," he told her.

"But you've given me so much already. . . ." Brandy glanced up at him in surprise. He looked so handsome tonight that her heart ached. She remembered their waltz and his kiss, and almost wished that their coming marriage was real.

He drew out the box and presented it to her.

She stared down at the jeweler's box wrapped in a velvet bow and gave a soft gasp. "Oh . . ."

"Here . . ." He pressed it into her hands. "Open it."

Brandy was almost afraid to, but she carefully untied the perfect bow and then lifted the lid on the small box. Even though the light in the carriage was dim, the diamond glittered before her.

"It's lovely . . ." she breathed, unable to believe that he was actually giving her an engagement ring. She lifted her gaze to his, her heart beating rapidly at the beauty of the gift. She almost believed . . .

But it was then that she saw the cold, almost calculating look in his eyes, and the more tender emotions that had filled her died. This was no romantic gift from a man who loved her. It was a prop in the play of their courtship. It was part of the act designed to convince onlookers that theirs was truly a loving arrangement.

"Thank you," she said stiffly, the magic of the moment gone forever. His presentation of her engagement ring was as romantic as his proposal.

Brandy took the ring out of the box and slipped it on her finger. For some reason, it irritated her even more to find that the ring fit perfectly. Was this man so calculating in everything that he did that he'd even managed to find out her exact ring size?

"It fits?"

"Yes."

Rafe sat back, greatly pleased with himself.

Brandy sat beside him, feeling chilled to the depths of her soul.

Rafe escorted Brandy to dinner in the dining room of his hotel. She noticed the admiring glances of the other men in the room as she entered on Rafe's arm, but she took no pleasure in them. She couldn't help but wonder what they'd think if they knew the truth about her. She doubted any of them would even want to be seen in public with her had they known she was Miss Brandy, the lady gambler from *The Pride of New Orleans*.

The food was delicious, but Brandy found it tasteless. She merely picked at her food. Ironically, she knew Claire would be proud of her, for one of her first lessons on being the perfect lady was an admonition never to eat a lot in public. Well, there was no worrying about that tonight. She had no appetite whatsoever.

"I've arranged a meeting in the morning with the priest who is to marry us," Rafe told her as they finished the meal.

"All Claire has planned for tomorrow are etiquette lessons, so I'm sure there will be no conflict. Is there a particular day that you want this wedding to take place?"

" 'This wedding' is our marriage," he corrected,

wondering why her clinical phrasing bothered him. It was, after all, a business deal between them. "I thought it would be best if we married next week, perhaps Thursday or Friday."

"Are we going to leave for Natchez right afterward?" Suddenly faced with the reality that her fate and future were soon to be sealed with his, she felt a bit nervous.

"I do want to start home as soon as possible, but I thought it would be best if our wedding night was spent somewhere other than on a steamboat."

"I see." Brandy went cold inside. He had already planned the who, what, when, where, and why of their wedding night without even consulting her. If she'd cared, it might have hurt her to be excluded from the planning. But she couldn't allow herself to care.

They said little as they left the restaurant and drove back to Claire's home. He escorted her to the door and stayed with her until she was safely inside.

"You two do understand the importance of what you're undertaking, don't you?" Father Finn asked, looking from Rafe to Brandy and back. There was no doubt they were mature enough to marry, yet he sensed an underlying, unspoken tension between them and that was unusual in young couples in love.

"Oh, yes, Father."

"Marriage is a very serious commitment meant to last a lifetime . . . 'til death do you part." He paused, waiting for them to say something. When they didn't offer any comment, he went on, "Perhaps you two would like to wait, take a little time to think about what it is you're doing. It's always better to be cautious than impulsive with this kind of decision. Getting married is not a frivolous matter."

"This is not an impulsive decision for us, Father," Rafe said firmly. "We're taking it very seriously. I've waited my whole lifetime for Brandy, and now that I've found her, I don't want to wait any longer."

"And you, young lady? Are you sure about this marriage?" Father Finn turned his gaze on Brandy.

"I'm sure, Father," she replied without hesitation. "Rafe means more to me than I can say. There aren't words to describe how I feel about him."

The priest fell silent, studying them thoughtfully, his fingers steepled before him. After a long, quiet moment, he overruled the caution he felt. "All right. If you're certain that you have no doubts about the commitment you're about to make to each other, we'll proceed."

"Thank you, Father," Rafe said, glancing at Brandy with a warm smile.

"Have you thought of what day you'd like to have the wedding?"

"A week from Friday is our first choice, if you can do it."

"All right. We'll have the service in the small chapel in the back of the church. Is seven in the evening satisfactory?"

"That will be wonderful."

They thanked him for his kindness and accommodation, then left the rectory. They were relieved that everything was going so well.

Father Finn stood in the doorway watching them go, wondering if they would live happily ever after. He hoped they would. They seemed like nice people.

The rest of the week passed in a blur of activity. Claire kept Brandy busy almost every waking hour with her instructions on running a large household, basic etiquette tips, rules on hosting a large dinner party and the correct way for a lady to speak. The last lesson had come when Brandy had cursed after accidentally smashing her finger doing a household chore.

"A lady should never use such language," Claire corrected.

"But it hurt!"

" 'Ouch' is sufficient. Others will know that it hurt from that. There's no need to put so much—er, colorful emotion into your exclamation."

"I see. Let me get this all straight now. . . . I'm not supposed to eat. I'm not supposed to speak my mind. I'm not supposed to have an opinion contrary to a man's. I am supposed to smile sweetly all the time and always tell men how smart and handsome they are, even if they're dumber than dirt and twice as ugly. And I am always supposed to be a perfect lady in thought, word and deed."

"Exactly," Claire said triumphantly. "Marc told me you were a quick study, and he was right."

"Just because I'm a quick study doesn't mean I like what I'm studying. How do 'ladies' live through all of this?" she asked.

"It's a way of life, Brandy. Civilization is based on it."

"What kind of civilization insists that you hide who and what you really are?"

"You don't hide it. You simply disguise it to become socially acceptable."

"But when do I get to be myself again?"

"In the privacy of your own room, you can be whoever you like. But when you are in society as Mrs.

Rafe Marchand, you have a duty and responsibility to act the part."

"Sometimes that's what it feels like—like I'm acting out a part in some play."

"Don't worry. Soon all these things will become second nature to you."

"Yes, but will I really be a better person for it?"

"Only you can know what's in your heart. I think you're a wonderful person. You are kind and thoughtful, not to mention smart and quick-witted. You're going to be a tremendous success when Rafe introduces you to society. I'm sure of it."

The feeling of restriction and gloom that had hovered over her lifted at Claire's gentle, reassuring words. Unable to help herself, Brandy gave her new friend an impulsive hug.

"No matter what the rules of society say, if I want to hug a friend, I'm going to do it. And I don't care whether we're in public or not."

"You'll be glad to know that gestures of friendship are always welcome in polite society." Claire returned the hug. "I'm so proud of you. At first, when Marc spoke to me about this job, I wasn't sure what to expect, but you've made it a joy. It's a pleasure to work with you."

"Let's hope Monsieur Hebert thinks so after tonight," Brandy said, grinning wickedly.

"Why are you worried about the dance instructor?" Claire was curious.

"Because the poor man may not be able to walk when he gets through with me."

The women enjoyed a good laugh.

"He's our instructor from the academy, so I know for a fact that Monsieur is used to young ladies who are . . . um, shall we say, unskilled in the art of dance?"

"I hope I tread lightly on him."

"I'm sure it will go very well."

"Rafe did try to teach me to waltz on the steamboat."

"And?"

"And it was very romantic. The waltz is wonderful."

"Yes it is, but there are many other steps you need to know besides the waltz. Monsieur will teach you all of them if he has time."

"I hope I can remember everything."

"You will, and if you don't, I'm sure your new husband will be glad to help you."

"He is an excellent dancer." Brandy thought of that night in the moonlight and how it had felt to be in Rafe's arms, being swept about the deck. Heavenly . . . She wondered if dancing with Monsieur Hebert would be as wonderful. It would be an interesting experiment to find out.

Rafe knew it was getting late, but he wanted to speak with Brandy and Claire about the important dinner meeting he had scheduled for Saturday night. He had arranged to dine with Steve Gibson, the owner of the shipping line he had invested in, and his wife, Geraldine, and he wanted Brandy to accompany him. The Gibsons had been eager to meet her, after learning about his upcoming nuptials.

As he approached Claire's home, Rafe was surprised to hear the sound of music coming from the house. He passed the parlor window on his way to the front door, and it was then that he saw the figures waltzing about the room.

A sense of irritation filled him as he stopped to watch. It annoyed him to find Brandy dancing smoothly about the room in the arms of another man. His hands clenched into fists as he looked on, and when he saw Brandy throw back her head and laugh in delight at something the other man said as he twirled her around the room, a muscle worked in Rafe's jaw.

Rafe scowled, wondering where Claire was. He wondered who the man was. He was tempted to storm through the door and demand some answers, but somehow he managed to keep a rein on his temper. Instead, he stalked to the door and knocked.

"Good evening, Mr. Marchand. We weren't expecting you. Won't you come in?" Della greeted him, obviously surprised by his arrival.

Her surprise bothered him even more. Had Brandy planned this, knowing he wouldn't be there?

"I need to speak to Brandy, please." He managed to sound cordial in spite of his anger.

"They're in the parlor. It's serving as a ballroom tonight as you can see," the maid said, smiling and directing him that way.

The music was flowing from the room as Rafe appeared in the doorway. He stood in silence watching Brandy dancing with the other man as the two musicians played a waltz for them. He saw Claire standing on the far side of the room by the musicians and realized then that he was overreacting.

"Why, Rafe, good evening!" Claire said when she spotted him across the room. "Come meet Monsieur Hebert. He's the dance instructor from the academy."

She made the introductions as Brandy looked on.

"Sir," Rafe said as he moved forward to shake the other man's hand.

"Your fiancée is very light on her feet. She's learning so quickly that she may not need more than one other lesson."

"Oh, really?" Rafe looked over at Brandy.

She was smiling brightly at the instructor's praise, her cheeks were flushed, her eyes were aglow. A shadow of annoyance crossed his face as he gazed at her.

"You were right, Rafe. Dancing is wonderful." Brandy said, remembering their dance. She now knew many more steps, so she could dance with him in public without embarrassing him. "Monsieur Hebert is a wonderful teacher. I've learned so much from him tonight."

"You have? Shall we see what he's taught you?" He found himself gritting his teeth.

Claire's brows rose at his words. He sounded positively jealous.

"Of course," Claire insisted, stepping back. "Monsieur, can you ask them to play another waltz?"

"My pleasure. I will enjoy watching you demonstrate all that I've taught you tonight." He spoke quickly to the musicians and went to join Claire to watch them.

Brandy looked up into Rafe's eyes as his hand settled possessively at her waist. She noticed a certain almost dangerous glitter in his eyes, and it made her heart jump and her pulse race.

"Is something wrong?"

"No. Nothing's wrong," he answered tightly.

Without another word, he squired her out onto the makeshift dance floor. His hand was firm and commanding at her waist, and he was amazed once again at how tiny she seemed to him. He found himself gazing down at her as they began to move about the floor.

"Shall we see just what Monsieur has taught you?"

She lifted her gaze to his and smiled at him. It was a tender, serene smile that touched something deep within him, easing the anger that had held him. Suddenly, a part of him wanted her to look that happy always. They were moving together then, their bodies swaying in unison, ebbing and flowing with the music, lost in the beauty of being in each other's arms.

Rafe discovered that she had, indeed, learned a lot from her lesson, and a surge of some strange emotion challenged him. He told himself it was ridiculous to feel this way. This was only a dance. She was just showing him how much the instructor had taught her. But he couldn't help feeling jealous that she had learned so much more from the other man.

"You learned a lot today," he told her as he made a fancy move, and she kept up with him without missing a step.

"Thanks to you. If you hadn't allowed Claire to hire Monsieur Hebert, I think you and I would have been practicing every night for hours to get this far."

"Would that have been such torture?"

Brandy looked up at him quickly, wondering at his tone, wondering at his question. His expression was curiously bland, though, so she assumed that he was only teasing. "The torture would have been yours. Heaven only knows what I would have done to your feet, stepping on you."

"Heaven is right. It would have been heavenly duty teaching you all the intimacies of waltzing. I enjoyed our first lesson on board the *Pride*."

"So did I," she said in a breathless voice. He didn't sound like a man who was marrying her strictly as a business proposition. He actually sounded as if he wanted to be with her, as if he wanted to dance with her. "Perhaps you wasted your money. . . . I enjoyed my lesson with him, but you certainly would have been my first choice for an instructor."

The music stopped.

Rafe stood looking down at her. "Don't worry. There are other things I'll teach you that we won't have to hire an instructor for."

Her pulse quickened at his words, but they weren't given any time to say more, for Claire interrupted them.

"Beautiful . . . just beautiful. You two dance marvelously together. No one could tell that you were even slightly unaccustomed to waltzing, Brandy." She turned to the dance instructor. "You did a fine job, Monsieur Hebert. I think we'll only need one more night of instruction before she's ready for her grand debut in society."

"Tomorrow, then?" he asked as he motioned for the musicians to gather up their things and prepare to leave.

"Tomorrow evening will be fine. We'll be expecting you."

He took his leave with the musicians, and Claire turned to Brandy and Rafe.

"Things are going very well. Brandy's a delightful companion and one of the quickest learners I've ever worked with."

"Brandy is special."

"To what do we owe the honor of this call?" Claire asked.

Rafe quickly explained his arrangement with the

Gibsons for Saturday night.

"That will be perfect. It will be your trial run, so to speak," she told Brandy brightly. "Your wardrobe will be ready. You'll have completed your dance lessons, and we'll have another two days worth of etiquette lessons completed."

"Good. How do you feel about this, Brandy?"

"I'm looking forward to it."

"After watching you tonight, I'm sure no one will question your dancing ability."

"Thank you. I do enjoy it."

Rafe prepared to leave. "I have meetings again all day tomorrow. But I'll stop by to see you in the evening, if that's all right with you?" he asked Claire.

"That will be fine. We'll see you then."

With that, he was gone.

Once he'd disappeared down the steps and into the night, Brandy turned to find Claire standing behind her, smiling.

"What are you smiling about?" she asked.

"Your fiancé, my dear. You are one lucky woman. Rafe Marchand is madly in love with you."

"You really think so?" She was surprised by the conviction in Claire's voice. She knew their charade was working, but she was still surprised by Claire's conviction that he was "madly in love" with her.

"Of course," she insisted. "Didn't you see the look in his eyes when he came into the room and saw you dancing with Monsieur Hebert?"

"No, actually, I didn't even know he was there until the waltz had ended. I was too busy concentrating on the steps, and I didn't want to tread on Monsieur Hebert again."

"Well, believe me when I tell you that Rafe was jealous. Once he realized that this was just your dance lessons, he relaxed a bit, but he wasn't at all happy when he came into the room and saw you in another man's arms."

"I've never thought of Rafe as the jealous type."

"I would start thinking that way," she advised her. "And what a wonderful thought . . . to have a man like him jealous of you."

"Well, Rafe has no reason to be. He's the only man I plan to marry." A flicker of hope that he might come to care for her stirred in her breast, but she fought against it. Thinking like that would only make things worse.

"The two of you are going to be very happy," Claire predicted.

"I hope so." Brandy didn't have the heart to disillusion her. It was good that they were making everyone believe they were in love. It was good that strangers thought they were crazy about each other. Obviously, they were both better actors than they thought they were.

"And the two of you are going to make such beautiful babies. . . ." Claire sighed at the thought of their offspring.

Her innocent words struck pain in Brandy's heart, yet somehow she managed to keep an outwardly calm expression.

"Well, I think I'll go on to bed for now. What time do I have to be up in the morning?"

"We don't have to go to the dress shop for your fitting until ten. So you can sleep later than usual."

"Good. I need it."

"Sweet dreams, Brandy. You're doing beautifully."

Claire's praise fell on deaf ears. The pain in Brandy's heart was too great to allow her even to think about anything so trivial as etiquette and dance lessons.

Rafe had made a bargain with her, and he was going to hold her to it—no matter how much he acted as if he cared.

Chapter Fifteen

It was after midnight, yet Brandy could not sleep. She hated to admit it, even to herself, but she was nervous. She paced her bedroom at Claire's house, alternately staring out the window at the darkened street below and praying fervently to be saved from the night to come.

Brandy didn't want to do this. It was true, she'd had dreams of becoming a fancy lady when she was young, but that was all they'd been—dreams. She'd never really thought she'd get to this point, never really thought the time would come when she would honestly be trying to fit in with the upper crust of society.

She drew a strangled breath and went to dig through her valise. She knew she had them somewhere. She knew they were there. She'd made a point to pack them when she'd left the *Pride*. Brandy almost gave a cry of delight when she found them.

Her hand closed over them and she smiled. Her security . . . They were there. . . . She hadn't left them behind.

Brandy felt triumphant as she drew the deck of cards from her suitcase. She went to sit at the small table and began to play. Solitaire was a wonderful, mind-numbing game, and right now, she needed something to soothe her anxious soul. She didn't know how long she'd been playing when the knock came at her door.

"Brandy? Are you all right?" Claire sounded concerned.

Brandy opened the door to find the other woman standing there in her wrapper, looking very worried.

"I hope I didn't disturb you . . ." Brandy began to apologize.

"No, no. You weren't disturbing me. I just got up to get a drink of water and saw your light. I was worried that you were ill." She glanced past Brandy into the room and saw the cards strewn about the table. "You're playing cards?"

"I couldn't sleep. I was too worried about tomorrow night."

"You're going to be fine," Claire assured her.

"How can you be so sure?" Brandy asked in frustration. "What if, after all our hard work, I make some awful faux pas and ruin everything? I'd be so embarrassed and I doubt Rafe would ever forgive me."

"You're not going to make any faux pas. You've worked too long and too hard to let a simple dinner party unnerve you. You're Brandy O'Neill, lady gambler. Where's your nerve? Where's your confidence?" Claire tried to buoy her spirits.

"I'm not sure . . ."

"What game were you playing?"

"Just solitaire to pass the time."

"Well, how about teaching me how to play poker? I've heard men talk about the game for years, but no one's ever offered to show me how to play."

"You want to learn how to play poker?" Brandy was astonished. Claire was a lady of quality. Why would she want to play cards?

"It sounds like fun . . . betting and bluffing and winning . . ." She was smiling.

"But you don't always win."

"Ah, but you always think you will, don't you? And that's all that matters. Come on. If you can't sleep, you may as well lose some money to me." Claire didn't wait to be invited in, but marched straight over to the table and picked up the cards. "Here. Deal. Now it's your turn to teach me a few things."

An hour later, had they been playing for real money, Claire would have been much lighter in the pockets.

"You're terrific at this! No wonder you were doing so well on the *Pride*," Claire declared as she lost yet another hand. "And you bluff so well."

Brandy flashed her a winning smile. "Thanks. You're a wonderful loser, too."

"That's my life," Claire chuckled. "I always lose. I'm used to it."

"You should never get used to losing. There's always some way to win, if you just keep trying and work hard enough."

"Think about what you just said to me. Are you really going to let a little thing like dinner with some of Rafe's business associates make you nervous?"

Brandy's smile turned rueful. "I see your point."

"Thank you."

"Now, about you . . ."

"What about me?" she asked, surprised.

"Why are you so convinced that you can't win what you want?"

"I never have," she said with a shrug. "After so many setbacks, you give up hoping."

"You shouldn't."

"But Brandy, sometimes losing hurts so much that it's better never to have wanted it in the first place. It's better to insulate yourself and protect yourself. Then you can never be hurt in any way."

Brandy couldn't imagine what had hurt Claire so badly in the past, but she knew it must have been terrible. "We're going to have to work on you. If you can transform me, then I can certainly transform you."

"What do you plan to change me into?" Claire asked. "An old-maid schoolteacher who can play cards?"

"There have been worse things." Brandy laughed.

"Like what?"

"How about an old-maid schoolteacher who can't play cards?"

The two women laughed easily together, sharing a mutual respect and camaraderie.

Brandy's eyes narrowed as she studied Claire across the table. She had potential. It was just that she was so accustomed to the teacher role that she'd never thought about making herself more attractive. True, she was a bit old. Brandy thought she'd mentioned that she was twenty-nine, but that shouldn't discourage them in their hopes of snaring her a husband. Claire had told her that a lady should always look her best, no matter what her circumstances. She wondered, too, about her glasses, and whether she really needed to wear them all the time. . . .

"Didn't you tell me a few days ago when I was suffering through all those fittings that a lady should always present her best image, no matter what her circumstances?"

"Well, yes. Why?"

"Because you aren't following your own advice."

"What are you talking about?"

"Look at the way you dress."

"What about it?" Claire stared at her, puzzled. She thought she dressed perfectly for her job.

"You look like a schoolmarm."

"That's what I am," she said in exasperation.

"But is that what you want to be? Did you always want to be a teacher?"

Claire was startled by Brandy's insight. No one else in all these years had ever asked her what she really wanted out of life. No one else had cared, and after a while, she'd almost stopped caring, too. She'd concentrated only on what was safe.

"I never wanted to be a teacher," she said softly, her vulnerability revealed.

Brandy couldn't believe that Claire was opening up to her. "What did you want to do when you were just out of the academy?"

"I wanted to marry and have children. But the man I wanted . . ."

Brandy sensed this was the story that had altered her life. "What about him?"

"The man I fancied myself in love with didn't love me. He married someone else . . . one of my closest friends."

"He just ditched you and married your friend?" Brandy was outraged.

Claire smiled, thinking this was the first time anyone had defended her. It almost brought tears to her eyes, to think that Brandy actually cared enough about her to be angry for her.

"You are so sweet," she said, smiling at her tenderly. "But no . . . he never knew that I loved him, and I never told my friend. They were perfect for each other. I was happy for them. I really was."

"You're a saint," Brandy muttered, hearing the painful truth in her words.

"There's nothing saintly about me. She was beautiful, inside and out. Everyone loved her. Even I loved her. I was glad they were together."

"You're a much kinder person than I would have been."

"But there's no point in wanting what you can't have."

"Who says you can't have it? Just because that one didn't work out, surely there's been someone else you've cared about since then."

"Actually, there hasn't been," Claire answered simply. "And to tell you the truth, he didn't even know how I felt at the time. Not that it would have mattered."

"Well, we're just going to have to make a few changes in you, just like you're working on changing me."

Claire smiled at Brandy's enthusiasm. "I'm a few years older than you are."

Brandy made a dismissive noise. "Who cares? There's more than one man out there who would love to have a woman of your culture and breeding by his side."

Claire laughed out loud. "I wish you luck."

"Luck will have nothing to do with this. You're an intelligent, lovely woman. We're just going to let everyone know it. Not to mention the fact that once I'm through with you, you're going to play a mean hand of poker."

They laughed again in delight with each other, pleased with their growing friendship.

"Tomorrow morning, first thing, we're going to start transforming you. That'll help keep my mind off that dinner party tomorrow night," Brandy told Claire.

"Why am I more nervous now than you were earlier?"

"Don't be nervous," Brandy said with a grin. "Just trust me."

And for some reason, Claire did.

The following morning, they ate a late breakfast together.

"Are you willing to put yourself completely in my hands?" Brandy asked her as they finished eating.

Claire looked up at her. "Yes."

"You don't sound very convinced."

"Maybe because I'm afraid. What you're asking of me . . ."

"Is the same thing you're asking of me, and I haven't balked yet, have I?"

"Good point," Claire agreed. "All right. I'm as brave as you are. What are you planning to do to me? I already bought that dress the other day. What more do we need to do?"

Brandy looked thoughtful. "I've been thinking about it all night, and I have a few ideas. We need to start with your hair."

"My hair?" Claire put a hand protectively to her bun.

"Wearing it that way makes you look so—so old. You're a pretty woman. There's no reason to wear your hair pinned back like that. Let's go upstairs and see what we can do with it."

Claire sat there for a moment staring at Brandy. She told herself that this was what she'd been wanting—some adventure in her life, some excitement. Well, it didn't get much more exciting than changing her whole look. She was going to Natchez. She was going to be seeing Marc regularly. Things couldn't be any worse for her than they had been. At the very least that could happen, she'd have a new hairstyle and a new wardrobe.

"All right. Let's do it."

An hour later Claire sat before the mirror at her own dressing table staring at her reflection. She blinked several times, for she almost didn't recognize herself.

"Oh, my . . ." she breathed, enchanted by her mirror image. "I look so . . ."

"Pretty?"

"Well, yes . . . and different."

Claire kept gazing at the woman who was staring back at her. Her hair had been washed and brushed out and styled into a tangle of soft curls, then pulled up away from her face so the heavy mass could tumble down her back. The style took years off her.

"Do you like it?" Brandy asked, rather proud of her handiwork. She'd gotten good at styling her own hair when she worked on the steamer, and she'd enjoyed working with Claire's thick, heavy tresses.

"Yes. Yes, I do," Claire answered firmly.

"Good. Now, about your glasses . . ."

"What about them?"

"Do you really need them?"

"I'm afraid so," she said softly, having always been

self-conscious about wearing them. "I can't see well at a distance."

"Ah, but when you're in a social setting, all you really need to see is who's sitting next to you, right?"

"Well, I guess so . . ."

Brandy carefully took the spectacles off Claire, then studied her thoughtfully. "You really have beautiful eyes. It seems a shame to hide them that way. From now on, only wear the glasses when you absolutely have to."

"If you say so," she agreed, grinning at her "teacher."

"That's what I like—a cooperative pupil. Now, do you have any great objections to trying a little makeup?"

"I've never worn any before." She looked a little scandalized at the thought.

"Then it's time to try it. We'll be careful how much we use. We'll apply it very lightly and see how it looks. All right?"

"I'll try anything once," Claire declared.

They shared a look of daring as they began to experiment.

"There . . . Now, all you need are a few new dresses to complement your new look, and we'll be ready."

"Ready for what, though?"

"Romance, adventure . . . who knows? For life!"

"You know, once I come back from Natchez and have to resume my teaching duties, I'll have to put all of this away and go back to pinning my hair in a bun again."

"Why?"

"Because it's expected of me."

"Do you always do what's expected of you?"

Claire was thoughtful for a moment. "I suppose I have . . . up until now."

"Good. We're both changing, and for the better, I hope."

"So do I," she said. "Now, Miss O'Neill, it's time to concentrate on you again."

"I was afraid you were going to say that."

"There's no escaping me. Tonight is your first test. We're going to find out just how good a tutor I am. How much are you going to eat tonight at dinner?"

"Next to nothing—no matter how delicious everything looks."

"Very good. And what kind of language will you use?"

"Only language suitable for a lady. Even if I hurt myself desperately, I will smile and bear up quietly."

"Wonderful, and finally, what kind of conversations will you have?"

"Inane ones." Brandy sighed wearily. "I'll keep smiling and saying all the sweet things everyone wants to hear. That way, when everyone goes home and they think about me, they'll think I'm the nicest, most wonderful lady in the whole wide world."

"Magnificent."

"Just because I learned it doesn't mean I like it. There's much to be said for honesty and forthrightness."

"You're not being dishonest when you're being a lady. You're just projecting an image of cool control and unflappability. When you're acting ladylike, you appear to be able to handle any situation with aplomb. To all the world, it seems nothing can disturb you, that you can handle anything, no matter how tragic."

Brandy nodded. "I know, but so many of the quality ladies I've met over the years have been cruel and mean-spirited."

"Then you just make sure that you're one of the ones who's not. Always defend the defenseless. Always champion the weak. It will make you a better person and a more caring one, too. Sometimes wealth does strange things to people. It's always good to remember where you came from and how you got where you are."

Unbeknownst to Claire, her words had struck at the very heart of Brandy's dilemma. She knew exactly where she'd been, and she would never forget how she had come to be where she was. Paying her debt to Rafe had landed her here, and while there were moments when she thought that maybe, just maybe, some good would come of it, she could never forget what the ultimate outcome would be. For her own sake and for any children she might have in the future, she would learn all these lessons well. But she would never, ever forget who she really was.

At seven o'clock that night, Brandy was ready for her dinner engagement with Rafe's business acquaintance.

"In all honesty, what do you think?" Brandy asked her tutor, twirling like a debutante in front of her for Claire's final stamp of approval.

"I think you look like a lady," she complimented her.

"Really?" Brandy turned questioning eyes to her one last time.

"Really. You are a vision to behold, and you move with a confidence that marks you as a woman in control. You can handle any situation that arises."

"Right."

"And you're going to have a wonderful time tonight. I want you to remember that."

"If you say so."

"I do."

They heard the knock at the door downstairs then and Della going to answer it. The deep sound of Rafe's voice drifted up the steps to them, and Claire glanced at her.

"Are you ready?"

Brandy drew a steadying breath and nodded.

"Wait here. I'll go down and greet him, and then you can make a grand entrance."

"Is that necessary?"

"Yes. I want you to be able to gauge his reaction when he first sets eyes on you. I want you to see how he feels about you. He won't be able to disguise it. You're far too beautiful to ignore."

"If you say so."

"You'll see. You missed it the other night when you were dancing with Monsieur Hebert. I want to make certain that you don't miss it tonight. Give me a minute, then follow."

Claire swept from the room and down the steps to welcome Rafe. She was still wearing her hair down the way they'd styled it earlier that day, and she noticed Rafe's surprise at the change in her appearance.

"Good evening, Rafe. It's good to see you tonight," Claire greeted him.

"It's good to see you, too. Your hair is different, and without your glasses . . . You look very nice," he said approvingly.

"Why, thank you. Brandy and I were experimenting today, and I thought I'd try something a little different."

"It's very becoming."

Claire smiled, pleased with his response. She knew that if he hadn't liked it, he wouldn't have said anything. "Brandy will be right down. She's excited about tonight."

"It should be an enjoyable evening."

"You're dining with a business acquaintance?"

"Yes. Steven Gibson and his wife, Geraldine. I'm thinking of investing in his shipping company, so it's an important dinner."

"Well, I hope it all goes very well for you."

It was then that Brandy appeared at the top of the staircase. Rafe saw a movement at the landing and looked up.

Claire couldn't help but smile broadly at his reaction. She watched him carefully as his eyes widened and a slow, appreciative smile curved his lips.

"Good evening, Rafe," Brandy said softly as she descended toward him.

"Brandy," he managed, his voice sounding just a bit hoarse.

"Do you like the dress?" she asked.

Her gown was an off-the-shoulder creation that fitted her perfectly, enhancing the fullness of her bosom and the slightness of her waist. Deep rose in color, it set off her fair skin and made her look fabulous.

"You look beautiful," he told her, meaning it. He noticed his diamond sparkling on her hand, and he felt a surge of male pride in knowing that she was his. Even as he thought it, though, he was taken aback. He didn't want a wife. He'd never wanted a wife. He was taking one for convenience's sake and nothing more. Yet still, the idea that she was his pleased him enormously, and he refused to analyze his feelings further.

"Shall we go then?" Brandy said sweetly as she moved past him to claim her light wrap.

"Your carriage awaits." He gestured toward the door in a gallant motion. Then Rafe glanced back at Claire. "Don't worry. I'll have her back before midnight."

"That will be fine. I'll be waiting for her."

Brandy shot Claire a glowing look as she disappeared from the house on Rafe's arm.

Brandy was very quiet in the carriage and drew a puzzled look from Rafe.

"Is something bothering you?" he asked, sensing that she was tense about something.

"No . . . er, yes . . . Oh, I don't know."

"What is it? Is something wrong?"

"No, nothing's wrong. I'm just nervous, that's all."

"But why? You look more beautiful than ever. Everything's going to be fine."

"I'm glad you think so. It's just that I'm afraid we'll run into someone who will recognize me, and it will ruin your whole evening."

"Brandy, I'm sure a lot of men will recognize you. You're a beautiful woman who's not easy to forget. But I'm not ashamed of you," he told her forthrightly.

"You're not?"

"No. If anything, I'm proud of you—of the way you've worked to support yourself and your mother."

"Then why did you insist on the tutor and the chaperone?"

"To help you, not to insult you. I want to make this transition as easy as possible. That's why I told Claire that money was no object when it came to your wardrobe. I want you to have everything you need. I don't want you to lack for anything."

Brandy looked up at him, a new softness in her eyes. "Thank you."

"And you're going to be all right. Don't worry. Steve Gibson's a very nice man, and I'm sure his wife is just as nice. Things will be fine."

"I'm glad you think so. I don't want to disappoint you."

"You won't disappoint me, Brandy . . . ever. . . ."

He gazed down at her, seeing the pure beauty of her, seeing the look of innocence in her eyes. His gaze went over her, and he couldn't help himself. He bent to her and kissed her. It was a soft kiss, a gentle kiss. One that explored and coaxed, but did not demand.

Brandy had been gazing up at him, hearing him say that he was proud of her and would never be disappointed in her, and she couldn't believe it. She wanted to think that he was telling her the truth. She wanted to think that he really meant it. When he kissed her ever so sweetly, her heart lurched in her breast.

This was not a man demanding favors from her. This was not a man wanting more than she could give. This was a man who was giving, not taking.

Brandy relaxed against Rafe, wanting the reassurance that she did look pretty. She had seen his admiring expression as she came downstairs. Now, he was being kind to her and she found she liked it . . . maybe too much.

Right now, though, it didn't matter, for his lips were on hers and the night was spinning out of control.

The carriage pulled to a halt just then at the door of the hotel, and with a groan, Rafe was forced to release her.

"Everything is going to go just fine. You'll see," he promised, touching her cheek gently before pressing one last quick kiss on her lips.

The carriage door flew open, and they were forced to descend. As they did, Brandy's cheeks were flushed and she looked like a woman who was madly in love.

Chapter Sixteen

"It is lovely to meet you at last," Geraldine Gibson said as she greeted Brandy for the first time in the restaurant. "I've heard so many wonderful things about you."

"Oh?" Brandy was a bit taken aback by Geraldine's statement, yet her expression revealed nothing but pleasantness.

"Why, Rafe here has done nothing but sing your praises to us all week. I'm just so glad that we're finally able to find some time to spend together."

"It's a pleasure to meet you, too," Brandy returned as she slipped into the chair that Rafe was holding out for her. She cast him a sweet smile as she did.

After their orders were taken, Geraldine leaned intimately toward Brandy.

"I've been waiting all week to ask you, and now that we're together, I must hear the whole story! Tell me all!"

Brandy looked at her wide-eyed. "What story?"

Rafe leaned over to take her hand, and Brandy was reassured by the strength of his warm, steady grip.

"Geraldine's a hopeless romantic, sweetheart. I mentioned to her our whirlwind courtship, and she had been dying to hear the entire story ever since."

"You did?" Brandy's eyes were wide and innocent as she looked at her "beloved." "Well, I'll tell you, Geraldine, men like my Rafe are so rare. . . ."

"Oh, I know it. He's a man after my own heart—a romantic just like my Steven," the other woman told her as she looked at her husband. "We've been married for over fifteen years now, but he's still a hero to me. He swept me off my feet and to the altar so quickly, I didn't know what happened. I've never regretted it, though."

"That's wonderful," Brandy sighed, giving Geraldine a truly warm smile. It must be heavenly to be that devoted to each other and that much in love. She wondered what it would feel like.

"So, now, how did this all happen? Rafe told us that the first time he saw you was on board the steamship on the trip up here."

"I remember the first time I saw him, too. He was so handsome and there he was, just standing there watching me. Later, I saw him dancing with another woman, and I just couldn't wait until I was the one in his arms."

Rafe met her regard levelly, his eyes dark with meaning, and he was smiling ever so slightly.

"And now you are." Geraldine sighed loudly. "Oh, my. This is so exciting. You knew you were meant to be together just as quickly as Steven and I did."

"It didn't take long for me to know that Brandy was the woman for me," Rafe said.

Brandy knew he meant it, too, for as much as it pained her to admit it, no other woman of his acquaintance could be blackmailed into the arrangement he'd set for her.

"And your wedding is next week?"

"Yes. It's going to be a small, private ceremony. Neither one of us has a large family, so we're keeping things intimate."

"I wish you both so much happiness. There's nothing more sacred than marriage. It's a lifelong commitment that grows stronger with each passing year, and then when the day comes that you're blessed with children . . . Why, children are the most important thing in life."

"How many do you and Steve have?"

"We have three—two boys and a girl," Steve offered proudly. "One of these days, I'll bring the boys into the business with me, and we'll just keep getting bigger and better."

"Do you plan to have children?" Geraldine asked.

"Oh, yes," Rafe said. "In fact, it was one of the few things we talked seriously about before we decided to marry. We both want to have children and as soon as possible."

"I can just see you now, Brandy, holding a dark-haired little boy who looks just like your handsome husband," Geraldine sighed contentedly.

How Brandy managed to control herself, she never knew, but she gave the credit to years of poker playing and Claire's lectures on control.

Brandy's smile was sweet. "I love children. I think having a baby will probably be one of the most important moments of my life."

Rafe tensed subtly at her words. Obviously she couldn't wait to bear his child so she could be free of him and of their arrangement.

"Well, dear, you must keep in touch with me and let me know all the news after you go home. I'd like us to be friends. It seems we have so much in common." Geraldine reached over and patted her hand.

"I'd like that." Brandy had been pleasantly surprised so far, for Geraldine did seem to be a genuinely nice person.

The conversation continued on to business, and then the meal was served. It was during the main course that another couple came into the dining room and was seated across the room from them. Brandy noticed Geraldine's expression turn sour, and she wondered at the reason.

"Is something wrong?" Brandy asked, as the men continued to speak of the shipping business.

"I can't believe it!" Geraldine said in a low, scandalized voice.

"Can't believe what?" Brandy glanced around trying to figure out what had upset Geraldine.

"I can't believe that they let *her* into this restaurant," she huffed.

"Who?" Brandy asked.

"Why Nila Sanders, of course," Geraldine said pointedly, motioning slightly toward a nicely dressed woman who'd just been seated with an attractive man escorting her.

"She looks fine to me. Is there something wrong with her?" Brandy couldn't imagine what the problem was.

"Of course she looks fine. Clothes are always the *first* thing they buy. White trash isn't always poor, you know," Geraldine carped. "That woman shouldn't be welcome here."

"What do you mean by 'that' woman?"

Bobbi Smith

"She's just one step out of the gutter. She used to work down on the riverfront in one of those . . . saloons." She said the last word with utter disdain. "She's hardly out of the gutter, and yet they allow her in here with us . . ."

Steven looked at his wife fondly, but there was an edge of impatience in his tone when he spoke. "Geraldine, honey, I want you to think about what you're saying. You should be proud of that woman for working her way up to a better life."

"Proud of her? She should stay with her own kind," Geraldine insisted.

Rafe was listening to the discussion in disbelief. He was shocked by Geraldine's bigoted views. He glanced at Brandy. He was proud of her tonight. She looked the lady, and she was acting the lady. Even Geraldine hadn't recognized her mean beginnings. Little did Geraldine know that her comments about Nila Sanders applied to Brandy, too.

His gaze caught and held Brandy's. He saw a flash of hurt in her eyes that was quickly followed by fiery anger, and he knew he had to speak up—and quickly. "You know, Geraldine, not everyone has been born with our wealth, comfort and security. Your family and mine have been very blessed. Some people work long hours all their lives just to keep food on the table and never get ahead. I agree with Steve. You should be applauding that woman's efforts."

Geraldine didn't look the least bit chastened until Steve spoke up again. "Sweetheart, you might as well admit it. My family is just one generation away from living in that gutter you're talking about. My grandfather was only a step above an indentured servant when he came over, and it's taken us this long to get where we are. You should remember that everybody

214

doesn't have the strong family ties that we did to help each other out."

"Steve's right, Geraldine," Rafe went on, wanting to erase that pain he'd seen in Brandy's eyes. "Sometimes fate plays cruel tricks on people, and they're forced by circumstances to do whatever they must to survive."

"I suppose you're right." Geraldine backed down, but it irritated her to do it.

"I know they are," Brandy managed, finally calming herself enough to speak without rancor. "It's always best to be kind and to give everyone the benefit of the doubt. The woman you're speaking about has obviously worked hard to get where she is today. We should be celebrating her willingness to take matters in her own hands, to work hard and do what had to be done. I shudder when I think of what the alternative would have been for her."

Geraldine found herself rethinking her condemnation of the other woman. "It's just that I was so shocked to see her after all the gossip I'd heard about her last week."

"Perhaps it's time to stop listening to the gossips and to start forming your own opinions."

"Perhaps you're right."

After that, Brandy couldn't wait for the evening to end. They bade each other a polite good night about a half hour later, and Rafe summoned a carriage for them.

"You were magnificent," he told Brandy as the vehicle rumbled off toward Claire's house.

"No, you were," she said, looking into his eyes. "Thank you."

Her words were soft, yet filled with meaning, and Rafe couldn't stop himself. He did what he'd wanted to do ever since they'd reached the hotel hours before. He took her in his arms and he kissed her, this time passionately.

It was an explosive embrace. Brandy had known that what had been happening between them when they'd arrived had been unfinished, and she was glad now that they would not be interrupted for some time. She linked her arms around his neck to draw him closer as she savored the ecstasy of his lips on hers.

Rafe drew her across his lap, cradling her against his chest. The feel of her breasts crushed against him, the seductive scent of her perfume and the hunger of her mouth against his sent a shudder through him. Desire pounded hot and heavy through his body as his hand sought the soft swell of her breast.

Brandy gasped at the intimacy of his touch. There had been several times in the past when a man had cornered her and tried to touch her this way. But her reaction had always been revulsion. She had always managed to escape from their unwanted pawings, but still she'd felt soiled.

But this . . . This was different. Her body reacted instinctively to Rafe's caress. She arched toward him, unconsciously offering him more.

At her sensuous move, Rafe groaned and broke off the kiss, his lips moving to explore the sweetness of her throat. He felt her tremble at his touch and then moved lower to trace a fiery path over the tops of her breasts, bared as they were above the bodice of her gown.

"Rafe . . ." She whispered his name hoarsely, not knowing whether it was a plea or a verbal caress. His mouth was a heated brand upon her. An aching emptiness began to grow deep within her. She told herself this was crazy. True, he'd been kind and attentive to her tonight, but that was no reason to lose her head. He did not love her, and she did not—could not—love him. "Rafe . . . stop . . ."

He froze at her words. His sanity returned coldly, quickly, and he silently cursed his own weakness. He was acting like a randy youth. He'd had trouble concentrating on business all evening because Brandy had been sitting next to him. It seemed that all he'd been able to think about was how beautiful she was. Then, when Geraldine had unwittingly insulted her, he'd felt compelled to defend her, to protect her from the hurt of the woman's unkind words. And now that they were finally alone on their way home, he couldn't keep his hands off her.

Rafe told himself this was ridiculous. Brandy was a lovely woman, but she was just one of many. He gave her a half-smile as she moved away from him to sit back on the carriage seat.

"You're right. It's best we behave ourselves. Claire wouldn't approve."

Brandy was glad for his mention of Claire. It helped her keep her sanity. She gave Rafe a slight smile in return. "I have a feeling she would be lecturing both of us on the proper way for a lady and gentleman to behave."

"True, but this time next week, we won't have to worry about Claire's lectures anymore."

"I know." Brandy's smile did not falter, but she felt a definite lag in her confidence. Considering how she reacted to his kiss and his touch, she wasn't sure what was going to become of their union. Had they cared about each other—really cared about each other—she would have been thrilled to be his wife. But the future stretched before her in a bleak, heart-breaking landscape. Though she found that she was attracted to him, it had to be a purely physical thing. It couldn't be love.

He helped her down from the carriage when they arrived a short time later at Claire's home and then escorted her to the door.

"Good night, Brandy."

"Good night, Rafe," she said, turning back toward him once the door was open.

But he was already walking away.

Brandy felt strangely bereft and wondered why it bothered her so much that he hadn't kissed her good night.

"How did it go?" Claire asked as she came out of the parlor to find Brandy standing in the front doorway staring after Rafe.

Brandy was glad to find that her friend had waited up for her. She came inside and closed the door behind her. The smile she wore was triumphant.

"It went well?" Claire pressed, eager to know. She'd been worrying about Brandy all night.

"It went more than well—It was fantastic! You would have been so proud of me," Brandy said.

"I would have been proud of you no matter what, but you made it through unscathed."

"Yes, I did, although there was a moment there when I almost reverted to my old unladylike self. Rafe was right in hiring you. It could have been a disaster."

"What happened?"

They moved into the parlor and sat together on the sofa as Brandy told her all about Geraldine's remarks. Claire looked stricken.

"Yet you managed not to say anything . . ."

"I didn't have to. Both Rafe and her husband spoke up."

"Oh, your Rafe is such a hero." Claire reached out and patted her hand. "You're one very lucky woman to have him. Of course, this Geraldine had no idea that she was indirectly insulting you. No doubt, she would have been mortified if she'd known how you were taking what she was saying."

"In keeping with what my tutor has been teaching me, I think Geraldine is basically a good person and she probably means well. But I don't think she's ever in her whole life had to worry about missing a meal or about being her own sole support."

"You're being kind," Claire said.

"Isn't that what you've been teaching me to be?"

"You were always kind. I didn't have to teach you that. But you're right, I am proud of you. Did you say anything to her about it?"

"I just told her that she should be celebrating the fact that the woman was brave enough and strong enough to try to improve her lot in life."

"What did she say?"

"Not much. I think the three of us gave her something to think about."

"Good." Claire rose, trying to stifle a yawn. "I'm not used to these late hours. I'm going on to bed."

"You'd better get ready. Once we find you a beau, you're going to be up later than this," Brandy teased.

"I'm waiting in breathless excitement for that moment, but until then, I'm going to get some sleep. Good night, Brandy. I'm glad you had a good time."

"Good night."

When Claire had gone, Brandy stood and wandered to the windows that overlooked the street. It was dark and deserted outside, and she felt very alone. She wondered what she'd gotten herself into, and she wondered, too, if she was going to be able to pull it off.

Chapter Seventeen

"Are you about ready?" Claire asked as she knocked lightly at the door to Brandy's room.

"I guess," Brandy answered. "Come on in and see what you think."

Claire opened the door to find Brandy standing in the middle of the room in her wedding dress. The dress looked fantastic, but Brandy looked a bit pale.

"What's wrong? Are you feeling all right?" The days leading up to the wedding had passed quickly for them, but during all that time Brandy had never mentioned that she wasn't feeling well. Claire was worried that she might be taking ill.

"I feel fine," she answered. "I'm just nervous. I've never gotten married before, you know."

Claire laughed. "I know, and I've never been in charge of shepherding a bride to the chapel before either, so that's two of us who are nervous."

Brandy managed a smile. "You've been a good

friend to me over the past week. I can't thank you enough."

"You don't need to thank me. I just want you to marry the man of your dreams and live happily ever after."

"That's all I want, too," Brandy said, her double meaning lost on Claire. She drew a ragged breath. "So, do I look good enough to become Mrs. Rafe Marchand?"

Claire stepped back and studied her from every angle. The white satin gown she wore was simple, yet fashionable. It was full-skirted and trimmed in lace. Her slippers matched the gown. Her hair was styled up and held in place by pearl-studded combs. The bodice of the gown was demurely cut. At her throat and ears, she wore pearls that emphasized the beauty of her skin. The veil that she had yet to don was fastened to a crown of pearls.

"I have never seen a more beautiful bride," Claire said in all honesty. "He'll be so proud when he sees you. You're lovely."

"Thanks. How soon do we have to leave?"

"All I have to do is slip into my gown and I'll be ready. I gave instructions for the carriage to be here at six-fifteen. That should give us plenty of time to get to the church."

Brandy glanced at the clock to see that it was only 5:45. "Let me know when you're dressed. I want to see how you look, too."

"Don't worry. I expect a full critique from you. Tonight is the first night we're trying out the new me. It will be interesting to see how everyone reacts," Claire said. She sounded light-hearted about the evening to come, but she was really excited. She couldn't wait for Marc to see her. She hadn't spoken ·

222

with him since the day she'd agreed to take on the job, and she wondered what he was going to think about the "new" Claire.

Getting a grip on her runaway hopes, Claire told herself not to think about Marc, that she was doing this for herself, not him. But she knew his opinion would mean the world to her. She had loved him from afar all this time, and now, at last, she knew how to fight for him. She wasn't admitting that this was her last chance in life to find happiness, but it would be her one and only big chance to try to attract the man of her dreams, and she fully intended to do her best. She wasn't the shy, insecure Claire any more. She was Claire, the old-maid schoolteacher who had learned how to play a mean hand of poker.

Ten minutes later, Brandy made her way to Claire's bedroom to find her friend looking like a different woman.

"I cannot believe this," Brandy said with real awe as she stared at her. "It's hard to imagine that you're the same teacher I met just a few days ago."

"That's good?"

"That's better than good. Look at you! That gown is absolutely gorgeous!" Brandy circled her, smiling widely at the changes they'd wrought.

The emerald gown was demure in style, high-necked and long-sleeved, and enhanced all of Claire's good points. Her eyes shone with an inner radiance. Her skin was flawless. A light blush stained her cheeks, and she wore just the slightest touch of color on her lips. She'd obviously remembered every trick Brandy had taught her about using makeup.

Claire took one last look at herself in her full-length mirror and had to admit that Brandy's encouragement had wrought big changes. "It's all because of you, Brandy. I would never have had the nerve to do this on my own."

"I'm just glad we did do it." Brandy gave her an impulsive hug.

"Shall we go get you married, young lady? And I do not use the term 'lady' loosely."

For a moment, Claire saw a slightly haunted look in Brandy's eyes, but it was quickly masked.

"Yes. Let's go. It wouldn't do for us to be late. Not today. I have to get a few things from my room and then I'll meet you downstairs."

"I'll be waiting."

Brandy went back to her own room and closed the door for a moment. She stood there looking around the comfortable bedroom that had been her safe haven. This was the last time she would be here. Claire had made arrangements for her things to be delivered to the hotel while they were at the wedding. After the ceremony, she would go there with Rafe, and the following day, they would leave for Natchez.

Brandy swallowed tightly. There was no longer any pretending that this wasn't happening. There was no denying her fate was sealed. In a little over an hour, she would be married . . . married to a man she'd known only a few weeks.

She realized then that she was trembling; she had never been this afraid before. It enraged her that she was afraid now. She stared around, looking for the one thing she needed, the one thing that might help calm her. And she saw them, already tucked into her valise.

Grabbing her deck of cards, she stuffed them into her small drawstring purse. She didn't know why having them with her made her feel better, but they did. She took one last glance around, then picked up her veil and quit the room. Brandy made her way downstairs to where Claire awaited her.

A short time later, they arrived at the church. Father Finn was there to welcome them, but there was no sign of Rafe or Marc and the children yet. He showed them into the chapel and they prepared for the ceremony. Claire and Marc were to be the witnesses and the children the only other guests.

When Brandy was left alone with her thoughts, she took the opportunity to wander out of the chapel and into the semi-darkness of the church itself. It was serene and completely peaceful, unlike the turmoil that was filling Brandy as she faced her uncertain future.

Slipping into a pew midway up one aisle, she tried to gather her thoughts, but as much as she tried to feel brave, she only felt lost and alone. Claire was her friend, but she was being paid by Rafe to be her teacher. She was totally alone tonight, and she longed for the comfort of her mother's understanding nearness, or, at least, Ben's gruff affection. But she had no one to turn to. No one who really cared about her.

Tears burned in her eyes as she gazed up at the altar. She wondered what had brought her to this, the lowest moment of her life. She had always imagined her wedding would be a beautiful, loving affair with friends and family. But it was going to be nothing more than a cold sealing of a business arrangement—an arrangement that only she and her soon-to-be husband knew about.

Brandy drew a ragged breath and knew there was nothing she could do. She had agreed to his terms, but only because she'd had no choice. She had to go through with it.

Lifting her eyes heavenward, she began to pray silently. She hoped that God was listening and that he would hear her plea for help and send an army of angels to rescue her. But somehow she knew that no warrior angel was going to show up just in the nick of time with the money she owed Rafe. No, as much as she longed to be rescued, if there was any rescuing to be done, she was going to have to save herself. Brandy swore then and there that no matter what happened over the coming months, if she did conceive and bear Rafe a child, there was no way she would ever leave her baby. Somehow, some way, she would find a way out before that time came. There was no other way she could go through with the wedding and live with herself.

A touch on her shoulder startled her, and she looked up to find Father Finn standing beside her.

"It's time. Rafe and Marc are here," he said softly, frowning slightly in concern as he saw her expression. "Brandy . . . Are you sure about this?"

Brandy quickly forced a smile. "Oh, yes, Father. Everything's fine. I was just missing my mother and wishing she was here with me."

"Oh, all right," he said, relieved. He'd had his misgivings about this union, and he wanted to make sure it was the right thing for them to do. "We'll begin as soon as you're ready then."

She nodded, girding herself for the future she was about to face. There would be no turning back. "Thank you, Father." She rose and stepped from the pew, walking with him back to the chapel.

Rafe had taken extra care with his appearance, even buying a new suit for the occasion. Marc had picked him up in his carriage, and they'd made the trip to the church together. Merrie's endless chatter on the ride there had made the time pass swiftly, and Rafe had answered all her questions with good-natured ease.

"You seem very calm tonight for a man who never wanted to get married," Marc had remarked as they'd neared the church. Rafe had always fought the idea of wedded life, and Marc was surprised that his friend wasn't showing any last-minute doubts about his decision. "Are you that sure Brandy is the woman for you?"

Rafe had looked at his friend. "I'm that sure. You were right that first night when you said she'd make the perfect bride for me."

Marc had given a disbelieving shake of his head. "I'm glad you're doing this, and I hope you're very happy. You both deserve happiness."

"Thanks," Rafe had said, feeling like a cad listening to his friend. If Marc had known the truth behind his proposal to Brandy, he might not be so pleased with the coming ceremony. But then, it was none of Marc's business. Rafe would worry about telling him everything later. Much later.

They'd entered the church to find Father Finn in the chapel, deep in conversation with a woman they hadn't recognized.

"Father . . . ?" Rafe had said.

When Father Finn and the woman looked up, both Rafe and Marc had been startled to find it was Claire he'd been speaking to.

"Claire?" Marc had blinked in amazement. Her glasses were gone. Her hair was brushed out about her shoulders in a thick mass of curls. Her dress fitted her enticingly, hinting at but not revealing the very womanly curves beneath it. She looked mature, sophisticated and elegant, and he had only been able to stare at her as he'd tried to reconcile what he was seeing with the Claire he knew.

"Good evening, Marc," she'd said sweetly, smiling at him, her focus only on him. He looked handsome. So handsome, in fact, that he took her breath away, and she remembered all too clearly that night so many years ago when she'd lost her heart to him. It pained her a little now to know that those feelings were still alive deep inside her.

"You look . . . lovely," he'd managed with a smile.

"Thank you." Her gaze had been riveted on him. She was seeing only him. All else was a blur—in more ways than one.

"Yes, you do look beautiful, Claire," Rafe had complimented her. Then he'd looked around for Brandy. When he'd seen no sign of her, he'd known the strangest moment of panic. He feared she'd flown . . . That she'd decided to renege on their deal and not marry him . . . That she'd gone . . .

"Where's Brandy?" Marc had asked the question that was burning in Rafe's mind.

"She went out into the church," Father Finn explained. "I'll go get her now that we're all here." He disappeared into the cavernous church to bring her back.

"Papa, who is that lady?" Merrie asked.

"Merrie, Jason . . . This is Claire. She was a friend of your mother's. Claire, this is my daughter, Merrie, and my son, Jason."

"Hello," Claire said softly as she looked down at the two children standing beside Marc. As her gaze met the little girl's, she caught her breath. Merrie was the image of Jennette, and a shaft of pain went through Claire's heart. She hadn't realized until that moment just how much she'd missed her friend— her laughter, her love of life, her good nature. "Merrie . . . You look so much like your mother. You're absolutely beautiful. And Jason . . . You look just like your handsome father."

Jason turned red and looked uncomfortable. Merrie eyed Claire with interest.

"You knew my mama?"

"Yes, we were friends when we were growing up." Claire found herself bending down to talk to the little girl. "If you like, I'll tell you all kinds of stories about the adventures your mother and I had when we were little."

Merrie was beaming at her. "I'd like that."

"What about you, Jason?" Claire's eyes were twinkling with mischief as she spoke to the sturdy, handsome little boy who was trying so hard to look manly. "Shall I tell you about the time your mother and I decided to have a mud fight in her backyard and how mad your grandmother was when she saw us?"

Jason's eyes rounded. "My mama did that?"

"Oh, yes," Claire said with conviction.

"My mama was fun, wasn't she, Miss Claire?" Merrie said with a giggle.

"Your mother was a lot of fun," Claire told her, her heart warming to Jennette's most precious legacy. They were so beautiful and so much like her. She smiled as she looked back at Marc. "So you've all come to see Rafe get married, have you?"

"Oh, yes," Merrie said in a very adult way. "Uncle Rafe is going to be very happy married to Brandy. I just know it."

"I think so, too," Claire agreed with her.

They heard footsteps echoing in the silent church,

and Father Finn entered with a veiled vision in white that Rafe knew was Brandy. He could only stare, his gaze feasting upon her as she moved with the priest to stand at the front of the chapel. She looked so beautiful that he felt as if the breath had been knocked out of him. She seemed to float, not walk. She was the very essence of femininity—exquisite and enchanting—and Rafe was enthralled.

"Rafe, if you will join us here," Father Finn directed.

Rafe wouldn't have moved if the priest hadn't spoken to him. When he did, he went quickly to stand at Brandy's side.

"If you're ready, we can begin."

At their silent assent, he began the ceremony, intoning the vows before God that bonded them together in His eyes.

Brandy listened intently to all that Father Finn was saying. She knew this was a farce, but she couldn't run now. She would go through with it and pray that she could find a way out.

Casting a sidelong glance at Rafe, Brandy couldn't help noticing how very handsome he looked. Her heartbeat had quickened when she'd entered the chapel and seen him standing there. He'd looked so tall and powerful. She'd remembered the heat of his embrace and just thinking of it had set her pulse to racing. Tonight was her wedding night. Tonight, she would not have to stop him. Tonight, they would be man and wife, in the eyes of God.

Rafe was listening to every word Father Finn was saying. He was getting married. It was hard to believe. He'd never wanted a wife, never wanted to open himself to the pain that that kind of relationship could bring, but what he'd arranged with

Brandy wouldn't be like what his father and mother had had. This would be different. He was attracted to her, and that was good. She was a lovely woman. He would suffer no hardship taking her to his bed, and when the time came for her to go, he would feel no pain, for they had no emotional commitment to one another. They each knew what to expect, and they had agreed to the terms. It was a means to an end, a marriage of convenience for both of them. They each were getting what they wanted out of the relationship.

"Do you, Brandy O'Neill, take this man, Rafael Marchand, to be your lawfully wedded husband, in sickness and in health, for richer or poorer, 'til death do you part?"

"I do," she said in a voice just above a whisper.

"And you, Rafael Marchand. Do you take this woman, Brandy O'Neill, to be your lawfully wedded wife, in sickness and in health, for richer or poorer, 'til death do you part?"

"I do." His voice was deep and steady.

"Do you have the ring?"

Rafe slipped the band onto Brandy's finger.

"By the powers vested in me, I now pronounce you man and wife. What God has joined together, let no man put asunder," Father Finn concluded. "You may kiss your bride."

Rafe turned slowly to Brandy and lifted her veil. He gazed down at her, seeing the question in her eyes. With infinite tenderness, he kissed her. It was a chaste kiss, a gentle kiss, but when he drew back, a flame shone in his eyes that hinted at the passion of the night to come.

Brandy was looking up at him, not sure what to expect. She saw a glow of desire in the depths of his gaze, and an answering heat flared to life deep within her. She didn't know what the night to come would bring, but she knew she would never be the same again. She was no longer Brandy O'Neill. Now she was Brandy Marchand.

"Thank you, Father," Rafe told the priest before turning to speak to Marc, Claire and the children. He knelt down before Merrie first. "I've married another woman, but you'll always have my heart."

Merrie threw her arms abut his neck and kissed him soundly on the cheek. "That's all right, Uncle Rafe."

He chuckled as he stood up. "I must not be as wonderful as I thought. She's fallen out of love with me already."

"Women are fickle; what can I say?" Marc said wryly, then he turned to Brandy and kissed her cheek. "Brandy, you look positively radiant tonight. May you always be as happy as you are at this moment."

"Thank you, Marc. Thank you for everything."

"Oh, Brandy, the ceremony was lovely," Claire said, hugging her. "You should have everything you need at the hotel when you get back there. And tomorrow, the steamship leaves at three in the afternoon, so I'll meet you on board. How's that?"

"That'll be wonderful. You know Marc is returning to Natchez with us tomorrow, too?"

"He is?" Claire looked over at Marc, unaware that for the briefest of moments everything that she felt for him was revealed in her expression. "I didn't know that."

"We'll all be making the trip together." Brandy saw the look in Claire's eyes and wondered at it.

"That'll be nice. It will be fun spending time with

the children. I think you're going to be a little too busy with your husband to spend much time with me."

Brandy blushed at her words, and Claire gave a soft laugh.

"I wish you so much happiness."

"Shall we go, Mrs. Marchand?" Rafe asked, turning to her.

Brandy wanted to say no, she didn't want to go with him. She wanted to go home to her mother. She wanted the safety and security of being Brandy O'Neill, not the uncertainty of being Brandy Marchand. But it was too late.

She had made her bed, and now she would have to sleep in it. And from the look she'd seen in his eye, she doubted there would be much sleeping tonight.

They thanked Father Finn again and then left in the waiting carriage.

Once they'd gone, Marc turned to Claire. "Would you like to join us for dinner?"

"Why, thank you." She was completely taken aback by his unexpected invitation, but was not about to pass it up. "I'd love to."

"Oh, goody!" Merrie said eagerly. "You can tell us more stories about Mama."

"It would be my pleasure," Claire said. But even as she said it, she was saddened by the knowledge that Marc hadn't asked her because he wanted to be with her. He'd invited her along to talk about Jennette.

She stifled a sigh and fixed her sights on her goal. She'd taken this job on a wild whim, and she was going to see it through. If she had to talk about Jennette in order to have time with Marc, so be it.

Father Finn had been talking to the children, and when Marc came to him, he looked up and smiled.

"You've done a wonderful job with them. They're lovely children."

"Thanks. Would you like to go to dinner with us?"

"I'd love to, but I can't tonight. Please let me know how you're doing."

"I will. Thanks, Father."

As they left the church, Marc took Claire's arm to escort her down the steps. When she smiled up at him to thank him for his thoughtfulness, he was struck again by the change in her. She looked so pretty that he was having a hard time reconciling this woman with the one he'd interviewed just the week before.

"I still can't get over the change in you."

"Well, I'm just glad you approve."

"I more than approve. You're stunning."

"Stunning? I'd hardly call myself stunning, but it did take a lot of nerve. Brandy encouraged me, and looking back now, I think she was right."

"She was very right. She's been as good an influence on you as you've been on her."

"Not only that, she's taught me something else I never knew."

"What's that?" He looked puzzled.

"She's taught me how to play poker."

Marc threw back his head and laughed. It was a laugh of pure delight. "Brandy is one special young woman. I hope she and Rafe live happily ever after."

"I do, too," Claire agreed as Marc handed her up into the carriage, and as she settled in, she added a second wish for herself. She hoped that she would live happily ever after, too.

Chapter Eighteen

Rafe opened the door to the suite of rooms he'd taken for the night.

"I hope you approve of this suite," he said as he swept her up into his arms and carried her inside.

"Oh!" she said as she clung to him. His gesture surprised her, and she was blushing as he set her on her feet. "This is beautiful," she remarked, gazing around the luxurious sitting room. Lush and well-appointed, it was the picture of elegant living.

"I've ordered dinner for us. I didn't know if you'd had time to eat before the wedding."

"Thank you. That was very thoughtful of you." Brandy was nervous. There was no denying it. Claire was not hovering nearby to protect her virtue, for she was a married woman now. She no longer needed a chaperone. She was completely alone with her husband, and, tonight, there would be no interruptions.

"Would you like to change?" Rafe asked as he

slipped out of his coat. "I directed the bellman to put your things in the bedroom when they were delivered, so everything you need should be in there."

There was something so intimate about watching him shrug out of his coat in such a casual motion that Brandy had to put some distance between them. She moved across the room toward the connecting door to peek inside the room. She almost gasped out loud at the bedroom they would share that night.

The room was dominated by a huge bed; the satin spread upon it had been turned back, and huge fluffy pillows lined the headboard. A table had been set up in the middle of the room and was covered with a fine linen tablecloth and set with china, silver and crystal for the meal. There was a smaller room off to one side, and as she ventured closer, she could see that it was a good-sized dressing room complete with a bathtub. She had known the *Pride* was fancy, but these were by far the richest surroundings she'd ever been in.

"Rafe, this is magnificent."

"There's nothing too good for my bride," Rafe said as he came up behind her.

Brandy was startled by his unexpected nearness, and she moved quickly away. "I think I will change into something more comfortable," she told him.

"Do you need any help?" he asked.

"No," she answered too quickly. "No, I'll be fine."

"Just call if you need me."

"I will."

He sensed her nervousness and retreated to give her the time she needed to relax. He glanced back at her as he reached the doorway, then left the room and closed the door quietly behind him.

Only when she was sure she was alone did Brandy

manage to relax a bit. She took off her veil and laid it gently on the dresser. She found her things neatly arranged in the dressing room and located what she was looking for—the gown and wrapper that she had chosen for her wedding night. It was a sleek, silk negligee, deep rose in color, and she knew from trying it on at the dress shop that it clung to her every curve, revealing nothing, yet suggesting everything. She wondered now how she'd been so brazen as to pick that one. Surely there must have been something in high-necked flannel that she could have bought. She smiled wryly at the thought of what Rafe would say to a flannel-clad bride. Their deal hadn't said she had to be a temptress, but for some reason, she wanted to look her best tonight. It was her wedding night, no matter what the underlying circumstances.

Brandy readily admitted to herself that she wasn't sure what to expect. This was a business deal, her payment of a debt of honor. She had to go through with it, yet dread filled her. She clutched the negligee in her hands, meaning to change, yet somehow she couldn't—not yet.

All through her childhood, her mother had told her stories of how much in love she'd been with Brandy's father. Their wedding night had been simple, spent in their own small home, and yet the love between them had made the small dwelling seem a palace. Brandy longed for a love like that.

Her gaze dropped to the gown she was holding, and she shuddered. This whole thing was demeaning, and yet there could be no forgetting that the minute he touched her, she wanted him. A light knock at the door drew her attention.

"Yes?"

"Brandy, our dinner is here."

"It's all right to have them bring it in," she told him, putting the nightgown back in the dressing room.

The door opened and the maids carried in their dinner. Silver tray after silver tray was arranged on the table along with an iced bottle of champagne before the servants disappeared. Rafe locked the door after them, then returned to the bedroom.

"I'm sorry you didn't have time to change. Do you want to eat?"

"Yes, please," she said eagerly, glad for the distraction. And she had to admit that she was hungry. She hadn't had a bite to eat since breakfast, and the food did smell delicious.

Each dish was a gourmet's delight, and they enjoyed every one. Brandy sighed as they sampled the dessert—a small wedding cake he'd ordered just for the two of them.

"Thank you," she said, lifting her gaze to his.

"You're welcome." His voice was deep, and his eyes upon her were warm with the knowledge of what was to come now that the food was finished. "It was delicious."

"Every bite." She knew she was sounding inane, but she could think of nothing else to do or say that would delay the inevitable any longer.

Rafe had been watching her during the meal. Her nervousness was very apparent, and it bothered him. He'd wanted the night to be special for her. She was his wife now, and he wanted her to have all the things she'd never had before. Her nervousness was making him decidedly uncomfortable.

"If you'll excuse me for a while, I believe I'll go downstairs for a drink in the bar."

Brandy couldn't believe she'd gained a reprieve.

She almost smiled at the news, until he stood up and came toward her. Without another word, he kissed her, a hot, passionate exchange that took her breath away.

"I'll be back soon," he said.

With that he was gone, and she was alone, still wearing her wedding dress.

Rafe lingered in the bar drinking a single bourbon for as long as he could nurse it. He wanted to give her time to relax. He wanted the night to be one they would both remember. When he could delay no longer, he quit the bar and headed back up to their rooms. Surely, she'd had time enough alone.

He entered the room using his key and found the door to the bedroom open. He walked in unannounced to find Brandy sitting at the table still clad in her wedding gown. A space had been cleared before her, and she was playing solitaire.

"You're playing cards?" he said in amazement.

She looked up, her eyes wide, to find him standing there. "I, um . . . I always play when I'm nervous. It helps me relax."

He walked to her side and looked down at the game, studying her cards. "It looks like a lost cause. You might as well give it up."

"I know," she said, reading double entendres in his words.

"Here . . . I have an idea . . ." He scooped up the cards from the table and began to shuffle. "Would you like to play for a while? The two of us?"

"You'd like to play cards with me? Now?" She stared at him, shocked.

"Sure. I like to play cards with you anytime, but if it will help you relax, right now would be great. I get to pick the game, though," he said.

Brandy felt her confidence returning. She knew cards and gambling. She could handle this, and him. For a fleeting moment, she considered running up the betting so she could win back what she owed him. That was, until she found out what he had in mind. "What are we going to play?"

Rafe looked up at her, his eyes alight with a wicked glow. "Poker . . . Strip poker."

Brandy stared at him. "Are you serious?"

His smile was her answer, and she was infinitely thrilled that she was still completely dressed, except for the veil. "You're on."

Between the two of them, they managed to clear the table they'd dined on and then sat down facing each other.

"Shall we draw to see who deals first?" Brandy asked.

He nodded, waiting as she shuffled the deck thoroughly. She put the cards in the middle of the table and sat back as he cut the deck to choose his card. He held his up. It was a nine. With a casualness born of confidence, she cut the deck, too, and drew a jack. She smiled at him triumphantly.

"Are you ready, Mr. Marchand?"

"Absolutely, Mrs. Marchand. Deal the cards." His eyes were glittering as he watched her shuffle and deal.

He picked up his first hand and was disappointed. It had nothing the least bit exciting. He threw down three and waited.

Brandy studied her cards and couldn't prevent a smile from creeping across her face. A pair of tens. Not too shabby. She kept the one queen she had and threw down two. She dealt Rafe his cards, then her own. She was disappointed to find that she'd drawn

240

nothing else she could use. Still, her pair looked good if he was throwing away three cards.

"Let's see what you've got," she said, laying her pair out for him to see.

Rafe grunted in irritation to find she'd beaten him. He threw his cards in.

"Looks like you're the winner," he said with a smile. He'd donned his jacket before going downstairs to the bar, so he took that off first. "Let's go again. I'm ready."

Brandy dealt smoothly. Rafe picked up his hand and this time he smiled widely. He didn't care the least bit about bluffing, and it didn't matter to him at all if he won or lost. Still, he knew it would be fun to win, and, with that in mind, he appreciated the two pair, ace high, hand she'd dealt him.

"I'll stay," he said with confidence, grinning widely at her.

"I'm taking two."

Brandy looked less than pleased with her draw and reluctantly laid down her cards. All she had was a pair of twos. It was better than nothing, but not by much. Rafe revealed his hand, and at his easy win, she took off one earring. She was very glad that she hadn't changed into the negligee yet.

"Your deal." Brandy shoved the cards across the table to him.

She did not notice his slight of hand or that the ace he'd been holding was not in the cards he began to shuffle.

The playing continued, and to Brandy's dismay, she was losing more than she was winning. It hadn't mattered at first, for she was shedding jewelry, then petticoats, shoes and stockings, but as they got closer and closer to actually removing garments, she tried harder and harder to concentrate with poorer and poorer results. It occurred to her that Rafe had always been a good card player and that his win that night onboard the *Pride* hadn't been a fluke. She focused solely on her hand, wanting to beat this man once and for all.

"Three eights," she announced proudly, laying out her cards.

"Beats me," he admitted, tossing in his hand and unbuttoning his shirt.

Brandy tried not to look the least bit concerned that he was going to be half-naked, but she had never been in a bedroom with a half-naked man before. Oh, sure, she'd seen the men working on the levees without their shirts on, but this was so much more . . . intimate, that she found she was holding her breath.

Rafe was very aware of Brandy's gaze upon him as he shrugged out of his shirt, and he loved it. Under normal conditions, he would never have dreamed of cheating, but tonight the time had come. He had hidden the few cards he needed while she'd been distracted, and he was ready to attack. At any other time, he would have been appalled at planning such a deceitful strategy, but this was more than war. This was his wedding night.

He dealt to himself from the bottom of the deck and waited.

"I'll take three," Brandy announced, disgusted with the hand he'd given her.

She picked up the cards and stared down at the pitiful assortment of numbers and colors. Nothing. Absolutely nothing. She swallowed nervously as she waited to see what he would do. She had nothing left to take off except her gown.

It was bad enough, sitting there staring at Rafe's tanned, lightly furred chest. There was something so intimate . . . so raw about seeing him exposed that way. Not that he was unattractive. Far from it. His shoulders were wide and powerful, his arms heavily muscled. She wondered what it would feel like to touch him, then brought herself up short at the thought, wondering what was wrong with her.

"I'm staying," Rafe said easily. "What have you got?"

Brandy laid out the cards slowly. She was not good at handling defeat. Of course, there was always the off chance that Rafe had a worse hand than she did.

Rafe did not speak but smiled widely as he spread out his hand—a full house.

Brandy flushed and bit back a groan of mortification.

"Will you need any help, my love?" Rafe asked.

"I'll manage," she said tightly as she rose and started for the dressing room.

"Where are you going?"

"I was going to undress in there."

"There's no need. Right here will do. Go ahead, I'm in no hurry to continue play. I'll just sit back and enjoy the view."

Gritting her teeth, she worked at the buttons at the back of her gown, finally freeing them far enough down so she could slip out of the dress. She let it fall, and it dropped to the floor at her feet in a white silken pool. Clad only in her undergarments, she gracefully stepped out of it, then picked it up and spread it over a chair nearby. She glanced up to find Rafe's gaze upon her. She could almost feel the heat of his regard as it raked over her. A flush stained her cheeks, yet she did not cower or try to hide herself from him. Giving a defiant lift of her chin, she moved back to the table.

Rafe thought he had never seen a more magnificent woman in his entire life. He still remembered that first night when he'd seen her on the steamer and how lovely she'd looked then. But that night had been nothing compared to now.

He watched her every move as she walked toward him. Her body was perfect, her legs long and shapely. The chemise she wore covered just enough to titillate his imagination—and he had a very active imagination.

The realization that she was his wife, and before the night was over she would be his, sent a surge of desire through him. He picked up the cards and began to shuffle once more. In all his wildest dreams, he'd never thought he'd be playing poker on his wedding night, but right now, he found there was nothing else he'd rather be doing. Never before had he wanted a woman as badly as he wanted Brandy. He was determined to win.

He dealt quickly, then watched and waited. They were down to two garments apiece. This shouldn't take long. He let his gaze slip past her to the bed beyond. It looked wide and comfortable, and he had a vision of laying her gently upon its softness.

Brandy was concentrating with all her might on her cards, but things weren't going quite as she'd hoped. She'd thought that by getting him to play she might distract him from the purpose of the night. She'd thought maybe he would drink too much and maybe he would be tired and fall asleep, so she'd be saved—at least for tonight. All her plans were for naught, though. Rafe had barely touched the champagne, and he seemed more determined than ever to see this through to the end.

She picked up each card saying a silent prayer that it would be better than the one before, but to her dismay, she'd been given a dismal mix again. As she looked at her last card, she was relieved. At least now she had a pair of fives. It wasn't much, but it was better than her last hand. She schooled her expression to one that revealed nothing as she looked up at Rafe.

"I'll stay," she announced. She looked over at him, wanting to project an image of confidence. Instead, she found herself staring at the way his muscles rippled as he reached for his own cards. She had not thought that watching a man move could be sensuous, but she was fascinated by the play of his muscles and the way his skin gleamed golden in the lamplight.

Rafe studied his hand, then looked up at her as he announced, "I'm taking three."

He slid the three discards to the center of the table, then dealt himself three more. One by one, he picked them up, studying each one judiciously, revealing nothing.

Brandy could feel the tension within her growing as she watched him. She knew now there was no saving herself from her fate. He was her husband, and no matter what happened in the card game, by morning, she was going to be Mrs. Rafe Marchand in more than just name only.

"Let's see your cards," he said, his gaze boring into hers across the width of the table. He had read her look of confidence, but he'd also known from the nights of playing her on the *Pride* that she didn't have a very good hand. She had not changed the way she was sitting, and she had not straightened her shoulders as she met his regard.

He waited eagerly to see her cards. He knew what was coming next. His shameless trickery had been worth it to claim her as his prize. His gaze swept over her again, taking in the swanlike arch of her neck and the tops of her breasts revealed now above her chemise. Her skin looked satiny, and he wanted to reach out and touch her, to caress that silken flesh, to . . .

Brandy laid out her hand, hoping against hope that her pitiful pair would take the day. She knew instantly that it was over as his gaze darkened with the heat of his intent.

"It looks like you've lost, my sweet," Rafe announced, showing her his hand. He was holding three aces.

She nodded, her breath catching in her throat. She knew she should stand and shed the chemise brazenly. But this defeat was too much like the one she'd suffered on the *Pride*. He had beaten her. She had lost. There was no escape.

As she thought it, though, and as Rafe rose from across the table from her, looking tall, and handsome and powerful, she wondered fleetingly if she really wanted to escape.

Escape what? She knew to her despair how wonderful his kisses were. She knew to her despair how devastating his touch could be. And tonight . . . tonight . . . she was his wife.

A sad pain knifed through her. If only he truly cared about her. If only it had mattered that she was his wife. But it didn't. To him, she was nothing more than a brood mare, acquired through a financial arrangement and being put into service to deliver a child. Nothing more.

But as Brandy watched him coming toward her around the table, her soul was crying out.

If only. . . .

"Let me help you with that," he said in a husky voice. He wondered how he was ever going to continue to play and to concentrate with her sitting across the table from him naked to the waist. It wouldn't be easy.

Brandy lifted her eyes to his and saw the hunger there. She couldn't stop herself from slowly rising from her chair, and she stood before him—an offering . . . waiting.

Rafe reached out and untied the ribbon that held the chemise at her breasts. He unlaced the garment in a sensuous exercise, caressing the inner curves of her breasts as they were partially revealed to him. As he finished, he paused to let his burning gaze sweep the length of her body. Her breasts were almost fully revealed to him now, and desire jolted him to the depths of his soul. Bending toward her, his mouth sought hers, and as their lips met she moved closer into the circle of his arms. It was that movement, that surrender, that defeated his control, and he crushed her to him.

"I want you. . . ." he growled, any thoughts of poker gone forever.

Chapter Nineteen

Rafe's kiss was urgent and devastating, and all Brandy's resistance crumbled. She hated to admit it, but she had wanted this . . . she had wanted him. The preamble of his kisses in the carriage was nothing compared to his uninhibited passion now. A low whimper came from her as he stripped away the chemise, baring her breasts completely to his gaze and touch. She shivered before the power of the hunger she saw in his expression.

"Rafe . . ." She said his name in a whisper.

He did not speak but gathered her up in his arms and carried her to the bed, lowering her onto it with infinite care, then following her down. His touch was bold as he stripped away the last vestige of her clothing that had barred her complete beauty from him. He settled beside her on the bed.

"You're more beautiful than I ever imagined," he told her as he kissed her again and drew her against him. Desire pounded through him and hardened his already firm resolve to know all of her love this night.

Brandy felt shattered. Rafe's embrace was proving to be her heaven and her hell. She couldn't stop herself as she responded wantonly to his every kiss and caress. She had never known loving could be this way. His touch was gentle, yet arousing, driving her need to higher and higher peaks until suddenly sensations unlike anything she'd ever known before burst upon her, sending her to ecstasy. Desperate to be closer to him, she grasped at his shoulders, clinging to him, needing him, wanting to feel his hardness against her. It was mindless passion that left her clinging to him, and as the rapture swept over her, tears streamed down her cheeks.

But Rafe wasn't through. He moved away from her only long enough to shed his pants, then moved over her. He saw the widening of her eyes as she saw him for the first time and realized that all Ben had told him might be true. She had carefully safeguarded her reputation on the *Pride*, but Rafe had never seriously considered that she was a virgin until this moment. The knowledge thrilled him.

"I'll be gentle," he promised, moving between her trembling thighs and positioning himself to claim her.

He kissed her, his mouth on hers in a loving exchange that swept her up and away from reality. He truly meant to be gentle, but as he thrust forward, the heat of his desire rent that which was the proof of her innocence. Brandy tensed and cried out softly, surprised by this passionate male invasion.

"I'm sorry," Rafe murmured. Her innocence had been no lie.

He wanted to tell her how special the gift of her

innocence was and to ease her fear of what had to be a frightening experience for her, but he could not deny the driving need of his body. Later there would be talk. For now there was only love.

Rafe couldn't stop himself. He began his rhythm, seeking to please her again as he claimed his own release. The tightness of her body, the sweetness of her kiss, the softness of her womanly curves against him drove him mindless with need, and he strained against her, seeking, then reaching, that peak of passion that could not, would not, be denied. He loved her.

Rafe lay with his weight still upon her, their bodies melded in love's embrace, savoring the moment. He had known many women. He was no inexperienced youth, but nothing in his past had prepared him for what had just taken place with Brandy. Even Mirabelle, with all her skillful, learned ways in the art of love, was no match for the sweet gift of innocence that Brandy had just given him. She had been so responsive to his touch. Her kiss had been as sweet as wine and her loving pure ecstasy. Rafe kept his eyes closed, savoring the moment, relishing the rapture of their joining. He had known when he'd made the bargain with her that making love to her would not be an unduly harsh duty, but it had turned into a reward more exciting than anything he'd ever known. Unconsciously, he tightened his arms around her.

Brandy hadn't been sure what to expect. She had heard tales of what making love to a man was like, and had seen enough of the drunks from Natchez-Under-The-Hill to have an idea of what to expect, but she had never thought it would be like this. She knew Rafe to be a harsh, unyielding man. True, she had seen him be kind on a few occasions, but she'd thought it mostly an act. She hadn't been certain what would happen once they were alone, and now she wondered why she had been so afraid. His kiss had been thrilling, his touch ecstasy. She had thought he would be quick, harsh and thoughtless in his taking of her. She'd had no idea he could evoke such feelings within her body. She trembled as she remembered the force of the rapture that had throbbed through her willing body. She had been pliant in his hands, unable to deny him, unable to refuse him anything. His gentleness had aroused her completely, where anything else would have left her unmoved and in control.

A lone tear trickled down her cheek. It would have been so much better if he had been hard and cold with her. She could deal with him that way. It would have been business between them from the start. But now . . . now, she didn't know what to think or what to do. . . .

Brandy had learned the hard way how to deal with the cruelties of life. She did not know how to deal with the gentleness. She knew a moment of terror as she realized how precarious her situation was. It was one thing to have lost that hand to him and be forced to be married to him this way, it was another completely to lose her heart and her soul to him.

Rafe stirred and levered himself up above her on his elbows. He kissed her again then, and once again all rational thought fled Brandy. There was only Rafe, and his touch, and his kiss, and the sensuous world he created for her.

They loved through the night, and only slept as the sky in the east lightened.

Brandy came awake first, and she lay quietly,

studying the slumbering man beside her. Rafe was handsome when he was awake, but asleep she found him even more devastatingly attractive. The guardedness about him was gone, leaving him looking almost youthful. She wanted to reach out and touch him—his arm, his chest, his cheek—but she didn't dare. She was safe while he was sleeping—safe from the power he held over her, safe from the confusion of her own emotions.

An ache grew within her heart. It had been one thing to contemplate his demand that she bear and abandon a child. It was another to fall hopelessly in love with him and then be forced to give him up, too.

As she gazed at Rafe, she hardened her heart. She couldn't afford to feel this way about him. True, he had introduced her to the beauty of physical love, but he did not love her. He never had. He never would.

Brandy turned to stare at the ceiling, and after a few moments, she knew what she had to do. She had to find a way to get the money she needed to pay him off. She wracked her brain in desperation, seeking a quick solution to her problem, but found none.

As time passed, she became so desperate that she even considered the possibility of approaching Claire with her dilemma and asking her for a loan. But as quickly as she thought it, she dismissed the idea. Claire had proven to be a friend over these last two weeks, but she had been hired by Rafe specifically to be that—her friend. Claire worked for Rafe. If she confided in her, Claire might go to him and tell him what Brandy was planning, and she couldn't let that happen. She had to get the money on her own to pay him back.

Finally, Brandy came to understand what she

would have to do. She would pretend to be Rafe's loving bride; although, in truth, it would not be a difficult role. She would bide her time, doing what he expected of her, but when the opportunity came, she would do whatever she had to to survive. Her sanity depended on it.

Brandy did not fall back asleep, but lay silently in her marriage bed until Rafe stirred and came awake over an hour later.

"I wondered how long you were going to sleep," she said teasingly as he turned to her.

He braced himself up on one elbow to look down at her.

"How long have you been awake?" Rafe asked.

It surprised him that she looked even more beautiful this morning than she had last night. He rarely spent the night with a lover, and the few times he had, the women definitely lost their appeal in the bright light of day. Not so with Brandy, though. She looked fresh and beautiful and well loved.

"A while," she said softly. "But if you'd slept much longer I was going to see about changing our reservations on the steamboat."

"You could always have gotten me up," he said in a low growl of a voice as his gaze roamed over her.

From her flushed cheeks, to the swell of her breasts beneath the sheet, to the length of her silken leg pressed against his, she was all woman—his woman. He hardened just at the thought of tasting of her again. Rafe reached for her hungrily, wanting more of her sweetness, wanting to prove to himself that last night's loving hadn't been a dream.

Brandy had no time to answer as he kissed her with sweet passion. She tried to hold herself back. She tried to deny the effect his touch had on her, but as his hands skimmed over her, rioting her senses, she lost all logic, all restraint. She knew it was wrong to allow herself to feel this way, but if only for this little while, she would take what she could. She gave herself over to Rafe's masterful touch, clinging to him in her need. She had learned much from him during the long dark hours of the night, and she boldly caressed him now as he caressed her. Caught up in a frenzied need, they were catapulted to rapture and beyond.

It was much later when they finally left their bed, and Brandy's mood was almost regretful. As long as she was wrapped in his arms, she could pretend that he wanted her there, that he wanted to love her. Once they left the bed and this room, she didn't know what was going to happen. Rafe left her alone as he went downstairs to order breakfast to be brought up to the room, although it was almost closer to time for the midday meal than breakfast.

Brandy sought a hot, soothing bath while he was gone. She eased her slender body down into the water, eager to soak and relax. She had just begun to wash with the scented soap when she heard the door open and looked up to find that Rafe had already returned.

Rafe paused in the doorway to stare at the sight of her, her hair pinned up with just a few loose tendrils escaping, her skin flushed from the heat of the water, her eyes aglow with the look of a woman well loved. He said nothing, but stripped off his shirt as he walked toward her.

"What are you doing?" she asked nervously, seeing the burning, wild look in his eyes.

"You'll see," he said as he bent and pressed a kiss to her lips and then sought the sweetness of her neck.

The Lady's Hand

A thrill of excitement shot through her, and she arched her back at his ploy. He took full advantage of what she offered, seeking each breast with heated kisses. Not wanting to wait another minute, he scooped her up dripping wet and started for the bed.

"But Rafe . . . You're getting soaked. . . ."

His grin was devilish and lusty. "I didn't notice."

He fell upon the bed with her in his arms. Within moments, the rest of his clothing had been discarded, and they came together in a whirlwind of desire. He sought the womanly heat of her and made her his. They came together, man and woman, giving and taking, until passion's peak exploded around them, and they were lost in the perfect beauty that was their loving.

Rafe had always considered himself a man in complete control. He did not let his emotions interfere with what he had to do in life, and yet with Brandy, it seemed all that was changing. One look at her, so seductively revealed in the bathtub, had unleashed a wild passion within him that had had to be sated—then and there.

Rafe didn't know what it was about Brandy that made her different from the other women he'd known, but she was. He had never felt this way before, and he wasn't sure what to make of it—of this driving need to be one with her, this overwhelming desire to be buried deep within the silken confines of her body. The ecstasy of loving her was almost too much to bear. He sighed as he held her close, unmindful of the wet sheets and his wet clothes strewn around.

Only the knock at the door a few minutes later drove them apart.

"I forgot to tell you that the food would be coming

soon. Wait here." He laughed as he pulled on his damp pants and dry shirt. As he went into the sitting room to admit the servant bringing their food, he closed the door to ensure Brandy's privacy.

As she heard him moving about the other room with the servant, she slowly rose from the bed. She caught sight of herself in the mirror over the dresser and stared at her own image as if seeing another woman. Her color was heightened, her body alive with the knowledge of loving a man.

Brandy had never known such passion was possible. Even now she ached with wanting him again, and he'd only been gone from her for a few minutes. She knew it was crazy. She knew she had to control these feelings, but it was so beautiful between them that she wanted more of this intimacy. She never wanted it to end.

She returned to the tub and quickly finished bathing. The water was tepid and did not encourage lingering. She had stepped from the tub and was wrapped in her silken robe when Rafe came back into the room.

"He's gone now. Are you hungry?"

"Famished," she told him. Her gaze was upon him as she wondered if her answer referred to food or to him.

Rafe held out his hand to her and she took it.

"Your breakfast awaits you." He gestured expansively toward the delicious fare.

"Thank you, sir. You have seen to my every need."

"Have I?" he asked, drawing her to him, enjoying the feel of having her in his arms again.

Her kiss was his answer, and when they broke apart they were hard pressed to think about eating.

"We'd better eat while we can," he finally said, reluctant to let her go. "If we don't, we might grow weak from lack of sustenance."

"I can understand why," she said, giving him a seductive grin.

Her smile was so captivating that she almost took his mind off food. Only his rigid self-control kept him from taking her again, right then on the sofa. It was an intriguing thought, though, and he considered it for later, after they'd partaken of the meal.

"We've never had much of a chance to talk about Claire," she said, needing to distract herself temporarily from her sensual thoughts of Rafe. "She's been such a great help to me. Where did Marc meet her?"

After watching Claire with Merrie and Jason last night, Brandy had sensed there was something she didn't know about their relationship. She wasn't sure what, but she wanted to find out if she was right or not.

"From what I understand, Claire was one of Jennette's friends."

"Did Marc know her, too?"

"As a matter of fact, he did. He hadn't heard from her in years, but when Jennette's parents suggested he hire Claire, he immediately thought it was a good idea."

"So they knew each other before Marc married Jennette. . . ." she said thoughtfully.

"I don't know how well, but I do know that she and Jennette were friends and she was at their wedding. Why?"

"Oh, I don't know. I just thought they were well-suited. She seemed to get along with Merrie so beautifully."

"And Jason, too. Whatever possessed her to change the way she dressed so completely?"

"I told her that if she had to work on me, she had to work on herself, too. I even taught her how to play poker."

"You taught her how to play poker?" Rafe was choked with laughter at the thought. "But Claire's a schoolteacher!"

"That doesn't matter. I just hope she plays better than I have the last few times," she said, thinking of the strip-poker game.

"Has losing to me been all that dreadful?" He was thinking about how lustily their last game had ended, and how he wouldn't mind beating her again that way.

Brandy looked up at him as the strip-poker game was forgotten and she remembered all too clearly gambling away her very life. Rafe saw the haunted look in her eyes, and he was immediately sorry he'd said what he had. If he could have taken back those words right then, he would have. For that one small moment in time, they had been comfortable together and enjoying each other's company.

"I've lost more than money to you. It seems I've lost my soul." She stood up and excused herself. "I'd better get dressed now if we're going to make the steamboat on time."

He watched her walk from the room. The heat in his body faded as she distanced herself from him, not only physically, but emotionally, too. He rose from the table and started to follow her into the bedroom to begin his own packing. As he did, he cast one last longing glance at the sofa that had fueled his erotic fantasy while they were eating. Forcing his wayward emotions back under his usual rigid control, he focused on the business of getting them to the riverfront on time.

Chapter Twenty

Claire stood on the deck of the *Mississippi Belle* with Marc, watching for Rafe and Brandy to arrive. Louise had taken the children off to play, and they were left alone to enjoy a moment of adult conversation. They had boarded early just to make sure they were on time and were now eagerly awaiting the newlyweds.

"I wish they'd hurry up and get here. I want to see how Rafe survived his wedding night," Marc said with an easy grin.

"I'm sure he survived just fine," Claire told him. "They certainly made a handsome couple, didn't they?"

"They certainly did. I never thought I'd see the day when Rafe took a wife, but he actually went through with it."

She looked at him curiously. "Why didn't he want to get married?"

"His mother wasn't exactly the most loving woman in the world, so Rafe didn't have the best of feelings toward women. He never wanted to marry one . . . until Brandy."

"It looks like Brandy changed all that."

"She must have. Why else would he have married her so quickly?"

"I know another courtship that was a quick one," Claire told him with a smile, remembering how quickly he and Jennette had fallen in love. "It didn't take you and Jennette long to know."

"All I had to do was take one look at her. . . ." He got a faraway look in his eyes. "But that kind of love only comes once in a man's lifetime." He sounded regretful. "I still miss her, even after all this time."

"I miss her, too. I hadn't realized how much until I saw Merrie, and then it all came back to me . . . how much Jennette had enjoyed life. You were lucky to have her."

"I was."

They shared a poignant look as they remembered Jennette and all the happiness she'd brought into the world.

"I'm glad you two were so happy together, and your children are truly a gift from God."

"I don't know how I would have gone on without them. It happened so fast. One minute she was fine, and the next, the fever had taken her. If it hadn't been for Merrie and Jason . . . They gave me a reason to get out of bed in the morning, a reason to eat and drink and keep going."

Claire couldn't help herself. She reached out and touched his arm in a friendly gesture. "You've done a great job all by yourself. You should be proud. I know Jennette would be."

He nodded, but didn't speak for a moment. "Thanks. It's good to talk about her. I doubt that I'll ever get over her completely, but I'm getting better."

"I think you're doing fine."

"I'm trying." He saw a carriage pulling to a stop on the levee then, and Rafe climb out. "Look, there they are!"

"Oh, good," Claire moved closer to the rail to watch Brandy alight from the vehicle. "They're both smiling. Everything must be wonderful with the world."

"Good. It's nice when things work out right. Let's go meet them."

Brandy appeared the smiling bride, but her heart was encased in ice. After their disastrous conversation, she'd silently berated herself for forgetting the most important thing about their arrangement. This man didn't love her and never would. She'd been foolish to forget that for even a moment. Her body might betray her when he touched her, but she couldn't let her heart.

When she saw Marc and Claire waiting for them on the upper deck, she was relieved. The tension between her and Rafe had been palpable in the carriage, and she was glad to see her friend. It would be good to be with someone she could relax with for a while. What pleased her even more was the fact that she and Marc looked very relaxed and comfortable together. She hoped these few months they were going to spend in close proximity would spur something between them, especially after what Rafe had told her last night.

Brandy had been putting two and two together and realized that Marc had to be the man Claire had loved all those years ago. Why else would the cautious schoolmarm have cast her fate to the wind so quickly and so willingly, except for love? Their stories definitely coincided, especially since everything she'd heard about Jennette had been how beautiful and wonderful she'd been. No wonder Claire had thought it was hopeless to win Marc's love. But that had been then, and this was now. It pleased her to note, too, that Claire was wearing one of the new daygowns they'd had made for her. She looked sophisticated and lovely, and Brandy intended to keep herself distracted with trying to get the two of them together.

"Hello, newlyweds!" Claire greeted them as they reached the deck where they were waiting. She hugged Brandy and gave her a kiss. "It's so good to see you! How are you?"

"We're fine," Brandy answered. "And we made it to the ship on time."

"I'm proud of you," Marc said to Rafe. "I might have been a bit distracted with such a beautiful wife."

Brandy blushed becomingly, and Rafe just laughed.

"We had to make the steamboat so we could chaperone you," Rafe told them. "You did such a good job for us, we must return the favor."

"That's right," Brandy teased. "Now you're the unattached woman and Marc is the unattached man. We're going to have to keep an eye on both of you."

Marc was smiling easily. "You're too late. I had Claire all to myself last night."

Claire blushed, while Brandy and Rafe both looked at the two of them with renewed interest.

Seeing their expressions, he quickly amended,

"Well, I had her almost all to myself. We did have Merrie and Jason to contend with."

"You're reputation is safe, then," Rafe said to Claire. "Merrie is probably the perfect chaperone."

"Indeed, she is," Claire agreed. "I don't think she left us alone for a minute. She's so cute, and bright, too. It was fun spending time with her and Jason . . . and Marc," she added when he looked her way.

The conversation remained general as they made their way down the deck. Brandy was almost relieved when Marc and Rafe decided to go down to the men's saloon and have a drink. She needed time away from him, time to get her thoughts in order. She needed to get her runaway emotions under control, and being with Claire would help calm her, even though she couldn't talk about what was troubling her.

"Tell me about last night," Brandy said as they sat on deck together. "Marc invited you to dinner with him?"

"Yes," Claire said, her eyes aglow as she related the events of the evening just past.

"I'm so glad you got to do that. You look so happy today."

"I suppose I am. Marc is a nice man."

"Claire . . . you can tell me it's none of my business if you want to, but there's something I want to ask you."

"What?" She couldn't imagine what it was Brandy was hesitant to ask about.

"Is Marc the man you were in love with when you were just out of school? I've been watching you with the children, and there were a few things I heard in conversations during these past few weeks that made me think he might have been. I asked Rafe about the two of you last night, and he did say that you had known each other for a long time. Is he the one you've loved all these years? Is he the one who never knew that he held your heart?"

"Yes." The word was almost torn from Claire. She looked miserable, but when she saw the look of delight on Brandy's face she was confused. "Why are you so happy?"

"This is wonderful!"

"What is?"

"That Marc's the man you love."

"I'm glad you think so."

"A lot of time has passed. You're two different people now. Things are different."

"No, they're not. I'm still the same Claire he knew back then."

"Oh, no, you're not! Look at all you've accomplished! You're one fantastic woman. You're a fine teacher. You're gentle and intelligent, and I can attest to the fact that you're an excellent chaperone. Not to mention that you can now play a mean hand of poker."

Claire was smiling. "But what does all that have to do with anything?"

"It comes down to this. Do you want Marc LeFevre or not? You need to make that decision. Once you do, then we'll know what we have to do."

"Of course I want him, but does he want me? He doesn't even think of me that way," Claire said a little sadly.

"But he will," Brandy said with confidence. "Don't you remember that woman in the teal gown who stared back at you in the mirror in the dress shop? That's the woman who's going to win Marc's heart."

"Do you really think we can do it?"

"Not we—you. And, yes, I know you can."

A look Brandy had never seen before shone in Claire's eyes—hope . . . love . . . excitement.

"You're right. I'm being given a second chance to win Marc. I have to try."

"Everything will work out, but we have to be prepared. Aren't you glad you bought all those new dresses now?"

Claire grinned at her conspiratorially. "I'll say. All right, my chaperone and teacher, what do we do first?"

They put their heads together and began to plot their strategy.

It was late that night when Brandy and Rafe entered their cabin. They had dined in splendor in the steamboat's dining room and had spent several hours just talking with Marc and Claire. To all outward impressions, they were in love and completely happy. Only they knew the truth.

Brandy wasn't quite sure what to expect when Rafe closed and locked the door behind them and started to undress. She had felt numb inside all day since his remark about losing to him in the card game that morning, and she knew it was going to be very difficult being alone with him now. It had been one thing to be cordial with people around. It was another to deal with him when they were alone. But even as much as she wanted to walk out of their room and never come back, she knew she couldn't. Hers was a debt of honor. She'd agreed to the payment terms, and she had to hold to it.

Their room was small and felt almost cramped after their luxurious suite at the hotel. It unnerved Brandy to know that she had to undress in front of

Rafe. It had been one thing in the poker game; it was another now. Whatever happened tonight would set the tone for the rest of their marriage, and the realization unnerved her.

She watched Rafe surreptitiously, but he seemed to be having no problem with the intimacy of their quarters. He had already undressed and gotten in bed while she'd had her back to him. Whatever chance she'd had of avoiding being watched had been erased by his quick action. Now, he lay there, the covers only up to his waist, his arms folded behind his head, watching her.

"Are you coming to bed, my bride?" he asked, his eyes dark with passion's intent.

"Yes . . . in a minute . . ." she mumbled, wishing for a way out, finding none. Her gaze was drawn to the wide expanse of his chest.

"Take your time. I'm enjoying the view, and I'm sure it's going to get much more interesting before the evening is through."

The intimacy of his remark sent a flush of heat through Brandy, and she turned away and began to undress. She thought that if she took her time, he might fall asleep, and then her dilemma of the evening would be taken care of.

What she didn't know was that Rafe found her deliberately slow movements even more erotic than if she had been standing unclothed before him. As she shed each garment, his desire for her grew until he could barely keep himself from leaving the bed and taking her, quickly, hotly, excitingly.

Rafe regretted that things had changed between them since that morning. She had withdrawn from him, and he wanted back that intimacy they'd shared through the night and into the early morning hours.

Brandy knew he was watching her every move, and despite all her prayers that he would fall asleep, it wasn't happening. She could delay in removing her gown no longer and began to unbutton her dress.

Rafe watched as she slipped the buttons free of their restraint, and as she did, her chemise was revealed to him. He remembered far too clearly for his own quietude how she'd stood before him and he'd helped her unfasten the chemise during the poker game last night.

"If you like, we could play poker again," he said with a rakish grin, his gaze searing upon her, tracing the paths his hands and lips would soon be taking.

Brandy looked up at him quickly, seeing the desire in his expression and knowing there would be no escaping him tonight. She told herself that she would be fine. She told herself that she would hold herself aloof from him; that way she wouldn't be in danger of forgetting herself and the only real reason she was there.

"There's no need. I'm not an innocent any more," she said with quiet calm.

Her choice of words bothered him for some reason, but he shrugged it off as he held out his hand to her. "Then come here. I'll help you with what's left."

Across the width of the small room their eyes met, and Brandy moved slowly forward to join him on the bed. The sheets were cool against her, and she shivered as his hand took hers.

"You're cold?" he asked, surprised.

"A little."

"Let me warm you. . . ."

Then there was no more need to talk as his mouth claimed hers in a fiery domination that stirred to life the glowing embers of the passion she'd discovered the night before and had tried so hard to deny all day. An inferno engulfed her, the heat of his loving branding her for life.

Brandy wanted to fight him, wanted to fight the need that overwhelmed her, but she didn't have the strength. She surrendered to him, accepting her weakness, and losing herself in the heaven of Rafe's arms. His strength, his passion, his caress, erased any vestiges of resistance in her. As his body moved over hers to claim her in love's most intimate fashion, she did not resist, but opened to him willingly, almost crying out to him in the joy of knowing he would soon be one with her. And when they came together, their limbs entwined, theirs hearts beating as one, there was no telling where one began and the other ended. Brandy matched him caress for caress, kiss for kiss, forgetting everything she'd told herself about holding herself apart from him, of keeping her heart aloof and unattached.

They sought the peak of passion, and they crested there together. The splendor of their loving left them breathless and sated in each other's arms. They lay, their bodies still one, quietly reflecting on the wonder of their joining. Neither spoke.

When Rafe finally moved away, Brandy turned from him and pretended sleep. He did not see the tear that slipped from her eye.

Rafe lay staring at her slender back. He longed for the woman who had been so open to him and so insatiable last night. He longed to have her back in his arms, loving him, wanting him, needing him. She had come to him tonight without a word, yet it wasn't the same. He didn't know how to recapture the glory that had fleetingly been theirs, but he wanted it back. He almost reached out to her to love her again, and he knew he wouldn't be denied, but he held himself back. He would wait. He would give her time. And then one day, she would come to him openly because she wanted him.

Rafe lay back and stared up sightlessly at the ceiling. He would have been amused by his plight had it not troubled him so. Of all the women in the world who wanted him and wanted to share his bed—and there were more than a few—he had now married the one female who had no great desire to be his wife or his lover. He wondered if he'd made the right decision with Brandy, forcing her to his will as he had. He knew only time would tell.

Brandy lay beside Rafe, her back to him, seeking sleep, wanting sleep, wanting to forget, if only for a little while, how traitorous her body became the moment he laid a hand upon her and how easily he roused her to passion with just a touch and a kiss.

"I have an announcement to make," Marc informed them the following evening at dinner.

"Really?" Rafe looked at him askance, wondering what he was up to.

"Yes. I would like to host a reception for you and your lovely bride when we get back to Natchez. What do you say?" he asked, looking from Brandy to Rafe. "It's important that Brandy gets to meet everyone and has a proper introduction to society. That's why I thought she'd be more comfortable if she does it in friendly surroundings like my house. I might prove a little rusty, since I haven't been entertaining the last year, but I'll manage, if you'd like me to."

"It's a great idea, Marc. Thanks," Rafe told him.

"Yes, thank you, Marc. That is so sweet of you, but

I've got another idea. Why don't you let Claire help you plan it? If she's as good at parties as she was at teaching me, your party will be a smashing success," Brandy offered, seeing an opportunity for them to work together.

Marc looked at Claire. He had been hard pressed to keep his eyes off her all night, for she was wearing a teal gown that was stunning on her. "I'd love to have your help, if you have the time?"

"I'd be honored. Thank you for asking," she returned, her heartbeat quickening at the thought of being in such close contact with him.

"When would you like to have it?" he turned back to Rafe. "How much time do we have to plan?"

"Brandy will need at least a week to get settled in at Bellerive. We'll be home in two days. Do you want to plan on the Saturday after next?"

"That should be fine. Claire and I will take care of everything. All you and Brandy will have to do is show up."

"Sounds like my kind of party," Rafe said, laughing.

They talked of the guest list as Brandy and Claire listened. They shared bewildered looks every now and then as the two men talked of people they didn't know but were quickly learning about from Rafe's and Marc's humorous stories.

"What about Mirabelle?" Marc asked, deliberately bringing her up. He knew there would be no avoiding her in their social group, and she would have to be dealt with eventually.

"Ah, the lovely Mirabelle . . ." Rafe paused, knowing that a confrontation was inevitable.

"Who's Mirabelle?" Brandy found herself asking when she noticed the change in Rafe's expression.

"An old friend," he answered, then turned to Marc. "She'll have to be invited. To exclude her would wreak more damage than to invite her."

"My thoughts exactly, but you'd better be prepared."

"Oh, I will be."

Claire and Brandy glanced at each other, curious now.

"Just what should you be prepared for?" Claire asked.

Rafe realized the best thing to do was tell them the truth so they could be prepared for her, too. "Mirabelle and I have known each other for some time."

That was all he had to say for Brandy to understand. He had told her on the night that they'd come to terms about their marriage how women were always chasing him, wanting to marry him. She'd seen it with the Demers girl. "So she's like Lottie Demers?"

"You could say that," he said blandly, wanting to avoid any further discussion about Mirabelle.

Marc was tempted to tell Rafe to have Brandy pack her gun that night to chase the women off, but he didn't think his witticism would draw many chuckles right then. "I'll invite her. The worst that can happen is she'll make a scene and then it will reflect badly on her, not you."

"She's bound to find out sooner or later. Better from us," Rafe agreed.

They talked until late, making plans and finalizing the guest list, then retired for the night. Marc offered to escort Claire to her room, and they went out on deck together.

The night was oppressively warm and dark. Heavy clouds hung low, and thunder echoed in the distance.

"They always say storms are more intense on the river," Claire remarked as she walked to the railing and turned her face to the wind. She loved thunderstorms, the gusts of wind, the scent of the coming rain. The unleashed power of nature thrilled her.

A jagged streak of lightning rent the heavens, illuminating the river and shore in a flash of bright light, and the thunder that followed rumbled about them. Claire did not flinch, though, or shy away in fright. She merely closed her eyes and savored it.

"Aren't you afraid?" Marc asked coming to her side. He leaned one elbow on the rail as he studied her and not the coming storm.

Marc was surprised by her fearlessness. He was amazed at all he was learning about her—about the real Claire. He had known her for years, yet had always thought her a quiet woman who stayed in the background and drew little attention to herself. The better he got to know her, though, the more he was discovering what she was really like—bright, witty and downright pretty now that she'd put away the schoolmarm clothes and was dressing in a more stylish fashion. The dress she'd appeared in tonight was elegant, and he'd stared helplessly at her when he'd seen her enter the dining room.

"No. There's nothing to be afraid of," she said softly, still not opening her eyes. "I'm here with you."

The moment was one of revelation for Marc as a warmth he'd thought long dead stirred deep within him. He had thought he would never feel this way again about a woman, yet something about Claire touched his heart. She was kind and funny and wonderful with the children, and he liked her. Yet, tonight, right now, he realized that she was a beautiful woman. His gaze settled on the soft curve of her lips, and without thought, he moved toward her. Cautiously, gently, Marc lifted one hand to cup her cheek, and then he dipped his head to seek the sweetness of her kiss.

Claire did not move. She couldn't believe that her dream, her fervent wish, was coming true. She remembered that when the lady at the dress shop had sold her the dress, she had hoped that when Claire wore this dress her fondest wish would come true. And it was. Marc was kissing her.

The thought came and went in a flash, and then she thought no more, but gave herself over to the joy of the moment as lightning flashed and thunder rumbled and the wind picked up around them. His lips upon hers were everything she'd ever dreamed, and she found herself lifting her arms to link them around his neck. It had been forever since she'd allowed herself to think of this moment, but now . . . he was actually with her and she was in ecstasy.

As she looped her arms around his neck, Marc gave a low guttural groan and moved closer, bringing her against him. He deepened the kiss, parting her lips and seeking the sweetness of her. They were lost in the wonder of the moment, unmindful of anything but each other. And then it happened.

Later, Claire would believe that the gods had been conspiring against her, but the crash of thunder, followed by cold, pelting rain, drove them apart and left them breathless in the dark of the night. They stood in the blowing rain, staring at each other in awe, neither able to fully grasp the full import of what had transpired. Then, suddenly, they were laughing, like children caught in mischief, and Marc slipped an arm around her waist as they ran for her cabin door.

"Good night, Claire," he told her huskily as he saw her inside.

"Good night, Marc. Sweet dreams," she said as she gave him one last smile before closing and locking the door.

Sweet dreams. . . . he thought. It seemed forever since he'd last had any kind of dream, let alone a sweet one, but maybe the time had come.

Maybe it had, indeed.

Chapter Twenty-one

It was late the following night, and Brandy was in bed, awaiting Rafe's return. He had gone to the bar with Marc after dinner, and she had retired to their cabin to pack so she would be ready to disembark when they arrived in Natchez the next morning. She was tired and could have slept, but she needed to talk to Rafe about the way she was going to meet with her mother and tell her of their sudden marriage. She'd finished her packing several hours before and had been expecting him to return ever since, but it was near midnight, and he still hadn't returned.

Brandy told herself that she didn't miss Rafe, that she was glad he had gone with Marc. But as the hours had passed and she lay alone in the bed they'd shared for the nights of the trip, she couldn't help remembering the excitement of his hands upon her, the sweetness of his kisses, and the power of his love-making. In frustration, she rolled over onto her stomach and tried to get comfortable.

She had almost fallen asleep when she heard the door open and Rafe come in. She had left a lamp burning low, and he turned it up only slightly as he began to get ready for bed. Knowing there would be no better opportunity, she sat up to speak to him of what was on her mind.

"Rafe, we need to talk," Brandy told him.

"I didn't know you were waiting up."

"It's important. It's about my mother."

He made no comment as he continued to unbutton his shirt.

"When we get to Natchez, I want to have the time to meet with her alone."

"Why?"

"Because I want time to explain things to her."

He stiffened, wondering just how much of their agreement she was going to reveal. "Like what?"

"Like how I met and fell in love with you so quickly that I couldn't resist you. I'm going to tell her about how you swept me off my feet, and how I couldn't wait to return home to marry you because I wanted you so very much."

He heard the note of bitterness in her tone, and it stung him. "Do you think she'll believe you?"

"I hope so," Brandy said in almost a whisper. "I cannot allow anything or anyone to hurt my mother. She's worked hard all her life. Nothing has ever gone easily for her, and I refuse to let her be hurt now."

He looked at Brandy. "Are you saying you think I might somehow intentionally hurt her?"

"The truth about us would devastate her. I want your solemn word that you will never tell her the truth of our marriage." She met his gaze and held it.

"I give you my word that I will not tell her about

us, but won't she figure it out once the baby is born and you leave?"

At the mention of his only reason for taking her as his wife, she tensed. Silently, she prayed again for the opportunity to find the money she needed to pay him off before that horrible, fateful day arrived. "I'll worry about that when the time comes. Who knows?" she found herself taunting him. "I may be barren."

"You aren't," he growled, low and forcefully. His mood turned dark at her words. His gaze bored into the depths of her soul.

She sensed she'd pushed him too far, and quickly went on, "I want to go home by myself first and have an hour or so with her before I introduce you. My mother's going to be very shocked, and I want this to be a happy time for us. We can worry about the rest of it later."

"All right, Brandy. If that's what you want, that's what you shall have. Claire and I can find some way to stay busy while you tend to your mother."

"Thank you," she said quietly as he came to the side of the bed.

He stood there looking down at her, and then moved over her.

There was no reason for them to say any more. Their bodies spoke for them in a language as old as time.

The following day, Brandy sat nervously in the carriage as it wound its way through the streets of Natchez-Under-The-Hill, heading for the small rented house where she knew her mother awaited her return. For the first time ever, she was almost thankful for her mother's failing eyesight. Brandy hoped she wouldn't be able to see through her phony smile and carefully practiced expressions of joy. Her mother had always been able to read her like a book. Brandy had never been able to lie to her or to sneak anything past her. She hoped this would be the first time. She hoped, too, that she could convince her mother that her feelings for Rafe were real and that they truly did love each other and want this marriage.

As the carriage drew to a stop, Brandy took a steadying breath and descended. She paid the driver and then headed inside, ready to tell the biggest lie she'd ever told in her whole life to the one person she loved the most.

"Mama?" she called out as she let herself in and found the tiny sitting room deserted.

"Brandy! You're finally home! You were gone so long this time, I've been worrying about you," Libby O'Neill called out excitedly from the kitchen where she sat with Althea, the lady who watched over her while Brandy was away. Libby was a diminutive woman, but one of great courage and wisdom, and there was nothing in the world, right then, that was going to stop her from going to her daughter. Frail though she was, she managed to get up and hurry through the house toward the sound of her daughter's voice.

Brandy rushed toward the kitchen and found herself enveloped in a much-needed motherly hug. "I'm home, Mama," she sighed, tears choking her voice.

Libby heard the emotion in her words, and, after giving her daughter a loving embrace, she held her back and peered up into her face. It proved an exercise in frustration for her, for although she could make out Brandy's features, she could no longer clearly discern the look in her eyes or the details of her expression. "What's wrong, sweetheart? Is something troubling you?"

"Oh, no, Mama. Nothing's troubling me. I'm just glad to see you. I've missed you."

"Not nearly as much as I missed you. How are Ben and all your other friends?" she asked as she drew Brandy into the kitchen to sit at the table.

"Miss Brandy, it's good that you're home all safe and sound," Althea told her. "I'll go on now and give you some time together."

"Thanks, Althea. I'll talk more to you later."

"Yes, ma'am."

With that she left, and Brandy was alone with her mother.

"Tell me all about this trip. You were gone so long. I don't like it when we're apart this much, but I know you have to do it."

"Not any more, I don't," Brandy announced. She'd been trying desperately to think of a way to ease into the subject of her impromptu marriage, but finally decided the direct approach was best.

Libby frowned. "What do you mean?"

"I mean, I never have to leave you again."

Libby's expression turned incredulous and hopeful. "I don't understand. . . ."

"Mama," Brandy said gently as she knelt before her and took her hands in hers. "While I was on this trip, I met a man. . . . His name is Rafe Marchand, and you'll be meeting him soon."

"What about this Rafe Marchand?"

"Mama . . . Rafe and I were married while we were in St. Louis."

There was a stunned silence, just as Brandy knew there would be.

"Are you sure you made the right decision?" Libby worried. She knew her daughter was a smart girl, but sometimes things could be done in the heat of the moment that would be regretted later.

"Oh, yes, Mama. I made the right decision." Brandy spoke the truth this time.

"Good . . . good . . ."

It was then that she saw the tears silently streaking down her mother's cheeks.

"Mama?" Brandy was suddenly frightened, unsure of her mother's reaction. She didn't know if she was happy or sad.

"It's all right, sweetie. It's all right. . . ." Libby hugged her to her heart. "This is the best news I've ever had. I've been praying and praying for a miracle to help you. My prayers have finally been answered, and his name is Rafe Marchand."

Brandy relaxed against her mother, allowing herself to feel young and small and protected for just that little while.

"Oh, Mama . . . I can't wait for you to meet him. He's very handsome, and from what I understand, he owns a plantation outside of town. We're going to go live there . . . at Bellerive."

Libby's face was alight with an inner glow as she smiled at her only child. She caressed her daughter's cheek as Brandy gazed up at her adoringly. "You're a beautiful woman, Brandy. I am so glad you've found your man."

"So am I."

"When do I get to meet him? Soon, I hope. He must be wonderful to have won your heart so quickly."

"He's a very special man, Mama. I hope you like him."

"If you love him, I'll love him, too," Libby stated firmly. "After all, he had the good sense to marry my daughter, didn't he? How could I not like him?"

They shared another mother-daughter hug.

"He'll be here shortly. I told him to give us a little while alone so I could tell you all about our whirlwind courtship and everything."

"So tell me everything!"

"But we have to get you packed, too. We'll be leaving for Bellerive as soon as he gets here."

"Today?"

"Today. Tomorrow morning, you'll be waking up at Bellerive Plantation."

"I truly can't believe it! I tell you what—get out my one valise, and we'll pack while you tell me the whole story. It must be wonderful."

"Oh, it is."

And as Brandy talked, she packed her mother's things, preparing both of them for a brand-new life.

It was over half an hour later when Rafe and Claire arrived at the small house. Feeling as he did about mothers, Rafe was not particularly looking forward to this encounter. He descended from the carriage, then helped Claire down.

He eyed the neighborhood critically, seeing how rundown it was and understanding more and more of what Ben had told him about Brandy's background. It might not be a fine home, but it seemed they kept it neat and clean.

"I'm looking forward to meeting Brandy's mother," Claire said eagerly. "Aren't you? She must be a special person to have raised Brandy."

"That's true," Rafe remarked noncommittally as they approached the dwelling. He knocked at the door and it was opened almost immediately by Brandy.

"I'm so glad you're here," she said, greeting them with a smile as she held the door wide for them to enter. "My mother's excited about meeting you."

Claire entered first and Rafe followed. He hadn't been sure what to expect. From Brandy's tale of her mother's failing health, he had almost expected her to be bedridden, but the aura of vitality about the fragile-looking, gray-haired woman who stood across the room surprised him.

"Mama, I want you to meet my friend Claire— she's the one I told you all about—and this is Rafe." Brandy led Claire and Rafe over to meet her.

"Claire, Brandy has told me all about you and your poker playing. I think you're going to need a few more lessons to keep up with my girl," Libby said with a teasing smile.

Claire fell in love with Libby O'Neill immediately, and she pressed a warm kiss to her weathered cheek. "I'd give anything to be as good as Brandy is, and she's trying to teach me. Maybe one of these days I'll beat her."

They laughed, and Libby turned her attention to Rafe.

"So, Rafe Marchand, you've fallen in love with my daughter, have you?" Libby asked as she tilted her head back to peer up at him.

"Yes, ma'am, I have," he answered, and for some reason, even though he knew he was doing what Brandy wanted, he felt really rotten for deceiving her mother.

"Come a little bit closer so I can get a good look at you," she insisted.

Rafe stepped closer, and Libby studied him thoughtfully.

"From what I can see of you, you're as handsome as Brandy said you were."

At her frank assessment, Rafe actually found himself blushing a little. "Why, thank you."

"No need to thank me, young man. You'll find as you get to know me better that I always speak my mind and I always tell the truth. Life is much easier that way. People always know where you stand, and you never have to remember that you lied and what it was you lied about."

"I'll remember that." The strangest wave of guilt swept over him, but he shrugged it off. The truth as she was to know it was that he loved her daughter and had married her so quickly because he couldn't live without her.

"You're going to take good care of my girl, aren't you?"

"Yes, ma'am."

"Good." She reached out and took his hand, feeling the strength and power there. She patted it in a warm, loving gesture as she motioned for him to stoop down to her. When he did, she kissed his cheek as she said to her daughter, "You've got yourself a good one, Brandy. I understand why you married him as quickly as you did."

"So you like him?" Brandy asked lightly, smiling as she looked from her husband to her mother.

"Oh, yes. I think Rafe and I are going to be very good friends," Libby said confidently.

Rafe wasn't sure what to think about this little woman. She was unlike any female he'd ever met before. There was something about her, about her kind touch, her gentle words, that made him want to be his best for her and made him want to make sure that no harm came her way. It was a foreign emotion for him, this feeling of wanting to safeguard a woman, and it puzzled him. Still, her over-whelming acceptance of him at face value touched him in a way he'd never been touched before, too, and left him half smiling as he gazed down at her.

"Mama's things are all ready to go," Brandy spoke up, gesturing toward the small pile of belongings that were her mother's life's possessions. "I sent word to Althea of our plans and an extra week's pay for letting her go on such short notice. I also notified the landlord that we were leaving. We can be on our way as soon as you're ready."

"Let's go then," Rafe said, picking up Libby's things and taking them out to the driver. He came back inside as the women were taking one last look around.

"Is it a long ride?" Libby asked Rafe.

"We should be there in about an hour and a half."

"Before dark, then."

"Yes."

"Good, I'm interested to see what your home looks like," she said.

"'Our' home," he corrected, though he didn't know why.

Libby looked up at him again. "Will you do me the honor of escorting me to our carriage, sir?"

"It would be my pleasure," he agreed without hes-itation, surprising Brandy.

Libby tucked her hand in the bend of his arm and, looking like a queen, allowed Rafe to lead her to the carriage and hand her inside.

Brandy and Claire shared a look as they hesitated a moment, then followed.

"I think she likes him," Claire said with certainty.

"But does he like her?" Brandy couldn't help worrying, knowing what she did about his past.

"How could he not?" she asked. "Your mother's precious. You're very blessed to have her."

"I know. She's the wisest woman I've ever met, not to mention the sweetest."

"She takes after you, does she?"

Brandy laughed. "Hardly. I think I must have tested her good nature sorely as a child, but spunk is a good thing to have sometimes."

"You wouldn't be where you are today without it," Claire agreed.

Brandy went silent at her friend's observation, wondering if being where she was, was good or bad. They climbed into the carriage, assisted by Rafe, and he settled in beside Brandy for the ride to Bellerive.

"Tell me about your family, Rafe," Libby asked as their journey began. She wanted to learn more about this man who was now her son-in-law.

"There's not much to tell, Mrs. O'Neill," he began.

Libby stopped him right there. "Just one minute, young man. You are officially family now. What is this 'Mrs. O'Neill' business?"

Rafe actually looked like a surprised and chastened schoolboy at her scolding.

"Call me Libby or even Mother, if you like. But Mrs. O'Neill? Never."

"Yes, ma'am."

She gave him a look. He grinned at her, completely taken off guard by her personality. He'd never met a mother like her before.

"Yes, Libby," he answered respectfully.

"That's better," she said sweetly. "Now, about your family . . ."

Rafe answered succinctly, "My parents are dead, and I was an only child."

"Ah, but now you have Brandy," she said. "You're not alone any more."

"That's right," he told her, taking Brandy's hand in his and smiling down at his bride.

Brandy looked up at him and gave him a grateful smile. He was as good as his word.

Conversation remained general as they made the trip to the plantation. Libby took an immediate liking to Claire, too.

"My little girl has worked long and hard trying to make things better for us. It's wonderful that you're helping her this way, and it was wonderful of Rafe to think of hiring you." She looked at Rafe, then asked Claire, "Has Brandy given you much trouble?"

Claire stifled a grin at Brandy's quick look. "No, Brandy was fine. Now, on the other hand, her poker lessons with me haven't gone quite as well as my lessons with her. I'm not nearly the quick study that she is. I'm afraid I'm woefully lacking in talent in that area."

"That's all right. If we play any more, it won't be for money. It will just be for fun," Brandy said.

"I enjoy playing just for fun, too," Rafe added, giving Brandy a knowing look as he remembered their wedding night.

Libby looked contentedly at her daughter. "You're very good at poker, darling, but I always worried about you being on that steamboat. You're going to be so much happier with Rafe. I just know it."

Brandy didn't answer, for she didn't want to boldly lie to her mother. *Happier with Rafe?* Hardly. The days before their fateful card game seemed unreal to her now. Since then, her life had changed so dramatically that she almost didn't recognize herself any more. She was a lady of quality now . . . Mrs. Rafe Marchand.

It was over an hour later when Rafe announced that they were almost at Bellerive.

"How much farther?" Brandy asked, surveying the surrounding fields with interest.

"We've been on Bellerive land for the last ten minutes, but the house is still a few miles ahead. Once we're on the drive, you'll be able to see the house off to the right in the distance."

When they turned up the drive a short time later, they were impressed by the way the tall oaks arched magnificently overhead. As the carriage emerged from the trees, Brandy caught sight of the plantation house, and her heart went to her throat.

Off to the right, set in majestic splendor among another lush grove of oaks, was Bellerive. Three stories tall, glistening white in the light of the late afternoon, it was a testimony to the glory of Greek Revival architecture.

Brandy gasped. "Oh, Rafe . . . Your home is beautiful."

Claire was staring in silence, while Libby sat back, knowing there was no point in her making the effort to see anything just yet.

Rafe turned his gaze to the house that held so many memories for him. He knew it was an impressive piece of architecture, and he admired it for that, but Brandy looked so awestruck that he tried to put from him the memory of his mother's betrayal and his father's death within those walls, and see the house through the eyes of someone who had never been inside it and did not know its history. For an instant, he recalled how excited he used to be coming home, the warmth of his father's counsel, the joy of an unburdened childhood, and he smiled.

"This is home," he said simply.

But as he was gazing at the house, the front doors opened. He expected to see one of the servants come out. He was totally unprepared for the sight of Mirabelle coming across the veranda, her arm lifted in greeting as if she were the mistress of the place welcoming her husband home.

Brandy saw the woman and glanced over at Rafe. She was surprised by his strange expression. He seemed to be scowling, and a muscle was working in his jaw.

"Who's that?" she asked innocently, thinking it had to be someone close to him.

"Mirabelle," he answered tightly.

"The same Mirabelle you and Marc were talking about on board the steamboat?"

"The same."

Brandy and Claire exchanged looks as they waited for the coming confrontation.

"This should be interesting," Rafe said with a growl as the carriage pulled to a stop.

Chapter Twenty-two

"Rafe, darling!" Mirabelle exclaimed as she saw him step down from the carriage.

Before he could answer, she was down the steps and into his arms. She'd been thinking about him the whole time he'd been away and had merely stopped in at the house today to see if there had been any word on the date of his return. It was a delightful surprise to find that he was arriving while she was there. Surely, fate was putting them together for a reason, and she hoped to be celebrating that reason all night in his arms.

"Mirabelle . . ." was all he had time to murmur as she kissed him full on the mouth.

"I think I understand what Rafe and Marc were talking about the other night," Claire murmured to Brandy inside the carriage as she watched the other woman in action.

"I think I should take things in hand—what do you think?"

"Excellent idea," Libby agreed. Mirabelle's display was too flagrant to be missed by anyone.

"Darling," Brandy drawled as she climbed out of the vehicle on her own. "Do *we* have guests?"

It all happened so fast that Rafe had little time to escape. As Brandy made her move, he grasped Mirabelle by her upper arms and held her away from him.

" 'Darling'?" Mirabelle demanded. Her face still flushed from the kiss, she looked past Rafe to where a beautiful woman was climbing down out of his carriage.

"Hello," Brandy went on casually as if it were an everyday occurrence to have women brazenly kissing her husband in public. "I'm Brandy Marchand—Rafe's wife. And you're—?"

Rafe released Mirabelle as if he'd been burned. Mirabelle's mouth dropped open as she stared at the perfectly dressed, perfectly coiffed, absolutely beautiful young woman who'd just appeared before her. Her shock lasted only an instant, though, for it turned almost immediately to fury. Outraged, she turned her glare on Rafe.

"Rafe, honey, who is this person?" Mirabelle asked as she put a possessive hand on his arm.

"This is my wife Brandy, Mirabelle. Brandy, I'd like you to meet Mirabelle Chandler . . . an old friend." Rafe slipped out of his "old friend's" reach.

"An *old* friend . . ." Brandy emphasized the word as she moved forward and took Rafe's arm in a casually intimate gesture. "Hello, Mirabelle, it's so nice to meet you after all Rafe and Marc have told me about you."

"Your wife?" Mirabelle recovered enough to turn on Rafe. "Is this some kind of joke? Who is this woman?"

"I assure you this is no joke," he stated with authority. "Brandy and I were married in St. Louis."

"You're married?" she repeated, looking from the young woman at his side to Rafe.

"Very married," Rafe told her, smiling down at Brandy with a look of affection that left no doubt of the state of their relationship. He pressed a soft kiss to her lips.

Mirabelle was trembling with the force of her anger. She was about to lose her temper completely when she heard another voice from the carriage.

"Rafe, dear, would you help me down? I'd love to meet your friend Mirabelle," Libby called to him.

He turned to the old lady, and with two hands at her waist set her lightly to the ground.

"You are such a dear boy," Libby said, patting his arm affectionately before turning to the other woman. "It's so nice to meet you, Mirabelle. And what a wonderful welcome-home surprise to find one of Rafe's friends here waiting to greet us."

"Who are you?" Mirabelle demanded haughtily, staring at the plainly dressed little old woman in disdain.

"I am Rafe's mother-in-law. You may call me Libby. All my friends do," she said happily.

"You're his mother-in-law? Rafe Marchand . . . !" Mirabelle ground out his name as she turned on him only to see him helping another lovely woman out of the carriage.

"And, Mirabelle, this is Claire, Brandy and her mother's traveling companion. Claire, Mirabelle Chandler."

"Ooooh! I hate you, Rafe!" she hissed as she took one last look around, then stalked off to where her own carriage was waiting. She yelled in a very unladylike fashion for her driver and climbed into the vehicle unassisted to await him.

The last they saw of Mirabelle was her stony profile as her driver fled the premises as if he were a fox and the hounds were at his heels.

"You are truly a gentleman, Rafe Marchand," Libby observed, feeling quite satisfied with the way things had turned out. "I trust she won't be back?"

"I thank you for the compliment, and as to the answer to your question . . ." He paused to stare after the departing carriage for a moment. "You can never be sure about anything with Mirabelle. Come, let's go inside. I want you to meet the servants and get a look at the house."

He escorted them indoors and called the servants together to introduce them. George, Tilda and several of the other maids gathered round to hear who these women were. They'd been watching as Miss Mirabelle left in a huff, and they were wondering what was going on.

"This is Mrs. Libby O'Neill, Miss Claire Patterson and this, everyone, is Brandy, my wife."

"Your wife, sir?" George looked at him in astonishment.

"Yes, George, my wife."

The butler broke into a wide smile. "Congratulations, Master Rafe. That is positively the best news we've had here in years. Yes, sir, it is. How do you do, ma'am?"

"It's nice to meet you," Brandy returned, smiling happily at this warm welcome.

The astonishment on the servants' faces reinforced

everything he'd told her about himself. It had been common knowledge that he had not wanted to marry, and her arrival was a complete surprise, but not, from the looks of things, an unwelcome one.

"I hope no one is too disappointed that Miss Mirabelle isn't the one arriving here in my position?" she asked daringly, a twinkle of mischief in her eyes.

George rolled his eyes at her words and was grinning as he answered, "Oh, no, ma'am. We are more than pleased with everything. Welcome to Bellerive."

"Thank you, George," Brandy said, immediately warming to this man as she saw the kindness in his eyes.

They were given the guided tour, starting there on the main floor. All were impressed by the well-appointed rooms with their plush furnishings.

"What's in there?" Brandy asked, as they passed a closed room on their way down the main hall toward the steps to the second floor.

"That room is not used. It's kept locked," Rafe said tersely, offering no further explanation.

Brandy was puzzled, since every other part of the house had been open to them, but she said nothing. They went up to the second floor and were equally impressed with all the bedrooms. As they were about to enter another room where the door was shut, Rafe spoke up again.

"That room is kept locked, too. There's nothing in there worth seeing. Why don't we go out on the balcony?" he invited them, diverting their attention.

"Bellerive is beautiful," Brandy declared as they stood on the second-floor balcony overlooking the wide expanse of perfectly manicured lawn.

"It was my father's dream," Rafe said simply, yet he was profoundly touched by the awe and respect with which Brandy, her mother and Claire had admired his home.

"And you've kept it up and improved it. Your father would be proud of you," Libby said firmly.

Rafe looked over at the little woman. He saw the sincerity in her expression and felt a jolt of an emotion he'd not allowed himself to feel in years. "Thank you," he said.

Claire and Libby were given spacious rooms on the second floor at the far end of the hall from Rafe's room. They agreed to meet downstairs in an hour for dinner.

Rafe and Brandy entered his room, and he closed the door behind them, giving them privacy for the first time since they'd left the ship that morning. Brandy smiled at him.

"I appreciate your kindness to my mother—for being gentle with her and for bringing her into your home."

"Now that I've met her, I understand your concern about her. You were right in suggesting we bring her here."

"And you truly don't mind?"

"Not at all. In fact, now I know where you get it from."

"Get what?"

"She took on Mirabelle without batting an eye. Your mother's one brave lady."

"That she is. She's always had to be. There was never anyone to defend us or take care of us."

Her words were not spoken to evoke sympathy, but simply to state the facts. Still, Rafe found himself wanting to be the one to make sure these two women were never again left without protection. When he realized the direction of his thoughts, he gave himself a mental shake.

Going to Brandy, Rafe took her gently in his arms and kissed her. "Welcome home."

She almost believed he meant it. After all, they were alone in his room with no audience to judge their performances, but her logical self cautioned her not to read anything into his words or actions. "I love Bellerive. You're very blessed to have it."

He smiled at her. "I think I'll go on downstairs and see how things have been while I've been away. I'll be in my study when you come down."

She nodded, and he left her alone to finish unpacking.

Downstairs he went into his study to go through his papers. He had just settled in when he looked up to find George in the doorway.

"Did you want something, George?"

"Mrs. O'Neill is on her way downstairs, and I wondered if you'd like her in here with you or shall I take her into the parlor?"

"Bring her in, George, and thanks. By the way, her vision is impaired so she will need extra help with a few things," he told the butler, enlisting his help in keeping an eye on Libby.

The servant nodded and went to meet her at the foot of the staircase.

"Will I be bothering you if I join you?" Libby asked as George directed her inside.

"Absolutely not," Rafe told her, standing as she entered the room. "Please, come in and sit down. Are you all settled in?"

"Yes, thanks. With all your servants to help me, it didn't take any time at all to put my things away. The room is lovely, too. I appreciate your thoughtfulness."

"It's my pleasure." He waited until she'd taken the seat before his desk before sitting back down in his own chair.

Libby couldn't see well, but she could make him out, looking powerful and in control behind his massive desk. Her instincts were telling her that he was a good man and obviously a kind man, yet she sensed a hesitation in him, something that he was holding back. She was beginning to understand why as she listened to him talk about himself and his life. Since he'd lived alone for so long, it was no wonder so many people were surprised that he'd married unexpectedly. But then, they'd never seen or met Brandy.

"We certainly surprised your friend Mirabelle this afternoon, didn't we?" she said.

"That we did. I'm sure it will be quite a while before she recovers from the shock of it."

"Really? Had she thought you were going to ask for her?"

"No, that was never a consideration. Mirabelle knew all along that I had no desire to marry," he said, then quickly added, "until Brandy."

"I understand, believe me. When my husband and I met, it was the same way. We knew instantly that we were meant to be together. Sometimes, I think love is heaven-sent, don't you?"

Rafe knew Brandy didn't think there was anything heavenly about their marriage. "Yes."

"I just hope the two of you are as happy as we were. My husband died while Brandy was still very young, but the few years we had together were so special. . . . I was blessed to have him, and even more blessed to have Brandy. I'm glad you love her. I was praying for you to come to her, you know."

"You were?" He looked at her, startled.

Libby's expression was loving. "Oh, yes. I've been praying about you ever since I knew my eyesight was failing. I knew that as long as Brandy had me to worry about and care for, she'd never take the time for herself. As willful as she is, I knew she needed a strong man, and I sense you're more than a match for her."

"And that's good?"

"Very good."

He felt uncomfortable with her praise, for since his father's death no one had ever taken the time to tell him his strengths and make him feel as if he were doing the right thing. He'd been on his own, alone now for so long that he didn't know how to accept this kind of compliment, especially from an older woman. As he thought about it, he realized that he'd never been around a grandmotherly woman before, and he wasn't quite sure what to do or how to act. That very realization bothered him more than anything, for he was a man accustomed to being in control.

Rafe heard Claire and Brandy in the outer hall then, and he was almost glad. Talking to Brandy's mother disturbed him in a way he couldn't understand. He just knew it troubled him, and he wasn't sure if that was good or bad.

Brandy and Claire found them in the study, and George announced dinner shortly thereafter. As they ate the sumptuous fare, the talk turned to the coming party.

"Did you speak with Rafe and Marc about the plans for the party while you were waiting at the steamboat this morning?" Brandy asked.

"Yes, and he said that Marc and I would need to start working on things early next week."

"Good," she said with a nod.

Rafe looked from one woman to the other. "Why do I get the feeling that more is going on here than I know?"

"Nothing's going on," Brandy said innocently. "Although, if you don't mind, I do need to purchase a dress or two for Mother, especially with the party coming up."

"That's fine. The carriage and driver are at your disposal. You can set up an account with the dressmaker and just instruct all the bills to be sent to me."

"Rafe, it's not right that you should be paying for my clothes," Libby protested. "I have a few dollars put away for just such occasions."

"There is no need for you to use your money. While you are under my roof, I will be glad to pay all of your expenses."

"You are as wonderful as Brandy said you were." Libby had never known anyone like Rafe, and she got teary-eyed at his most recent act of kindness. "That is so sweet of you."

Rafe looked at Brandy for a long moment; then, for some reason, he wanted to make Libby smile. "My motives are purely selfish. I love being surrounded by beautiful women."

Libby smiled at him, a smile that told him she thought he was the most magnificent man on the face of the Earth.

Rafe found he liked it, and he fought the scowl that immediately followed.

"So have you and Marc planned what days you'll be needed at his home?"

"No, we haven't gotten that far yet. He said he would stop by some time this week."

"Good. We'll firm everything up then."

When dinner was over, it was late and everyone was tired. Brandy helped her mother to bed, then entered the bedroom that was hers and Rafe's. She found him already in bed, waiting for her.

"It's been a long day," she said wearily, thinking of how very much her life had changed since she'd arisen that morning. Until this moment, she could pretend that she was still Brandy O'Neill, playing at being Rafe's wife.

"And I hope a longer night," he said with a seductive grin as his gaze met hers.

She could see the flame in the depths of his eyes, and she knew what he wanted. Her body's answering response let her know that despite all her denials, she wanted him as much as he wanted her.

"No poker tonight?" she asked archly.

"Are you nervous?"

She paused to consider his words. For some reason, she did not feel uncomfortable even though this was her first night as Rafe's wife in his home. "No . . . No, I'm not. You made it easy for me, even with Mirabelle." She thought of the other woman in his arms, her lips on Rafe's, and a surge of unwanted jealousy went through her, moving her toward the bed . . . toward him . . . toward her husband.

His grin widened. "It was a surprise finding her here."

"Is she always that brazen?"

"Yes."

Brandy looked thoughtful as she came to stand at the side of the bed. "I do suppose you bring out that quality in women. . . ."

"I do?"

She kissed him then, hotly, passionately. She wanted him to remember only her kisses and her caresses. She wanted to erase any thought of the other woman from his mind.

They spoke of Mirabelle no more that night.

Brandy came awake shortly after dawn to find that Rafe was already up and was getting dressed.

"Where are you going?" she asked in a voice husky with sleep.

"I have to meet with the overseer this morning. I'm sorry I woke you. I was trying to sneak out without bothering you."

"The bed felt lonely without you," she said in an unguarded moment.

At her words, Rafe paused in dressing and turned to look at her. In the softness of the early morning light, she looked more ravishing than ever. Her hair was a riotous tumble of curls about her face and shoulders. Her cheeks were flushed with the memory of their loving, and her eyes held the secrets of the ages. He felt the heat settle in his loins as he stared at her.

"Do you have to go so early?" she asked, lifting a hand to him in invitation and in memory of the ecstasy they'd shared through the dark night hours.

"I promised I'd meet him in . . ." He glanced at the clock. "In about fifteen minutes."

Brandy's smile widened at having that much time, and she seductively drew the covers away so he could see her. "How long will it take you to dress again?"

"Not long," he growled. The importance of meeting the overseer was suddenly lost on him as he gazed upon the perfection of his wife's slender body.

*   *   *

Claire had known that once they traveled to Rafe's home in Natchez, Brandy's need for her would diminish. Brandy had accomplished everything she'd hoped she would, and after the party at Marc's, no doubt she would be set in society. Still, she knew she had at least another week or two left on the job that Rafe hired her for, so she decided to take everything one day at a time. Regardless of all else, she would have Marc to herself on several occasions as they planned Brandy's and Rafe's reception.

When Marc arrived at Bellerive the following day, Claire was thrilled, though she managed to act calm as she came downstairs. She had missed him dreadfully. She still ached with happiness from their embrace on the steamboat, and she was eagerly hoping they could find some time alone together soon.

"Marc . . . Good morning," she greeted him when she found him standing in the foyer talking with Rafe.

He looked up, and a slow smile spread across his face. "Good morning, Claire. You look lovely today."

"Thanks. Are you ready to talk about the party?"

"I was just going over things with Rafe. Why don't we sit down together and figure out what we have to do in order to put this together in time."

They settled themselves in the parlor and an hour later knew what had to be done.

"Then you want me to come with you now to see your home and decide exactly what to do?"

"That would be wonderful, and I promise I'll have you back at a reasonable hour."

Claire's heart was singing as she rode from Bellerive at Marc's side. It felt right, so right to be with him this way. The only thought that troubled her was that he was thinking of her as a paid employee and not as a friend who wanted to help. But if nothing else, as a paid employee she would be able to speak to him whenever the need arose, and she planned to need him often over the coming days.

Chapter Twenty-three

The ballroom in Marc's home was crowded with friends, well-wishers and more than a few broken-hearted young females all waiting for the entrance of the newly married couple. Talk had flown fast and furious about Rafe's unexpected marriage. Tears had been shed among the debutantes, each of whom had fancied herself the one woman who could get Rafe Marchand to propose, and more than a few men had shaken their heads in the defeated knowledge that the one man they'd thought would never succumb to a female's charms had at long last fallen.

"Ladies and gentlemen, may I introduce to you Mr. and Mrs. Rafe Marchand," Marc announced as he stood at the doorway to the ballroom.

At his announcement, Rafe entered the room with Brandy on his arm. They looked marvelous together. Rafe, devastatingly handsome in his perfectly tailored suit, was a dark power beside Brandy's vibrant beauty. She'd chosen her most dazzling gown for tonight, a full-skirted, low-cut, rose satin creation that set off her coloring and drew men's gazes to her like a magnet. Her hair was styled artfully, with matching rose-colored ribbon wound through the curls.

The men who'd bemoaned his passing from bachelorhood understood Rafe's decision immediately at their first look at his bride.

"Where did he find her?" Charles Kerrin asked his friend, Pierre Martin.

"I don't know, but I wonder if she has a sister?"

Their eyes brightened at the thought, and they knew they'd have to ask Rafe as soon as they could get him alone.

The music began, and Rafe squired Brandy to the center of the dance floor. Taking her in his arms, he swept her around the room in graceful precision. They looked the fairy-tale couple, and many a young woman watching wished she was the one in his arms, being held close to him, earning that look of devotion from him.

Mirabelle stood in silent fury apart from the others. She'd heard all the gossip about the romantic wedding, but instead of being happy about it for Rafe's sake, she had only grown more and more angry. He had graced her bed, and she had been good enough for him there—more than good enough judging from his reaction at the time. But when it had come to marriage, he had not given her a thought, but had wed this one instead—a simpering little miss who looked as if she could be easily manipulated.

Mirabelle found it hard to believe that he preferred this Brandy to her. She hardly thought the debutante type would keep Rafe's attention for long, and she wondered just how soon he'd be back, seeking her out. Since the day of Rafe's return with his bride, she had been trying to find out more about this Brandy O'Neill. No one she'd spoken to in their circle of friends had ever heard of her. Still, she wouldn't stop trying. She wanted to know why Rafe had chosen to marry Brandy.

Nearby, standing at her mother's side, young Cynthia Harris was equally disturbed by the sight of Rafe so obviously in love with his new wife.

"Oh, Mama . . . I thought he was going to marry me. . . ." she said in a choked voice as she struggled not to cry.

"Cynthia," her mother said sternly as she spoke to her in low, private tones. "I told you before we left the house that if you couldn't control yourself, you shouldn't come tonight. Now, stop. Right now. Rafe Marchand may be off the marriage market, but there are many other available men here tonight. Start looking around. Surely, one of them is just as promising as Rafe was. Maybe more."

Cynthia fought back her tears and pasted on a bright smile. She knew her mother was right, but that didn't ease the pain of knowing Rafe would never be hers.

"So far, so good," Brandy said, looking up at Rafe as they circled the dance floor, all eyes upon them. "I haven't tripped yet."

"And you won't. You're as light on your feet as you are beautiful, Mrs. Marchand," Rafe told her with a warm smile. He knew how nervous she'd been on the trip to Marc's house, and he wanted her to be at ease.

"Why, thank you, sir. I had a wonderful teacher."

"Our first lesson was . . . special, wasn't it?" His

eyes glowed at the memory.

She grinned mischievously as she teased, "Why, Rafe, I was talking about Claire."

He spun her around in an expert move that thrilled her, and she matched him step for step, laughing at his daring.

"What were you saying about your first dance instructor?"

"Oh, my *dance* instructor . . . He was magnificent."

"Not Monsieur Hebert?"

"No, not Monsieur Hebert." She managed a laugh.

All day Brandy had been tense about the reception. The dinner party in St. Louis had been an important first test, but this—this was her telling moment. If she was accepted and welcomed by Rafe's friends without question, then she had truly mastered all that Claire had tried to teach her.

Brandy drew a deep breath as she continued to follow Rafe's lead. There was one other concern that haunted her. Rafe had told her that it wouldn't matter to him if someone recognized her, but she knew how condemning Southern society could be. If anyone learned of her past, she feared the worst—that she would be scorned and ridiculed, that her shame would fall on Rafe, too. Struggling not to dwell on those thoughts, she kept a serene expression in place and tried to just enjoy being in Rafe's arms.

Rafe looked down at Brandy and thought he'd never seen a more beautiful woman. Her eyes were bright, and her cheeks were flushed from the dance. His gaze dropped to her mouth, and he found her lips slightly parted, as if waiting for his kiss. The need to kiss her was powerful, overwhelming his common sense, and in the middle of the ballroom, as they waltzed about the spacious dance floor, Rafe bent to her and, without missing a stride in their dance, kissed her, a soft, quick kiss on the lips.

Brandy was touched by his daring. A thrill shot through her that he cared enough to publicly show his affection for her. She smiled openly now for the first time, and he smiled back at her. The intimacy of the exchange touched them both, and they finished the waltz dreamily, their arms linked as the music ended. Then they went forth to greet everyone.

"They look so perfect together," Claire remarked to Marc as they watched Rafe and Brandy making their way around the room, talking with everyone. "I'm so glad everything's worked out for them."

"I am, too. If anyone deserves some happiness in his life, it's Rafe."

"He is a strong man, and Brandy is just what he needs. She loves him dearly. Have you noticed, too, how well he's getting along with her mother?"

"I have, and that's good."

"Brandy and her mother are going to make a big change in his life."

"I hope so."

Claire sighed as she realized that her time in Natchez was almost over. After tonight, Brandy would be introduced and accepted into society. She wouldn't be needing her services any more. It was almost time for her to return to St. Louis and her job at the academy.

"Why the sigh?" Marc asked. "You sound unhappy about something."

"No, not unhappy . . . not really."

"Then what?"

"Well, it just occurred to me that very soon, Brandy won't be needing me anymore. After tonight, she'll be accepted into society. She's learned everything I had to teach her, and since she no longer needs a chaperone, my duties here are complete."

Marc was surprised by the sense of loss that filled him at the thought of Claire returning to St. Louis. Their spontaneous kiss that night on the steamboat had left him unsettled, stirring feelings he'd thought dead and also arousing not a little guilt in him. He had not approached her again in that way, but had maintained a warm friendship with her as they'd planned the reception for tonight. He thoroughly enjoyed being with her. He enjoyed her quick wit and endless good humor, and the way she seemed to truly like spending time with Merrie and Jason. He didn't want to think of their time together ending.

"Shall we dance?" he asked, his mind racing to think of some way to delay the inevitable.

When Libby had arrived with Rafe and Brandy, she had felt like a fairy princess, in spite of her age. It was the first time in her whole life that she had had a fancy ballgown and had been invited to a party like this one. She'd been worried beforehand that she might commit some faux pas, but both Brandy and Rafe had assured her that she would be fine. When they'd reached Marc's home, she had been immediately taken over by Marc's maternal aunt, Sophie, a dear little widow lady who loved making new friends. They sat together on the side of the dance floor now, enjoying the bustle of the evening.

"Your daughter is lovely. She and Rafe certainly make a good pair," Sophie told her. "It's about time that boy married and settled down."

"I'm glad they found each other."

"Now, if only Marc could find someone . . . It's tragic that Jennette died so young, but Marc is too young and too handsome to stop living now."

"There's another woman out there. It will just take him time to adjust, that's all. After all, his wife's only been gone a little over a year, hasn't she?"

"You're right, I know. I just like everybody to be happy. It's my worst trait."

"Everyone should have such a terrible trait," Libby quipped, laughing at her new friend.

"Thanks. There are those who don't appreciate my worrying so much about them."

Libby patted her hand. "Believe me, they'd miss it if you didn't."

They shared a knowing smile.

"How do you like living at Bellerive?"

"It's a fantasy come true for me," Libby answered honestly.

"And it will only get better once those grandchildren start coming," Sophie remarked, and then launched into telling her all about her own grandchildren and how much fun they were.

In Sophie's talkative company, Libby relaxed and enjoyed herself, grateful for the other woman's attention and friendship. Libby knew she was going to love her new life here.

Brandy had been stolen from Rafe's side soon after they'd made their first round of the room to meet everyone, and she hadn't been back to him since, as each man in the room had sought the honor of dancing with her. As the current waltz ended, she thanked her partner, and, a wee bit hot and weary, she moved toward the refreshment table alone to get a cup of punch.

"Well, well, well, if it isn't the blushing bride," Mirabelle said nastily as she appeared nearby. She'd been watching and waiting for a chance to talk to Brandy, and now was the time. The little bitch had dared to steal Rafe, and she was determined to do her best to ruin everything for her if she could. With no one around right then to overhear their conversation, it was safe for her to have her say.

"Hello, Mirabelle," Brandy said coolly as she glanced over at the other woman. Mirabelle was a force to be reckoned with, and somehow Brandy had always known this moment would come. Brandy was going to let Mirabelle lead the conversation, but she was not about to play the sweet little wife tonight. She had to let this woman know she was her equal.

"You know, Brandy. I'm really very confused about all this." Mirabelle gestured around at the celebration.

"What is it you don't understand? Rafe fell in love with me and married me. This party is to celebrate that. It's really very simple."

Mirabelle was caught by surprise at the challenge in Brandy's tone. She'd thought her a simpering idiot. This spirit in Rafe's little wife was something she hadn't expected, and it only angered her more. Who was this chit that she thought she could talk to her that way?

"My dear," she replied, "anyone who knows Rafe knows this marriage is completely unlike him. He's never married because, as I know so well, he could never be satisfied by just one woman."

"He seems satisfied with me so far," Brandy returned.

"So far, yes," she agreed smoothly. "But, darling, you've only been married a few weeks. I've known the man for years."

"And he's never chosen to marry you, has he?" Brandy was deliberately cold, wanting this conversation over as soon as possible.

Mirabelle's temper grew hotter. "That was my choice, my dear. I like my life the way it is, doing what I want, with anyone I want, whenever I want."

"I'm happy for you, Mirabelle," Brandy said in an uninterested drawl. "What's your point?"

It outraged her that Brandy was giving as good as she got. "My point is this. You're just a child, a baby really. You may have Rafe's name, but you'll never keep him. He's been my lover for years, and we both look forward to continuing our . . . how shall I say it . . . our 'association.' "

Brandy was trying to be a lady. She was mentally reciting to herself all the rules Claire had taught her about self-control and behaving herself at all times in public; however, Claire had never met or dealt with anyone like Mirabelle. The time had come for Mirabelle to have a talk with the real Brandy O'Neill Marchand.

"You know, Mirabelle, it took Rafe only one week to fall in love with me and decide to marry me. As you've said, you've known him for years. That should answer any questions you have about our relationship. He is my husband now."

"In name only."

Brandy gave a soft, deriding laugh at her statement, yet her heart was breaking, for there was more truth to her words than Mirabelle knew. "You played your hand and you lost. It's time for you to give it up and move on."

"Rafe's mine! He's always been mine."

"Cut your losses while you still have your dignity," Brandy cautioned, knowing Mirabelle's kind and

how to deal with them. "*This* lady won the hand."
She held up her hand so Mirabelle could see the
flashing diamond and wide gold band that pro-
claimed her as Rafe's wife. "You didn't."

Mirabelle stared at the large diamond and looked
at Brandy, seeing the confidence and cool nerve in
her expression. In a moment of revelation, she realized that she had lost—and to this woman. In fury,
she squared her shoulders and stalked away.

Brandy stood there for a moment unmoving,
watching her go. For all that she looked outwardly
calm, confident and happy, inwardly, her pain was
intense. No wonder Rafe wouldn't be back to her bed
once she'd conceived. He had Mirabelle waiting for
him. She hoped with all her heart that she never had
to speak with the woman again. It would be devastating enough to know that Mirabelle would be back
in Rafe's arms as soon as she had completed her part
of their "arrangement."

It was then that Brandy heard the sound of soft
applause coming from somewhere from behind her;
shocked, she glanced around to see who'd witnessed
the exchange with Mirabelle. When she came face to
face with Sam Foster, she knew a terrible sinking
feeling in her stomach.

"Sam . . ." She said his name breathlessly. Her ve-
neer of calm was shattered by the sight of the gen-
tlemanly poker player she'd played so often on the
Pride of New Orleans.

"Miss Brandy." He gave her a slight, courthy bow.
"I can't tell you what a delight it is to see you again.
And I must say that I have never been so glad to see
anyone put in her place as much as the lovely Mirabelle. She's needed it for years. Congratulations on
your wit and nerve. You handled her perfectly. I

doubt she'll cause you any more trouble."

"Thank you." She was cautious. Sam had always seemed to be a nice man, but this would be the telling moment.

Sam could not miss how pale Brandy had turned when she'd seen him and how quietly she was talking to him. He hastened to reassure her about his intentions.

"Brandy, dear, there's no need to look so terrified," he told her. "You don't have to be afraid of me. You're a wonderful young lady and you deserve this happiness. As far as I'm concerned, Mrs. Rafe Marchand, this is the first time we've met."

Brandy's sense of relief was so great that tears threatened and she almost threw her arms around him. She stopped herself, though, for she knew she'd have a hard time explaining it. "I always knew you were a very special man, Sam."

"I just want you to be happy, Brandy, and I think Rafe is one very lucky fellow. How he ever won you over is a mystery to me. I'm going to miss our games, though. You were the highlight of many of my trips. If you ever want to play again, you let me know. I'd love to have the chance to win back some of my losses from you."

Brandy was smiling brightly at him. "I'd kiss you right now, if I wasn't a married woman."

"I'm afraid Mrs. Foster might have an objection, too," he said with a chuckle.

"Is she here? I'd love to meet her."

"Come with me, my dear. I'll introduce you right now."

Brandy followed Sam to meet his wife of many years.

Across the room, Rafe had been trapped in a conversation from which there seemed no escape. He'd kept saying the right things at the right times, but concentrating had become almost impossible once he'd seen Mirabelle corner Brandy. He'd wanted to cut the conversation off and rush over to help her, but there had been no way he could do it without offending someone. So, helplessly, he'd watched the scene unfold between the two women, hoping that Brandy could hold her own against the sharp-tongued widow.

When Mirabelle had finally walked away, Rafe had been able to tell that she was furious, and he couldn't help smiling to himself. Brandy had taken on Mirabelle and won. He'd glanced her way again to find that Sam Foster had joined her and was speaking with her. Rafe had known a pang of jealousy, seeing her with another man. He'd wanted to be the one with Brandy, not stuck where he was discussing crops and the weather. Finally, a few minutes later, desperate to be with his bride, he'd found the opportunity to make his excuses and seek her out.

"Good evening, Annette, Sam," Rafe greeted the Fosters. "I'd like to steal my bride away, if you don't mind?"

"You take good care of her, Rafe. She's a lovely lady," Sam said with a kind smile.

"I will," he promised. "Darling, would you like to dance again?"

"I'd love to. It was nice to meet you, Annette, and you, too, Sam."

With that, Rafe whisked her out among the other couples on the ballroom floor.

"So?" he asked, once they could talk.

"So, what?" she returned, for some reason wanting

to make him suffer a little in his search for information about Mirabelle.

"I couldn't help noticing your encounter with Mirabelle. Did it go well?"

"As well as it could, considering that she told me that you had been lovers and that there was no way you could ever be satisfied with just one woman."

Rafe's jaw tightened at the abuse Brandy had been subjected to. "I'm sorry."

"For what? For my finding out the truth about your relationship with her?" she said coldly. "We are fine actors, you and I, but we both know the underlying truth about our marriage, don't we? The truth is, Mirabelle was right in everything she said, but I didn't let her know it. She said you didn't love me, that I was your wife in name only, that I might be able to keep your name, but I would never be able to keep you. She's a very perceptive woman."

Her words knifed at Rafe, yet he could not deny them. "Brandy, I . . ."

"It's not necessary for you to say anything right now," she said, smiling up at him as if she were thrilled to be in his arms. "This is our belated wedding reception, remember? We must enjoy ourselves. We must convince everyone that ours is a love match."

He smiled back, but it was not a smile that reached his eyes . . . or his heart.

Marc found Claire talking with Libby and Sophie. "Would you like to dance again?"

"I'd love to." She quickly rose and went into his arms.

Marc generally talked to her while they danced, but this time he was unusually quiet as they moved about the room. Claire wondered at his mood, but said nothing. She just enjoyed being in his arms. When the music ended, she started to move away from him, but he caught her hand.

"Claire . . . Would you mind stepping out on the balcony with me for a moment? There's something I wanted to ask you."

He sounded so serious that she didn't know what to make of his invitation. She nodded her answer and allowed him to draw her along with him.

Claire was breathless as they stepped outside. She was wearing the teal ballgown. She was alone with Marc in the moonlight once again, and this time not by accident—he had invited her there. She did not speak, but moved even farther away from the house so they would have some privacy. She stopped in a quiet, shadowed corner and turned to look up at Marc. Her pulse quickened as her gaze went over his features. Oh, how she loved him . . . He meant the world to her . . . He always had. His expression was serious, and she wanted desperately to know what was on his mind.

"Was there something you wanted to ask me?" she said softly.

Marc was staring down at her in the moonlight, seeing how lovely she was, remembering their kiss in the thunderstorm. With an effort, he forced his thoughts to the solution he'd found for his dilemma.

"Yes," he said, clearing his throat. "Since your time working with Brandy is almost over . . . I was wondering if . . ."

"Yes?" Her heart was pounding as she imagined all kinds of wonderful things.

He began again. "I was wondering if you'd like to come to work for me."

Claire blinked as she stared at him. In all her wildest dreams, this had never been the question he'd posed. "Work for you?" she repeated rather dazedly.

"Yes," he went on quickly. "You get along with Merrie and Jason so well, I thought you might be interested in staying on and tutoring them. The children certainly adore you. I think it might work out perfectly."

How Claire kept the pain she was feeling from showing in her expression, she never knew. She wanted to slap him for being so blind about her feelings, but then she remembered her own advice to Brandy and managed to control her wayward emotions. She smiled at him sweetly as she answered, "That's a wonderful idea, Marc. I do love your children, and I would enjoy working with them."

He smiled quite happily at her answer.

He was completely unaware that he'd broken her heart.

Chapter Twenty-four

Claire was up early the next morning and already at the breakfast table when Brandy came down. Rafe had already left to take care of business, and Libby always slept late.

"Good morning," Brandy said as she found her friend in the dining room. "You're up early today."

"I had a lot to think about. I'm glad you came down now so we can talk."

"Is something wrong?"

There was a silence; then Claire answered, "I don't know. I don't think so, but things aren't turning out quite the way I'd thought they would."

"Did something happen between you and Marc last night?" Brandy asked hopefully.

"Yes and no." At her friend's confused look, Claire quickly explained, "He invited me out onto the balcony. He said he wanted to ask me something. The moon was out. It was a beautiful night. I had on the teal gown. . . ."

"Yes?" Brandy was eager to hear what had happened.

"Do you know what he wanted to ask me? He wanted to ask me if I'd go to work for him as a tutor for the children after I'm finished working for you."

"A tutor?"

"A tutor," she repeated flatly.

The two women shared a pained look.

"Obviously, this man is going to need some more encouragement. I thought the two of you working together on the reception would help, and I suppose it did a little."

"I don't see how."

"You have to be more optimistic, Claire. Think about it this way. He likes you and respects you. He realizes you're going to be leaving and he doesn't want you to go. His emotions are still raw from Jennette's death, and he can't admit that he cares for you yet, so he asks you to be a tutor so you'll stay."

"You're a romantic, Brandy. I'd like to think that you're right, but I don't know."

"What have you got to lose? You obviously need more time with him, and this is the best way to get it. It could be worse."

"I know. He could have realized I was leaving and merely said good-bye."

"Did you give him an answer?"

"I told him yes, of course," Claire said with a sad smile. "You've taught me a lot about going after what I want."

Brandy smiled gently back at her. "Some of me is rubbing off on you."

"Yes, and I'm enjoying it, too."

"How soon did you tell him you'd start?"

"Whenever you thought we were done here."

"Why don't you plan on staying with me another week or two? Let's just let Mr. Marc LeFevre wait a little while for his 'tutor,' shall we?"

"Yes, but what do you want to do in the meantime?"

"Well, I've been thinking about taking riding lessons. Want to take them with me?"

After eating, Brandy and Claire sought out George, and he arranged for them to start riding that very day.

The days that followed passed quietly as a routine was established. Rafe was gone from early morning until dusk, returning to the house during the day only for the noon meal. At night, he and Brandy came together in heated matings, loving long into the early morning hours.

Brandy alternately dreaded his coming to her and longed for his embrace. She continually had to caution herself to remember why she was there, but there were times when for just a little while she was able to forget. Especially when she watched Rafe with her mother. As distant a man as he was, for some reason he seemed taken with her mother, and it was a mutual admiration, for her mother was constantly singing Rafe's praises to her. The trouble was, most of what her mother told her about Rafe was true, yet Brandy had to protect her heart. She knew what the future held for them.

Rafe returned to the house early one afternoon, his work in the fields done for the day. As he rode up the drive, he was pleasantly surprised to see Libby sitting in the shade on the veranda. The old woman's charm was winning him over, despite his best efforts to remain immune to her good and loving nature, and he smiled as he saw her finally recognize him and wave. He dismounted and was heading up the walk to the steps when it happened.

"You're back early," Libby was saying as she rose and started forth to meet him. She was concentrating on looking at Rafe and did not realize how close she was to the steps. She missed the top step and stumbled.

"Libby!" Rafe was only a short distance away when she fell, but he was unable to reach her in time to catch her or break the fall. He watched in horror as she landed heavily, and he was at her side in an instant. "Are you all right?"

She lay unmoving and the sight of her so hurt unnerved him. He scooped her up in his arms and ran up the steps, kicking open the front door and bellowing for George.

"What happened?" George came running from the back of the house.

"She fell. Send for the doctor! I don't know how badly she's hurt!" Rafe ordered as he took the stairs two at a time and rushed to lay her upon her bed.

George sent one servant for the physician and another to the stables to get Brandy and Claire. He went to Rafe as quickly as he could to see if there was anything more he could do. He found Rafe sitting on the edge of the bed, holding Libby's hand and talking to her in a soft, reassuring voice.

"Is she all right?"

"She's conscious, but she hit her head when she fell, so I want the doctor to take a look at her."

"I'll be all right," Libby said in a weak voice. "I just hate not being able to see well anymore. . . ."

Rafe squeezed her hand supportively. "You're going to have to learn not to rush."

"But I was so glad to see you. I was so glad you were home. I just wanted to talk to you for a while."

Her words touched him deeply. No one seemed to care if he was home or not, except Libby. "Well, talk away. You've got me all to yourself."

They were deep in conversation when Brandy, followed by Claire, came charging into the room.

"Mama?" Brandy cried frantically, seeing her mother lying on the bed.

"She's going to be mad at me," Libby said aside to Rafe, sounding much like a little child in trouble.

"Maybe for a minute or two, but as long as you're fine, she'll get over it," he returned with a half-grin.

"What happened?" Brandy asked as she knelt beside the bed.

"I wasn't looking and I fell," Libby offered. "Rafe rescued me."

Brandy looked up at her husband, her eyes filled with tears. "Is she all right?"

"She's going to be sore, but I don't think anything's broken. I had George send for the doctor, just in case."

"Thank you."

"I'm just sorry it happened," Rafe said.

"So am I," Libby said with a grimace. "From now on, I'll behave myself and stay as far away from those steps as I can, unless someone is with me."

"That's a very good idea," Rafe stated firmly. "I like women falling all over themselves for me, but this wasn't what I had in mind."

Libby laughed at his dry humor, and Brandy managed a smile. They stayed with her, keeping an eye on her until the doctor came and pronounced that she was bruised but would be fine in a few days.

When he'd gone, Brandy and Rafe retired to his study downstairs. Rafe had just poured himself a glass of whiskey and had gone to look out the window.

"I understand now," Rafe told her as he took a deep drink of his whiskey. For some reason, he felt the need of the liquor's reinforcement tonight.

"Understand what?" Brandy looked at him curiously.

"I understand why you felt guilty about leaving her while you were working on the *Pride*. She's a very sweet lady, and she needs someone with her to keep watch so nothing happens to her."

"I had Althea, but if something bad had happened while I was away, it would have been awful."

"Well, it's good that you're here now."

He wasn't looking at her as he spoke, but was still staring out the window. Brandy wondered if he really meant it.

Rafe continued to drink all night, which was unusual for him. He did not understand the strange, troubling emotion that gripped him. He had felt helpless in the face of Libby's accident. It had torn him apart to see her fall, and he was angry at his own inability to stop her from hurting herself. The only good thing about the whole situation was that she hadn't been seriously injured.

Brandy had already retired when he made his way to bed that night. His mood was unsettled as he entered the bedroom. He undressed in silence, knowing she was asleep. But as he lay down beside her, he had to touch her, to feel her warmth surrounding him, to bury himself within her and forget everything but the sweetness of being one with her.

Neither of them spoke as he reached for her. In silence, he sought her lips, the softness of her throat, the fullness of her breasts. She held him to her, savoring the feeling of peace between them tonight. She dared not question it. She didn't want to ruin the poignancy of their coming together.

When at last he moved over her and claimed her for his own, she took him deep inside her, and they moved together, giving and sharing, until love's glory swept over them. They slept, their limbs entwined as well as their hearts.

It was almost a week before Libby was up and moving around normally again, and another week before the day arrived for Claire to move to Marc's. Marc came for her, and her parting from Brandy was bittersweet.

"I'm going to miss you." Claire gave her a hug.

"If you ever want to play poker, you just send word," Brandy told her.

"I will. I'll keep in touch."

"Please do. I'll be thinking about you."

"I'm so glad you and Rafe are happy. I'm so glad everything worked out for you."

"So am I," she answered, ignoring the bite of her conscience. Claire had come into this arrangement not knowing the truth, and she would go away still blissfully ignorant. That was good. No one else needed to know her torment.

Rafe left on a two-day business trip the following week, and the time passed slowly for Brandy. The days were quiet and the nights, alone in their bed, seemed interminable. Brandy had thought she would welcome the reprieve, but she missed the warmth of him next to her, the excitement of his caress and the ecstasy of loving him. There were times when she found herself fantasizing about a normal relationship with Rafe, of being a wife who was loved and who loved. Often, she found herself thinking of him, longing for his kiss or just wanting to hear the sound of his voice. Her mother talked about him endlessly, telling Brandy how wonderful he was, until she thought maybe he should have married her mother instead of her. When news came at last that his carriage was returning, she and her mother both hurried out to greet him. This time Libby stayed wisely back, waiting for Rafe to come to her, rather than risk a fall.

Rafe caught sight of them waiting for him and felt a stirring in his heart. He glanced down at the boxes he held and wondered why he felt so anxious about giving them the gifts he was bringing. He'd spent several hours the day before trying to find just the right present for Libby, and he'd finally located a beautiful embroidered shawl that would look lovely on her. He knew she didn't have anything like it, so he bought it for her without a thought, cost be damned. He'd also bought Brandy an engraved wooden jewelry box. He hoped she'd like it.

As soon as the carriage stopped, he climbed out and went to meet them.

"Hello, Brandy . . . Libby."

"Welcome home, Rafe," Brandy said softly, unsure how to act with him. Her heartbeat quickened at the sight of him.

"This is for you," he said, giving Brandy a quick kiss as he handed her the gift. Then he turned to Libby, and he couldn't help smiling.

"It's about time you came home," Libby declared,

giving him a big kiss on the cheek as he went to her.

"Miss me, did you?"

"Absolutely. It was too quiet around here without you."

He grinned at her openness. "Here, this is for you," he said, handing her the remaining box.

"You brought me a present, too?" she asked, wide-eyed at the thoughtfulness of his gesture.

"I hope you like it." He waited to see her reaction to his gift.

"I'll love it, whatever it is, because it's from you," she assured him as she lovingly touched the box and then untied the ribbon. When she finally opened it, her expression was rapt. "Oh, Rafe . . . It's the best present I've ever had."

Libby looked up at him as her hand caressed the soft fabric of the shawl.

"You like it?"

"I think it's beautiful. You are the dearest boy. . . ." She kissed his cheek again as she moved inside to show Brandy the special gift Rafe had brought her.

At her approval, he suddenly felt ten feet tall and strong enough to defeat an entire army. He glanced at Brandy and saw her poignant expression.

"Do you like your present?" he asked gruffly.

"Yes, it's lovely. . . ." She was clutching the jewelry box to her heart, but it wasn't his gift of the box that had touched her heart, it was his treatment of her mother. As she stared at him, she saw a man who cared about small children, a man who was tender and concerned about a little, old, defenseless woman, a man who was a magnificent, responsive lover, a man who couldn't possibly be as harsh as the Rafe Marchand who'd blackmailed her into marriage.

Something blossomed within her, and in that moment, Brandy knew a terrible secret. Somehow, some way, this man had won her heart. She loved him.

Suddenly needing to get away from him, she started inside. "I'd better stay with her and make sure she's all right."

He merely nodded and watched her go, wondering at the sudden strain that had developed between them.

A few hours later they had dinner, and Libby came downstairs to the table wearing his shawl.

"I thought it might be a bit cool this evening," she told him with a proud smile.

They all knew the night was sultry and warm, but it didn't matter. Libby was happy, and that was all that mattered.

Later, after they'd eaten and Libby had gone upstairs to bed, Rafe went into his study to work for a while. Brandy had debated going on up to their bedroom to wait for him, but she so desperately wanted to talk to him, to tell him how much his kindness to her mother meant, that she followed him.

"Rafe?"

He looked up at her interruption, his expression questioning.

"I just wanted to thank you for being so good to Mama. You know how much she loves you, and your thinking of her this way is . . . well, special. Thank you. No one has ever treated her this way before."

"Your mother is one of the nicest women I've ever met. I like her."

"And your mother did a fine job in raising a son to be so caring and thoughtful of others' needs."

At the mention of his mother, Rafe recoiled. It was

impossible for him to think of Libby and his mother in the same context. For a short time, he'd been enjoying the feeling of family that Libby encouraged, but at the mention of his mother, his past came slamming back with a vengeance.

"You know, it's strange," Brandy was saying as she slipped into the chair before his desk, "but you've never told me about your mother. What was she like?"

"There's very good reason why I don't speak of my mother."

Brandy heard the harshness in his tone and was surprised. "You didn't get along with her?"

He wanted nothing to do with the memories Brandy seemed intent on dredging up. He had to slam the door on them and on Brandy. He couldn't let her that close. He had been without a family for all these years, and he didn't need to change things now. He was just fine alone.

"You want to know about my mother," he said coldly. "What do you want to know? How she cheated on my father every chance she got? How she publicly humiliated him?"

"I'm sorry, I didn't know." She heard his pain and rage and wanted to say or do something to help, but she knew there was nothing she could do.

"There's more that you don't know. Shall I tell you?" He didn't wait for a response, but went on with a vengeance, "The reason the one bedroom upstairs is never opened is because that's the master bedroom suite where my father and I came home and found my mother in bed with another man."

She gasped, shocked. She could imagine the effect walking in on such a scene would have had on a young boy, and she wanted to go to Rafe, to ease the horror that must still live within his soul. But his icy look froze her where she stood.

"And the room next door?" He gestured toward his father's study before she could speak. "That's the room where my father decided he couldn't go on without my mother after she deserted us. That's the room where he took his own life rather than face a future without her. So, you're right. I don't speak of my mother. She died several years after my father, and I didn't mourn the loss."

"But your family . . ." She thought he must have had aunts and uncles who cared about him. Surely, there had been someone . . .

"I have no family, and I like it that way. Don't think that I'm going to change, because I'm not."

"I had just hoped that—"

He cut her off. "You and I both know why you're here. There is no more to our relationship than that. If I'm kind to your mother while she's living here with me, it's because it pleases me to do so, and for no other reason. Now, if you'll excuse me?" He gave her a dismissive look. "I have work to do."

Coldly dismissed, Brandy quit the room, leaving him alone. She had gone in to see him with such high spirits. She had even entertained the faint, but desperate hope that he was beginning to have feelings for her, as she did for him. But hers had been a fool's dream. Rafe didn't love her and he never would. She managed to hide her tears until she was alone in their bedroom. She couldn't let him know that she cared.

The nausea started early one morning a few weeks later. At first, Brandy thought she was just sick, and she lingered in bed longer than usual that day. When it returned the next two mornings, but disappeared by afternoon, she began to realize the truth. She could only thank heaven that Rafe had left the house early enough so that he was not a witness to her telling behavior.

Frantic, Brandy counted the days since her last womanly time, and there could be no denying the truth of it. She was with child. She had already missed a cycle.

A sense of gloom and crushing despair overcame her. She wanted her child—her child and Rafe's child. Yet the bargain she'd made would force her to give up the baby. She could tell no one of her condition—not her mother, not Rafe, not the servants. She had to pretend this wasn't happening and try to find a way to escape what fate had dealt her. There had to be a way out, if only she could find it.

Night after night, she prayed fervently for some idea to free herself—a plan, a way to buy her way out of the debt that bound her, a way to claim freedom for herself and her child. It all came down to money. She needed money if she was to save the baby, and money was the one thing she did not have.

It was then that she remembered her encounter with Sam Foster the night of their reception at Marc's home. He had told her if she ever wanted to get up a poker game, just to let him know.

Poker . . . poker . . . That would be her salvation, she just knew it.

Brandy began to plot. If she was careful, she could gather enough cash around the house to start the game. The big thing would be getting word to Sam and arranging the game so Rafe would never find out. She didn't want him to know what she was doing. She didn't want him to know she was even pregnant. She would win enough playing with Sam Foster to pay off her debt entirely, and then she would be free of Rafe and the heartbreak of their sham of a marriage forever.

Chapter Twenty-five

Rafe stood at the rail of the steamboat staring sightlessly out at the passing countryside. Things had been tense between him and Brandy ever since the scene in his study, and he was glad now that he'd had to make this trip to New Orleans so he could get away. He needed some time to think.

Remembering that night, now, and the look on Brandy's face after he'd told her that he had no family and liked it that way, Rafe once again felt the pain that had struck him then. It hadn't been until that moment that he'd realized how closed his life had been and how tightly he'd held his emotions in check all these years.

Rafe gave himself a mental shake. He didn't understand what was happening to him. He almost wished Marc was there with him so he could talk to him about it, but there was no way he could confide in Marc without telling him the whole truth—and that could be ugly. He knew how much Marc liked and respected Brandy, and he could well imagine what his friend would say to him about the "arrangement" he'd forced her into.

Inwardly grimacing, Rafe started to go into the dining room for dinner, then changed his mind and headed for the men's saloon. A whiskey sounded much better to him than food did right then.

One whiskey led to another, and it was near midnight when Rafe finally decided he was having his last drink. He'd been sitting alone at a quiet table all evening, thinking and drinking—neither of which had done much to settle his dilemma. He'd only grown more befuddled and more miserable as time went on.

He'd been about to call it a night when he heard several men at the bar talking about Miss Brandy on the *Pride*. Sitting back, he'd listened to what they had to say, and he smiled ruefully at their talk of how wonderful Brandy was, how beautiful she was, and how utterly unattainable she was. The men at the bar all agreed that the man who won her was going to be one lucky fellow. As drunk as he was, Rafe was tempted to introduce himself to them as her husband, but he stayed where he was, even more confused than ever.

It was in the early morning hours when he finally made his way to his cabin. He fell upon the solitary bed still fully dressed, and, in a benumbed stupor, he reached for the wife he'd left behind at Bellerive. The reality of his lonely bed sent a shock to the core of his being and jarred him to face the reality of his life and of his feelings.

He wanted Brandy more than he'd ever wanted any woman. All he had to do was lay a hand upon her, and he couldn't stop himself from loving her.

Loving her . . . ?

Rafe frowned into the darkness. Did he love her? A few months before, the thought would have disturbed him greatly, but in this moment as he lay alone in the night, it seemed right. He let his thoughts drift over Brandy and the memories they'd made together. He remembered the first time he'd seen her on the *Pride,* how lovely she'd been and how very good at poker. He thought of her dangerous encounter with Jackson, and a cold sweat beaded his brow as he realized how close she'd come to being killed that night. Rafe drew a ragged breath. If something had happened to her then, he would never have known the beauty of her love. He thought of the drunken Jones, too, and grew angry at the thought of the other man's hands on her. Brandy was a woman made to be loved, not abused. The memory of her first kiss as she'd rescued him from Lottie Demers brought a chuckle from him, and it was then that he had the answer to the question that had been tormenting him for days.

In the darkness, Rafe smiled. Brandy was everything those men had said about her and more. He admired her more than he'd ever admired any woman. Where his own mother had been a liar, Brandy was always honest. Where his own mother had not known the word honor, Brandy had lived up to every commitment she'd made. She was kind and gentle, brave and smart. Her spirit was indomitable, and Rafe finally admitted to himself that he did love her. He wanted to spend the rest of his life with her, loving her and making her happy.

When Rafe fell asleep a short time later, his dreams of Brandy were sweet. He was up at dawn, mentally preparing a battle plan for how he was going to handle his lovely wife. First things first. He would conclude his business as quickly as possible and get back home. He wanted to talk to her face to face, to tell her that he loved her and wanted their marriage to be a real one—forever. The thought excited him, and he couldn't wait to return.

He took a room at the hotel and sent word to his business associate asking if their appointment could be moved up to that afternoon. He had told Brandy that he would be gone a week, for he'd intended to pay other business calls while he was there, but all that mattered to him right now was getting back home to his wife. When he received word that the other man would see him that very day, Rafe was pleased. If all went well, he would be home the next evening. The thought appealed. Two nights without Brandy would be rough; three without her would be devastating.

With several hours to pass before his meeting, Rafe decided to do some shopping. Apart from the flowers he'd brought her on board the *Pride*, he'd never truly courted her as she deserved to be courted. With that in mind, he began to shop in earnest, hoping to find something that would be a keepsake, something that would remind both of them of the importance of this trip and how he'd finally awakened to the knowledge that he loved her.

Rafe knew she was probably still very hurt by his cold cruelty that night in his study. He regretted that night more than he could ever say, but he knew there was no going back. They had been close, and he had been frightened by the intensity of what he'd been feeling. It had been a purely defensive move on his part to shove her away from him as he had. He hadn't had that intimacy with anyone since his mother's betrayal, and learning to trust again was going to be difficult for him. Difficult though it might be, he wanted a future with Brandy, so he would have to learn. He only hoped that she cared enough about him to help him through it.

As Rafe walked the streets of New Orleans anticipating his homecoming, a single fear still haunted him. He had not bared his soul to anyone since his father's death, and the possibility remained that he might return home to tell Brandy he loved her, only to have her scorn him. The possibility was disturbing, but he found the thought of a life without her far more devastating. He wanted her to be his wife because he loved her and because she loved him, too, and not for any other reason.

Rafe looked up then as he passed a small shop that carried china and crystal, and in the window he saw a crystal heart. It occurred to him that the heart was the perfect symbol of his love for Brandy. He had protected his own heart for so long, afraid to lose it for fear that it might be broken. When he went to Brandy to tell her that he loved her, he would give her the fragile heart and ask her to treasure it and guard it with care, for it represented his love for her.

A few minutes later, he was on his way again with the small wrapped package in hand. He was smiling as he headed for his business meeting. He couldn't wait to get home.

Brandy was nervous, but she was doing everything in her power to hide it. She had maintained an outward calm all day, and there was only a short time left now.

She swallowed nervously as she rested a hand on

her still-flat stomach. She wondered if she was doing the right thing, then realized she had no other choice. Rafe had taken all choices from her when he'd forced her into this unholy union. Her hands were trembling, and with an effort, she brought her nervousness under control.

It was working out perfectly. She had nothing to be nervous about. The plan had come to her that night when she'd been praying for a way out of the horrible situation she found herself in. She was pregnant with Rafe's child, and she had to find a way to get the money to pay him back so she wouldn't be forced to leave her baby after it was born. It was out of that desperation that her idea to contact Sam had come, and she had sent him a discreet message the day Rafe had left only to hear back from Sam the very next day. It seemed his wife had gone out of town to visit her ailing aunt, and the following night would be the perfect time for a poker game—if she could make it.

Brandy had told the servants that she'd been invited to dinner with the Fosters, which wasn't altogether a lie, and she was now just about ready to go. She'd gotten together enough money to start her off, and she prayed even harder that she would win a hand or two early to bolster her finances. Her mother had gone to bed early, so there were few questions to answer there. She'd donned one of her gambling dresses from the *Pride*. The carriage was to be brought around front for her at seven-thirty, so she was due downstairs in just a few minutes.

Standing before the mirror, Brandy studied her reflection, wanting to make sure she looked her best. Sam had assured her in his note that none of the men who were invited tonight knew Rafe, so her identity would be safe. It was all in good fun anyway as far as Sam was concerned.

Brandy was the only one taking this evening seriously, and that was because her whole future hinged on her winning big tonight. She had to do this. She had no alternative. How else could she face what the future held for her? How could she possibly tell her mother the terms she'd agreed to before marrying Rafe? And even more devastating, how could she possibly leave her very own baby? Desperation drove her as she dabbed perfume at her pulse points and took one final look at her reflection before turning to leave the bedroom.

Rafe couldn't remember the last time he'd been this excited about returning home. Soon he would be with Brandy. That was all that mattered.

The trip upriver had seemed to take forever, but at last they had landed at Natchez and now he was on the last leg of the journey home. Home . . . The word felt right now. Before he'd always been going to Bellerive, and he might have occasionally called it home, but tonight it truly felt like a homecoming.

There was no denying that he was nervous. It wasn't going to be easy for him to bare his soul to her, but he was going to do whatever he had to, to let her know that he loved her and wanted a future with her.

The carriage seemed to be going at a snail's pace. He was tempted to tell the driver to step down, that he'd take over the team himself, but he controlled himself. It was only a matter of a few minutes now and he would be with her again. He smiled.

Rafe glanced down at the gift-wrapped present he held. He'd refused to put it in his bags for fear that it might be broken. It was too important for that. It symbolized his life and how he felt about Brandy. It had to be perfect when he gave it to her. He slipped it into the pocket of his jacket for safekeeping as they turned up the drive that led to the house.

It was just beginning to get dark, so he was eagerly looking forward to the long, quiet evening ahead of them. He could hardly wait to see Brandy and give her his gift.

As soon as the carriage stopped, Rafe was out the door. He hurried inside, surprising George, who hadn't been expecting him, but who had come to the front of the house to see who'd pulled up in the drive.

"Why, Master Rafe . . . It's you," the old servant greeted him. "You're back early, sir."

"I know," he said, smiling happily at the man who'd been through so much with him. "I was missing my wife. Is she upstairs?"

"Yes, sir," George told him. He thought it was good that Rafe was back, so he could accompany Miss Brandy to the Fosters'.

Rafe thought about climbing the stairs at his normal pace, but he was so close to her now, he took them two at a time. He had to see her. He wanted to kiss her. He needed to see the look in her eyes when he gave her his heart.

The bedroom door was closed, and he didn't even bother to knock. Without a thought, he threw it wide and walked in.

"Rafe!" Brandy said his name in shock as she dropped the vial of perfume she'd been using.

"Brandy, I—" he began, and then stopped cold at the look of guilt on her face. His heart constricted painfully as he stared at her. She was wearing one of her gambling dresses and was standing before the mirror obviously getting ready to go out some-where—but where?

Memories of another time slashed at Rafe, and he remembered the scene with his mother. In crystal clarity, it all came back to him—the horror of finding her naked in bed with the other man, the misery of listening to her fight with his father, the pain of dis-covering that she'd never wanted him or loved him and never would.

"What are you doing?" he asked, trying to come to grips with what was happening. He advanced into the room slowly.

"Nothing . . . just trying on an old dress, that's all," she lied, and her nervousness showed. "You're back early."

"Obviously," he drawled as he spied her drawstring purse lying on the bed. In two strides he was there, grabbing it up and finding all the money she'd put away just for tonight. "Going out, were you?"

He lifted his gaze to hers, saw the turmoil there and was filled with a terrible fury. He had thought she was different from other women. He had thought that he loved her. What a fool he'd been!

Rage at her for proving to be just like his mother, and loathing at himself for being so easily fooled, filled him.

"Answer me!" he snarled as he cast her purse aside in a furious gesture that sent the money flying about the room.

Brandy saw the anger in his eyes and knew there was no point in trying to lie her way out of the sit-uation. She had never dreamed he would come home ahead of schedule, but he had, and now she was caught. There was no alternative but to face him with the truth. She gave a defiant lift of her chin.

"Yes, I was going out!" she snapped, her fury matching his but for completely different reasons. She had wanted to save her baby, and now she had no hope. "I was to be the hostess at a poker game at Sam Foster's home tonight."

"Sam Foster?"

"He's an old friend. He gambled with me often on the steamer, and he told me at the reception that if I ever wanted to play poker again, to let him know. So Miss Brandy of the *Pride* was going to make a command appearance tonight. The stakes were going to be high, and I was praying with all my might that I would win and win big so I could get out of this sham of a marriage!"

At her words, his outrage grew. He had fallen in love with her, but she wanted nothing more than to get away from him!

"Well, madam," he said in a low, lethal voice, "if you're so intent on getting out of this marriage, why don't we just work on making that possible?"

He tossed off his jacket and began unbuttoning his shirt as he stalked toward her, the predator toward his prey.

"No . . . Rafe . . ." She backed up.

"Oh, yes. You said it yourself. You want out, and we know the terms of the agreement, don't we? I know exactly how to get you out of this 'sham of a marriage'. . . ."

He snared her wrist in an unyielding iron grip and pulled her along with him toward the bed. Tonight, he would not be denied.

Brandy felt sick inside. She'd seen Rafe angry before, on the steamboat, but it had been nothing like this. This was a cold fury that frightened her far more.

"Rafe . . ."

"There's really no need for talk," he told her as he pushed her down on the bed. "We have nothing left to say to each other anyway."

Rafe joined her on the bed, reaching for her, caressing her through the silk of her gown. He'd meant to demean her, to make her realize what her betrayal had done to him, but as he held her body against his, his anger fled. Passion, hot and driving, exploded within him. Brandy was his. . . .

Brandy had been trembling when Rafe came to her. She'd feared his anger and had not known what to expect from him, but at the touch of his lips on hers, hard and demanding at first, but then becoming soft and coaxing, her trembling was for another reason. Even though she knew he didn't love her, she could never deny her need for him.

His clothes were discarded and her gown was shed. The silken material ripped in their haste to be close, but neither noticed. Their need was too great, their desire too wild, to care about such things. They needed to be together. Nothing could keep them apart.

Rafe's hands upon Brandy aroused her to a fever pitch, and she returned his caresses, wanting to excite him in the same way. His body was hard against her, and she accepted him as he came to her. Theirs was a turbulent, desperate mating. Driven by passions they couldn't control, they moved together in a frenzy of physical need, seeking, then finding that ultimate release.

After their lovemaking, they always lay together, savoring the closeness of being one, the joy of holding each other. But not tonight.

As Rafe's passion cooled, his sanity returned, and

he went cold inside. The fury that had driven him earlier had been erased now, and in its wake, he felt nothing for her—nothing at all.

Rafe withdrew from Brandy without a word and began to gather up his clothes. He dressed, then picked up his jacket and left the room. This was one night he would spend in his study.

Brandy had wanted to cling to him as he left the bed, but she had not dared. She had suddenly felt naked and exposed before him, and she'd drawn the sheet up over herself. When he closed the door silently behind him, it terrified her more than if he'd slammed it in a fit of rage. Outbursts of anger she could handle. Cold indifference would be terrible to deal with.

Alone, Brandy could no longer hold back the tears. Great sobs wracked her as she realized that there could be no going back. What had existed of their fragile relationship had been destroyed, and her one hope to earn enough money to buy her way out of the marriage was gone. Her future with Rafe stretched before her, bleak and unforgiving. She wondered how she would ever survive.

Rafe came downstairs to find the carriage waiting at the front door.

"George!"

The servant appeared almost immediately. He'd expected Rafe to be in a good mood, having come home so early, and he was surprised to find that he was surly. "Yes, sir?"

"Send a note to Sam Foster telling him that Brandy won't be coming over tonight, and dismiss the carriage. Nobody's going anywhere this evening."

"Yes, sir."

"I'll be in my study and I do not want to be disturbed—by anyone. Is that clear?"

"Yes, sir."

Rafe went in and locked the door. As he moved to light the lamp on his desk, he tossed his coat across a chair. It was then that the small package fell out of his pocket, and Rafe was reminded of how happy and excited he'd been about coming home just a short time before.

He stared at the box, then went to pick it up after lighting the lamp. His expression was filled with loathing as he looked down at it in his hand. Striding to the small bar, he poured himself a tumbler of whiskey and downed it in one fiery swallow. He poured another ample draught into the glass, then walked to his desk to sit down. In disgust, he threw the box he'd so carefully brought back from New Orleans on the desktop.

It was several hours and many whiskeys later when he finally opened the box. As he looked at the crystal heart, he cursed his own stupidity in believing Brandy was different from other women. How could he have forgotten all the lessons he'd learned through the years? He would never forget again . . . never.

Rafe took the crystal heart out of the box. It felt cold to his touch, and he thought that most appropriate right now. For an instant, the memory of how excited he'd been when he'd first seen it in the shop window returned, and in a flash of uncontrollable anger he threw the heart with all his power against the wall. The heart shattered into a thousand tiny fragments on impact, and crashed to the floor.

Rafe had thought that he would feel some satisfaction at having destroyed it, but he only felt empty and alone. He drank another whiskey and waited for morning.

As dawn brightened the eastern horizon, he emerged from the study. He called George to him.

"I want you to open the locked bedroom today and see that Miss Brandy's things are moved in there."

"You want her in the locked room?" George repeated, shocked by Rafe's order. No one had been in there in years.

"That's what I said. I'll be gone for most of the day. See that it's done before I return tonight."

"Yes, sir."

Brandy passed a quiet day with her mother. Brandy told her how Rafe had come home early and was already back at work out on the plantation somewhere. Libby expressed her wish that he'd come back to the house so she could see him. Brandy said nothing.

It was mid-afternoon when a great weariness overcame Brandy, and she excused herself to go upstairs for a nap. As she went down the hall, she saw that the door to the locked bedroom was open. Curious, she went to see what was going on. Tilda, one of the maids, was busy putting clean linens on the bed.

"Tilda? Why is this room open? Rafe told me it's always locked."

"I know, ma'am, but this morning, Mr. Rafe said that we were to move your things out of his bedroom and put them in here."

Brandy felt all the color drain out of her face as she stared at the servant. She recovered only after an awkward moment of stunned silence. "Yes, yes, of course. That's fine. I was going to lie down for a while, so I guess I should do that in here now."

"Yes, ma'am. I've already put all your things in the closet and dresser."

"Thank you."

Tilda quickly left, and Brandy walked slowly into the room where Rafe and his father had found his mother in bed with another man. She could almost picture the horror of that night so long ago, and she realized why she'd been banished to this room—Rafe believed her to be no better than his mother.

Pain stabbed at her heart; yet, even as she was hurt by his rejection of her, in the long run, she knew it was for the best. If they were separated this way, it would be possible for her to hide her condition from him for a little longer, and the one thing she needed was time. . . . Time to find a way out of her dilemma . . . time to save her baby and herself . . . .

Brandy sat down on the edge of the bed cautiously, testing its softness, and then lay down. Though she was nearly exhausted from her emotional turmoil and from the new and precious life she carried within her, sleep would not come.

Chapter Twenty-six

It was late, long after midnight. Brandy lay in her solitary bed unable to sleep. She was tired, but that wasn't unusual, for it seemed she was tired all the time now. Still, she needed to sleep, and sleep wouldn't come.

Since that fateful day when Rafe had returned from New Orleans early, he had not made love to her or shown her any outward affection. She had thought living with him before had been difficult, but this was becoming unbearable. Night after night, she'd waited, anticipating his coming to her bed, but he had made no effort to seek her out. Several nights, she'd heard the sound of a horse and had gotten up in time to watch him ride away into the darkness. She'd never known what time he'd returned, for she'd always fallen into an exhausted slumber before then. Her heart ached and misery haunted her soul, for she was certain on those lonely nights that he was seeking out the warmth of Mirabelle's bed. It crushed Brandy to think of him in the beautiful widow's arms, but there was nothing she could do. It was clear that he wanted nothing more to do with her.

Her mother had noticed the coolness between them. When she'd remarked on Rafe's aloofness and the fact that Brandy now had her own bedroom, Brandy had made up a plausible story that he had been used to living alone so long that he needed more privacy. Her mother had seemed to believe her, but sometimes Brandy wondered.

The days passed in an endless stream. She'd forced herself to keep busy so she wouldn't have too much time to think. She'd received an occasional note from Claire letting her know how things were going with Marc and the children, but other than that there was a tedious monotony to her life. Keeping her pregnancy a secret from everyone had become her foremost goal. She had to hide her condition until she could find a way to escape from the hell her marriage had become.

Sighing, Brandy rolled over and sought comfort, but there was no peace to be found, only desolation and fear for her baby's future.

Rafe sat in his study, downing another shot of whiskey. He held the empty glass up and studied it thoughtfully in the lamplight. There had been a time in his life when a few whiskeys had helped him to see things a bit more clearly, but not anymore. He'd been relying on the liquor's blessed numbness for many days now, and nothing was any clearer to him. If anything, his life seemed even more complicated.

He still loved her. . . .

He'd tried to deny it. He'd tried to ignore the feelings that swept through him every time he saw her, but he could only hide from the truth for so long. He did love her, and all the whiskey in the world couldn't wash away the truth of it.

Rafe considered having another drink, but decided against it. Past nights had proven that more whiskeys didn't help. He might sleep for a few hours, but when he awoke, the torment was still there.

Shoving the glass aside on his desk, he stood up. He swayed, a bit unsteady, then got his bearings. He felt like a sea captain on a rolling deck, and he grinned stupidly at the image that conjured up in his liquor-soddened mind. *Captain of my ship . . . Master of my fate . . .*

He gave a snort of derision. He couldn't even master his own runaway emotions—how could he possibly be the master of his own fate?

Brandy . . .

She slipped sweetly into his thoughts again, and he felt the heat settle in his body. Even after all that had happened, he still desired her, still wanted her. He had never known bliss as wonderful as making love to her. He had considered seeking out Mirabelle, had gone so far as to ride halfway to her house several nights, but in the end, he'd just spent long hours on horseback, riding to the wind, trying to find solace for his soul.

Brandy . . .

Visions of her played in his mind and would not be dismissed. He remembered how nervous she'd been on their wedding night and how he'd cheated at the strip-poker game. He thought of her innocence and how responsive she'd been. Memories of how sweet her kisses were, of how silken her skin was to his touch, of how perfect it had felt to be one with her sent desire pounding through him. He had hoped the liquor would dull his need, but it hadn't. He wondered if this was how his father had felt about his mother. He might despise her, but, God help him, he still wanted her.

Driven by demons that he could not banish, Rafe left his study and started up the stairs. He did not pause before her door, but threw it open and stood silhouetted in the doorway, staring at her where she lay in his mother's bed.

"Rafe . . . ?" Brandy had just been about to drift off when the door opened, and, startled, she sat up in bed, clutching the sheet to her breasts.

Rafe stood unmoving in the doorway. On the way up the steps, he had been determined that nothing was going to stop him from making love to her. But as he stared at her now, the memory of his mother hit him with such force that all his passion and need drained instantly from him. He remained where he was, watching her, his expression inscrutable. Then, in complete disgust, he turned abruptly and walked away.

For just a moment when the door had first opened, Brandy didn't know what to think. She'd known a flicker of hope that he was coming to her because he couldn't live without her anymore, because he wanted her and loved her, but as quickly as the thought had come, she'd pushed it away. This was her real life, not a childish fantasy. And then he was gone without a word, leaving her feeling even more terrible than she had before.

Rising, Brandy closed the door, and then leaned heavily against it as silent sobs wracked her. She didn't know how much longer she could keep this up. Surely, working as a maid somewhere would be far better than living like this. All her life she had thought the worst thing was not knowing where your next meal was coming from, but now she had learned a bitter lesson and knew better. She would rather be hungry and know she was loved than to have all the riches money could provide and be alone and hated.

Brandy stumbled back to her bed and curled up there, resting one hand protectively on the curve of her stomach. She did not sleep at all that night.

Rafe returned to the house early one afternoon the following week. He was leaving on another business trip to St. Louis the next day and had some paperwork to complete before he could go. Libby was in the parlor, and she came to meet him as he entered the house.

"Well, this is a pleasant surprise," she told him with a welcoming smile. She thought the world of him and was worried about the coolness she'd noticed between him and Brandy.

Rafe couldn't help but smile back at Libby. She was, indeed, the only bright spot in his days anymore. "I've got to go to St. Louis tomorrow for another meeting, so there were things I had to finish up here first."

"Oh, you're leaving us again. . . ." Libby was truly disappointed and it sounded in her voice.

"Don't worry. I'll be back."

"Lunch is almost ready. Do you want to eat with me? I've been rather lonely at lunch lately."

"I'd love to eat with you, but why have you been lonely? Where's Brandy?" he asked.

"She hasn't been feeling well these last few days,

although she probably didn't tell you because she didn't want to bother you."

"Not feeling well?" He frowned at the thought that she might be ill. "What's wrong?"

"She never says exactly, but I do know she's been a bit pale lately and resting a lot in the afternoons."

Tilda came to tell Libby that the meal was ready, and Rafe let her know that he would be eating, too. He and Libby passed a relaxed meal together, talking of everything except Brandy. When they were through, Rafe stood to excuse himself.

"I think I'll go check on my wife, and then be about my work."

"I hope you get it all done."

Leaving Libby in the dining room, Rafe went up to Brandy's bedroom and stopped outside the door. He hesitated there, wondering exactly what he should do. If she was asleep and he knocked, he'd wake her, and Libby had said that she wasn't feeling well. The thought of her suffering in any way troubled him, and he wanted to make sure she was all right before he left for St. Louis. Cautiously and quietly, he opened the door to let himself in.

The sight of Brandy sleeping, curled on her side on the bed, did not affect him today as it had the other night when he'd been drinking so heavily. He moved into the room silently and came to stand at the bedside. His gaze was warm as it swept over Brandy. She was wearing just her chemise; the light cover she'd been using was a tangle about her hips. Rafe saw right away that Libby had been right. Brandy's color was pale. She looked fragile almost. He let his gaze drift lower, and it was then that he saw the undeniable swell of her stomach.

Rafe felt a burst of joy as he stared at the proof of

her condition. Brandy wasn't sick. Brandy was having his baby! He wondered how he could have been so unseeing not to have known that she was with child.

As the moment of Rafe's excitement passed, though, reality bared itself to him. She had wanted a way out of their marriage, and now she had it. This was the beginning of the end.

Brandy came awake slowly, her eyes fluttering open to find Rafe standing over her with the strangest expression on his face. Realizing her state of undress, she quickly grabbed for the cover and shielded herself from his view. "Rafe? What is it?"

"When were you planning to tell me?" he demanded.

"Tell you what?" she countered defensively, hoping against hope that he hadn't seen, but somehow knowing just from his look that he had.

"That you were pregnant," Rafe said flatly.

She saw the cold look in his eyes, and the pain of all that had happened between them welled up inside her. "Never, if I'd had my way!"

Her words were almost a physical blow to him, and he fought back, sneering, "Ah, but you should be happy about the baby, Brandy. You said yourself that all you wanted was to get out of our marriage, and we both know the terms."

"Yes, we do know the terms, don't we? When this is all over, you'll have just what you wanted, and that's all that really matters to you, isn't it? That Rafe Marchand gets exactly what he wants, when he wants it."

He smiled thinly at her. "Rest well, madam."

He left the room.

The door closed behind him with a finality that

crushed Brandy. She stared after him, wanting to cry, but no tears would come. Instead, a cold, hard logic filled her, and she knew what she had to do. She had to get away with her baby while she still could.

Brandy agonized through the night, trying to decide what to tell her mother, and finally she decided that the only way to handle it was with the truth. She waited until Rafe had departed the following day, then took her mother upstairs to her bedroom where she knew they could talk in private.

"What's the matter, honey?" Libby asked Brandy when they were alone. "Rafe was worried about you yesterday after I told him how you hadn't been feeling well. Are you feeling worse today?"

Brandy almost gave a heartless laugh at her mother's observation that Rafe had been worried about her. She was certain he hadn't come up to her room because he was concerned—puzzled maybe, but worried about her? Never. "Actually, I'm feeling better today, Mama."

"Then why all this secrecy? What do you want to talk about that couldn't be said downstairs?"

Brandy took her hand and led her to one of the chairs in the room. "Sit down, Mama. There's something important I have to tell you."

"You think I need to be sitting down to hear this?" Libby looked at her questioningly.

"Yes."

Libby did as she was told, frowning and worried now. Something was very wrong with her daughter, and she didn't know what. "All right. I'm sitting down. Now, tell me. What in the world is going on?"

Brandy stood there before her mother for a moment, trying to get her thoughts in order. She'd known it was going to be difficult, but she hadn't imagined just how difficult until now.

"Mama . . ." She glanced at her mother and saw her expectant look, then forged ahead. "Mama . . . I'm pregnant."

Libby's expression went from puzzled to joyous in the blink of an eye.

"Oh, Brandy!" she exclaimed, jumping up to hug her. "This is wonderful! Does Rafe know? Have you told him yet?" She couldn't imagine that he knew, for he had been very quiet last night and again this morning. His conversations with her when they'd been together before he'd left had been polite, but he'd said nothing to suggest that he knew he would soon be a father and she would soon be a grandmother.

"Oh, yes. Rafe knows."

Libby heard the change in her voice. "But he didn't seem excited. In fact, for the last few weeks, he's been acting more than a little withdrawn. I mean, he's always cordial, but things definitely have changed between the two of you. What is it, Brandy? Doesn't Rafe want a baby right now?"

"This is why I wanted you to sit down. I have a lot to tell you, and, honestly, if I could have avoided this moment forever, I would have considered myself blessed. But I can't keep the truth from you any longer."

"What are you talking about?" Libby was completely baffled.

"It's about me and Rafe . . ."

"Yes?" She waited expectantly.

"I guess I'd better start at the beginning. . . ."

"That would help."

And Brandy did. She told her mother how she'd met Rafe on the *Pride*, and how attracted she'd been to him. She told her how he'd saved her from the drunken Jones and how she'd returned the favor by rescuing him from Lottie Demers. Libby laughed heartily at that story.

"I don't know what happened after that night. I had liked him up until then, but as I was leaving his cabin, he accused me of being in on the scheme and asked me what I wanted out of him."

"Rafe did?"

"Oh, yes. I told him I wanted nothing from him, and the next night when he came down to gamble, I was determined to beat him."

Brandy paused as she remembered her humiliation.

"What happened?"

"I didn't beat him."

"You lost?"

"Badly."

"How badly?"

"Thousands."

"Brandy!" Libby gasped.

"I know. I had a decent hand. I thought I had him beaten. I didn't, and I didn't have enough money to pay him what I owed him."

Libby's eyes were wide as she whispered, "I always worried that you'd be hurt that way some day. How did you get the money?"

Brandy drew a strangled breath as she prepared to tell her mother the ugly truth of their marriage. "I arranged to meet with him the following morning, in hopes that I could borrow the money from Ben. But Ben had only a portion of what I owed, so I had to go to Rafe and offer to make payments to him until it was all paid off."

"What did Rafe say?"

Brandy swallowed nervously. "He refused to let me pay it off a little at a time. He made me a counter-offer."

Libby nodded, waiting.

"He said that he would forgive the debt if I would marry him, bear him a child and then leave. He said he had no need or desire for a wife, but that he'd always wanted children and this seemed the perfect way for him to get what he wanted."

"Rafe couldn't have said that!" Libby was completely taken aback. The callousness of his offer seemed totally at odds with the man she'd come to know and love there at Bellerive. Rafe was a good man, a loving man. Surely, this couldn't be true.

"I'm sorry, Mama. But that's the truth of how we came to be married."

"And you agreed to those terms?"

"What else could I do? I owed him money—a lot of money."

"But to agree to leave your own child . . ."

"I never planned to go through with it. I had hoped to find a way to earn back the money before I got pregnant. That way I could pay him off and be free of my debt. But it didn't work out that way. You know the night he came back early from New Orleans?"

"Yes. I went to bed early that night."

"And it's good you did. You missed what happened. I had already realized I was pregnant, and I knew I had to do something fast. I made arrangements to be the hostess for a poker game. Rafe wasn't supposed to be home for days, and yet he showed up that night just as I was getting ready to leave."

"That was when he moved you into this bedroom, wasn't it?"

"Yes. He was furious. And then yesterday, when he discovered I was pregnant . . . Well, it was awful, Mama."

Libby stood up and went to her daughter, gathering her in her arms and holding her close. "I'm sorry, sweetheart. I'm so sorry. I never knew. I realized that you two seemed tense around each other, but that's normal in marriage. There are always things that have to be worked out. But I never suspected that it was anything like this. . . . It just doesn't make sense, his acting this way." She was still having trouble trying to reconcile the Rafe she knew with the man Brandy had just described to her.

"I understand why he's doing this." At her mother's questioning look, Brandy quickly told her of his parents' tragic marriage and the hurt he'd suffered at the time. "But it doesn't make it any easier for me to accept. That's why I'm telling you this. That's why we have to leave here, now."

"But Brandy, think about what you're saying. Do you really want to leave Rafe, to just walk away? He's the father of your child."

"I have to, Mama. He doesn't love me. He doesn't even want me. All he wants is our baby, and I cannot, will not, abandon my child."

"There's one thing you haven't told me yet," Libby said quietly.

"What?" Brandy couldn't imagine what it was. It seemed she'd poured her heart out about everything.

"You haven't told me what your feelings are for Rafe. I can't help believing that you care for him. I know you would never have agreed to his marriage terms if you'd had no feelings for him."

Brandy was forced to face the truth of her emotions. It hurt, but she did. "I love him, Mama. I love him so much, but he doesn't love me. He never has, and he never will. He made it plain from the start that he didn't want a wife. He only married me for convenience's sake after his encounter with the Demers girl. I made things easy for him, and providing the baby was just a bonus for him. He would get exactly what he wanted without the complication of having to deal with a wife, for I'd be gone, my debt to him forgiven."

Tears were streaking down Brandy's cheeks as she finished relating the truth of her feelings for Rafe, and Libby held her even closer, trying to absorb her pain, wanting to ease her heartbreak.

"What do you want to do?"

"I have to leave here—now, while he's gone. I can't let him have this baby. It's my child, too. I don't want my child to be raised by a man who cannot love."

Libby nodded. She knew what had to be done. "All right. How soon do you want to leave?"

Brandy looked at her mother in surprise. "I know how much you love Rafe. I thought you were going to argue with me and try to convince me to stay."

"I do love Rafe, and it's almost impossible for me to reconcile the man you've told me about with the man who's been so kind and loving while we've been here. But you are my daughter, and this is my grandchild. We have to leave soon, if we're going to leave at all. Do you have any money?"

"Just a small amount."

"Where did you plan to go?"

"I thought if I found Ben, he would help me. But I don't know when he'll be in town next. Trouble is, we only have about ten days before Rafe is due back. Whatever I do, I have to do now."

"We'll leave today. Have the servants bring around the carriage and tell them we're going to take a short trip downriver to visit some friends."

"Let's just take a few things with us, so no one is suspicious. When we get to Natchez, we can catch a steamboat upriver and wait for Ben in another town. That way no one will know where to look for us."

"Good. I'll be ready to go when you are." Libby had enjoyed living at Bellerive, but comfort meant nothing next to her daughter's happiness and her unborn grandchild's welfare. Things would be difficult for them, but somehow they'd manage. She was sure of it. They'd done it before.

"I'll meet you downstairs. I want to leave a letter for Rafe so he understands why I've done this."

Libby nodded, knowing Rafe deserved at least that much from them. "I'll go tell George about our little trip and have him get the carriage."

Alone in her room, Brandy went to the small desk and took out paper, pen and ink. It took her a long time to write that final missive, but she did it. When it had dried, she folded it and slipped it into an envelope, then took it into Rafe's room and left it on his nightstand. She hoped he'd understand, but somehow she knew he wouldn't. She was glad she was going to be far away when he read the letter.

Brandy and her mother acted normal and appeared happy as they left Bellerive in the carriage with just a few bags. They did not look back.

The ride into town was nerve-wracking, for Brandy feared every minute that Rafe would return unexpectedly, as he had from New Orleans, and her escape would be foiled. When they reached the levee, they dismissed the carriage, then checked on Ben's schedule and departures that very day for upriver.

As it turned out, Ben was only one day behind them. They used almost all their money to book passage on a steamboat leaving that afternoon for Memphis. Brandy knew Ben's family lived there, and he would be heading home next. They could meet him in Memphis. She hoped he could take them somewhere where they could start a new life.

It was late that afternoon when their steamboat pulled out of Natchez. Libby stayed in their cabin, but Brandy went out on deck and watched until the town had disappeared from view. She wondered if she would ever see Natchez again.

Chapter Twenty-seven

"Brandy? Libby? What's happened? What's wrong?" Ben asked as he hurried into the room at the inexpensive hotel where Brandy and Libby were staying in Memphis.

"I'm so glad you came," Brandy said as she went straight into his arms to give him a hug. "I was afraid you might not get our message."

"They gave it to me as soon as I docked. I haven't even been home yet. Why are you here?" He looked past Brandy to where her mother sat quietly in a chair by the window.

Brandy looked up at him, ready for him to know the whole truth. "I've left Rafe. I had to."

"I thought you were going to be happy. . . ."

"Sit down. This is going to take some explaining."

Ben took a chair by Libby and listened attentively as Brandy began to talk, telling him everything from the very beginning on the boat.

He was scowling when she finished. "I thought something was wrong between you. I had a feeling . . ."

"I know. I wanted to believe I could figure a way out of this by myself, but now that I'm pregnant, it's too late. I have to think of my baby."

"I understand. What do you want me to do? Name it and it's done."

Brandy had tears in her eyes as she gazed at her dearest friend. "We need a place to live where Rafe can't find us. I'll be able to get some kind of work. Surely, there's a maid's job somewhere that I can take until I'm farther along in my pregnancy. I'm going to pay Rafe back a little at a time. I owe him, and I will not run from the debt. It's just that I cannot give him my child. I can't—"

"It's going to be all right," Ben promised with certainty, already thinking of the best place for her to stay. She needed to be where she could get lost in the crowd and not be noticed when her pregnancy was advanced. "I have friends in St. Louis who own a boarding house. I'm sure we can get you a room there."

"But St. Louis . . ." Brandy looked nervous at the thought of returning to the place of her marriage.

"It's a big town. It wouldn't be easy for Rafe to find you there."

"Thank you."

Both Brandy and Libby were more than grateful for his friendship in this, the greatest hour of their need.

"I'm due to stay in Memphis overnight and leave tomorrow late afternoon. Why don't you come home with me for dinner?" he invited them, knowing his family would be glad to see them again.

"We'd love to." The thought of being surrounded by friends appealed to them both.

Rafe was not in a good mood as he made the final leg of the trip back to Bellerive. Brandy had been in his thoughts the entire time he was away, and it annoyed him that he could not forget her. He told himself that he only had to deal with her for a few more months and then she would be gone from his life. He had thought that the prospect of a life without her would please him, but it didn't. His mood turned even blacker as he rode up the drive to the house.

"Welcome home, Mr. Rafe," George said as he met him on the veranda.

"Hello, George. Where is everybody?"

"Everybody, sir?"

"Brandy and Miss Libby."

"Why, they're not here, sir."

Rafe stopped and stared at him. "Where are they?"

"Miss Brandy and Miss Libby left the day after you did. They said they were going to visit some friends downriver."

"What friends?" As far as he knew, they had no friends downriver.

"They didn't say, sir, but Miss Brandy did leave a letter for you in your room."

Rafe walked past him without another word. He mounted the stairs and stalked into his bedroom to see the envelope on his nightstand. He muttered a vile curse under his breath as he grabbed it and ripped it open.

Dear Rafe,

If you are reading this letter, then you already know that Mother and I have gone. I am sorry I

*had to leave this way, but I could not bear to stay
on at Bellerive with the way things are between
us.*

*I know that I still owe you a debt, and I give
you my word that it will be repaid. However, I
cannot and will not repay that debt with the life
of my child. The debt is mine, not my baby's. I
could not leave my child to grow up as you did,
believing it was unloved and unwanted by its
mother. I want my baby. I love my baby already,
and I cannot even consider a life without this
child.*

*Please do not try to find me. I do not think it
would be wise for us to see each other again. It
would be too painful for both of us.*

*I will see that the money is sent to you as I earn
it. It may take some time, but I will repay every
cent.*

I wish you happiness.

Brandy

Fury filled him as he read and then reread the missive. Brandy had gone. She'd actually run from him.

"George!" he bellowed.

The servant appeared in the doorway of his room.

"How long ago did she leave?"

"The day after you did, sir."

Rafe again swore violently under his breath. "Have
my horse saddled and brought around."

"Yes, sir." He hurried off to do Rafe's bidding.

Rafe stood in the middle of his room feeling totally
lost, and that didn't sit well with him. He headed
down the hall to Brandy's room and went in to find
that all her new clothes were still there. She'd taken

nothing with her that he'd bought her. Not even the jewelry box. He started back downstairs and happened to glance into Libby's room to see her shawl folded neatly on the bed. Sadness and a terrible sense of loss filled him. They were gone. He was alone.

Coldly furious, Rafe knew where he had to start his search. He would go first to Marc and Claire and see if they had spoken to Brandy or seen her in the last week. He hoped they had. Brandy had such a headstart on him now that it could prove next to impossible to find her without some kind of lead. But find her he would. She was having his baby. He could not let her go.

When his horse was brought around, he mounted and rode across country to Marc's. He made the trek in record time. His horse was lathered as he reined in before the house, but he didn't care. He had only one thing on his mind—finding Brandy.

"Rafe? What are you doing here? Is something wrong?" Marc asked, meeting him at the door.

"It's Brandy. Have you seen or talked to her lately?"

"No, I haven't. Why?"

Claire appeared at the top of the steps with the children. "Has something happened to Brandy?" she called down worriedly.

"I just got back from St. Louis to find that she's gone."

Claire knelt down to speak with Merrie and Jason. "Children, why don't you go play while I talk with your Uncle Rafe for a minute, all right?"

"Sure!" Jason and Merrie raced off, delighted to have a break from their studies.

Claire quickly went downstairs to join the two men. She knew she was only an employee in the household, but this was different. Brandy was her friend.

"You don't know where she went?" Claire asked as she saw how grave Rafe's expression was.

"No, that's why I came here. I thought you might have an idea where I could find her."

"How long ago did she leave?"

"Over a week ago."

Claire pressed him. "Why? You were so happy together."

Rafe looked from Marc to Claire and decided to tell them everything. "I think there are a few things you need to know—both of you."

Marc suggested they go into his study to talk. When they'd settled in, Rafe told them the whole story.

"You blackmailed Brandy into marrying you?" Marc stared at him in disbelief.

"It seemed like a good idea at the time. After all, you were the one who said she'd make me the perfect wife. But I thought by marrying Brandy this way, I could take care of all the Lottie Demers who were pursuing me and have a child, too."

"But you wanted Brandy to go after she had the baby," Claire said, looking at him sadly. "Surely you must have realized how cruel that was."

"Now I do, but then . . . Most of the women I'd had contact with were just like my mother—self-centered and vain. My mother left us when I was young because she didn't want me or my father. When Brandy agreed to my terms, I thought she was the same way. Now, I realize I was wrong . . . about a lot of things."

"What are you going to do about it?"

"I'm going to try to find her."

"But why?" Claire interrupted the two men. "If you don't love her, why do you want her back? Why don't you just leave her alone? Hasn't she been tortured enough? You forced her into a marriage she didn't want. You were trying to take her baby from her. She's given you her word in her letter that she'll repay your money in full. So why don't you just let her get on with her life?"

Rafe stared at Claire, hearing the painful truth in her words. He knew he should do what she asked of him, but there was one problem. . . . He couldn't.

"I can't just let her go, Claire."

"Why not?" she retorted, wanting to force him to admit the truth.

Rafe lifted his tormented gaze to hers. The words were wrung from him, "Because I love her, and she's going to have my baby."

Claire's smile was bright. She realized what his confession had cost him, and she admired him for being strong enough to acknowledge his true feelings. "It's wonderful that you love her. It's just a shame that it took you so long to recognize it. Have you told her how you feel?"

"No. I had intended to when I got back from New Orleans, but that was when I found her dressed as Miss Brandy again, ready to be the hostess at a poker party. She told me that night that she was doing it because she wanted to earn enough money to get out of the marriage."

"Of course she would say that, especially if she'd just found out that she was pregnant and didn't want to be forced to give up her child."

"Things deteriorated after that, and now . . ."

"Now you have to find her so you can tell her that you love her."

"I know. I just hope it's not too late."

"Who would ever have thought that things could get so complicated?" Marc said with a grin. "The good news is that congratulations are in order. You're going to be a father! I think this deserves a toast."

"Save the celebrating until I find her and bring her home. I'm in no mood today."

"You should be," Claire told him. "You've just admitted for the first time out loud that you love Brandy. I hope you find her and soon."

"So do I."

"Where are you going to look next?" Marc asked.

"I'm going to find her friend Ben. If anyone knows where she and her mother have gone, it's Ben."

"Good luck, and if you need any help, just let me know," Marc told him.

Marc and Claire walked Rafe outside and watched until he'd ridden away.

"I hope he finds her soon," Claire said softly, thinking of the pain both Rafe and Brandy were enduring, separated by a sea of misunderstandings, each not knowing the other's feelings. "I know how terrible it can be to love someone and lose him."

Marc had never heard Claire talk this way before, and he glanced over at her to see the strained look on her face. He had lost Jennette, so he knew how painful it could be, but he'd never thought Claire had lost anyone. They had never talked about the loves in her life. "You sound like you know firsthand what it's like to lose a loved one."

"Oh, yes," she said with a brittle laugh. "It's a terrible thing when someone dies as Jennette did, but it's also a terrible thing to lose someone you love because of a misunderstanding or simply because they didn't know how you felt."

Marc thought about Rafe and Brandy. "If they'd just been more honest from the start. If they'd just told each other the truth, they could have avoided all this heartbreak and been happy."

Claire couldn't believe what Marc was saying. She looked at him and found his gaze upon her. In that moment, she knew she could no longer hide her feelings for him. She had waited all these months and years. She'd been patient, hoping that he would see the truth of her feelings for him and come to her, but it hadn't happened. And now she realized there would never be a better time. With all the nerve that Brandy had taught her, she decided to forge ahead. She had absolutely nothing to lose and everything to gain.

"Marc?" Her gaze searched his for a hint that he knew what was coming and felt the same way she did, but she found nothing in the depths of his eyes but gentleness and understanding.

"Yes?"

"I've been wanting to say this for a long time, but I've been afraid. . . ."

"What is it?"

"Marc, I love you. I always have and I always will."

Silence reigned as they stood on the veranda staring at each other.

Claire feared immediately that she had ruined everything. In that instant of silence, she prayed fervently that she could take back her every word and plead temporary insanity, but there was no going back.

"You love me?" he repeated, dumbfounded.

"Oh, yes, and I have for years. Even before you met

and married Jennette. Why do you think I took the job with Brandy so quickly? Why do you think I agreed to tutor Merrie and Jason? I did it so I could be near you."

"Claire, I . . ."

"I know," she said wearily, all the fight suddenly going out of her. She had played her hand, and she had lost. She should have remembered that she wasn't that good at poker. She was contrite for having embarrassed him, and she was glad that there had been no one else around to overhear. "I'm sorry. I never meant to embarrass you. It's just that, after listening to Rafe's sad story about Brandy, I couldn't go on pretending anymore. I wanted the truth to be out between us. I love you. I have for a long time, and I'm not ashamed of it."

With all the dignity she could muster, Claire turned and started to walk away.

But Marc, too, had been goaded to reality by Rafe's tale of woe. In two steps, he was beside her, touching her arm to stop her progress away from him.

"I hadn't realized until just now how special our relationship is. If we're going to have confessions here, I want to tell you that I offered you the job with the children because I couldn't bear the thought of your going back to St. Louis. I didn't recognize it for what it was then. I guess I still hadn't recovered enough from Jennette's death to say the word 'love' then, but Claire . . . I can now."

"Oh, Marc . . ." Her heart was in her eyes as she looked up at him. She was trembling with excitement as she realized that he cared for her.

"I love you, too, Claire."

He drew her close and his lips sought hers in a sweet, possessive exchange that left them both breathless. They drew apart, realizing that it was broad daylight and anyone might be watching.

"Will you marry me, Claire?"

"Yes, yes! Oh, yes!" she cried, launching herself back into his arms.

They kissed again, and then forced themselves to maintain some semblance of dignity.

"We'll be married as soon as possible. Is that all right with you?" Marc asked, loving the feeling of having her in his arms, not wanting to let her go.

"Tonight?" Claire asked with a laugh of pure happiness.

"If only we could," he growled, unable to resist stealing another kiss. "I'll send word to the priest right away."

They shared an adoring look for a moment, but then Claire turned serious as thoughts of Brandy intruded. "I only hope Rafe isn't too late to save his marriage to Brandy. She's a proud woman, but they're so perfect for each other."

"It will work out," Marc reassured her. "When Rafe sets his mind to getting something, he gets it, and he loves Brandy very much."

"I hope you're right. They deserve all the happiness they can get."

"Just like us," Marc added.

Claire looked up at him, all the love she had for him shining in her eyes. "Just like us."

"Shall we go tell Merrie and Jason?"

She knew a moment of uncertainty. "Do you think they'll be happy? They loved their mother very much."

"Yes, they did, but you're not trying to erase Jennette's memory. You're going to build on that and create new memories for them—and new love."

"Just as I will with you," she said softly as she lifted a hand to caress his cheek. "I want to make you smile again, Marc LeFevre. I want to make your life heaven on Earth."

He was deeply touched by her words, and he gathered her to him once more. She had brought sunshine to his darkest days, laughter to his home and love back into his heart. "You already have, Claire."

Rafe was a man on a mission as he rode for town. He was looking for Ben Rodgers of the *Pride*, and he wasn't going to stop until he'd found him. He went straight to the shipping office and learned that the steamboat would be back in Natchez in a week. He was outraged that he would have to wait that long to speak to the man, but he knew there were other things he could do in the meantime. He checked at the various shipping offices to see if there was a record of Brandy and her mother leaving, but their names did not appear on any of the passenger lists. Frustrated, but not defeated, Rafe prepared to wait for Ben's return. He was going to find Brandy and bring her home where she belonged. Nothing would stop him.

The week passed slowly for Rafe, but when the day finally arrived that the *Pride* was due in port, he was in town early in the morning, more than ready for the confrontation.

The minute the gangplank had been lowered, Rafe boarded the ship and sought out the captain.

Ben was on the top deck and saw Rafe board the ship. He had known this moment was coming, and he was glad that Brandy was already safely settled in her new home with her mother. She was as happy as she could be considering her circumstances, and he intended for her to stay that way. He had promised her he would keep her new location secret.

"Rodgers, I want to talk to you," Rafe called out as he reached the deck to see the captain walking the other way, his back to him.

Ben stopped and turned to face him. His expression was stony, his regard condemning. "What do you want, Marchand?" He spoke with utter disdain, as if it pained him to talk to the other man.

"I want my wife back. Where is she?" Rafe demanded as he closed the distance between them, coming to stand before Ben.

"Sorry, I can't help you."

"Like hell you can't! You're the one she'd run to if she wanted to get away—now where is she? I want to take her home."

Ben could barely control his temper. "I don't suppose it occurred to you that she doesn't want to 'go home,' and that's why she's gone?"

"Where is she, Rodgers?"

"Marchand, you're in no position to demand anything of me," Ben sneered, disliking Rafe intensely for the pain he'd caused Brandy. This man had forced her into a loveless marriage and then had bartered her child to pay a gambling debt. Ben thought he was a lowlife, and he itched to set him straight.

"I'm going to find her."

"She doesn't want to be found—not by you. So leave it alone. Brandy's started a new life, and it's one without you. And she's happy."

Ben's honest words lashed at Rafe, striking his every vulnerability.

"She's my wife."

"Then you should have treated her like one. If I'd known the terms of your marriage in the beginning, the wedding would never have taken place. You are one cold bastard. It's a good thing you weren't here when she told me. I might have—" Ben's blood was boiling, and his control was threatening to break as he remembered Brandy's desperation and pain. "Might have?! Hell, I'm going to!"

Without warning, Ben's temper won the battle with his self-control. He hit Rafe full force, knocking him to the deck. He shook his fist as he stood over him. "Now, get off my ship, Marchand. If I ever see you again, it will be too soon."

Rafe had been caught totally unaware by the blow, and it took him a second to recover and get up. Blood seeped from the corner of his mouth, and his jaw was aching. The man packed a good punch. He should have remembered Ben was Brandy's protector as well as her friend.

"Right now, I'll be the first to tell you that I deserved that," Rafe said, looking Ben in the eye. "But there's something more that you need to know. Things have changed."

"Right," Ben snarled, tempted to hit him again, but controlling himself with an effort.

"No, I didn't get the chance to tell her before she decided to leave, but I love her. She's going to have my baby, and I want us to be a family." He knew he was taking a chance opening up to Ben this way, but he wanted to get to Brandy as quickly as he could.

"Sorry, Marchand, I can't help you. Now, get off the *Pride*." Ben turned and walked away.

Rafe rubbed his sore jaw as he started from the steamboat. He was certain that Ben knew where Brandy was. In fact, Rafe had anticipated just such a reaction from Ben Rodgers and already had another plan ready to set into motion.

As he left the steamboat, Rafe nodded slightly to a man waiting on the levee with his bags, looking to all the world as if he were sailing on the *Pride*. The man returned his signal and mounted the gangplank to board the ship.

Rafe waited in town until the steamboat pulled out that afternoon. With his man in place, it was only a matter of time now until he received word on Brandy's whereabouts. Until then, he could only sit and wait. The prospect wasn't appealing, but for the time being he was thwarted.

Chapter Twenty-eight

The knock at the door jarred Rafe from a sound sleep.

"What is it?" he growled, sitting up in the darkness, wondering what time it was.

"There's a gentleman downstairs, sir," George told him through the closed door. "A Mr. Hampton. He says he has important information for you and must speak to you now."

At the mention of Hampton's name, Rafe was out of bed and pulling on his clothes.

"Show him into my study, George. I'll be down directly."

In the two weeks since Hampton had boarded the *Pride* to keep an eye on Ben Rodgers during the trip north, Rafe had had no word whatsoever from him. At times, the tension of waiting for news had nearly driven Rafe to drink, but he'd sworn off after Brandy left. He was glad now that he had, for he would be able to think clearly while dealing with the man. His instructions to Hampton had been clear—follow Ben Rodgers whenever he left the boat at each port and see if he visited two women—one pregnant, one elderly—then report back.

Rafe made his way downstairs. He tried not to be too excited, but he hoped the man was bringing him good news.

"Mr. Hampton, a pleasure to see you," Rafe said as he entered his study.

The other man stood and they shook hands.

"Would you like a drink?"

"No, thanks, Mr. Marchand. I knew how quickly you wanted this information, so I hurried out here as soon as my boat docked."

"I appreciate it." Rafe went to sit behind his desk as Hampton sat back down in the chair before him. "Well, what did you find out?"

"Captain Rodgers was very cautious about his activities, which made this quite a challenge, but I managed."

"And?"

"And I do believe I've located your wife."

"Where?" Rafe came to his feet.

"She and her mother have taken a room in a boarding house in St. Louis, sir." He handed him a sheet of paper with the address on it.

Rafe looked up at the man. "You do good work, Hampton."

"Thank you."

Rafe unlocked his top desk drawer and took out an envelope. "Here's the other half of your fee, plus a nice bonus for you. I appreciate your discreetness in the handling of this matter."

"I'm glad I could bring you good news, sir."

George showed Hampton from the house. When he came back in, Rafe was standing in the hall waiting for him.

"Pack my bags, George, and order the carriage brought around. Brandy's in St. Louis, and I'm going to bring her home."

"Yes, sir!" George said happily. He knew there would be no peace in this house until Miss Brandy was back where she belonged.

The trip upriver passed slowly, but Rafe had expected no less. He consoled himself with the thought that Brandy awaited him at the end of his journey. Just seeing her again would make it all worthwhile.

When at last St. Louis came into view, Rafe was certain he could have jumped overboard and swum to shore quicker than the steamboat could churn its way to the levee. He gripped the rail to calm himself as he waited for the lines to be thrown and the vessel tied up. Finally, it was time.

For the whole trip north, Rafe had been confident, believing he could convince Brandy to come home with him, but now a sudden, terrible doubt assailed him. He feared that she truly did despise him and wanted nothing more to do with him. It was a humbling possibility, but one he knew he should face. He would go to her and tell her that he loved her. Until he did, nothing else mattered.

Rafe hired a carriage and made the short trip to the boarding house where she was living. He paid the driver handsomely to wait for him, then went up the steps to the house, knowing that the next few minutes would determine his whole future. He knocked on the door and waited.

"Can I help you?" an older woman asked as she answered the door.

"I'm here to see two of your tenants, Brandy and Libby. May I come in?"

"Theirs is the last room, upstairs on the right."

"Thank you."

Rafe hurried up the steps and down the hall. He knocked on the door and was rewarded when he heard Libby call out.

"Who is it?"

"It's me, Libby. . . . Rafe."

There was a silence, then the sound of footsteps, and the door opened. Rafe found himself staring down at Libby. She was looking up at him, tears streaking her cheeks.

"You came . . ." She kept her voice cautious as she tried to gauge his reason for seeking them out.

"Where's Brandy? Is she here?" he asked urgently. He had come all this way; he needed to see her.

Libby held the door wide. "No, she's not, but come in. I want to talk to you." She motioned him inside.

The room was small, but neat, with two beds, a table with two chairs and a dresser. He sat down at the table, and she joined him there after closing the door.

"Why did you come, Rafe? Why are you here?" Libby wasted no time in getting straight to the heart of her fear for her daughter. Rafe had broken Brandy's heart once; she would not let him hurt her again.

"I want to take Brandy, and you, home," he said.

"Why? So you can claim your winnings?"

"No, because a wife belongs with her husband."

"You never allowed her to be a wife to you. You told her over and over you didn't want a wife. Why the change now?" Libby was close enough to him that she could make out his expression, and she could see the anguish there as he answered her.

"Because it took my losing Brandy to realize how much she means to me, how much I need her. I love her, Libby. It wasn't easy for me to admit—or to recognize it for that matter. I've never loved a woman before, and it was more than a little frightening when I realized that I needed Brandy so desperately. I'm used to being alone. I'm a solitary man. I'm not used to needing people or to being needed. It's a new experience for me."

"And?"

"And I found that once I'd lived it, I didn't want to be without it."

Libby's heart softened, for she knew his words were from the depths of his soul. "You do love her, don't you?"

"Yes, ma'am. More than I've ever loved anyone, and I can't bear the thought of living without her."

"Well, what took you so long to find us?" Libby said with a little laugh.

He looked shocked. "I had to have Ben followed in order to track you down. When I went to see him in person, he wasn't too amenable to helping me." Rafe rubbed his jaw in memory.

"Ben's a good man. He loves Brandy, too. I'm glad you've come, but I do have to say one thing to you."

He didn't speak but waited for her words of wisdom.

"Brandy is my daughter. The child she's carrying is my grandchild. I do not want this baby to be brought up unloved and unwanted. I raised Brandy without a father, but she was loved. I will not stand by and watch this baby be used as a pawn in any struggle between the two of you."

"I understand, and I promise you, Libby, that if Brandy doesn't want anything more to do with me, if she wants to end our marriage, then I'll go."

Libby studied him, then nodded. "I believe in you, Rafe. Deep in your heart I know you're a good man. But now you have to prove it to my daughter."

As if her words had conjured her up, Brandy came through the door right then. At the sight of Rafe sitting at the table talking to her mother, she stopped dead, shock showing clearly on her features.

"Get out!" she said in a low, frantic voice. She had wondered who the carriage parked out front belonged to, and now she knew.

Rafe didn't speak, but only gazed at her. She looked more beautiful than ever to him, and he ached with the need to hold her and tell her he loved her. But he saw, too, the panic in her eyes, and he knew he had to be gentle.

"Hello, Brandy," he said softly.

"Get out! I want you out of here! You got my letter, didn't you? I'll get you the money! Just go away and leave us alone!"

"I can't," Rafe said simply, rising and going to her.

"I think I'll go downstairs for a little while," Libby excused herself.

"Mother!"

But Libby closed the door behind herself as she left the room, and they were alone.

"What do you want from me?" Brandy demanded, furious that he'd found them.

"You look beautiful, Brandy," he told her, his gaze warm upon her.

"I want you to go, Rafe. I give you my word I'll pay you the money back, but please . . . just go. . . ." Her nerves were stretched taut. This was her worst nightmare come true. He had found her, and he had come after her only to take her baby away.

Rafe sensed the rawness of her emotions. "Brandy, please listen to me. I didn't come here to hurt you. I came because I needed to see you again . . . to talk to you. . . ."

"About what? About how I'll be free of the marriage in just a few more months?" she challenged him bitterly.

"No," he said calmly, realizing how desperately he'd hurt her. "I came to talk to you about us."

"Us? There is no us."

"I'd like there to be."

He took her hand, but she snatched it away from him as if it burned her.

He went on, "Brandy, there's something I have to say to you, and when I'm done, if you still feel the same way you do now, I'll go."

Brandy moved across the room, wanting a distance between them. It hurt her too much to realize how much she still loved him. For just an instant, when she'd come into the room and seen Rafe there with her mother, looking so handsome and wonderful, her heart had leapt with joy. She'd missed him— oh, how she'd missed him. But she kept her back to him now, afraid that what she was feeling would show in her eyes.

"Brandy . . ." Rafe began slowly, unsure of himself and of her. "I followed you here because I love you."

Brandy tensed at his words, but did not move or turn back. She did not trust herself or him.

"I know you have a lot of reasons not to believe me, but I had to let you know how I felt. In fact, I knew I was in love with you when I came back early from New Orleans that night. I had been ready to tell you then, but you said that you were going to the poker game only because you wanted to get out of our marriage."

At his words, she turned to look at him, her expression stunned.

"If you still feel that way, then from this moment on, I want you to know that your debt to me is canceled. You owe me nothing. You are my wife and you are pregnant with my child. I will support you, and take care of you, no matter where you want to live. All I ask is that you let me be a part of my child's life. You said in your letter that you didn't want our baby to grow up as I did, and you're right. I want to be there to love my son or daughter, too." He paused and drew a deep breath. "I love you, Brandy. I want you to remember that."

He waited for a moment for her to say something . . . anything. Each second seemed an eternity, but her only response was silence.

Defeat crushed him, and his shoulders slumped. He took one last look at her, standing across the room so proud and beautiful, and then he turned to go. His life lay bleakly before him, but at least, for a little while, he had known her love.

His hand was on the doorknob before Brandy spoke.

"Rafe . . ." her voice was choked with emotion. This was the man she loved! He had just told her that he loved her! And he was leaving! Walking out of her life. She couldn't let him go! She couldn't.

He looked back at her.

"Oh, Rafe . . . I'm sorry . . . so sorry. I didn't mean for things to be this way."

"I know," he said sadly, thinking he should leave. There was no point in going on. "Good-bye, Brandy."

"Rafe, no . . . Wait . . ."

He glanced back, questioningly.

"I love you, too," she said simply.

Their eyes met and then the distance between them was far too great. They flew into each other's arms, man and wife in all ways at last.

Rafe spun her around, holding her to his heart. "I'm sorry I hurt you."

"I love you, Rafe, and you love me. Nothing else matters now." She was crying in earnest, unable to believe the joy that was bursting inside her.

He kissed her then, his mouth settling over hers, telling her of his passion and his need.

"Oh!" Brandy said in sudden surprise, breaking off the kiss with a most stunned look on her face.

"What's wrong? Did I hurt you?"

"No . . . But I think your son just let me know that he approves. . . ." Her hand was resting on the mound of her stomach.

Rafe frowned, not understanding.

"I just felt him move. . . ." she said in wonder.

Rafe paled as he stared at her. " 'He'?"

"Of course. We're going to have a son, and he's going to be as wonderful as you are."

"A son . . ." Rafe was awestruck.

She was back in his arms then, kissing him, loving him. They finally broke apart only when things might have gone farther than they'd planned. Libby was just downstairs.

"We'd better tell Mother," Brandy said with a smile, high color staining her cheeks, her breathing quick and excited, her eyes aglow with happiness.

"Will you come with me now? Tonight? We can check in at the Planter's House again." His eyes darkened at the memory of their wedding night.

"The Planter's House?" Brandy gave him a wicked smile. "I think I'd like that."

"I know I would."

It was much later that night when they lay together in the comfort of a luxury suite at the hotel. Libby had elected to stay in the boarding house one final night, and so Rafe and Brandy had a night all to themselves. When they'd reached the room, he'd even carried her over the threshold again. Their loving had been poignant and beautiful, and neither of them wanted the night to end.

Brandy lay with her head on his shoulder and her hand splayed across the hard width of his chest. Her every dream had come true. Rafe loved her and wanted her as his wife in all ways. They were a family.

"I missed you," she told him, glorying in the warmth of his closeness.

"I missed you, too. The last time I was in St. Louis I stayed here, and I didn't sleep much because I kept thinking about you and our wedding night."

"So you enjoyed our poker game, did you?"

"Immensely," he chuckled. "I've never had that much fun cheating before."

Brandy sat up and glared at him, her expression indignant. "You cheated?"

He grinned lustily at her as he snared her wrist and pulled her back down across his chest. "Absolutely, and it was worth it, too."

His hands traced over her silken curves, pressing her more closely to him. She reveled in his touch. She had missed being with him, near him. It seemed she couldn't get close enough after all this time apart.

"I suppose I forgive you."

"Just 'suppose'?" He drew her down for a kiss.

She didn't need to answer him. Her actions let him know he was forgiven.

The following morning, Rafe arranged for their passage home. They returned to the boarding house to pick up Libby and all their things, and then were ready to go home.

Libby saw how Rafe and Brandy shared secret looks and smiles, and she knew now that her daughter had found true happiness. She was content. Her grandchild was going to grow up in a loving home with adoring parents.

The trip back to Bellerive was a far cry from their earlier desperate flight. The days were spent in sweet harmony for Brandy and Rafe, loving and learning to love. The nights were heated splendor as they gave each other the perfect gift of themselves.

Bellerive had never looked more beautiful to Rafe as the carriage made its way up the drive, and George's wide smile said it all when he saw Brandy and Libby emerge from the carriage with Rafe.

"Welcome home, Miss Brandy," he told her.

"Thank you, George, and you're right. I really have come home."

Epilogue

Marc and Claire were married a month after Marc
proposed. It was a small, quiet ceremony with only
family and a few friends. After Jennette's death,
Marc had thought he would never know this happiness again, but Claire's love brightened each day for
him and for the children, too, who adored her.

Charles Martin Marchand came into the world
with a lusty cry the following January. Brandy's delivery was slow and painful, but once she held her
dark-haired, blue-eyed son in her arms, all the pain
was forgotten. Rafe was at her side the whole time.
Charles was named after both his grandfathers, a
choice that made his Grandmother Libby cry. He
was loved.

The christening was held when he was six weeks
old, and his godparents, Claire and Marc, were
proud to take on the responsibility.

The Lady's Hand

Jason and Merrie weren't quite sure what to make of little Charles, for he didn't do a whole lot except cry when he was hungry.

A party was held at Bellerive after his christening, and it was then that Merrie got to hold him for the first time.

"Come sit here on the sofa," Brandy told her.

Once the little girl had settled in, Brandy carefully placed her sleeping son in her arms. Rafe was standing nearby, and he thought he would never forget the look of awe that shone on Merrie's face as Charles came awake and opened his eyes to look up at her.

"Oh, look, Aunt Brandy! He woke up!" Merrie giggled. "I think he likes me! He's not crying."

As quickly as she said the words, Charles began to whimper. Brandy took him again, rescuing Merrie from his tears.

"I like babies," Merrie said, snuggling close to Brandy's side so she could keep watch over Charles.

"Someday you can be a mommy, too," Brandy told her.

"Good. I think it will be fun. Papa?" Merrie called, and Marc looked up.

"What, Merrie?"

"Since Claire's our new mommy, can we have a baby, too?'

Marc and Claire shared a quick look of embarrassment and love.

"Well, er—uh, maybe."

"Good. I want a baby sister. Charles is nice, but I want a girl to play with."

"Ugh!" Jason said from where he sat across the room, watching the goings-on with a jaundiced eye. "If we have a baby, it had better be a boy."

"Well, we'll just have to see what happens," Marc

said, giving Claire a loving look.

Rafe was smiling as he listened to their conversation. He gazed at Brandy as she sat holding their son. Life was sweet. He would be forever grateful for the night he'd won his lady's hand.

Lone Warrior

Bobbi Smith

Marisa Williams learns how untamed the frontier can be when a party of raiding Comanche spirits her away to their village. Once there, they strip her and send her to a tipi to await her fate. When a virile warrior enters, she fears the worst. But his green eyes calm her fears, until his searing kiss enflames a passion that sets her shaking all over again.

Wind Ryder knows what being a captive of the Comanche means. Since he was taken many springs ago, he's become the best of warriors. The chief's gift of the blond beauty proves his prowess, but her silky skin and tender lips also haunt his dreams. Dreams that make Wind Ryder realize Marissa is the fiercest fighter of all, for she has won the battle for his his heart.

HALF-BREED'S

Lady

BOBBI SMITH

To artist Glynna Williams, Texas is a land of wild beauty, carved by God's hand, untouched as yet by man's. And the most exciting part of it is the fierce, bare-chested half-breed who saves her from a rampaging bull. As she spends the days sketching his magnificent body, she dreams of spending the nights in his arms.

___4436-6 $6.99 US/$8.99 CAN

Dorchester Publishing Co., Inc.
P.O. Box 6640
Wayne, PA 19087-8640

Please add $1.75 for shipping and handling for the first book and $.50 for each book thereafter. NY, NYC, and PA residents, please add appropriate sales tax. No cash, stamps, or C.O.D.s. All orders shipped within 6 weeks via postal service book rate. Canadian orders require $2.00 extra postage and must be paid in U.S. dollars through a U.S. banking facility.

Name_____
Address_____
City_____ State_____ Zip_____
I have enclosed $_____ in payment for the checked book(s).
Payment <u>must</u> accompany all orders. ❏ Please send a free catalog.
          CHECK OUT OUR WEBSITE! www.dorchesterpub.com

WANTON SPLENDOR
BOBBI SMITH

From Christopher Fletcher's simmering gaze to his lean strength, he infuses heat throughout Kathleen Kingsford's body. Caught amid her brother's foolishness and her enemy's greed, Katie longs for the solace Christopher promises. But can she trust this high-stakes gambler? As a vicious hurricane descends, she has no choice.

Katie appears at his door, her dress clinging to every curve, raindrops tracing tantalizing paths across her creamy skin. Ever since their first meeting, he wanted to be the one to protect her. And now she is here. Now she is his. Now they can finally surrender to their wanton splendor.

BRAZEN
BOBBI SMITH

Casey Turner can rope and ride like any man, but when she strides down the streets of Hard Luck, Texas, nobody takes her for anything but a beautiful woman. Working alongside her Pa to keep the bank from foreclosing on the Bar T, she has no time for romance. But all that is about to change....

Michael Donovan has had a burr under his saddle about Casey for years. The last thing he wants is to be forced into marrying the little hoyden, but it looks like he has no choice if he wants to safeguard the future of the Donovan ranch. He'll do his darndest, but he can never let on that underneath her pretty new dresses Casey is as wild as ever, and in his arms she is positively...*BRAZEN*.

Heart of Texas
Constance O'Banyon

Casey Hamilton has nowhere to go, no place but the Spanish Spur ranch to make a new home for herself and her little brother and sister. And when none of the local men will work for her, when trouble seems to dog her steps, she has no choice but to hire the loner with the low-slung guns strapped about his lean hips. She knows he is part Comanche, a man who'd fought his share of battles; is he a gunslinger as well? Is that why the past seems to haunt him? Either way, his silver eyes hold secrets too deep for telling; his warm lips whisper warnings she dare not ignore; and his hard arms promise that in his stirring embrace she will find the true...*HEART OF TEXAS*.

Crosswinds
Cindy Holby

Ty – He is honor-bound to defend the land of his fathers, even if battle takes him from the arms of the woman he pledged himself to protect.

Cole – A Texas Ranger, he thinks the conflict will pass him by until he has the chance to capture the fugitive who'd sold so many innocent girls into prostitution.

Jenny – She vows she will no longer run from the demons of the past, and if that means confronting Wade Bishop in a New York prisoner-of-war camp, so be it. No matter how far she must travel from those she holds dear, she will draw courage from the legacy of love her parents had begun so long ago.

TEXAS STAR

ELAINE BARBIERI

Buck Star is a handsome cad with a love-'em-and-leave-'em attitude that broke more than one heart. But when he walks out on a beautiful New Orleans socialite, he sets into motion a chain of treachery and deceit that threatens to destroy the ranching empire he'd built and even the children he'd once hoped would inherit it. . . .

A mysterious message compels Caldwell Star to return to Lowell, Texas, after a nine-year absence. Back in Lowell, he meets a stubborn young widow who refuses his help, but needs it more than she can know. Her gentle touch and proud spirit give Cal strength to face the demons of the past, to reach out for a love that would heal his wounded soul.

Dorchester Publishing Co., Inc.
P.O. Box 6640 _____5179-6
Wayne, PA 19087-8640 $6.99 US/$8.99 CAN
Please add $2.50 for shipping and handling for the first book and $.75 for each additional book. NY and PA residents, add appropriate sales tax. No cash, stamps, or CODs. Canadian orders require $2.00 for shipping and handling and must be paid in U.S. dollars. Prices and availability subject to change. **Payment must accompany all orders.**

Name: _____

Address: _____

City: _____ State:_____ Zip: _____

E-mail: _____

I have enclosed $_____ in payment for the checked book(s).

For more information on these books, check out our website at www.dorchesterpub.com.
_____ *Please send me a free catalog.*

THE COWBOY
WHO CAME CALLING
LINDA BRODAY

Glory Day has found the man who promises to solve all her troubles. Then an interfering stranger literally comes between her and the outlaw she plans to bring in for the reward money. And she accidentally shoots him! Worse, Luke McClain is no ordinary cowboy; he is an extraordinary lawman and a true gentleman to boot.

While Glory doctors his wounds, Luke humors her ailing mother and seems determined to help save her father from jail and her family farm from ruin. What is a woman to do with such a meddlesome admirer? After one kiss, Glory realizes she *has* collared the correct man: She'll rope him into hanging his saddle next to hers for life.

CARNAL GIFT

PAMELA CLARE

Her body and her virginity are to be offered up to a stranger in exchange for her brother's life. Possessing nothing but her innocence and her fierce Irish pride, Bríghid has no choice but to comply.

But the handsome man she faces in the darkened bedchamber is not at all the monster she expected. His tender touch calms her fears while he swears he will protect her by merely pretending to claim her. And as the long hours of the night pass by, as her senses ignite at the heat of their naked flesh, Bríghid makes a startling discovery: Sometimes the line between hate and love can be dangerously thin.